# HOW TO CARE
## FOR A
## HUMAN GIRL

# HOW TO CARE FOR A HUMAN GIRL

A NOVEL

# ASHLEY WURZBACHER

**ATRIA** BOOKS

New York London Toronto Sydney New Delhi

ATRIA
BOOKS

An Imprint of Simon & Schuster, Inc.
1230 Avenue of the Americas
New York, NY 10020

First Atria Books hardcover edition August 2023

ATRIA BOOKS and colophon are trademarks of Simon & Schuster, Inc.

For information about special discounts for bulk purchases, please contact Simon & Schuster Special Sales at 1-866-506-1949 or business@simonandschuster.com.

The Simon & Schuster Speakers Bureau can bring authors to your live event. For more information or to book an event, contact the Simon & Schuster Speakers Bureau at 1-866-248-3049 or visit our website at www.simonspeakers.com.

Interior design by Jill Putorti

Manufactured in the United States of America

1 3 5 7 9 10 8 6 4 2

Library of Congress Cataloging-in-Publication Data

Names: Wurzbacher, Ashley, 1985– author.
Title: How to care for a human girl : a novel / Ashley Wurzbacher.
Description: First Atria Books hardcover edition. | New York : Atria Books, 2023.
Identifiers: LCCN 2022059140 (print) | LCCN 2022059141 (ebook) |
ISBN 9781982157227 (hardcover) | ISBN 9781982157234 (paperback) |
ISBN 9781982157241 (ebook)
Subjects: LCGFT: Novels.
Classification: LCC PS3623.U79 H69 2023 (print) | LCC PS3623.U79 (ebook) |
DDC 813/.6—dc23/eng/20221212
LC record available at https://lccn.loc.gov/2022059140
LC ebook record available at https://lccn.loc.gov/2022059141

ISBN 978-1-9821-5722-7
ISBN 978-1-9821-5724-1 (ebook)

*For Twinkle*

For there is nothing either good or bad, but thinking makes it so.

—WILLIAM SHAKESPEARE, *HAMLET*

# 1

---

# JADA

**March 2018**

*Make an observation that defines a problem.*

Every experiment begins here, in the first step of the scientific method: a witnessing, the bud of a question opening. When Jada woke one morning at the gray genesis of dawn, she felt the problem in her gut before she registered it in her mind, the body always knowing what the brain, in dreams, forgets.

For a moment, when she opened her eyes, the world was blank, innocent in its emptiness. Then context settled on the day like a layer of dust, and things came into focus in all their flaw and detail, and she made her observations, remembered where and when and who she was. Where: Pittsburgh, her bedroom, her husband beside her. When: eighteen months since her mother's death. Who: a woman, grief-drenched and unexpectedly pregnant.

Next to her, Blake dozed, mouth hanging open. Here was the problem, bigger even than the pregnancy itself: although she knew he'd celebrate the news, she couldn't bring herself to share it.

The sun rose, and the hushed world grew dense and strained as though packed into a space too small. She felt a weight on her chest like ghost hands pressing down. One of her own hands went to her abdomen, the other to her heart. So sweet, she thought, and good— the steadfast organ pumping devotedly away. Jada pictured her heart like a plump strawberry ripe in the crate of her chest, and she felt for that diligent fruit the kind of grateful affection she had tried and so far failed to feel for the cluster of cells that had attached itself to her uterine wall.

She had always assumed she would be a mother, had been primed for it ever since her sister, Maddy, was born just before their mother's breast cancer diagnosis. Jada had become a surrogate parent at twelve, caring for Maddy while her mother underwent surgery and chemo, lost her breasts and her hair, her balance and control of her hands. Two bald girls in the house then, one in a bed and one in a crib, both crying inconsolably: mother and child. Before Maddy's birth—their mother was forty and not trying—their parents had referred to her as a miracle. But although Jada loved Maddy, she was plagued by an unfair but unshakable vision of her as a kind of inadvertent bringer of death. Her beginning had been the beginning of the end.

Besides, Jada no longer believed in miracles. She believed in data, in the scientific method. She was earning her doctorate in social psychology, researching the mechanics of choice and decision-making in intimate relationships. Whether it was because of this training or her time raising Maddy or some innate flaw in her character that she could not view her own pregnancy as miraculous, Jada could not be sure.

She'd known for three days, and yesterday, she had almost told Blake. At least, she had considered it. Or at least, she had felt a surge of disproportionate, overwhelming tenderness toward him when he opted to use a stepladder rather than the arm of the couch when reaching up to screw a light bulb into a wall sconce. Tears had welled in her eyes. But she'd said nothing then, and she said nothing now, a pressure in her throat, a pounding in her head.

In the silence and the stillness her hands found each other, as they had often since her mother's death—a childish habit, holding her own hand. She crossed them at the wrists and interlocked her fingers, and somehow it worked, even now; she felt calm, held. She should hold her husband's hand. She should reach for him. Instead she drew into herself, rubbing her finger with her thumb, insisting, *It's going to be okay.*

Then came the sudden, blaring hysteria of the neighbor's car alarm. Jada let go of her hand quickly, like she'd been caught by a watchful chaperone. Blake's alarm clock joined the chorus, a series of chimes and angry vibrations from his phone across the room, and he groaned, hauled his legs over the side of the bed, and stood. An impersonal morning boner tented his boxers. Jada closed her eyes and let one hand return to the spot over her heart.

The din of the day picked up around her: the whine of an ambulance siren, the squawk of a blue jay. Sunlight hardened into stripes like bars that crossed her blanketed body, locking her in a silvery cell. Her skin felt sore. But she rose from her bed, she smoothed the imprint of her body from the still-warm sheets. There was a day to be got through, a problem to be puzzled over. There were choices to be made.

She spent the day on the couch, laptop warming her thighs, a jasmine-scented candle burning beside her. She was working on the protocol for her latest experiment, a study of choice overload and reversibility on undergraduate daters, and she lost herself in the work until Blake got home—at which point, to her horror, she observed herself hiding from him in the hall closet.

It was an involuntary physical reaction that did not occur to her as problematic until she was settled, ankles crossed, arms wrapped around her legs. She was still in her pajamas when she heard the garage door yawn open and Blake's BMW pull inside, and at first she told herself the pajamas explained her sprint to the closet, as if she intended to doll up for his arrival like some fifties housewife. But the closet she fled to did not contain her clothes, and besides, she had observed this much in her going-on-two years of marriage: in the dream scenes that flashed before your eyes as you zipped your wedding dress and fixed the clasps on your heels, you pictured your-self always that clean and well-clothed, an advertisement for happi-ness and good hygiene. But this vision was a delusion; marriage was mostly pajamas.

Anyway: he killed the engine; she bolted. Shut the door behind her and sat down beside the vacuum cleaner, where she remained as he wandered through the house, calling her name. He still didn't know about the pregnancy. He didn't know, either, how sometimes Jada took out a letter her mother had sent her years ago, placed a clean sheet of paper over the page, and slowly copied the handwriting, one loop at a time. Or listened to old voicemails from her mother on repeat, even the three-minute butt dial that consisted of nothing but the garbled TV noise of *The Ellen DeGeneres Show* punctuated with her mother's occasional laughter.

What he did know, what they both knew, was that her desire was dead. When he reached for her, she rolled away. When he touched her, she flinched, floundered, too slippy to be held. The sex that had led to conception had been a chore, and now, with her legs crossed beneath her on the closet floor, Jada was forced to recognize this fact more directly than she had before. *Make an observation that defines a problem*: here she was; she was here. Now came the question: Why?

She'd left the candle burning in the living room and could smell the jasmine scent wafting through the crack under the closet door. Except for the vacuum and some winter coats, a few cleaning supplies, and the ukulele Blake had bought on a whim once in Maui and never played, the closet where she hid was empty. She and Blake had moved into the house shortly before they married—she'd owned almost nothing at the time—and it was bigger than they needed. He'd tried fireman-carrying her over the threshold but in the process had knocked the tender bone on the outside of her ankle against the doorframe, and this knocking now seemed like a symbol of something, some fundamental way in which she did not fit here on Fifth Avenue, in the too-fancy house he'd bought. She had cried out in pain, "My lateral malleolus!" and he'd dropped her, his chivalry spoiled. They were the first to live in the house, and its virginal purity—walls without scratches, pristine hardwoods—both delighted and unnerved her, satisfying her clean-freak tendencies but striking her, at the same time, as unmaintainable, unreal.

After ten minutes, Blake blew out the candle. Jada smelled the faint slither of smoke through the closet crack. She heard him ask the cat where she was, heard the cat meow apathetically, heard her phone ring from the spot on a shelf where she'd left it. He was calling her.

He padded past the closet, pausing outside it on his way down the hall, so close Jada could hear her phone ringing both in the living room and from the device held to his ear. Why was he letting it ring? Clearly her phone was home, and as far as he was concerned, she was not. Then the ringing stopped and the floor creaked, Blake shifting his weight from foot to foot, and she wondered if he could sense her presence. Equal to her fear of being caught was her fear of not being so; his finding her might indicate that they were connected by something, some invisible force capable of permeating doors, some connubial sonar in him that pinged in her proximity. She sat unbreathing in hope and fear until he moved back down the hallway, flopped onto the couch, and turned on the TV.

Even as her shame swelled—what kind of wife was she?—it occurred to Jada that there might be some strategic advantage to her position in the closet, that from its confines she might observe her way toward a better understanding of the man on the other side of the door. Fly on the wall, wife in the closet: same difference. She knew people changed their behavior when they knew they were being observed. She recalled the research, the psychologists concealing themselves in bathroom stalls or standing by soap dispensers in plain sight, counting the number of toilet users who washed their hands. The verdict was that most everyone washes—when they know they're being watched.

What was the handwashing equivalent that Blake might let slide outside of her presence? Entertaining this question was a useful way of avoiding a larger, tougher one—the question of why she was in the closet at all—and Jada gave herself over to it eagerly. She was entitled to this information, she assured herself; in marrying her, Blake had agreed that his intimacy with her would grow over time to heights neither of them could fathom at the moment they exchanged rings. Marriage: the quintessence of informed consent.

But she learned little, only things she already knew. He liked to recite frequently aired commercials alongside their narrators. He liked to talk to the cat, trilling the occasional syllable in an imitation purr. In the beginning his dorky humor and the confidence with which he dispatched it had been part of what drew Jada to him. ("I'll have the leg of salmon," he'd said to the white-vested server at their first fancy dinner out, and winked at her as the server fumbled, confused. "The pay's great," he'd tell someone at a party, describing his job as an anesthesiologist, "but the work is mind-numbing.") His jolliness took the pressure off her, allowed her to fade into the background, smiling and nodding, thinking and analyzing. She had always been the serious girl, the studious girl, and she had grown into a serious and studious woman, stressed out, living on a shoestring budget when she met Blake through a dating app, setting up her studies, wrangling research assistants, writing articles, driving home on weekends to visit her sick mother. How hungrily she'd gravitated toward the ease with which Blake glided through the world, opening his wallet, telling his jokes. She had wanted a slice of that ease for herself. She had wanted other things, too, back then.

For instance: frequent and athletic sex of the kind that, lately, had come to feel physically impossible to her. For instance: to be someone else. For instance: to truly believe, as he did, that things were generally okay and would remain okay no matter what happened, who lived or died, who was or wasn't president. To be cared for, cooked for; to be handed mixed drinks if he was home when she came back from class or a long day of writing; to arrive at his condo and find him chopping a bell pepper or crushing cloves of garlic under the blade of a knife. He worked with a group that administered office-based anesthesia for pain management and worked set hours, and he drew sharp boundaries between his work life and home life in a way Jada respected but couldn't bring herself to replicate. She could cook, as well—she'd fed herself through college, forgoing expensive meal plans; she'd fed Maddy when her mother was too shaky with neuropathy to hold a spoon—but it excited her to have the option not to. She could mix her own drinks but found herself glad to outsource the work. Gradually she began to understand how much of what she'd done throughout her childhood and adult life she had done not because she'd wanted to, but because she'd had to. Until she met him, she had not had the luxury of telling the difference.

At first it excited her that she and Blake had little in common. He'd never known debt or poverty; his parents had paid for his college and med school, bought him a condo in Philadelphia while he was at Penn Medicine, a house in Durham during his residency at Duke. Nothing terrible had ever happened to him, and he lived relatively free of any fear that it would. Yes, she'd read the research on heterogamy and homogamy, she had plumbed the meta-analyses, she had learned that while most of us claim to want a partner with opposite traits, in fact much of our attraction and relationship satisfaction is rooted in similarity. But you can know what the hot dog's made of and eat it anyway. You can know something is true and still think it won't be true for you. Rational choice theory has long been debunked; we are not rational choosers but creatures of want and whimsy.

Blake shut off the TV, and Jada heard him open the fridge, exclaim, "What! No milk?" and backtrack down the stairs, into the garage and into his car, rewinding his presence, and she scurried to the bathroom, turned on the shower, and prepared the lie she told herself was not one: she'd been for a run. (She had, yesterday. It was not untrue.)

He was a good man. He would be a good father. But as Jada stood with the water weeping down and scrubbed her skin raw, she understood with a clarity that was uncharacteristic of her that she would not have this child.

# 2

## MADDY

April 2018

"Obviously," he said, "you can't have it. I hope that's clear."

They'd met at the grocery store, having agreed that she shouldn't come over anymore. He carried a shopping basket containing a bag of baby spinach, a package of ground chuck, a family of onions—two large, two small—and a bottle of maple syrup. She pushed an empty cart with a squeaky wheel.

"Obviously," Maddy said, pasting a smile on her face as a shopper passed by, a woman in a shirt that read THE ONLY THING TOUGHER THAN A TRUCKER IS A TRUCKER'S MOM! Maddy was smart enough to understand the terms of their conversation without his having to lay them out for her: it was not a conversation at all, but a transaction, here in the canned goods aisle, and it should appear cheerfully formal. She had explained the situation to him over the phone—the test stick she'd peed on, its bold pink lines. *It's out of the question,* he'd said, *no matter how I feel about you.*

She'd been distraught on the phone, crying and shouting, but by the end of the call the force of her emotions had worn her out, and she was ready to behave. *Promise me you'll do the right thing,* he'd said, and she'd promised: *I will.* She'd agreed to meet him at Giant Eagle after she was done cleaning houses so that he could do what he did now: hand her a manila envelope, stuffed thick, nodding like, *Go on, take it, be a good girl.* So she took it, like a good girl, and placed it in her buggy's collapsible compartment, the place where children rode.

What could she expect? That he'd want her to have it, keep it? She didn't even know if she wanted it, and he wasn't even her boyfriend, just—she flushed at the word—her *lover.* She didn't know what else to call him. He didn't love her.

Her eyes needed somewhere to go, so she focused on a row of baked beans. She thought, for some reason, of her sister. What would Jada do? Not be in this situation, for starters. And if she was, she'd know exactly what to do, and she'd do it. Take charge. Call the shots, like she always did.

"Maddy," he said, and she realized her eyes had filled with tears. She kept her gaze on the beans, now blurry, and stood still. "You're going to be okay."

Anger welled inside her. Anger that he'd put her in this position. Anger that he expected her to do what he wanted automatically, without asking questions, moving her arms like a marionette, taking his money. Maddy felt a spark of determination not to give him what he wanted. She could not tell where this determination ended and her true desire began.

"That's just a thing people say to make themselves feel better," she snapped.

He shook his head. "You're stronger than you think you are."

"You could knock me over with your pinkie finger."

"That's not true." He shifted his basket from left hand to right, looked around to make sure no one was listening. Said softly, "You're one of the strongest people I know."

Always, even now, the anger she felt toward him was followed by a swelling shame that built, broke, and washed the rage away. She could whine *he, he, he* all day, but she had done this, too. She, Madelyn Jean Battle. She hadn't said no. Much worse, she'd said yes, ardently and often. It was her own desire, her own decision, that had led her here.

She glanced at him—he who had been so seasoned and so tender compared to boys she'd been with before, and who now stood framed by mustard bottles lined up in rows, buy-one-get-one tags flapping at their bases—and thought she saw pain in his eyes. At least some of what she'd believed he'd felt for her had to have been real. Didn't it? A bolt of hope, followed by a rumble of fear: he was as strong and solid as ever, and it was true that he could knock her over with his pinkie finger, regardless of how he might feel about it. It occurred to Maddy, not for the first time, that he could kill her.

Not here, though. Not in the baked bean aisle. He'd never seemed dangerous, and even now the thought of his physically harming her almost made Maddy laugh; but he was stronger than she was, and he was desperate, and desperation drove people to do things you wouldn't expect. Like destroy someone whose existence they found inconvenient, as he was capable of doing to her, as he was asking her to do to their child. Besides, horrible things happened all the time to girls like her, motherless, adrift. The only creature in the world that would miss Maddy if she disappeared, or at least the first who would notice, was an owl she worked with at the wildlife rehabilitation center where she volunteered, who courted her by leaving her gifts of his uneaten dead mice.

A thirtysomething woman in a pink camo hoodie, jean shorts, and flip-flops rounded the corner and shuffled down the aisle with a twelve-pack of Mountain Dew under her arm. Maddy's lover drew back against a shelf of Heinz condiments, standing as far from her as he could, and the sight of him cowering against ketchup rekindled her anger. She wanted to wound him. She needed him to know she didn't love him, to believe he had been nothing but an antidote to her boredom, her unbearable sadness. After the woman in camo turned the corner and disappeared, she said, "This was never about you, you know."

She meant it as a blow to his ego, which she pictured as something alive and compact and, for some reason, furry, like a hamster running forever in a wheel inside the iron cage of him. She had meant to make it sound like she was cavalier enough to use him for casual fun. But he only said, "I know, and for that I am truly sorry," and added a can of crushed tomatoes to his cart. "You have someone to drive you?"

She nodded, thought of Jada, three hours away and unaware of the pregnancy. They hadn't spoken in months, hadn't seen each other since Christmas. She knew Jada would want to be the first person she'd consult, would want to save her. For her, the solution to Maddy's problem would be clear. She would promise not to judge Maddy for choosing what anybody could see was the right option. Everybody always pretended they wouldn't judge you, but they did so assuming you'd come around to their point of view, assuming you'd choose correctly.

Maddy searched the library of her mind for her earliest image of her sister, thinking it might somehow be the purest, and found a hazy picture of Jada dressing for a school dance she'd gone to with Drew. She must have been sixteen or seventeen, Maddy four or five. Maddy remembered watching her emerge from her bedroom like a queen about to address a horde of stinky commoners, her mother zipping the back of Jada's dress up to a point between her shoulder blades. She saw the narrow stem of Jada's neck; she saw her mother dab powder from a compact onto Jada's nose, heard the compact snap shut; she watched her mother hold something out to Jada, heard Jada say, "No, no lipstick." Big sister went off to the ball bare-lipped while little sister smeared the rose-red stick across her mouth, perched on a step stool before the bathroom mirror, dreaming of dancing, clowning her face with wax.

A long silence had stretched in the baked bean aisle. He said, "Well, then," and stuck out his hand, looking both ways as if about to cross a busy street.

Maddy stared at the hand. The furry knuckles, the clean nails.

"You're still going to help me, right?" she said. "With the other stuff?"

"Of course."

"You promised."

He was still standing there with his hand out. "I'll do my best."

She took the hand. They shook. Then he said, "Take care, Maddy," and walked away.

*Take care, take care*—she repeated the words in her head until they clumped together, shifting shapes, their meaning loosening and finally separating from them. *Take care, take air, caretake.* Care of what? He could have meant a baby. *Do the right thing*—he hadn't said what it was. Maddy pushed her cart in the opposite direction from where he'd gone, moving toward meat, her stomach turning at the sight of raw chicken breasts on Styrofoam beds. It was cold in the store. Goose bumps formed on her arms.

*Did* she want a child? Did it matter? Like him, she'd thought at first that she should get rid of it. But then fear had clamped down on her heart like a claw. She'd seen those pictures of dead fetuses like mangled cocktail shrimp, bloody feet on roadside billboards threatening damnation. If asked, Maddy would have denied believing in hell, at least until faced with the prospect that she might go there. Now suddenly it loomed.

She looked down at the envelope he'd given her, turned it slot-side up, and worked the gold clasp out of its hole. He hadn't licked the adhesive. She peeked inside and thumbed the bills she'd later count to confirm: four thousand dollars.

She wanted her mother. Panic rose in her chest, and she paused, breathing from her belly the way the school counselor had taught her in the brief time that Maddy saw her before graduating. The counselor had given her mantras to repeat when the panic struck. *I am stronger than my grief. I am going to be okay.* The same things her lover had said to her just now, or thereabouts, as if he'd known their power. *I am going to be okay,* she recited, rolling her way down the candy aisle. It was a phrase she repeated to herself almost daily, it was the thing she worked hardest to believe, and yet now that he'd said it to her it felt cheap, canned. Maddy swiped a bag of gummy bears from a shelf, tore it open, and popped a rainbow of bears two by two into her mouth.

No, she didn't want a baby. But she didn't not want one, either. She wanted only not to be in the situation she was in. She wanted not to have to choose.

The Haribo bag was half-empty by the time she wheeled her buggy down the checkout lane. She sealed the bag and placed it on the conveyor belt, then opened the envelope. Crisp hundred-dollar bills, collated into bricks and gum-banded together.

"This all?" the cashier asked, scanning the gummy bears. Her name tag read KAITLIN. She was about Maddy's age and, Maddy noticed, also pregnant. Maddy slid a bill from its pack and studied Ben Franklin's face, the droopy eyes and pursed lips. Didn't he have glasses? She'd thought he had glasses. But what did she know about founding fathers?

"No," she said, folding and unfolding the bill, taking in the rows of tabloids and candy that surrounded her. "That's not all."

She grabbed a Snickers bar, then two. A box of mints. Two packages of bubble gum, the kind that only held its flavor for the first few glorious chews. A magazine: RADICAL SPRING BEAUTY: QUICK FIXES FOR HAIR & SKIN! A bag of Twizzlers, a stick of cherry ChapStick, two bars of Daffin's milk chocolate from a fundraiser box. Three bags of Peanut M&M's, her dad's favorite. She knew his new girlfriend Carole Ann's favorite candy, too—3 Musketeers—and grabbed one for her before thinking twice and putting it back. She bore Carole Ann no ill will, but neither did she wish to shower her in gifts, to suggest that the three of them were some sort of family—her father, his girlfriend, and Maddy, cleaning houses for money and nursing birds in her spare time and still living at home, not a third musketeer but a third wheel, as squeaky and sad as the one on the buggy she now pushed to the end of the checkout aisle. The cashier bagged her stash and rolled her eyes when Maddy handed her the hundred.

"You don't have nothing smaller?"

"No."

Kaitlin gave Maddy a suspicious look and held the bill up to the light.

"It's real," Maddy said, too loudly.

Kaitlin stuffed Ben into the register and sluggishly counted change. "Aren't you fancy," she said.

In her car, her mother's old Taurus, Maddy tore open a chocolate bar and stuffed the manila envelope crookedly beneath the passenger seat so that only an orange triangle poked out like a beak. She'd left the store with three thousand nine hundred seventy-some dollars, but the weight of the coins where the bill had been gave the illusion that she was leaving with more than she'd started with. That nothing had been lost.

Friday night, almost time for *Dateline*. Since her mother's death, Maddy and her father had feasted on late-night crime shows. She'd grown hungry for the sight of other people's suffering. Her fear that she could join their grisly ranks at any time, be stuffed in a trunk, buried in the woods, *a body found in a cornfield outside of town*, was a welcome reminder: she was alive, and she wanted to stay that way. She would not, as it was sometimes tempting to believe since she lost her mother, rather have died along with her.

Inside her parents'—her father's—house, Maddy hung her jacket on a deer-foot coatrack, slipping the collar over the ledge of a cloven hoof. She plopped down on the other end of the couch from where her father slumped, feet on the coffee table as her mother would not have allowed, boots untied but not removed. The house was dirty— a film of dust on the coffee table, the bent and broken mini blinds, the TV stand with the mystery gunk on it that never scrubbed off; crumbs on the couch cushions; balled-up burger wrappers giving off a greasy smell—but after cleaning other people's homes all day, Maddy could not bring herself to care about her own. She had not inherited her mother's dedication to cleanliness.

Blue light illuminated her father's face and the faded checkered curtains that had hung in the house's front windows for as long as Maddy could remember. Inside each box in the checkerbox pattern was a white goose with a blue ribbon tied around its neck. Maddy tried to imagine her young mother hanging these curtains, but the image was painful and strange (why geese? when?), and she shooed it away. The windowsill was a mass grave, fly carcasses heaped behind the curtains, and it saddened Maddy to think of the creatures dashing themselves against the glass. She passed her father one of the bags of Peanut M&M's, and he accepted it with a nod.

"*A murder case full of heart-stopping twists and turns,*" Andrea Canning narrated onscreen when the show began, "*culminating in a gavel-rattling revelation! At the center of it all, a stunning thirty-year-old wife and mother.*"

Normally Maddy consumed these mysteries in silence, but tonight she felt restless, cantankerous. She propped her feet next to her father's. She could feel the breeze from the ceiling fan, which wobbled and ticked above her like a metronome, kissing the exposed flesh of her toes and the pads of her heels through holes in her socks.

"Why do they always do that?" she said. "'A stunning thirty-year-old wife and mother.' Why does it matter she was pretty? Would it be less sad she got murdered if she wasn't cute, or if she didn't have a husband and kids?"

Her father gave her a sidelong look. "Don't know."

"*Kimberly lit up every room she entered,*" said the dead woman's friend. Her hair was perfect, her makeup was perfect. The sad people on these shows were always so clean. "*That girl had a heart of gold.*"

For some reason this jagged Maddy, too. "And that." She pointed to the screen. The survivors were always saying things like this. *She loved to laugh. She was always smiling.* "Just once I'd like to hear one of these people say, 'She was just okay. Kind of a dick sometimes.'"

"Watch your mouth." He was shouting, probably without meaning to. His hearing was shot from his years in the sawmill, certain sounds and frequencies inaccessible to him. It was easy to forget this, his raised voice a constant source of conflict between him and each of the family's women as, feeling yelled at, they responded in kind.

"'She didn't really have any interesting hobbies,'" Maddy went on. "'Never remembered birthdays. Was always forgetting to pick up the kids from school.'"

Her father glanced at her. "Who put a burr under your saddle?"

"It's not a burr," she said. "It's an observation."

Her throat tensed, and her nose got hot. She thought of her plump, now jingling package of cash, which she realized—oops—she'd left in her car. The episode dragged on—Kimberly's body found in nothing but socks, the tread marks of boots ground into her back—but it failed to work its magic on Maddy. Her stomach was a nervous tangle, her heart hammered in her ears. What the fuck was she supposed to do? Should she tell her father she was pregnant?

The phrase sprang to her lips, but she kept them closed. His ignorance on the matter made it feel somehow less final. It seemed to her that some form of patriarchal recognition was required in all things to make them fully true, to give them consequence and meaning. As long as her father remained in the dark, no matter how her body might change, she could entertain the illusion that nothing that was happening to her was real.

"It's gonna be the ex-husband," her father said, motioning to the screen, where dead Kimberly's friend described Kimberly's joy upon remarrying and finding herself pregnant.

"Nah," Maddy said. "It's gonna be the new husband."

The light from the screen made the room look cool and underwater, like a shark tank or the ocean Maddy had never seen. She imagined a hammerhead slithering through the blue air, the side-to-side, sexy movement of its tail. The mean slit of its mouth. She crossed her arms and hugged herself.

*Dad,* she said in her head. But what would happen if she said it out loud?

Probably this: he'd demand to know the father, threaten violence. To him, maybe to her. Or maybe he wouldn't be surprised. Maybe he'd even be happy. She wasn't a child, after all; she was nineteen, would be twenty in June. She'd finished school, wasn't really interested in college, no matter or maybe because of how often Jada bugged her about applying. She didn't have a great job, but she had *a* job. Other girls she knew had had babies.

What would her father say about her if she was gone? *She had a heart of gold?*

Abruptly he swung his feet to the floor and handed Maddy the TV clicker, smudged with fingerprints, the numbers worn off the buttons.

"Going out," he said, and tied his bootlaces.

"What?" she said, and he looked at her like, *What's the big deal?* Between his nights at Carole Ann's and his time at work, Maddy was used to having the house to herself. "You aren't going to watch?"

He rooted through the debris on the coffee table for the keys to his truck. "Catch me up tomorrow."

Maddy's blood raced. Her palms were sweaty. *Don't leave me.*
But he left.

"Hold down the fort," he said, closing the door behind him. "See you tomorrow, Chiclet."

When he was gone the house was too still, *Dateline* too loud and too creepy. Maddy got to her feet, as if she might need to run. She wrapped her arms around herself, touched her ribs. She had to get out of there.

The last thing she saw before she turned off the TV was the face of the man who had discovered the murdered woman's body. "Damned shame," he said, standing on a broken-down porch in the snow, a frozen field stretching behind him. "You never expect to find someone dead, least of all a pretty thing like her."

When she climbed behind the wheel and started the engine, she didn't know where she was going besides away from her father's house. Past the junkyards and the three Amish farms tucked among the trees, curtains swept to one side, buggies reposing in driveways; past one buggy on the road, single horse clopping, the driver holding up a hand in greeting as she passed; down between the Methodist churches standing across from one another at the nearest intersection (one Free, one United; the sign at the corner: EVERY DAY IS PRAY DAY). She could leave this place, drive to Jada's in Pittsburgh. At the stop sign between the two churches, she called Jada, but Jada didn't pick up, and Maddy didn't leave a voicemail. She did not want to need Jada, but deep down, she knew she did. It was a grudging need, and a futile one; Jada wasn't here.

The number one cause of injury to birds is being hit by cars, so Maddy drove carefully. Past Mrs. Shivers's Soft Serve Shack, not yet open for the season. Past a sign for stump removal (GOT STUMPS? GET 'EM DONE!); past a makeshift cross marking the site of a roadside death. Past the carcass of a groundhog, the carcass of a deer. A billboard for a gun raffle, another bearing the masked face of a raccoon: RABIES BITES! WILD ANIMALS DO NOT MAKE GOOD PETS! Past the Stumble Inn, its gravel lot packed, its sign, NOW SERVIN MOONS INE. Past yard sign after yard sign, flag after flag: MAKE AMERICA GREAT AGAIN MAKE AMERICA GREAT AGAIN MAKE AMERICA GREAT AGAIN. She was Kimberly, the murdered woman with the golden heart, the pregnant mother found in a field. The twist: it wasn't the ex-husband who put her there, and it wasn't the new husband, either. In this version of the story, in Maddy's version, it was the woman herself.

Eventually she found herself at the bridge. Approaching it, wiping her eyes, Maddy stopped at a railroad crossing and looked both ways. She pictured the pregnancy test she'd held in her hand, its two affirmative lines as parallel and cold as the steel tracks before which she brought her mother's car to a full stop, following instructions, like a model citizen. It did not occur to her until the car had rocked backward, settling into the stop, that this was not something a girl set on suicide would do. She would sail forward, driver's ed be damned, hurling herself toward the prospect of oblivion.

She bumped over the tracks. Past a sign for Stroup's maple syrup (she thought, in spite of herself, of pancakes), gathering her resolve. When she reached the visitors' center, she parked her car in the empty lot. The platforms and overlooks offering views of the collapsed railroad bridge were empty. On the platform just beneath the bridge, where the structure merged into the hill, she paused and stared through the hollow spaces between the remaining support towers, a latticework of rails and beams crisscrossed and foreshortened in the moonlight, looking like a tunnel to nowhere. At the end of the tunnel, Maddy knew, the bridge and its supports ended abruptly hundreds of feet above the valley floor. It was too dark to make out the other standing segment of the viaduct on the opposite side of its crumbled midsection, a thousand feet away.

She ducked beneath the chain blocking the entrance to the bridge and picked her way over its wooden planking, reinforced when the bridge was opened to pedestrians who came to take in its crumpled structure. She thought she had a vague memory of riding across the intact bridge on an excursion train more than a decade ago, but when she strained her brain to recall any definite detail, she realized it was unlikely the event had taken place; she'd been just three or four when the train stopped running, five when a tornado destroyed the central part of the bridge. The trip was probably one Jada had taken with their parents before Maddy was born, a joyride she had heard talked about and into which she'd only imagined herself.

She was, after all, an accident. Her family had been fine without her. They'd had a dog, Trigger, a Brittany that died when Maddy was a toddler. A photo existed of the dog licking Maddy's feet, but she had no memory of him. Jada and their father, on the other hand, still reminisced about him, conjuring a bygone, better time when the liver-colored spaniel had stretched at their feet, tongue lolling, eyes full of love. Many times Maddy had dreamed of reaching out a hand to stroke the dog's silky fur, but many more times she had dreamed simply of being qualified to join in her family's nostalgia for the dog, this creature that bound them, this shared object of memory like a moon Maddy could orbit but on which she couldn't land.

If she died, would they speak of her the way they spoke of Trigger? Or would Maddy, like her mother, become a subject of non-conversation, a topic they feared touching lest it burn them? What would their lives be like without her—a family of three, then four, then three again, then two? Her father would mourn her silently and then, as he'd done with her mother, let go. As for Jada, she'd suffer through the loss stoically, sturdier than this or any other, firmer bridge.

Maddy checked her phone. No messages, no missed calls.

What remained of the railroad bridge was a six-hundred-foot-long section of the original structure, which cut off chillingly midway across the gorge at a point three hundred feet aboveground. She trudged to the end of it, plank by plank, following the old tracks. Where the bridge broke off, the state had built an observation deck with a high wooden railing overlooking the valley, where Maddy stopped, squinting at the collapsed girders and twisted towers lying sprawled on the valley floor, lit by the moon's dim glow. She moved to the center of the deck and planted her feet on the inch-thick window where visitors could stand, appearing to dangle vertiginously above the structure of the surviving bridge.

*She was okay,* she eulogized herself. *Kind of a dick sometimes. In school she was voted "most likely never to be single." Worst player on the softball team until she quit. A mediocre cleaning lady, she is survived by her dad; her smart, successful sister; her smart, successful brother-in-law; and the residents of the Pennsylvania Wilds Animal Rehabilitation Center, among them Wilson, the Eurasian eagle-owl; Warren, the one-eyed red-tailed hawk; Seneca, the screech owl with a broken wing; and some doves with concussions.*

She bent her knees, wound up, and jumped. Stamped, stomped as hard as she could, landing with all her weight on the platform, the impact sizzling through her legs. One, two, three-four-five times on the glass—*slam, slam*—until she stumbled and fell on the platform, knees buckling. Her phone was thrown from her pocket. For a moment she sat there trembling, looking up at the railing, over which she could throw herself if only she could summon the courage. She looked down at the glass beneath her and imagined the plunge through the hole, her limbs pinwheeling and plonking against girders. She thought of her mother, lowered into the ground.

At the viewing before the funeral, Maddy had looked at her mother's face for the last time, turned uncanny by makeup, which her mother had rarely worn in life. "Mama," she had whispered. She'd looked around at the room full of guests, people she knew and people she didn't. Somehow it had never fully occurred to Maddy until that moment that her mother had been not only a mother but a woman, Ellen, with her own thoughts and relationships with people besides her family and doctors. She was a woman who may not have planned Maddy but who also hadn't aborted her, a regular person who, staring at the positive lines on a pregnancy test two decades ago, had looked into the future and seen Maddy there—small and bumbling, not an accident or a miracle, perhaps, so much as a surprise—and said yes.

"Mama," Maddy had said again. "Ellen."

Then she had turned and seen Jada across the room, stone-faced and dry-eyed, deader inside than Ellen in her black box, and her heart had cracked, and out of the fissure had seeped a molten anger. After everything that had happened, everything Jada had done and not done, she wasn't even crying at their mother's funeral. What was *wrong* with her?

A crash in the distance to Maddy's left—a branch, an animal, a man?—made her jump and swivel. She squinted toward the end of the skywalk and imagined something crouching in the darkness. Then came the sustaining fear she'd sought and failed to find in tonight's *Dateline* episode, crawling up her spine, reconfirming her will to survive. Her hand moved to her pocket and drew out her keys, ready to stab whatever might come for her in the dark. Baby or no baby, mother or no mother, she wanted to live, even if she was alone in the world, her father checked out and her sister far away, their lives running parallel like the train tracks on this bridge, sourced from the same ore and laid close together but not touching.

The glass beneath Maddy seemed suddenly vengeful, as if it might cave after all just to call her bluff. She scrambled to her feet. Around and below her, spring peepers peeped their froggy booty calls. A breeze troubled her hair, tossing the streak she'd dyed pink at the front, strands like cold fingers tracing lines on her neck. She gathered all the air she could fit in the chambers of her lungs. She held it in, and then she let it out.

The scream echoed through the hills, the valley full of wailing, invisible girls, their cries both hers and not hers, turned eerie by the distance they'd traveled. Maddy turned, spooked, her chest empty, and made her way back down the skywalk, back into her life.

On the drive home she noticed the billboard. PREGNANT? SCARED? YOU'RE NOT ALONE.

# 3

## JADA

**April 2018**

If on her first trip to the closet Jada was baffled, on her second, two weeks later, she was genuinely alarmed. Who was this woman, bolting at the sound of her husband's car in the garage? Who was this person curled in a corner of the closet, drawn back from the strip of light threatening the door? Somehow, it was her, scared and alone, feeling the minutes stretch in the dark until it became clear Blake was in for the evening. Pizza was delivered. The cat again refused to disclose Jada's location. She had her phone on her this time, silenced, and when the screen lit up with a call from Maddy, she ignored it. She could smell the pizza, the briny note of the olives he loved and she hated. She pictured the brown bodies of kalamatas belly up on the cheese like roaches, and disgust rose in her throat even as her stomach growled. She would have to come out and face him, pick the olives off the pizza. She would have to explain herself.

But what could she say? That last week, while he was at a conference in Florida, she had ended her pregnancy? That she was still bleeding, just spots and not enough to be concerned about (she'd called, panicked) but enough that the procedure seemed not entirely over? She couldn't tell him that, and she didn't know what she could tell him instead. She was sorry, but not in the way he'd expect; what she regretted was not the abortion but the fact that she had not upheld her promise to be honest with him, that she had not felt *able* to be honest with him, because he would want the child, and because he always got what he wanted. Until now.

Jada pressed her thumbnail into the painted wood of the doorframe to leave behind two indentations, one for this visit, one for her last, like a parent marking a child's growth spurts. How long could this go on, how many marks could she make? She touched her engagement ring, tracing the sapphire's edges. She disliked the idea that it was her marriage, rather than hard work or scholarship, that had raised her up the rungs of the social ladder. She feared the prospect of carrying the secret of the abortion for the rest of her life. She feared Blake's pain if she told him. She disliked the feeling that she owed him and always would, that she might cease to operate without him, that he could be the only thing that kept her functioning, like a long-lasting battery. When her mother was dying, he used to interlock his fingers and place them on Jada's head, resting his chin on them and pressing down as if to shrink her. She had loved that pressure, had wanted him to crush her. She had mashed her face into his chest. He told her everything would be okay, and she had done her best to believe him.

As she prepared for her exit, Jada gave herself over to a castigation far more intense than she could expect from Blake, hurling insults at herself as if to build immunity to them. Shitty wife, nasty woman, fucked-up girl! (Sometimes, she wasn't sure how to designate herself, "woman" still seeming like a milestone title she hadn't yet reached, "girl" retaining a footloose, fancy-free quality she wasn't ready to surrender.) She unleashed herself on herself until the only thing left was to soften and rush to her own defense: *Enough*. Whose words were these, whose voices? They were both hers and not hers; it was as if she had absorbed them through her skin. Everyone was always yelling at everyone these days. Everyone, if they knew where she was and what she was doing and what she had already done, would yell at her.

When she stepped into the living room, the pizza box open exactly as she'd pictured it, a video game on the TV screen, Blake jumped, gripping the controller as though prepared to beat someone with it.

"Jesus, Jada, I thought you were an intruder," he said. "I could have killed you."

"I'm sorry."

He set down the controller. "Where were you?"

She shook her head, no words, and sank onto his lap. He cradled her, confused but yielding. She nuzzled his neck and inhaled slowly. This deep breath, this way of taking someone in, often seemed more intimate to her than sex, and preferable. A clean, skin-scented inflating, no mess, no risk; a body buoyant with another's essence. Sometimes she wished she could burrow into Blake and live cased inside him, hiding at the core of the thing she hid from. But when his hand traced down her back, then dipped lower, she sprang to her feet: no.

He shed his tenderness, sulking. On the wall behind him hung the antique print of an opium poppy she'd given him for his birthday, *Papaver somniferum* in cursive at its base.

"Can we talk about this already?" he asked. A stress line had formed between his brows, as fine as an eyelash, but deep. "What's with you?"

"I'm not in the mood," she said.

"You're never in the mood."

He was right. Her pregnancy had been the result of a few missed pills, the missing of which had been the result of a growing sense of their unnecessity; she was practically abstinent.

"You rarely initiate," she deflected. "It's not like I'm constantly rebuffing you."

This claim was half-true and depended on how you defined its verbs. She had chosen not to acknowledge the potential of certain advances Blake made to lead to other, erotic ones. Instead she treated these advances—a back rub, the brushing of a strand of hair from her face—as self-contained and platonic. If she could pretend oblivious-ness, it seemed, she could not be blamed for not engaging.

"Because I know I'll get shot down," he said. "Besides, I don't have to initiate. The initiation is implied."

"Implied?"

"I'm a man."

"So?"

"So I'm ready all the time. The ball's in your court, babe."

Right again: Clark & Hatfield, etc. An army of attractive confed-erates loosed on unsuspecting undergrads in the seventies had con-firmed it, as had subsequent studies: in heterosexual couples, women are the gatekeepers of sex. When asked a series of questions of esca-lating intimacy—Would you go out with me? Would you come over to my place?—participants' responses revealed substantial gender dif-ferences in attitudes toward sex. While about half of both men and women agreed to a date, a significantly higher number of men agreed to an apartment visit, and a startling 80 percent of men agreed to sex with the hot confederate, while not a single woman did. In roman-tic relationships between men and women, research showed, there's virtually no correspondence between when a man *wants* to have sex and when a couple actually does. For women, this correspondence is approximately one to one.

Jada revisited the research in her mind, but her ability to contextualize Blake's complaint was of little comfort. It simply served as unwelcome confirmation that she was the problem.

But he hadn't read the research. She said, "So you're telling me you're out for a walk, or changing a tire . . ." This was a bad example; she doubted he'd ever changed a tire, but oh well. She hadn't changed one either, though she clung to a deep-seated if untested notion of herself as the kind of person who would. "You've got your . . . your lug nuts . . ."

"Lug nuts." He smiled tentatively.

". . . and your wrench . . . and you're thinking about sex. You're just pulsating with desire, on your back with the greasy pistons."

"I don't know about 'pulsating.' But if you came along and made an offer, yeah, I'd put down the tire iron."

She was approaching dangerous territory. A yellow light flashed in her brain. She'd had her shot at a tire-iron guy, and they both knew it. If she wanted to, she could pick back up with Drew tomorrow. And they both knew that, too.

Blake said, "Look, I miss you."

Jada's heart clenched, and she thought back to the day he'd proposed. Brunch at the Grand Concourse, oysters on the half shell, warm donuts birthed onto a conveyor belt, an interior like the first-class dining room of the *Titanic*. Her lot in life seemed to be to always feel just a little out of place, no matter where she was, and she'd been feeling that way among the stained glass and Corinthian columns when he'd tipped his half-full glass and spilled his water. Her lap was soaked. The waitstaff descended, armed with cloth napkins. Aronson, Willerman & Floyd, 1966: participants asked to evaluate the attractiveness of contestants on a fake trivia show preferred not the contestant who answered every question correctly and charismatically, but the one who answered correctly and then spilled his drink. Competence and confidence alone were not enough; competence and confidence with a hint of a flaw, a demonstration of basic human fallibility, made a fatal formula.

It had for Jada, too. It was as if the day had taken off its jacket, loosened its tie. Suddenly it could breathe; she could breathe. She could make him feel better by laughing off his blunder, chase the color from his face. There were things he needed that it was in her power to give.

After that, the symphony—she'd wept during Chopin's "Raindrop" Prelude, tried not to let him see, and loved him for his tact in pretending not to—and then he'd walked her past the house she would soon find out he'd bought and, rather than getting down on one knee, which she would have hated, took her hand and said, *I'm about to do something that terrifies me.* She'd been filled with a spinning terror of her own, and she stuttered out an *Okay, sure* before he even opened the velvet box.

She had known he was going to ask her well before the box appeared. All day she'd sensed a strange energy; all day, like a loyal dog, she'd smelled his fear, stuck close to him in an animal eagerness to assuage it. There were two ways of looking at everything, and looking back, she wasn't sure which one was true: had she said yes because she'd truly wanted to marry him, or had she said yes because she'd wanted to alleviate his suffering, reward his wanting? Because she'd been determined to win over his parents, John and Bernadette, who lived in Pine Township and seemed perennially dismissive of her? Because she knew her own mother wanted so badly to see her settled?

The answers she tried out shook her, first in one direction, then in the other. From one angle she could see the whole day—the prime rib at the Grand Concourse sliced under its heat lamp, the ice cubes spread over the wet tablecloth, her tears over the prelude, the fumbling proposal and her awkward *Okay, sure*—as romantic. She was a bumpkin, and he had plucked her from obscurity like a rare flower, his Fair Lady; he had offered her this life because he adored her; he'd pretended not to see her tears at Heinz Hall because he knew her well enough to understand that she'd want to keep them to herself; he respected her privacy; their engagement had been charmingly non-cookie-cutter.

Viewed from another angle, the day looked different. She was a bumpkin, and she didn't belong in his world, was square-pegging the shit out of the round hole of his life; he'd pretended not to see her tears at Heinz Hall not out of respect but because he didn't want to do the difficult work of acknowledging them; and she didn't want him to see them because she did not want to open herself to him that fully, as fully as she'd once opened herself to Drew, as fully as she might open herself to some other, more suitable man.

It was in her power to pick a story and stick to it. *What you water will grow,* her mother used to say. She ought to water the one in which her current situation constituted a happy ending. But then, she had spent the last hour cowering in a closet, and now here was her husband, standing in front of her, telling her he missed her as if she were a thousand miles away.

"I miss you too," Jada said, then played her trump card. "But you don't know what it's like to lose your mother. I can't just—"

"I know." Blake threw up his hands, and she knew the conversation was over. Ever since Ellen's death, she had blamed all her irritability on that single loss. She hadn't been wrong; her grief was a low buzz beneath everything, a constant ringing only she could hear, which had intensified her aversions to things like the feeling of her anklebones touching or the sight of fingerprints on glass, and that made her do things like clean what wasn't dirty or fall asleep next to the cat under the bed; Blake had caught her one day, half-smooshed beneath the frame, eyes red. She got a free pass to be weird, broken, and she was not not guilty of taking advantage. "I'm sorry," Blake said. "I know you're suffering."

She was sorry, too; he was suffering, too. *Try*, she told herself, *try. Want, want.* No one likes a frigid woman. No one wants a frigid wife.

She thought of her desire as a living but shut-down thing: a cat curled up and snoozing, each breath a purr. A sad tulip, sealed and pink, planted in the shade of her center. Why not water the flower? Why not coax those petals open?

But she was dry, rarely cried, that afternoon with Chopin an exception, the result of her rising consciousness of the pitter-pattering notes and their accumulation into a beautiful water torture that cracked her. Even at their mother's funeral, while Maddy was tear-streaked and salt-crusted, her cheeks blackened from smeared mascara, Jada had been dry. Looking at her from across the room, Maddy's red eyes had narrowed as from the midst of a huddle of mourners she mouthed the question Jada had been asking herself ever since: *What is wrong with you?*

# 4

## MADDY

**April 2018**

The New Dawn Women's Care Center was located in a boxy brick building, painted dark gray, between an auto parts store and a McDonald's a few towns over. Maddy had expected protesters, but there were none. Someone had stolen the *G*s from the sign out front: FREE PRE NANCY TESTIN WE CARE.

She parked by a dumpster behind the McDonald's and sat motionless in the Taurus for twenty minutes. *EMPOWER YOURSELF,* the center's website had read. *Okay,* Maddy had thought. It had taken her a few days to gather the courage to come here, during which time she'd continued to keep her pregnancy a secret. Jada still hadn't returned her call from the night of her trip to the bridge, but no matter: Maddy would figure out her own shit. Now, behind the wheel of the parked car, she took a deep breath and prepared to be empowered. The website featured pictures of women of all shapes, sizes, and colors cradling babies or their own bulbous bellies. *KNOW YOUR OPTIONS,* the site said, and this was all Maddy wanted.

In fleeting moments of optimism that broke over her like waves, she imagined that there might be plausible options of which she wasn't already aware: waking up from a dream, for example, or time travel. Maybe the test she'd taken had been wrong. She imagined dozens of options like frosted cupcakes arranged behind glass, pastel-toned and sprinkled. She saw herself pointing to one, making her choice, peeling away its wrapper and popping it into her mouth, as through her it spread: power, the rush of it, sharp as a sugar high.

Away rolled the wave. Gone were the cupcake options, the many sweet, uncomplicated solutions. In their place Maddy pictured packages of red meat, cold and wrapped in butcher paper, leaking blood. She gripped the steering wheel. On her right middle finger, the gold ring—her grandmother's—that her mother had given her. On her left, her silver wraparound snake ring, its little eyes staring. She told herself to breathe but found that she couldn't. Then, once another cool wave of hope swept over her—choices, power, choices—she let herself be buoyed; she crossed the parking lot; she entered the butt-ugly building. A sign on the door read TOUCHING HEARTS, TOUCHING LIVES.

"I need a pregnancy test," she told the receptionist, a woman in her fifties with short, dyed-red hair and even redder lipstick. "It's free, right?"

"That's right."

"You don't need insurance? I don't want my dad to get a bill."

"Nope." The receptionist smiled warmly. "Our services are confidential and free of charge. We're here to help you, not to make a profit. Did you take a pregnancy test at home?"

Maddy nodded.

"It was positive?"

Nod.

"We can verify that result for you, no problem. Did you miss your period?"

Nod.

The woman took Maddy's driver's license, then led her to a room whose cinder-block walls were painted a dusty mauve. Maddy took a seat on a floral upholstered love seat and heard, coming from a machine on a small table, a recording of nature sounds, waves set to a gentle piano accompaniment. On the walls hung pictures of infants with sausagey arms and round eyes, each enclosed in a gold frame. A television stood atop a bookshelf stocked with parenting magazines. Next to it, about a dozen pamphlets were arranged in a plastic holder. A photo of a Black woman in profile looking out a rain-streaked window below the words LIFE AFTER ABORTION. A photo of a pensive-looking white man below the words THINK SHE'S PREGNANT? A photo of two smiling teenagers below the words SEXUAL INTEGRITY PROGRAM. A photo of a woman sitting on a kitchen floor with her head in her hands below the words ABORTION PILL RESCUE. A photo of a woman's hands cradling her pregnant belly, her fingers and thumbs forming the shape of a heart, below the words ADOPTION: A LOVING OPTION.

The receptionist handed Maddy a plastic cup. "For your sample."

"Sample?"

"Urine," the woman said, then opened the door and motioned across the hall to a bathroom. "The test is self-administered. I'll help you when you're ready, okay?"

In the bathroom Maddy hovered over the toilet and held the cup between her legs. The ocean sounds helped. She missed at first. Some hit her finger. Embarrassing that after a lifetime of peeing, when it came time to harvest some she couldn't calculate where to place the cup.

*Well, get used to it,* she told herself. Babies peed on you all the time. Babies pooped on you, like birds. And it wasn't like she didn't have a wealth of experience cleaning up other people's pee, crusted on the rims of toilet bowls, caked on tile floors.

With her cup in hand, she returned to the room with the framed baby pictures. When she leaned close enough to one, her nose almost touching the glass, she could make out a grid of fine lines and tiny numbers showing through the babies' skin. They'd been torn from calendars. A seagull called from the sound machine. A statue of the Virgin Mary with a coil of unlit Christmas lights wrapped around her base stood on a built-in corner shelf. Maddy picked up the ABORTION PILL RESCUE pamphlet and read: *Chemical abortion CAN be reversed, but time is of the essence! Medical professionals can save 64 to 68 percent of pregnancies using the natural hormone progesterone! If you have taken the first of two abortion pills and are having second thoughts, you are not alone! CALL OUR 24/7 HOTLINE NOW!*

The red-haired woman reentered the room and motioned for Maddy to sit back down on the love seat. "You can set your sample there," she said, pointing to the small table in front of the couch. Then she unwrapped a pregnancy test stick like the one Maddy had bought at CVS. "Go 'head and dip it."

"It looks like the test I took at home."

"It's a medical-grade hCG urine test," the woman said.

Maddy dipped the stick into her pee.

"Good." The woman took the test and the cup from Maddy and waited as a small plus sign appeared. "Looks like a positive," she said. "I'll send someone in to talk through the big news with you, 'kay?" Then she reached for something—Maddy assumed she meant to take her blood pressure and held out her arm—that turned out to be a TV remote. She roused the TV from slumber, hit play, muted the sound machine, and left the room as a film began to play, showing three happy women with children—one infant, two toddlers—explaining how thrilled they were that they'd come to the New Dawn Women's Care Center seeking help.

"I was so scared," said a Black woman, Lia, on the screen. "But the people at New Dawn were like a second family to me." She wiped away tears, and the camera panned out to show the toddler squirming in her lap.

The scene changed, and the woman who had just taken Maddy's pregnancy test away appeared onscreen. "The first time I held Lia's son," she said, "it was like . . ." She began to cry. "The heavens shined down that day." She wiped away a tear. "After all she'd been through . . . they shined down."

When the film ended, the door opened again, and a new woman walked in.

"Maddy!" she said, as if she'd been waiting for her all her life. "It's wonderful to meet you. I'm Pat, and I'll be your client advocate."

She put out her hand, and Maddy shook it.

"Ooh, I *love* your earrings," Pat said.

Maddy touched her earlobes. She was wearing her peanut butter and jelly earrings—one piece of bread in each ear, brown on the left for peanut butter, purple on the right for jelly, each with smiley faces and peachy blush circles on their cheeks.

Pat was what people must mean when they called someone "big-boned"—tall and wide, statuesque in a way at once matronly and masculine. She was powerful-looking but with a softness about her, her edges seeming smudged, her face acne-scarred. She wore a short-sleeved, rose-colored sweater of a thick, bumpy bouclé, pillowy nodes of yarn bursting from it like tiny pink pieces of popcorn. Over it, she pulled a white lab coat that had been hanging on a hook in the corner of the room. A frizz of gray-blond hair was gathered in a low poof of a ponytail like a bird's nest at her neck, where there hung a gold crucifix. The clasp had worked its way to the front of the necklace and was pushing up against the cross.

"Do you have any questions about the video?"

Maddy shrugged.

"None?"

"Well," Maddy said. "I guess . . . why should I care how the workers here felt when they held those girls' babies?"

"I'm sorry?"

"It's just . . ." Maddy faltered. "They aren't *their* babies. Who cares how it felt for them to hold somebody else's kid?"

Pat removed a notepad and pencil from the shelf full of parenting magazines and opened the pad to a clean page. "That's a good question, Maddy. So, we here at the center are in it with our girls for the long haul. We care about you. We like to think of ourselves as a family."

Maddy flinched. She supposed that when other people said "family," they meant that you trusted each other, that you went around hugging or affectionately palming each other's shoulders and talking about your feelings. Things Maddy's own family did not do.

"Okay," she said.

Pat smiled. "So, may I ask if you participate in a faith tradition?"

The question surprised Maddy. Her family had attended the Methodist church at the end of their road—the Free one, with the sign out front bearing messages like GOD ALWAYS ANSWERS HIS KNEEMAIL—periodically throughout her childhood, hardly enough for her to call herself a member. Although her father had returned to the church after her mother's death—it was where he'd met Carole Ann—Maddy had not. Perhaps ironically, she felt compelled by the cross that hung from Pat's neck to lie.

"Christian," she said.

Pat clasped her hands awkwardly, her pencil still pinched between a finger and a thumb. Her breasts wobbled. "I'm so glad to hear that, Maddy! Me too."

"Okay."

"And I have to ask, Maddy . . . how many partners have you been with?"

"With?"

"*With.*"

Maddy felt the blood rush to her face. "Five?"

"Five. And how old are you?"

"Nineteen."

"Oh," Pat cooed. "So, you know, Maddy, your body is precious, and sex is a beautiful gift. It's not a thing to be wasted." She touched Maddy's hand. "'Do you not know that your body is a temple of the Holy Spirit, who is in you, whom you have received from God?'" she quoted. "'You are not your own; you were bought at a price. Therefore—'"

Maddy pulled away. She motioned to Pat's necklace. "Your clasp is in front."

Pat smiled and patted the cross back in place. "So," she pressed. "What's your relationship with your parents like?"

"What?"

"You get along with them? Are you close?"

"No," Maddy said. "I mean, yes. My mom's dead."

"Oh." Pat scribbled on her notepad, looking genuinely devastated, a tremor in her voice. "I'm so sorry to hear that. How long ago did she pass?"

"A year and a half." Nineteen months, almost to the day. *I am going to be okay,* Maddy incanted. *I am going to be okay.*

"And your dad?"

"No."

"No, you aren't close?"

"No, he's not dead."

"How is your relationship with him?"

"I don't know," Maddy said. "Fine." Pat watched her, waiting for more. "Okay, I guess."

She'd spent a lot of time being angry with her father for the safe distance he'd seemed to keep, over the years, from her mother. He was skeptical of every treatment she tried, spent what seemed to Maddy like more than his fair share of time in the woods, hunting or wandering or whatever. Only recently had it occurred to her that he might have been priming himself for the loss to come. Not that that was any excuse. Once, Maddy had overheard an oncology nurse say to a trainee upon hearing that one of their patients' husbands had left her, "Isn't that always the way? The partners seem so supportive during the chemo, then boom! They disappear." In the weeks that followed, Maddy had viewed her father with a paranoid skepticism. He had not disappeared, but he had detached, and one night after an argument over household chores she had spat at him, "Why don't you just leave already?" But say what you would about her father, he'd stuck around.

Pat was waiting for her to say something, and Maddy wondered if she'd missed a question. She said, "I really just want to know, you know. My options." She glanced from baby face to baby face on the wall. They all looked the same to her. "I want to know how much it costs."

Pat looked concerned. "Would you say you're abortion-minded?"

"I don't know."

She had always heard that ending a pregnancy was taking a life, though a vocal group of girls at her high school had argued otherwise. At school there had been a clear hierarchy of girls, with a left-to-right political spectrum running through them that Maddy had never worked too hard to place herself upon but had bounced along uncommittedly. Both her über-conservative classmates and their staunchest feminist counterparts had judged Maddy for the nudes that went around when she broke up with her ex, Bear—one side because she'd taken them at all and the other because she'd been so bad at it, the poses graceless, the lighting unflattering. And both sides would judge her if she had a baby—one side for having sex and the other for doing it irresponsibly, then brain-washily declining to exercise her right *not* to have a baby. My body my choice my ass, Maddy thought. Many of the girls she knew had been no more cautious than she had in their trading of sex and selfies, only luckier, but she felt that no matter what she did, in their eyes she'd be wrong. She could not do right by the women in her life any more than she could do right by the men.

"Honey," Pat said. "Is somebody pressuring you to have an abortion? Is someone trying to force you?"

Maddy wasn't sure how to answer. Force—it implied muscle, brawn. No, he hadn't used force. He had asked her to promise she'd do it, firmly but not forcefully, when he promised her the money, and she had agreed.

"No," she said.

Pat scribbled on her notepad. "So, I know abortion can seem like an easy answer," she said. "But, see, a lot of women rush into it without knowing the facts. So then they come in here later looking to use our abortion recovery services—which we do offer, we do offer those—and every one of them tells us she wishes she'd known the facts beforehand."

"Which facts?"

"Oh," Pat said, "people will tell you it's no big deal, right? But you know how much doctors get paid to do abortions? They're making the big bucks, Maddy. So then the women, the victims, they end up with depression, they can end up with PTSD. It's like being at war. And did you know that every abortion you have increases the likelihood you'll develop cancer?"

At this Maddy rocked in her seat. It was as if Pat had physically pushed her.

"We just want you to know some of the health risks so you can make an informed decision," Pat said. "For instance, you should know it can puncture the cervix. In some cases, the intestines"—she lowered her voice, as if a gang of intestines might be listening in— "well, Maddy, they get sucked through the hole."

"I never said I wanted it," Maddy said.

"Of course." Pat smiled a wide, warm smile. "And you know, we're not here to judge you. We want you to make the choice that's best for you. We just want you to really take the time to think before you choose. Are you making a decision that you can live well with for the rest of your life? That's what we want you to think about."

"Okay."

"Let's just get through these questions, shall we? Then we'll do a quick ultrasound to confirm that you have a viable uterine pregnancy."

"Viable." Again, the cupcakes under glass, sugary-shiny.

"That's right. About one in four pregnancies ends in miscarriage, you know, Maddy, so there's no need for an abortion. It's all done naturally."

Naturally. Of course Maddy knew some pregnancies ended in miscarriage, but she did not know much about them. Why didn't she know this stuff? Why was she like a baby, wide-eyed and trusting, in this place where people came to learn about having babies?

In middle school health class the teacher had taken two sheets of
construction paper, one red and one white, pasted them together,
and then near the end of the class session pulled them apart so that
each sheet was covered in torn chunks of the other, scraps rimmed
by sticky residue. *This is what sex does,* the teacher said, *and this is
what happens after*: bits of this one stuck on that one, bits of that
one stuck on this one. You could never take them back. In health she
had learned a lot of facts about chlamydia and genital warts, but she
had not seemed to learn anything she could draw on here, now. Years
ago, Jada had tried to supplement Maddy's sex ed, but her attempt
was embarrassing and largely ineffectual. She had given Maddy two
books about bodies and sex. One was dry and full of pen drawings,
the artist-rendered curlicues of pubes making Maddy gag. The other
was mushier and encouraged her to lie on the floor and hold a mirror up to herself to celebrate the real thing. Jada had set the books
on the desk in Maddy's bedroom and muttered, "Let me know if you
have any questions."

But Maddy had not done the thing with the mirror and did not
tour the most intimate parts of herself until she began snapping selfies for Bear and a couple of other guys. She'd pushed the books to the
back of a shelf and forgotten them. She didn't need books; she had
plenty of online content, and she'd said as much to Jada, delighting in
making her feel old, the out-of-touch millennial who'd come of age
during dial-up. It must have worked, because Jada did not press her,
and now here Maddy was, seated across from Pat, who was asking,
"Have you told the father?"

Maddy hadn't expected to be asked about him. "Why?"

"It's okay, Maddy," Pat pressed. "I just want to help. Does he know?"

"He knows."

"And how does he feel about becoming a daddy?"

"Not great."

Pat nodded. "It's okay, honey. It's good that you shared your news with him. It can be scary for Dad, just like it's scary for Mom sometimes. What's his name?"

Maddy was silent. *I am going to be okay.*

"Nothing you tell me leaves this room, hon, I promise." Pat put a hand over her heart. "I'm just gathering the facts in case I need to follow up with you later."

What difference did it make, his name? She couldn't tell. She couldn't open that box, not now and maybe not ever.

She needed a name, though, and fast. In her panic all possible men's names had seemed to disappear, becoming blank spaces in her mind.

"His name is Blake," she said, and Pat set aside her notepad.

Pat led Maddy to another room, gave her a paper skirt to cover her lower half, and told her to lie on a table positioned next to an ultrasound machine. It would have to be done transvaginally, Pat said, and parted Maddy's knees.

"Scoot closer to the edge," she ordered. "There—perfect."

Maddy was at once terrified and curious. A part of her had wondered whether what was growing inside her, stopping her period and making her ill, was not a baby at all but a family of tumors come to claim her. Now she would know for sure. Her body went rigid when she heard gel splitching out of a tube and felt a cold, wet wand probing her. She grabbed the edges of the table.

"Just relax," Pat cooed.

Maddy studied the tiles on the drop ceiling, the grid they made like the ones showing through the framed baby faces on the walls.

She rose and sank on waves of nausea. Pat's gray-blond presence hovered next to her on a stool. All of this was real.

"Now, this isn't a medical ultrasound," Pat said, herding Maddy's knees apart each time they tried to press themselves together. "It's just to check, okay? Then we can refer you to an ob-gyn."

Maddy closed her eyes and thought of cupcakes, tried to focus all her senses on the thought of a delicious meal, but it was hard to feel hungry with a probe inside you. She had a vision of a cooked chicken sitting on its haunches in a pot like a decapitated baby in a broth bath, and she retched, her whole middle clenching around the wand. She concentrated on a warm ache in the center of her forehead, a zit starting.

"Oh, honey," Pat exclaimed, "do you want to see?"

"No."

"Looks like you're nine weeks along."

"No, that's not right." Eight weeks, no more.

"This right here, this is the yolk sac," Pat said.

"Please don't say 'yolk sac.'"

"And this here is the baby!"

"Please don't say 'baby.'" What a curse that you couldn't refuse a thing without also acknowledging it, could not say "Don't say 'baby'" without saying "baby." Maddy turned her head and saw a white-rimmed circle inside a fuzzy dark universe. Inside the circle, a flickering blob.

"See that fluttering?"

"No," Maddy lied.

"That's the heartbeat." Pat clicked on something with a mouse, and a series of lines appeared on the screen. "We can measure . . . ," she was saying.

"Stop." Maddy pulled out the probe and sprang up, not bothering to wait until Pat left the room to change, struggling to hold the paper shield over her front, grabbing her underwear and balled-up jeans from the chair beside her. She dropped the paper gown and pulled on her panties, soaking them with lubricant.

"Okay, Maddy, it's okay," Pat was saying.

Maddy hauled up her jeans without buttoning them and threw the jelly-spattered paper shield on the floor. She fled the room, then the building, and stumbled to her car, the gel slick between her legs. It wasn't until she reached the Taurus that she realized she'd left her phone and keys behind.

She did her best to collect herself in the parking lot before going back in. She zipped and buttoned her pants, wiped her eyes. She was repulsed by the yolk sac in her body but also protective of it, as if she and this creature the size of the head of a nail had survived something together, a raid they'd withstood in solidarity with one another. Could it be this way, she wondered—the two of them a team, united against the world and its jellied probes?

She breathed in, she breathed out. An SUV circled through the McDonald's drive-thru, and she watched as a back window rolled halfway down and someone's hand appeared and dropped a snow of crumpled straw wrappers onto the pavement. Then she burst into tears.

God, what had gotten into her? A baby, of course; but this was not like her, weeping over a little litter. The SUV drove away, and Maddy thought that although she might be a royally fucked-up fuckup, she could do better than that, she could at least teach a kid not to treat the world like its own personal trash can. She could create a person who might turn out not to be so bad, who could cancel out someone else's badness. Maybe her own.

She breathed out, she breathed in. She jogged over to the straw paper where it lay just beyond the drive-thru window, picked it up, and threw it in the appropriate bin.

When she reentered New Dawn, Pat was waiting for her, Maddy's phone and keys and a fistful of pamphlets in hand, which Maddy accepted. She felt that an apology of some sort was due—to Pat or by Pat, she couldn't decide.

"I know what you're going through, Maddy," Pat said. "I know it's hard, but you're not alone. I care about you."

This woman—she was either off the rails or an angel of God. That she would offer love like this, that she would claim to care for some random girl and some random girl's yolk sac, shook Maddy. A moment ago Pat had seemed aggressive, probing, but now here she was holding out this love, a golden chalice inlaid with gems glittering like lizards' eyes. Could she really just *take* it?

The next thing Maddy knew, she was in Pat's arms, her nose smashed into Pat's shoulder. Pat shushed her, stroked her hair. Maddy inhaled the fuzz of her sweater, choked, swallowed mucus. Her arms pinned beneath Pat's, she could not move. She could not remember the last time she'd hugged another person like this. It was an embrace like a straitjacket, and it was just what she hadn't known she wanted. Her body softened, swaddled.

When at last she unwrapped herself, Pat guided her into a room stocked with gently used baby clothes, bottles, packages of diapers, and used toys arranged on shelves. "All this goes to helping our girls," she said, "through our First Steps program. You can take our classes to earn points to get free supplies through baby's first year." At the door she handed Maddy a printed ultrasound photo, white crosses at each end of the fetus to mark the points measured from. Then she pressed something else into Maddy's palm, closing her fingers around it.

"Pray, Maddy," Pat said. "God will not forsake you." Then Maddy exited through the gift shop as if she'd visited a museum.

Outside, she uncurled her fist. Inside it was a rubber fetus doll, about two inches long and looking like a tiny beige beluga whale with its big forehead, shuttered eyes, and beaky mouth, ankles crossed into what looked like a tail and arms folded inward like fins. Maddy breathed in, breathed out. *I am going to be okay.* She pinched the rubber head so that it warped and elongated. There was a hole in it somewhere; escaping air wheezed.

She couldn't stay here. Whatever was going to happen next could not happen within the boundaries of her normal life. She would finish this week's cleaning jobs and shifts at the wildlife center, cancel the rest, and go to Jada's. There was nowhere else to go.

Maddy folded the fetus back into her palm and squeezed. She decided that she would play a game, an un-fun game that would require her to imagine the kind of constant responsibility parenthood would entail and to consider how her life would need to rearrange itself if she took it on. The only rule: to keep the doll always on hand, remain vigilant and aware of its location as if it were a living child. She slipped it into her pocket.

She could do it, she thought. She could care for a person, whether rubber or real. Wash, feed, soothe, and shush to sleep. She knew she could do it. She had done it before.

# 5

## MADDY

### May 2016

Against her sister's advice and in preparation for her sister's arrival, Maddy fills a liquid measuring cup with food-grade hydrogen peroxide and pours it into her mother's bath. She swirls the peroxide through the warm water, feeling its caustic fizz, then moves aside to help her mother climb in.

"They say it's like breathing," Ellen says, as Maddy helps her lower herself into the tub. "Like breathing through your skin." She'll soak for thirty minutes, then rinse with clean water. The bath is supposed to oxygenate her blood, slowing the growth and spread of cancer cells, and though Jada has claimed that the research it's based on is outdated, Maddy runs the water anyway.

She pulls the shower curtains halfway closed to give her mother some semblance of privacy and sits down next to her on the linoleum. There are little hairs all over the floor, but Maddy has neither the time nor the willpower to clean it. When she sits, she can smell herself—the natural antiperspirant leaves her armpits stinky, but if this is the price she must pay, so be it. She's on the hunt for the source of her mother's cancer, and almost everything is a culprit, deodorant included. The shower curtains she's tugged closed are fabric and PEVA, the old PVC curtain tossed out months ago. Her shirt is made of organic cotton.

She's just been dumped but has another boy waiting in the wings. Last Friday she rode home from a party smooshed between boy one and boy two, holding both their hands at the same time, surreptitiously brushing one set of fingers, then the other, hedging her bets. The new boy has already told her he loves her, has been courting her with texts for weeks: *ILY SWEATY.* ("Sweaty?" she said. "Sweetie," he said, and all she could do to keep from laughing was kiss him.) Jada told her once that, statistically and contrary to popular belief, men were the "first in and last out" of relationships, three times more likely than women to say "I love you" first. Maddy had not believed it until now, and although she's not particularly passionate about this boy, she can't help but feel that she owes him for his eagerness, that it'd be mean not to reward his persistence.

The old boy used to tell her she was a bad girl, and when Maddy reflects on her covert double hand holding, on her indifference toward the new boy despite his professions of love, she thinks maybe he's right.

"Oh, Chiclet," her mother sighs when Maddy tells her about the breakup, the boy on deck. Her head rests on the edge of the tub. Beads of sweat gather on her forehead. She is exhausted, and Maddy is part of what exhausts her. "What's the hurry?"

"You can't wait for Jada to get married."

"Jada's an adult."

"I'm an adult," Maddy tries.

"You're seventeen."

"Only for a few more weeks."

Ellen begins to cry. She cries all the time. Maddy's chest tightens, and she rushes to change the subject.

"Mrs. Mayhew asked about you today," she says. Recently, she's taken over her mother's cleaning jobs. Ellen has held several jobs in Maddy's lifetime: cleaning, working as a teller at Northwest, selling craft supplies at a store that's now out of business. Maddy tells herself she's filling in for her mother temporarily, sustaining relationships with the handful of well-off families who used to hire her to clean their homes or maintain their camps so that her mother can return to work when she recovers. She tells herself she'll never clean another house—not even her own—once this emergency shift has ended.

"What'd you tell her," Ellen says.

"I said you're good." Maddy dabs her mother's forehead with a dry washcloth. "She says I can call her Meghan." Although Maddy hates cleaning, she likes going to the Mayhews'. Theirs is not a large house, a split-level with green shutters, but it has a regal bearing, sitting back from the road behind a wide front lawn, stately in a country way. Like they ought to own horses. Meghan's husband, Jason, is running for state senate and has a campaign ad in which he appears in front of the house with Meghan and their one-year-old son. Beneath them, his slogan: MAYHEW, THAT'S WHO! Extending from the left leg of the *M*, an undulating pattern of stars and stripes streaks like the tail of a comet. Although she has no real interest in politics, Maddy likes the feeling of playing a small role in the Mayhew campaign. The house's windows, she notices each time the ad airs, are sparkling clean.

"You can call her Mrs. Mayhew," Ellen says.

"I knew you'd say that." But in fact, Maddy agreed to greet both Mayhews on a first-name basis. And, in fact, this afternoon she slipped into a purple tweed suit jacket Meghan had left hanging on her closet door, the lining silky and cool against her bare arms. This, like some of the details of her breakup—it involved a nude selfie, Maddy on her knees with her hips thrown to the side, her face duck-lipped, sent to the wrong recipient (oops) and circulated widely—Maddy keeps from her mother.

"You turned on all the lights while you cleaned?" Ellen asks. "You did the blinds?"

"I did."

"All of them?"

"All of them." Maddy wears gloves when she cleans to protect herself from potentially carcinogenic chemicals. But what's in the gloves?

"You did the ceiling fans?" her mother asks. "Baseboards?"

"Yes."

"Garbage disposal? Did you use the orange peels?"

"Lemon peels."

Ellen sinks deeper into the bathwater. She starts to cry again. "My girl," she says. "You work so hard."

Maddy panics. She's grown used to the sight of her mother crying, but naked crying is a singular horror. She says, "It's not that bad."

"You all work so hard."

"We're okay." Maddy searches for another topic to switch to. "I'm thinking I might quit the wildlife center," she tells her mother, to test if it's true.

In addition to school and cleaning, Maddy has begun volunteering a few hours a week at a local wildlife rehabilitation facility that used to accept patients of all kinds but now cares almost exclusively for birds. She is not allowed to take glove-trained raptors on her arms, as she'd imagined herself doing, but is limited for the time being to menial tasks like greeting visitors, preparing mailings, moving Rodent-Pro feeder mice from the freezer to the fridge to thaw, and, to her dismay, more cleaning: mountains of bowls and dishes waiting to be washed, heaps of dirty laundry, sheet after sheet streaked with goose shit. She resents her status as peon but suspects the center is testing her level of dedication, withholding more exciting work until she proves herself committed. But when will that be, and what does she have to do to get there?

Ellen wipes her forehead with the back of her hand. "No, you aren't."

"I have school," Maddy pushes. "And work."

"It's just six hours a week."

The volunteering was Ellen's idea. *You need something to care about,* she'd said, and Maddy said, *I care about you,* and Ellen smiled sadly and said, *Something else.* But Maddy doesn't care about data entry or goose poop or stuffing envelopes. She cares about the baby songbirds fed from eyedroppers, the eagle with the partially amputated wing, the wounded possum for whom the staff hides treats so he can forage for them as he'd do in the wild. In summer, during baby bird season, resident hatchlings will be hand-fed every half hour for up to sixteen hours a day by volunteers like Maddy. It's this tender stewardship she looks forward to, despite her threats to quit the center. Deep down, Maddy knows Ellen is right: she needs something besides her mother to care about.

"And I hate the polo shirts," Maddy says, referring to the green ones the volunteers wear.

"What's wrong with polo shirts?"

"They're for golfers," Maddy whines. "And wrestling coaches."

Ellen smiles. "LOL," she says, pronouncing the letters. Maddy has been teaching her text speak. "But you don't quit over a polo shirt."

"What do you quit over?" Maddy asks, but Ellen doesn't answer.

Maddy does not mention that she has also, over the past few weeks, been collecting money through a crowdfunding site she made

to travel with her mother to a clinic in Tijuana known for its experimental apricot seed extract therapy. The idea, the clinic's website
explains, is to kill only malignant cells, unlike chemotherapy, which
kills healthy ones, too. The cyanide derived from the apricot pits,
along with high-dose intravenous vitamin C, is supposed to provide
a healthy alternative to the more aggressive therapies that are, it's in-
creasingly clear, failing Maddy's mother.

This cyanide treatment will fit into the long chain of alternative
cures and questionable preventive treatments Maddy's mother has
sought out over the years, to her father's chagrin, in addition to the
hormone blockers and chemo pills: ginger and pau d'arco teas, the
ginkgo biloba nicknamed maidenhair, acupuncture, these peroxide
baths. Maddy has watched her mother lie out in the sun in the winter in an old swimsuit, her frayed canvas lounge chair surrounded by
snow, to soak up vitamin D. She has watched her mother guzzle green
smoothies that look and smell like blended grass. The cyanide treatment will take these remedies and raise them a sky without clouds,
smooth-centered conch shells, fresh fish tacos, fruit just off the tree.
The Mexican clinic's website boasts an impressive survival rate, an
in-house counselor who attends to patients' emotional health, and a
location on the Pacific coast where Maddy pictures herself and her
mother walking arm in arm beneath whispering palm trees with a
mariachi band playing happily in the background.

She hasn't told her father about Mexico, knows he'll go off about
drugs and gangs. He can't find out until it's too late to stop them.
Until they're at the airport. Until they're on the plane.

After the bath, Maddy rubs coconut oil into her mother's clean
legs and the soles of her feet, where a vicious rash has spread. She's
as intimate with her mother's body as she is with her own. Even as
a baby she was not so intimate; like an orphaned hatchling, she fed

mostly from a bottle—a bottle administered to her by Jada. Maddy both loves and resents this intimacy. She works the oil between her palms, spreads it across her mother's thin skin, tells her about feeding rescued chimney swifts on the wing, holding bugs in the air for them, pinched between gloved fingers.

Massaging her mother's legs takes Maddy back to bygone summers, to the public pool a half hour away where they used to swim and where Jada worked as a lifeguard. The version of her mother who took her there was in remission, health-conscious and wary but also functional and grateful, almost hyperactive—activities every day, the pool or the yard or the woods, working or swimming or walking or gardening or painting—as if she knew her wellness was temporary and wanted to make the most of it while it lasted. This version rubbed Maddy down with sunscreen (what was in the sunscreen?), spelling words in the lotion on her back and seeing if she could guess what they were, then wiping them away. She stood in the shallow end of the pool (the EPA has, so far, not classified chlorine for potential carcinogenicity) and parted these same smooth legs underwater so Maddy could dive down, grab calves or ankles, and push herself through.

Maddy is angry with her younger self for not fully appreciating moments like these when she was alive inside them, though she does not know what it would mean to do so. What could she have done inside those scenes but let them unreel at the same old pace? A minute is a minute whether you think about it or not; an hour is an hour. She could not have prolonged those turquoise afternoons with her mother, nor purified them, if she'd had the foresight of loss to realize what they'd one day come to mean to her. Probably, if she had had such foresight, it would only have spoiled the moment, injecting her innocence with preemptive grief.

She caps the coconut oil, gives her mother's legs a final, loving pat, and helps her into a loose-fitting dress. (What chemicals, she pauses to wonder, does this dream-blue Walmart shift contain? Flame retardants? Phthalates? Azo dyes?) No sooner is it over Ellen's head than Maddy hears Jada's car pull into the driveway and her feet crunch over the stones, then creak across the deck. There is a button on the dress that Maddy must fasten for Ellen, and as she works it through the buttonhole she can feel her mother drawing herself up, gathering her strength. It's like this every time; she puts on a show, pretends wellness, as if Jada is so fragile that she must be spared the sight of her mother as Maddy has just seen her, as Maddy sees her every day.

"You don't have to do that," Maddy ventures. The front door squeaks open.

"Do what?"

"Pretend for her."

But there is no time for Ellen to respond. The door swings open—they're a one-bathroom household, and privacy has always been hard to come by; growing up, their father was the only one in the family with door-locking privileges—and Jada breezes in. She is almost as tall as their father—nearly half a foot taller than Maddy or Ellen—and dressed in jeans, a black bomber jacket, and clean black booties, her hair pulled back in a bun that manages to look tidy in its messiness.

"There you are," she says, and takes their mother carefully into a hug. "You look good! Are you hungry? I picked up a pizza."

"We had pizza last night," Maddy says.

"Hello to you, too."

Jada holds Ellen with one arm, then reaches out the other to gather Maddy in.

"Phew," she says. "Still using that natural deodorant, huh?" She gives Maddy a teasing pat on the back.

Maddy studies her sister from inside her embrace. She wears no makeup except for a bit of mascara, and her beauty seems unaware of itself, as it always has, in a way that makes Maddy's chest ache with envy and admiration. But something is different about her now. There is something in the air. Something catches in Maddy's hair when Jada releases her, and Maddy turns to identify the source of the snag, and so it is that she's the first to see: on her sister's ring finger a massive sapphire sparkles, princess cut, the band rimmed in glittering diamonds.

In the living room, with the last of the day's light filtering through the goose curtains and the pizza box open on the coffee table, Maddy and her mother crowd Jada.

"Where did he ask? How'd he do it?" Ellen holds Jada's hand, her fingers resting at the base of the ring.

"We were walking down Fifth Avenue yesterday," Jada says, "and we stopped in front of this house. Turns out he'd made an offer." Gently, she pulls her hand back from her mother's, flexes and then closes her fist. She rests her unringed hand on top of her ringed one, hiding the stone.

"When?" Ellen asks, meaning the wedding. She's been doing this lately, cutting words from sentences as if to save herself the breath, and Maddy wonders if her mother's interest in text speak is more than casual curiosity about the ways of kids these days, if it is also a way of conserving her energy.

"I don't know." Jada studies their mother. "I'm thinking . . . soon." She turns to Maddy. "What about you, Mads? Still seeing . . . what was his name, Fish?"

"Bear." Maddy picks the pepperoni off a slice of pizza. "Nah. I dumped his ass."

"Maddy," Ellen chides. "Tell the truth." She turns to Jada. "He broke up with her, the jerk. Not good enough for our Chiclet."

"I'm sorry."

"I'm not sad," Maddy says.

"We have to celebrate," Ellen says, and it takes Maddy a moment to catch up—celebrate her breakup?

"We're celebrating now," says Jada.

"Where's Blake?" Maddy asks. "Why didn't you bring him?"

"I don't know."

"We'll have a party in the city," Ellen says. "See your new house."

"Good luck getting Dad there," says Maddy.

It isn't easy to get their father out of the woods. Jada has bribed him a few times—most recently, with a baseball game where during the seventh-inning stretch people in pierogi costumes raced across the field—but he's out of his element there, embarrassing. *Projects,* he'll say, passing a run-down building; *Apartments,* Jada will correct him. *Ghetto,* he'll say; *Neighborhood,* she'll counter. He's obsessed with drive-by shootings, which he speaks of as if they are scheduled events and which for a long time Maddy imagined as lawless parades where spectators, for reasons she could not fathom, knowingly took their lives into their hands. The irony of her father's fear is not lost on her: that a man who owns thirteen guns should be so disturbed by their existence outside what he considers their natural habitat—*his* habitat.

Once, after Jada spent her spring break with a college friend in New York, she sent Maddy a series of Photoshopped pictures into which she'd pasted the cutout image of their father crouched next to a pheasant he'd shot: their father and the pheasant on a nightclub dance floor, by the plinth of a Greek nude at the Met, at *Wicked* on Broadway, hunkered beneath the marquee. It was funny, and Maddy and Jada had laughed at the images together. But it made Maddy sad, too, and it makes her sad still, how more and more her father and Jada do not seem to speak the same language, or even to want to. She does not want to live in a world where her family, rather than being four-cornered, might become a rickety triangle in which she'll be the unwitting hypotenuse, stretched thin between her ever-diverging dad and sister.

"He'll come," her mother says, and here he comes now, home from the sawmill where he works as a lumber grader, kicking off his boots by the door.

"Jada's getting married," Maddy calls as he hulks through the room and helps himself to two slices of pizza, one piled atop the other, grease dripping.

"Really?"

"What do you mean, 'really'?" Ellen scolds. "They bought a house."

"Blake bought a house," Jada corrects her mother.

"For you," Ellen says proudly, and Jada looks like she might cry.

"Well," her father says. "Congratulations." He takes another double bite of pizza.

"Give her a hug," Ellen commands, motioning to Jada, who squirms in her chair. Their father, no more touchy-feely than his eldest daughter, is covered in sawdust. Last week, on speakerphone, he and Jada fought about the presidential campaign until she hung up on him.

"I will," he says, and moves to leave the room.

"Now," Ellen says. "Hug her."

The room goes still, silent. Ellen's body is weak, but in this weakness lies a kind of awful power. They will do as she commands.

Jada stands, faces him. His arms hover tentatively at her shoulders, barely touching them. Her hands flutter like injured wings at his back.

Ellen smiles. Maddy cringes. Her father steps away.

"Got to clean up," he says, and leaves the room.

"He works so hard," Ellen says, watching him go, and Maddy thinks she'll cry again. It's true: her father does work hard. A few years ago she accompanied him to the mill on Take Your Daughter to Work Day and was disappointed to find that she could not be near him on the job, could only watch from a room with a big window, where she sat in an orange plastic chair with a man who wasn't her dad who fed her Goldfish from a vending machine all day. No wonder her father was always tired, Maddy had thought as she observed him from behind smudged glass: on his feet all day, standing on moving lumber with a flexible scaling ruler he used to measure the width of boards whose length he could assess by sight. Flipping boards, inspecting, marking each with a grade before it was pulled away by a conveyor. Standing, flipping, marking all day—in heat, in cold, in his coveralls. Occupational exposure to wood dust is associated with increased risk of adenocarcinoma of the nasal cavity.

*How come you don't have any friends?* Maddy asked him once. She never saw him around other men, rarely saw her parents around other couples. There was the occasional cookout, a few company picnics (children diving into piles of sawdust, digging through its blond curls for coins and plastic rings), but that was all. Later, she would understand: the high turnover, the frequent injury, the constant noise. And, one October day: the one man with whom she'd seen her father fraternize, a man nicknamed Lady, feeding boards into the edger's row of chewing saws. A porcelain insulator from an electric fence grown into a tree, then into the board cut from it, missed by the metal detectors. The chunk of porcelain caught in the saw; two metal teeth broken off, thrown straight through Lady's safety glasses and into his now-missing eye.

Ellen turns back to Jada. "Honeymoon?"

"Italy?" Jada says the word shyly, as if she's sorry, and Maddy's heart catches fire. Why does her sister do this? If Maddy had what Jada has, she would not apologize, she'd . . . well, she doesn't know what she'd do.

Ellen nods in approval. "Like Diane Lane."

"Dad's crush," Maddy chimes in.

"Her and Dr. Quinn, Medicine Woman," Jada says.

Maddy thinks of her mother's words in the bathtub, her caution against hurrying in love. She thinks of the strain between her parents, her father grumbling at the natural cures her mother has tried, at the egg timer dinging to cue her meditation sessions on the living room floor. She knows little about her parents' love story, and it occurs to her that she might not have much time to ask.

"How did you know you wanted to marry Dad?" she asks.

Her mother dodges the question. "I didn't know," she says. "Just guessed." By now Maddy's father has come out of the bathroom and is rooting around in the fridge, within earshot.

"Would you do it again?"

"IDK." Ellen smiles mischievously at Maddy. "Maybe I'd marry a movie star."

Jada runs with it. "Which one?"

"Who'd be yours?"

"Easy. Gregory Peck, *Roman Holiday*," Jada says. "He and Audrey have such a nice day together. She goes back to her life with a new perspective."

"So you'd get together with the guy the star *doesn't* get together with?" Maddy asks.

"Well, yeah. I guess."

Ellen says, "Robert Redford, *Bridges of Madison County*."

"Ew," says Maddy.

"What about you, Mads?" asks Jada.

Maddy doesn't know, and something is stirring inside her, something blustery and gray. It's a dumb question, a false choice. She asked her mother a real question and got a fake answer, and this annoys her. Jada's head-hanging over her engagement annoys her, too. Maddy thinks of her first date with Bear, the boy who just dumped her. They'd gone for a walk by a reservoir with a spillway where people threw bits of bread to the thousands of carp that congregated there, roiling and churning and brown, like sewage come to life. There were so many fish that some were lifted fully out of the water on the bodies of others, crowd-surfing. A child's lost shoe bobbed on the scaly surface. The noise was nauseating—a nonstop slurping, the cold slaps of the carp's thrashing bodies—and when Bear hunched toward her for a kiss that afternoon she'd had to turn away, still seeing in his mouth the kissy O's of fish lips with their disgusting whiskers, opening for food.

*What was his name, Fish?* Jada had asked. And they want her to pick a celebrity? Why? If it were truly up to Maddy to choose whoever she wanted, she wouldn't pick an actor or a fictional character. She'd pick someone with money and a good job who didn't take her to feed Wonder Bread to carp and didn't pass around her nude selfies like they were candy at a parade and didn't just make her watch him play video games all day but occasionally handed her the controller. Someone happy and easy who could make her laugh.

Someone like, well, Blake. But she can't say that, now, can she?

"I don't want to play."

"Come on," Jada says.

"I said I don't want to." Maddy's face heats up. Something is not right here; everyone is acting too happy. Everyone is acting.

"It's just a game." Jada rolls her eyes.

"A stupid game." Maddy jumps to her feet. She needs out, needs air. "I'm going for a drive."

"Now?" Jada asks.

"No," her mother says. "Come on. Maddy, stay."

But Maddy doesn't stay. "Processed meats are a group one carcinogen," she says, and she tosses her plate of half-eaten pizza and rejected pepperoni on the table. She quits this moment; she quits this scene, over less than a polo shirt—over a game, a mood, an energy in the air. She gets into the car, even though she knows she might regret it later; she might feel bad about her childish behavior, kick herself for throwing away precious minutes with her mother, even if they were full of false cheer, even if they were spent fawning over Jada, who after all hasn't done anything except get engaged, and anyone can get engaged, anyone can wear a ring on their finger.

Her frustration propels her to the wildlife center, to the mews where the Eurasian eagle-owl sits patiently as if he's been waiting for her, orange eyes alert, prominent ear tufts sweeping upward from his eyes like bushy eyebrows. Maddy does not have a key to the mews, but she has a key to a room where a key to the mews is kept, so she lets herself in.

The owl has imprinted on humans, thinks he's one of them. It's only because of this delusion that Maddy can approach without frightening him, as she would frighten many of the center's other patients. Unlike them, the eagle-owl—who the center hopes will live fifty-plus years and who will remain nameless until he finds a sponsor—was raised in captivity, kept as a pet by someone without the proper exotic species permits until he was three years old. Maddy's had her eye on him ever since she first came to the center and heard his handlers talk to him, and him talk back, in a sweet interspecies call-and-response. She wants him to make for her the nests he assembles for his handlers inside his enclosure, moving rocks around and grouping them fastidiously, producing in his throat a special squeaky noise like a monkey's call and waiting in the hope that his handlers will fill his nests with eggs. Maddy loves him with a love that's sharpened, not dulled, by her knowledge of the length of his talons. She loves him for the futility of his labor, for his animal confusion, the trust he gives so freely and so blindly. She loves him for his absolute devotion to people who will inevitably fail him. It reminds her of her own.

She stands, now, and stares at him, hunched in his favorite corner, on the ground next to his water feature. "Hey, buddy," she says, and he stares back, blinking. Although she should not be here, although her heart races and she is aware of the eagle-owl's two-inch talons, there is a pleasure in her fear, which is largely self-indulgent. He won't hurt her. She looks at the citrus rings of his eyes, wide in the twilight, and feels the tension of the day begin to release.

"Who," she says, but the owl is silent. He shuffles in his corner, watching her. His vision is so sharp he can see each vein in the leaves outside his mews. His hearing is so sharp he can hear the beating of her heart.

"Who," Maddy says again, more softly this time.

She waits. It's cold, and she pulls the sleeves of her jacket over her fingers. She thinks of Bear, then of Blake. She thinks of her sister, who she has lost so many times now—to college, to grad school—

and who she fears she'll lose forever once she's married. She thinks of her mother. She holds each of their images in her mind for a few seconds, calling them up in full detail. Then she lets them go.

"Who," she tries one last time, and this time, the owl responds, his throat puffing out when he answers, "Who."

# 6

# JADA

### April 2018

A few days after her post-closet confrontation with Blake, Jada went without him to a gathering of psych graduate students and postdocs on the rooftop deck of a recently and cheaply renovated apartment building in Duquesne Heights. Twice a year the clinicals and experimentals came together en masse, once at a Halloween party, where the clinicals dominated at costumed beer pong, and once at a springtime bash like this one, hosted by a third-year clinical who studied brain differences in people with chronic pain. Jada rode the incline up the hill to the party with her friend Catalina. At the station they handed their fare to the woman in the booth with *The Price Is Right* playing on a TV screen behind her, then pushed through the green-lit door labeled THIS CAR UP to board the trolley.

Early on Jada had discovered that Catalina, like her, was the type who went around a party already cleaning up—wiping up spills, rinsing abandoned Solo cups and tossing them in the recycling, helping people into the rear seats of rideshares. Out of this discovery their friendship had bloomed. It was Catalina who had gone with Jada to pick out her wedding dress, which had in fact been a bridesmaid's dress plucked from the sale rack. And it was Catalina who had sat with Jada, held her hand, after she'd taken her second abortion pill.

Catalina was short, sprightly, easy to love. The grad school experience she shared with Jada lent their relationship a familial camaraderie, though their backgrounds were drastically different, Catalina the child of Chilean immigrants who had grown up in New York and still referred to it as "the city" despite living in this other, smaller one. There were times when, talking, Catalina would downshift into casual chitchat about the West Village or whatever, and Jada would feel thrown from the conversation. Still, their differences did not seem to come between them the way the differences between Jada and Blake did. When they met, he had known so many things she didn't—how to save money in a way that wasn't putting pennies in jars, how to order off foreign menus and travel on a train couchette (she'd been calling it a croquette for days before he corrected her, booping her nose: "A croquette is an appetizer, babe"). His intelligence was experiential, monied, SAT-tutored. Hers was bookish and scrappy and felt eternally precarious, so that no matter how much she learned, how familiar she became with the workings of the human mind, it did not seem like it would ever be enough.

"So, how are you?" Catalina asked as they creaked up Mount Washington in their red Mister Rogers box with its pressed copper ceiling, antique lantern swinging overhead, paper-bagged wine bottles wedged between their thighs.

"I'm fine," Jada assured her. "Really."

"Did you tell Blake?"

"No." Jada looked out the fingerprinted windows of the incline. Below spread a postcard view of the city, the fountain at Point State

Park, the butter-yellow arc of the Fort Pitt Bridge, colors saturated in the late afternoon light. A family of tourists sat on the opposite bench of the incline car, taking in the view.

"I don't know what's wrong with me," Jada said.

Catalina laughed softly. "Why does something have to be wrong with you?"

Jada shook her head.

"Your body"—here Catalina motioned up and down Jada's seated body with one hand, as if appraising a fine sculpture—"your choice," she said. "Right?"

Jada had held signs bearing the slogan before, marched in the streets after the election with her poster board and bubble letters, but the words felt newly charged, and she realized that until now the "my" in MY BODY, MY CHOICE had seemed not truly to apply to her but only to other women. She felt guilty, contrite, now that she had come to see her belief in her own exceptionalism for what it was. She had thought she could be smart enough, careful enough, impermeable enough not to need the rights she marched for. Everything had still been hypothetical then.

She turned to face Catalina. "Did I ever tell you I saved a child from drowning?"

"No."

"When I was a lifeguard, my first save was a little girl, barely smaller than my sister at the time. You never think you're actually going to use some of the things they teach you in training. I figured I'd only ever blow the whistle at kids goofing off, do some minor first aid. I had this funny tan line all summer where I'd hold my tube across my legs." They passed the descending trolley on the opposite track, full of waving passengers. "But then, one day, there this girl was, drowning, and there I was."

"That must have been scary."

"Yes. And exhilarating, once it was over and she was okay."

Catalina studied Jada. "Why are you telling me this now?"

"What do you mean?"

"I'm wondering," Catalina said, "if this is some way of justifying the abortion." She did not lower her voice when she said the word. "Some life-for-a-life-type thing."

Jada had not historically been prone to preoccupation with ideas of good and evil, but she was prone to preoccupation with ideas of success and failure, and getting pregnant accidentally had felt like a failure. Ending it felt like a failure. Hiding from Blake, coming to this party without him when she knew many of her colleagues would bring their partners, these things felt like failures. And yeah, maybe she had internalized the judgments all the people she hadn't told about her choice—Blake; her father; Maddy, probably; the woman seated across from them on the funicular with her downcast eyes and pursed lips, clearly eavesdropping; most of the people in her home-town, with their MAKE AMERICA GREAT AGAIN yard signs—would cast on her if they knew, and maybe she felt their weight. And maybe in her pain these last couple of weeks, she'd looked to the past to find solace in a time when she had, if not put life into the world, at least kept it there. That girl. Her pink bathing suit, its pattern of daisies.

She said, "Maybe."

Catalina nodded. "And I'm wondering," she went on, "why you need that justification."

The buzzer buzzed, the doors opened. Jada and Catalina stepped out of the car and into the upper station, with its old-school post-cards and window displays—THE BIG FLOOD, THE BIG FIRE—and ex-ited through the observation deck. Below, in the water, a sharp line where river met river, the Allegheny green and the Mon a murky gray, so that they seemed to remain divided at the very place where they converged. The sun was sinking fast.

"It's beautiful," Jada said.

Catalina smiled. "It's a sweet little town."

At the party, people gabbed about their research to anyone who'd listen, competing for the attention of polite partners and beer-fisted new recruits. Jada poured red wine into a chipped mug—I HEART BOSTON, a lobster where the heart should be—and made the rounds, splitting her time between the crowded kitchen of the host's apartment and the rooftop deck one floor up, where a pool glowed a brighter turquoise as the twilight deepened. Eventually she made her way back to Catalina, who stood by a table full of the catered tacos someone had sprung for, talking with her hands, her long hair tucked behind her ears and her silky tunic rippling in the breeze. Her dissertation involved creating a perceptual illusion to give pairs of friends the sensation of having exchanged bodies. Jada joined the cluster, taking a spot at the neck-high railing that enclosed the deck.

"Basically," Catalina was saying, wineglass tilting in her hand, "we simulated the sensation of waking up in someone else's body. What happened was that the participants' beliefs about their own selves, their own personalities, became more and more similar to their beliefs about their friend's personality the longer they inhabited that person's body. A few minutes spent inside someone else's shoes—literally looking down at your legs and feet and seeing someone else's pants and shoes—is enough to radically alter perspective and increase identification with the other."

Jada pictured Catalina's participants, pairs of friends lying on beds in goggles, each watching a live recording from a camera situated just above the other's head, generating 3D recordings from the perspective from which they were used to looking at their own body. Catalina and one of her assistants applied simultaneous touches to the same spot on each participant so that the participant felt the touch on their own body while seeing it on the body of their friend, the two bodies becoming blurred, the two identities blurring in turn. At one point, Catalina said, she had held the point of a fake knife to each participant's leg and measured their stress responses.

"Jesus," said Portia, a second-year health psychologist. "Our IRB approved that?"

"After much ado," Catalina said. "What better way to measure the genuineness of body ownership than by threatening the body? We see other people's bodies under threat all the time. We become desensitized to it. If the participants have a physiological response to the threat we create, it's a sign they're truly experiencing the body they're seeing—their friend's body—as their own."

At the end of the study, Catalina explained, a questionnaire was administered to assess the strength of the participants' perceptual experiences. *I felt that the body I saw was my own*, it read, or *I felt as if I had two bodies at the same time*, and the participants rated the truth of each statement: very false, false, neither true nor false, true, very true. *I felt that the touch I experienced was applied to the body I saw.* Very false, false, neither true nor false, true, very true. *I felt that my body was empty inside.*

Jada imagined looking down at the lower half of her prone body and seeing her mother's torso, legs, and feet. It was true there'd been times, even in her own separate shell, distinct from her mother's suffering, that she had taken the burden of that suffering on herself. She had thought she felt the catheter in her chest, the needle in her vein. She had seen the knife coming down; she had felt that fear. *I felt as if I had two bodies at the same time.*

To come home to her own splendid physicality after a day spent attending to her mother—to study her own strong legs, her breasts, her cheeks pink with health, her hair—had made Jada feel both thankful and ashamed. Her body had seemed like a betrayal.

"Think of the good this could do," Catalina continued. "Illusory embodiment can even shift racial attitudes. You think about people differently once you've learned what it's like to live inside their body. Body swapping isn't just the stuff of sci-fi anymore."

The talk at the other end of the pool deck had turned to politics, and Jada grew tense. They all agreed here, there was no real dissent; the talk was masturbatory, circular. She leaned against the deck railing and looked down. It was only a four-story building, but in the distance, at the bottom of the hill, the city sparkled: the bright nose of the Point, the rivers like dark mirrors, the spires of PPG Place. "You have to be willing to cut ties," someone was saying. "Friends, family, anyone who voted for him."

Her father. What would this crowd think if they knew? Jada finished off the last of her wine. How far from home she felt, moments like these, with the city yellow-lit and the Golden Triangle looking golden indeed and the distant noise of sirens punctuating everything—even though, to Catalina and most of her colleagues and professors, transplants from other cities, this one was practically rural, *a sweet little town*, a hamlet tucked among green hills. But Jada had known those green hills. She had known dirt roads, demolition derbies, isolation. She wasn't far from home at all, really, a matter of hours and deer-crowded roads, but on nights like this one, the space between here and home felt vast, like the space of many states. *Pittsburgh and Philadelphia*, someone once said, *and Alabama in between.* Also: *They cling to guns and religion.*

Well, Jada thought, yeah. They do. But didn't everyone cling to something? A gun, maybe, sure—or an outsized sense of one's own virtue. She should point to a few people who clung to that, too. She could point to a few people at this party.

"You have to show people there are consequences for their hate," someone sermonized.

"Is it hate," another voice asked, "or is it ignorance?"

It wasn't that Jada couldn't hold her own in these conversations; it wasn't that she didn't agree with most of what was said. It was that two years ago she'd gone around like Paula fucking Revere, warning of what was on its way, and half these very people had gone back to bed, not believing, grumbling in their sleep, *both the same* and *six or a half dozen*. And now hear them complain, hear them marvel, almost two years later: *Right here, among us! Here, of all places!*

Yep, Jada thought, here. Of all places.

When she'd started down this academic path, determined to live the life her mother wanted for her, she had done so in the belief that learning was about accumulation. No one in her family had been to college—that Jada was the first to go separated her not only from them but also from many of her fellow doctoral students, quite a few of whom were the children of academics—and she had expected to go, gather facts, skills, and credentials, and then cash them in while the general context of her life—her relationships, priorities, sense of self—remained intact. She had not anticipated the loss her education would involve. Goodbye, you said to your old life, to green hills or guns or religion. Goodbye to old beliefs; goodbye to the self that held them. She had abandoned so much in order to be here: her mother and sister, in their moment of greatest need (*Don't you dare give this up for me,* Ellen had said of Jada's acceptances to grad school, and yet Jada could not forgive herself for listening to her); Drew; peace with her father; her belief in the credulous, capitalist, all-will-be-well mentality that Blake still espoused and that her father clung to—there it was again, the clinging—even though it had never really served him. Perhaps these left-behind things were part of the structure of her life, load-bearing walls she could repaint but could not knock down. The sense she had of not belonging at parties like this one stemmed from her fear that others could see the things she'd tried to paint over.

We are both nature and nurture; they are an interminable marriage. She was her education, the books she'd read and studies she'd done. And she was the place, the people she came from, the origin point from which all her distances would always be measured.

Someone swept past and topped off Jada's glass. She thanked him—*tink*; cheers!—and then it was her turn to talk about her work. By now a few brave souls had taken the plunge into the pool and were floating and shrieking in the chill.

She was building a study that would examine the effects of choice overload and reversibility on online dating habits and daters' levels of satisfaction with their chosen partners. Her hypothesis was two-pronged: first, that participants who chose their partners from a large pool of options would be less satisfied than those who selected them from a small pool; second, that those who chose from a large pool would be more likely to want to reverse their selection than those who chose from the small pool.

"Take these tacos," she explained, gesturing to the food going cold. "We've got, what, four types to choose from? Say I grab a chicken, and it's good, it's fine, but I'm still likely to stay curious about those other ones. Would the carnitas be better, or the fish, or the veggie? Every choice entails a loss, right? Choosing one thing means not choosing something else. So as long as there are other options out there, some part of me is going to wonder if I chose poorly, if I could have done better than this perfectly acceptable chicken taco."

"And you think this has to do with relationships," said a man Jada had never met, probably someone's boyfriend.

"Sure."

He was waiting for an explanation. Dark eyes and feminine lashes; broad shoulders; a cocky twist to the lips, an involuntary smirk. He reminded her of someone.

"Maybe the taco example isn't a great one," she said. "It's low stakes. And most of the research on the topic has focused on similar low-stakes, everyday decisions like it. Often, they've been consumer ones, like which brand of marmalade to buy. We know that people have negative reactions to large choice sets in mundane situations. My study will test whether those reactions are replicated in more high-stakes, intimate situations, like partner selection."

"Or the Republican primary," Portia suggested.

The plan was to tell her study's participants that they'd be piloting an in-house dating system the university was developing. This was a lie—the vast majority of studies involved lying to participants, to greater or lesser degrees and as harmlessly as possible—but one that had become truer through her study's execution: as a necessary step in setting up the study, a fake online dating platform did have to be designed with the help of a staff member in IT. *Prowl*, Jada's team was calling it, in reference to the university's mascot and in spite of its predatory connotations. The system would present participants with diverse sets of profiles of potential partners. They would be prompted to choose the individual they'd most like to date, some from a pool of six options, others from a pool of twenty-four. Two weeks after the participants had made their initial selection, Jada's research assistants would follow up with them to ask how satisfied they were with their choice and whether they stood by it. Half the participants would be told that they could not reverse their choice; the other half would be told that they could. What the participants wouldn't know was that the faces they were browsing belonged to students at a different college across the country who had made photo profiles as part of a separate study conducted there by an acquaintance of Jada's. When the university's Institutional Review Board approved the study, they did so with the caveat that Jada's team would need to inform participants about campus mental health resources, lest they be distressed when they realized they would not be meeting the person they'd selected.

"What makes you interested in this topic?" asked the stranger. Jada caught a glimpse of his hand: no ring. "Why these questions?"

She always disliked answering this question. Anyone could be interested in anything; it was their right.

She said, "Do you feel sure about the things you do? The choices you make?"

"Yes," he said, and then Jada realized who he reminded her of: Drew.

"Well," she said, blushing, "I don't." She felt inadequate, envious, in the face of this stranger's certainty. "That's the reason. That's what interests me."

Constantly, in her mind, parallel worlds presented themselves, butting up against the one in which she was living. The world in which she'd stayed pregnant, where she stood at this party with a protective hand over her belly, turning down drinks. The one in which her child was born and grew. The one in which she hadn't married Blake, in which she was single and could, if she wished, go home with a man like the one she was now talking to, who had a look in his eye she knew (*The ball's in your court, babe*). The one in which she'd stayed with Drew. The ones in which she'd chosen other majors and careers from among the options that had been proffered to her as if in a colorful bouquet in college, where she was told she could be "whatever she wanted." The one in which she knew what she wanted. The one in which there was a woman president, in which her fellow citizens had chosen differently. The one in which her mother was still alive and would answer the phone when Jada called tomorrow to tell her about the party. She'd say, *Hey, Kit Kat*—that was Jada and Maddy, Kit Kat and Chiclet—then set the phone on the window ledge and talk while washing dishes, and Jada would strain to hear her voice over the sounds of water running and glass clinking and flatware scraping the sink.

"Who are you, anyway?" Portia asked the stranger. "You're in the program?"

"Nah," he said. "I live here." He swept a hand to the side to indicate the building before turning back to Jada. "2D."

Jada glanced across the blue hole of the pool at the darkened windows on the opposite side and caught a glimpse of her reflection: plain black formfitting tee, hair falling loose to the tops of her shoulders, flat gladiator sandals whose tops precisely met the cuffs of her jeans. Was she beautiful? Some people thought so. In any case, she did take a private pleasure in the precision of her appearance, in the touching of clean-cut hair ends to shoulders, shirt hem to the little gold sun of the button on her jeans. She liked clothes that fit like the pieces of a jigsaw puzzle. She liked being covered.

A tug on her arm. "Babe," Catalina slurred, squinting toward the makeshift bar at the far end of the pool where someone was mixing drinks, flaming an orange twist with a magician's flourish. "Isn't that . . . Blake?"

It was. He handed a drink to a first-year named Raymond, who took it, looking impressed. "Who is that guy?" Jada heard Raymond ask someone as she approached the bar.

"Hey," Blake chirped, greeting her as casually as if she'd been expecting him.

"Hey. What are you doing here?"

"Why shouldn't I be here? There's Miles," he said, nodding toward Portia's boyfriend, who looked back at him and waved enthusiastically. "There's Tess," nodding toward her friend Lainey's wife. "But you only tell me, 'I'm going to the spring party tomorrow,' not where, not what time, not 'Hey, Blake, do you want to come?'"

"It's work stuff," she said.

"How'd you get here, anyway? Your car's at home."

"Catalina and I took the incline." She tugged him away from the bar—limes in pools of liquid, puddles of wine—toward a quieter corner of the deck. "How did you know where the party was?"

"You're my wife."

"Yes," she said, "but how?"

"I looked at your calendar."

"You went through my phone?"

Jada's lab mate Marcos approached, waving, clapping Blake on the back.

"Blake! How many anesthesiologists does it take . . . to change . . . a . . ." He closed his eyes and tilted his head, pretending sleep.

Blake chuckled, suddenly illuminated. "Why can't you hear a psychologist using the bathroom?" he said. "Because the *p* is silent." He held up his drink—*tink*; cheers!—before Marcos moved away again, sucked back into the swirl of the party as if on a cloud, the distance between his outstretched glass and Blake's lengthening, like God's and Adam's fingers on the Sistine Chapel ceiling.

"I looked at your calendar," Blake said again, turning back to Jada. "You're my wife. I should know where you are."

"I didn't think you'd want to come." There was no good reason why she shouldn't have wanted him here; he was sociable, easygoing. Just as there was no good reason why she shouldn't have wanted to have his child; they were married, financially sound, capable. No good reason—but no, she told herself, that wasn't true. The not wanting *was* a reason.

"Who was that guy?" Blake demanded, puffing himself up, flicking his eyes toward the man from 2D.

"Somebody from the building. I've never seen him before."

"He was looking at you."

"We were talking," she said. "Don't do this jealous thing. It doesn't look good on you."

Blake unpuffed his chest. "Isn't that what you want?" he pressed. "For me to be more manly?"

"I never said that." Sure, Blake's model of masculinity was . . . pinker, cleaner than that of the men and boys she'd grown up with, who tended to be brusque, withholding, occasionally demanding—even Drew had been known to withdraw to the woods to sulk over some unspoken grievance or bellow "Ma!" at his mother in the next room to demand a roast beef sandwich. Jada had once been refreshed by the earnest religiosity with which Blake performed certain acts of self-care and housekeeping, like moisturizing or having his kitchen knives sharpened.

"You want me to claim you?" he asked. "Headbutt people with my horns?"

"No."

People were looking at them. Jada tried to sculpt an expression on her face that would say, *We're not fighting!*

Blake sighed. "Look at us," he said. "We're like people in some very serious marriage drama. Some movie I don't have any interest in watching."

"I like those movies."

"But this is your life," he said. "I know you like those movies. But do you like this?" He gestured back and forth between the two of them.

"No. I don't like this."

The party had gotten darker, drunker. Neighbors' lights had gone out. A group of rowdy students played giant Jenga. Jada heard Catalina's laughter carried on a cold breeze and wrapped her arms around herself. Blake was staring at her, waiting for her to say something, and she was just desperate enough and had had just enough wine that a half confession came sliding out: "Do you remember those days you came home from work and couldn't find me?"

"Yes."

"I was there."

He looked confused.

Jada hugged herself and looked at the ground, the pavement stippled with bits of shredded lettuce. The crisscrossed straps of her sandals, her unpainted toenails. "I was hiding," she said, nudging the lettuce bits into a pile. "I hid from you."

He looked at her like she'd confessed to an affair. "Why?"

She held out her hands as if to indicate her common befuddlement. This was as far as she could take him. She jumped as the Jenga tower came crashing down.

"Let's talk about this later," she said. "Let's not do this here."

"Do what?" Blake's eyes narrowed. "Jada, are you leaving me?"

"No." She answered before he'd finished asking the question.

Her phone rang. Maddy was calling. Jada turned from Blake and leapt into the call as into a lifeboat, shaken but grateful for escape.

"I have to talk to you," Maddy said.

"I'm kind of busy right now." Jada's hands shook, and she pressed the phone hard against her ear. "Are you okay?"

"Where are you?"

"At a party."

"You sound weird."

"I told you, I'm busy." Jada closed her eyes. Her mouth felt dry and winey. "Can I—"

"Sure, whatever."

She heard TV noise in the background. She pictured Maddy sitting alone in their empty house, and a spade of sorrow pierced her heart. "Are you safe?" she asked.

"Yeah." The TV sounds grew louder. "Have fun at your party."

"I'll call you back soon, okay?" Jada said, and Maddy hung up without responding.

She slid her phone into her back pocket and turned around slowly to find that Blake was unbuttoning his shirt, pulling his white undershirt over his head.

"What are you doing?"

He undid his belt. "I don't believe this," he mumbled, his chest aglow in the party lights, the T-shaped pattern of his chest hair rising and falling with his shallow breaths. "I cannot fucking believe this."

Off with the belt. Off with the oxfords, which he had the presence of mind to place side by side outside the likely splash radius, tucking them beneath the chaise where he dropped his clothes.

"Who is that?" someone asked. Jada abandoned the lettuce she'd consolidated into a disposable pile. Tonight she would not be the one cleaning up messes. Tonight, it was turning out, she and Blake were the mess.

A lesson in cognitive dissonance: she had thought she was an honest and okay person with her shit generally together. Now, new and ugly information: she could keep a secret from her husband, one bigger than the depth of her grief, which was less a thing she deliberately concealed than one she couldn't share if she tried. And worse: at the sight of him in crisis, publicly unhinged by pain she'd caused, she felt not tenderness but a churning disgust. How to reconcile these facts with her sense of herself as fundamentally decent? That she was ashamed of her disgust did not make it go away; it only made it worse.

"Blake," she said in a loud whisper, beginning to panic. "Come on. Let's go home."

Just once had she seen him like this. Driving across the country, somewhere in Texas, when a chain of tornadoes crossed their path. The dry streets flooded, the green-gray sky roiled, a siren wailed, hailstones struck the windshield. Jada veered the car partway beneath the roof of a gas station while Blake melted down in the passenger seat, shouting, *Oh, hell no, hell no, I will not die here, I will not die in*—but he did not know the name of the place where they were.

Off with his watch, which he stashed inside the right shoe. *Oh, hell no, hell no.*

It was Goodnight. Where the tornado had been. Goodnight, Texas. Jada's idea, taking the back roads, searching out some canyon.

"Blake," Jada hissed again. She looked around. The pool was empty, the air biting. Some people had begun to stare. Several, too drunk or distant to notice Blake's trembling, had begun to cheer. Someone yelled, "Yeah, baby, take it off!"

Sockless, shirtless, beltless in khakis, he moved to the side of the pool. Then he jumped in.

Onlookers whistled. Jada waited for him to pop up again. Wave to the crowd, make a joke of it all. But he appeared to be sitting on the bottom of the pool, encased in a net of bubbles like a whale. His ankles were crossed, his arms outstretched, his hair waving in the chlorinated current like seaweed.

Raymond said, "This is a joke, right? This is fun?" and pointed to the pool.

The Jenga tower crumbled again. Jada's heart pounded.

Across the pool, Catalina wobbled in her heels, blissfully inebriated. Their eyes locked, and Jada thought of their conversation on the incline, the drowning girl in the pool. *But then, one day, there I was.* Catalina must have thought of it too, that image of Jada in her red one-piece towing a body to safety, because her face lit up and her eyes grew wide and she motioned toward the pool, sloshing rosé onto the deck, teetering as the wind puffed her tunic like a bell.

"Save him!" she cried.

But Jada waited. Like her, Blake had been a swimmer in high school. He could hold his breath a long time. She could hold hers longer.

It was after midnight when Jada saw Catalina into the back seat of a friend's car and climbed, dry and raging, into the passenger seat of Blake's BMW. She had not jumped in after him but had waited for him to burst through the surface of the water like a performing dolphin, to the entertainment of his confused but delighted spectators. Now they sat in silence in the dark, the smell of chlorine thick in the air and three foil-wrapped leftover tacos in Jada's lap.

"You shouldn't have taken those," he said.

"I don't like to waste food."

"We have food at home." He wore a pair of the host's sweatpants, a hole in one knee. His wet khakis sat on the floor in a plastic Giant Eagle bag.

"I think I should get my own place," Jada said after a while.

He was right: it *was* like a movie. She heard her lines after she'd said them, but they seemed to come from somewhere else, someone playing her onscreen. She had the sensation of falling and put a hand to the car door to steady herself.

Across the Liberty Bridge, onto Boulevard of the Allies. She tossed him cliché after cliché, like little silver fish to a sea lion. She needed a break. She needed time, space. He swallowed the fish but was still hungry, barking, and she knew she owed him an explanation, something substantive if not palatable. It was his marriage, too. But anything she said could and would be held against her, so she shied away from specifics, trying to leave herself room to change her mind, handing him a cheap, prepackaged explanation, like a Happy Meal: break, time, space to work and think.

Over and over he asked, "What's wrong with me?" and each time her hands flapped in front of her like clipped wings: "Nothing!"

"I don't have back hair," he said. "Lots of men have back hair."

"You have a very smooth back."

"I have excellent vision. You think most guys have 20/20 vision at our age?"

"You have very good vision."

"I've never had a cavity."

She surveyed him top to bottom, praised his many fine attributes. In front of them flashed the glow of a car's taillights. He slowed to a stop, washed in red, still two or three car lengths away. He always left this vast, empty space between his car and the one in front; it drove her crazy. Involuntarily, her body scooted forward as if to nudge the car ahead.

"And," he said, "I'd be a great dad. Don't you think I'd be a great dad? What's wrong with me?"

"Nothing's wrong with you."

"What? What?"

"It's me," she tried.

"Yeah," he said, "it's you."

Okay, yeah, maybe; but also, it was science. There was a formula, an economic theory of personal relationships by which satisfaction was calculable: Outcomes = Rewards minus Costs. Satisfaction = Outcomes minus Comparison Level. Call Comparison Level CL, and define it as the perceived value of the outcomes one thinks they deserve—a value determined by one's level of self-esteem, culture, past relationship experience, the influence of friends and family. Jada had a PowerPoint on this she shared with students, but it was a lesson best shared in a classroom, and not in a car with one's dripping-wet husband. Anyway, did she really believe she *deserved*— she cringed—something more than what she had? She slept in a safe room on a bed like a cloud. He was kind, called his parents every day. Who did she think she was, to ask for anything other than what she had?

"A lot of women wish they could be with someone like me," Blake said. "A *lot* of women."

"I know," she said. "I'm sorry. I don't know what's wrong with me."

Dependence = Outcomes minus Comparison Level for Alternatives. Define Dependence as reliance on one's partner and, by extension, likelihood to remain in the relationship. Define CL for Alternatives as one's evaluation of whether being single would be preferable to the relationship they're in, of how likely they'd be to attract alternative partners better than the one they've got. Maybe, Jada said, stumbling her way through an explanation, she needed this time and space simply to clarify for herself that there was no one better for her than Blake, that . . .

"That's what dating's for, though," he said as the house came into view. "Shouldn't you have already done that?"

At home, they talked and argued for hours—from opposite sides of the shower door, putting on pajamas, sitting across from each other on the bed they shared—chronicling injustices and incidents that, in unhappy retrospect, took on a symbolic glow ("That time at trivia," he said, "with your friends, I could tell you were embarrassed of me"; "That time at Acadia," she said, "you just laid in the tent and whined"). Eventually Blake said, "Well, I could use some time, too. I want some time to think about alternatives to you."

"That is fair." She saw that, like her, he wanted this to be his idea. She saw too that, like her, he was wounded by that idea. He was making a show of swallowing a knife, walking over hot coals. It cut, it burned, but he persevered; he showed how manly he was.

"Like a trial period," he said. "A test."

Like a study. She was a professional who had observed a problem, which had given rise to questions, which had given rise to a theory: that it might be best for her to shed this life like the peel of an overripe fruit. Theories could not be proven, only disproven; no life experiment could demonstrate unequivocally that an action or condition would guarantee happiness. There was no right, only wrong and not-wrong. All she could do was test her theory to see whether it could be refuted, whether she sank when she let go of the buoy he'd been.

He went to the kitchen and poured the nightly glass of water he never drank, set it on its usual perch too near the edge of the nightstand. Already Jada had swept up the shattered remains of two of its siblings, knocked from that ledge weeks or months ago. She did not comment. On his trek to the kitchen he seemed to have pivoted toward positivity; he came back practically whirring with energy.

"This could be good for us," he said, as the clock struck four a.m.

She had a vision of herself in the closet, denting the doorframe with her thumbnail. A vision of the day she'd brought home the cat from the shelter, the spitting image of the one he'd had and loved as a kid, even though she was allergic and had to dose herself with antihistamines to live with it. A vision of herself and Blake a few days after her mother died, when she'd decided to go for a therapeutic run but had been so out of it she'd had to sit and hold out her foot so he could tie her shoes for her. ("That time at trivia," he'd said, "That time at Acadia," she'd said; not "That time you brought home the cat," not "That time you tied my shoes.")

Out of habit they climbed into bed side by side, their feet little peaks under the feather-down duvet. She began to feel sick, pulled the duvet to her chin. They lay there, not touching, until he rose, took his pillow, and shuffled to the spare room, and she heard the springs of the guest bed groan with his weight. Cold without him there to warm her, beneath the spinning ceiling fan, she pressed her face into her pillow. *I felt that my body was empty inside.*

The next day she put a deposit on a one-bedroom apartment in Squirrel Hill. She never did call Maddy back.

# 7

## MADDY

### April 2018

Once, Maddy watched a movie about a girls' home in Ireland where women went to have babies in secret, only to have them taken away and shipped off to adoptive families in America. At the time she'd struggled to imagine what it must have felt like to knock on the front door of a cold stone building, pregnant with nowhere else to go, and wait to be taken in by some stern nun with pursed lips and pasty skin. A gray place, dreary, nothing like Jada and Blake's town house on this bright twenty-first-century morning, and yet it was this memory of attempted empathy with a poor Irish maid that sprang to Maddy's mind when she stood on her sister's front stoop with a bladder full of Sheetz iced tea and a duffel bag on her shoulder and lifted her finger to the bell. Jada had not called her back, and perhaps it was better this way—Maddy was not giving her a chance to say no. Once the trouble was on your doorstep, surely, you could not turn her away. You might offer her hard crusts of bread with no butter, let her scrub the never-clean floors; you might make her kneel among the rats and scald her skin with lye, but you took her in. In the movie there was a graveyard out back where dead girls and babies were buried. Unmarked stones, creaky gate, rain and rain and rain.

She rang. The day was cloudless. It was eleven thirty on a sunny Sunday in America, and her rubber fetus was tucked inside her sweatshirt pocket. Maddy hoisted the bag on her shoulder. When the door opened, it revealed Blake, in plaid cotton pajama pants and a pitstained undershirt—*wifebeater.*

"Maddy?" He looked behind her, as if she might have brought some kind of entourage whose presence would explain her own.

She jumped right to it. "Can I stay with you guys for a while?"

He paused. His eyes narrowed. "Seriously?"

Maddy was taken aback. Also, she had to pee. She squeezed her thighs together.

Blake shook his head. "Sorry. It's just . . ." He looked past her again, lowered his voice. "She's not here."

"Where is she?"

"Moving *out.*"

Maddy shimmied and squirmed. Moving *out*? Out where? What was happening? Before her, Blake seemed to sway like a tree about to fall, and she felt suddenly nauseous. "I really have to pee," she breathed, her bag sliding down her shoulder, "and"—the need was sudden and overwhelming—"I think I might throw up."

She dropped her duffel on the stoop and ran past Blake, up the stairs to the house's main floor and into the hall bathroom. The nausea passed as she sat on the toilet, and she belly-breathed, in, out. *I am going to be okay.*

In, out. *I am going to be okay.*

She flushed, washed her hands, and stood gripping the edge of the vanity, staring at herself in the mirror: hunched and clammy in an oversized sweatshirt, hair a wild nest, its pink streak matted and greasy. She waited for tears that didn't come. Though she hated her grief, she had come to appreciate her tears, the way they transformed her pain into something tangible that could be delivered into the world and, once outside her, wiped away. Crying before a mirror was best, as it brought about a temporary and productive depersonalization; some gear inside Maddy shifted whenever she took in her own big-eyed, tragic image and pitied the reflection as she might a lost child or a baby bird. *Poor girl,* she would think, *poor thing, she needs help,* and a latent instinct deep within her—maternal, it occurred to her now—would be deployed. Poor girl, there there, *you are going to be okay.* Come on, Maddy; dry this sad girl's tears.

It was the same way she felt on those occasions when she thought of telling on *him.* To even entertain the thought, she had to split herself off from herself, to think of some other more innocent girl whose life she might save by telling the story of her own. She might not be able to speak in her own defense, but surely she could speak for the sake of this other girl, still uncorrupted, whom it was in her power to protect. It was in those moments she wanted him dead, she wanted to kill him. Then the thought would subside as she remembered that there was no other girl, she *was* the girl, the face in the mirror was her face, and the blade of her thoughts grew dull.

No tears came. Maddy looked around. This was the bathroom where Blake and Jada usually showered—the master bath contained only a large and luxurious tub with a handheld sprayer attachment—and the glass door of the shower stall was water-stained. Inside, Blake's body wash: Oak and Aged Bourbon.

Her phone rang from inside her sweatshirt pocket, a number she didn't recognize. For some reason, she answered.

"Maddy?" said a woman's voice.

"Yeah?"

"Hi, Maddy. This is Pat from New Dawn, just checking on you and the baby?"

*Pat from New Dawn.* Maddy liked the way it sounded: epic, like the title of a fantasy novel, a woman on the cover with futuristic armor and green hair. Entirely unlike the bumpy, lumpy woman in pink whose chest she'd sobbed into.

"Um," she fumbled, and felt her throat constrict. "Hi."

"How are you, Maddy? Is there anything you need from us?"

"Um," Maddy said again. She kept her voice low. "I don't think so?"

"Are you getting excited?"

Maddy didn't respond.

"And what about Blake?"

For a moment she was puzzled. Then she remembered: the name she'd given Pat when asked to name her baby's father. She turned her back to the door, covered her phone's speaker with her hand, and crouched low on the bathroom floor. "This isn't really a good time."

Pat was quiet for a few seconds. Then she lowered her voice, too. "Maddy. Are you in a safe place?"

"I'm fine."

"Is someone trying to coerce you?"

"No." Maddy could hear Blake moving around the house. "I just . . . I have to go."

"Well, you're doing the right thing," Pat said. "Choosing life? I'm proud of you. And I'm here if you need anything, okay?"

From the question mark in Pat's voice after "choosing life," Maddy gleaned that Pat was not convinced that she had decided against abortion. She wasn't just "checking in," she was on a mission, working overtime. Maddy sensed that her power was at its crux when she was a girl deciding, a girl able to be swayed. She was of interest—to Pat, to the world, maybe even to Jada—only so long as she was subject to influence.

"I have to go," she said again.

"Would you like to pray together?"

"No."

Maddy ended the call without saying goodbye and remained huddled on the floor by the shower stall, breathing deeply. She'd been in here long enough that it must be starting to seem weird. A tangle of Jada's hairs clung to the grille of the drain, and she reached for a tissue and half wiped, half tore the clot away. Birds could use it, but the window was closed and screened, so she threw the wasted nest away, gathered herself, and opened the door.

She found Blake in the kitchen, dressed, now, in dark jeans and a salmon-colored button-down, sleeves rolled. He seemed to have changed tactics—gone was the teetering tree of a moment ago, replaced by a clean and competent human host—and was opening a package of bacon. In a corner of the living room, a few cardboard boxes were stacked like building blocks. Maddy perched herself on a stool at the island. He had carried her bag inside.

"You okay?" He came around the island and held the back of his hand to her forehead. She felt her face fill with color.

"I didn't throw up," she said.

"Can I get you something?"

"A glass of water."

"Slice of lemon?"

She breathed out a tentative laugh. "What is this, a restaurant?"

Blake shrugged. "Are you hungry?"

She was. He took a silicone ice tray from the freezer and squeezed out two large cubes. He filled her glass with water, his with bourbon.

Maddy thought of how she'd noticed his body wash in the shower— *Oak and Aged Bourbon*—and felt embarrassed and titillated by this intimate knowledge. Funny, she thought, that he would want to drink what he bathed in.

Blake wiped the lip of the bottle with his finger. "Know what they call the bourbon that evaporates while it's in the barrel?" he said. "The 'angel's share.'"

He raised his glass to hers—*tink*—and they drank. She pictured tipsy angels singing and swaying outside a white marble saloon. Jada's house's walls were white, the windows large, the glass unsmudged. The chandelier over the island was spiky and modern, with gold-brushed arms reaching in all directions, juggling clear bulbs. At the center of each bulb, a tiny bolt of filament sizzled. Maddy gazed too long, then closed her eyes. Saw the hot, glowing scribbles printed on the insides of her eyelids. Where was Jada?

But what did she want from Jada, anyway? Another envelope of cash? Shelter from their dad? She knew what Jada would propose but wanted to see what it felt like to hear her propose it, and to refuse the proposal. Maybe that was why she was here: so she could run from Jada the way she'd run from Pat and listen to her heart, her gut, as she ran. Let her body show her the way, even if it was her body that had gotten her into this mess.

And Blake? What would he think, what would he say? Maddy watched him toss two slices of Italian bread into the toaster. He was spitting out a rapid, abridged account of the state of his and Jada's marriage: a chilly distance between them, a stone wall, and, it seemed, she had pushed him—or at least, she had not *not* pushed him—into a pool?

"... and I thought when I came back up," he was saying, "it might all turn out not to be real. But she was just standing there, looking at me like . . ." The toast popped up. He pinched the golden slices from their slots, shaking his head.

Maddy wasn't sure what to say. She touched her hair, trying to smooth the crazy strands. "Jada's always been like this," she tried, without knowing what she meant.

"Like what?" He straightened his back, butter knife in hand, as if drawing a sword to defend his lady's honor.

"You know," Maddy said. Even now, he'd defend her? "Just . . . hard to reach, I guess."

He resheathed his sword. "Yeah. Hard to reach."

"In her head."

"Yes," he said. "In her head."

Maddy reached into her sweatshirt pocket, where her fetus doll snoozed, and caressed the warm rubber. Her stomach growled as Blake slid two pieces of buttered toast across the quartzite in her direction. *Eating for two*—the phrase popped into her head, and a wave of nausea rolled over her, even as she salivated at the sputter of the first slices of bacon hitting the griddle.

"Did you hear the rumor about butter?" Blake asked.

"What?"

He waited a second for her to catch on, then said, "I'm not going to spread it," and gave her a sad grin.

Maddy rolled her eyes and laughed, as he clearly wanted her to do. She dug into the toast despite her nausea. The cat, Jake, approached, rubbing himself sexily against her foot where it dangled from her barstool.

"House cats kill four million songbirds a day in the US alone," she said, pulling back her foot. The floor's hardwood planks were arranged in a snazzy zigzag pattern that made Maddy think of zippers. "Even if the cat only carries the bird in its mouth, bacteria from its mouth kills it."

Blake looked at her blankly. "Jake's an indoor cat."

Maddy felt her cheeks go hot. She sounded like some freak, going on about cat bacteria when here he was, confiding to her about his marriage. She touched her hair again. Her mind flashed to the wildlife center, where she'd stopped early that morning to say goodbye to Wilson the eagle-owl. She'd found him, as usual, in the corner of his enclosure, picking up cobwebs like a feather duster. *I'll be back,* she'd told him, and lovingly plucked a wisp of web from his ear tufts. Her progress with Wilson was one of the only examples from her lived experience that suggested it was, in fact, possible to secure for herself the things she wanted.

Other things she wanted: a house like this one, a man like this one (her cheeks flushed again). To live on her own, away from her father and the decades-old decor of her childhood home, her mother's deathbed. What Jada had, she wanted.

It was a feeling that had solidified in her when at age nine she spent a weekend with Jada at college. That weekend had been Maddy's first taste of independence, and at the time that cinderblock dorm room had held all the allure of this town house. Her father had dropped her off in Happy Valley for two nights' stay, and Jada had taken her to a dance performance on campus, to Berkey Creamery for scoops of Death by Chocolate, and for dinner in a many-optioned dining hall. Back home, her mother popped supplements and crunched salads, but at college, Maddy let slice after slice of pepperoni pizza slide greasy-wet from a serving spade onto her warm and waiting plate, not yet knowing or caring about group one carcinogens. She accompanied Jada to Art History and fought to stay awake in the dark lecture hall. She had imagined herself a college girl, leaning over an exam sheet filling in answer bubbles with confidence and a number two pencil, nodding along to the art history lecture in understanding. But she had dozed off. Eventually she woke to Jada's voice in her ear—"Mads?"—and discovered with dismay the cascade of drool she'd deposited on her sister's sweater sleeve. Staring at the projector screen at the front of the classroom, at the image of a girl in an empire-waisted gown holding her small sister in her arms, their eyes downcast and a dark forest closing in around them, Maddy wiped her mouth.

Jada had lived with a fellow psych major named Brennan, a shot-putter with blond hair like straw, and on Maddy's second night, people crowded into their room to play music. A boy named Thomas had hunched over his guitar with his head tilted and black hair falling over his closed eyes, and Maddy had nodded along as he sang, moving her lips to lyrics she didn't know. He was good, good enough that when he put down the instrument and took a silly bow, she felt the urge to kiss his clean-shaven cheek. And then Jada *had* leaned in and kissed him—she and Drew were over by then—brushing his shoulder-length hair aside and curling her fingers behind his head, which she pulled with proud ownership to hers. At the end of the evening Jada ushered him out of the room with mumbled apologies, and he pulled on her hand as if to drag her away as she stood behind the door, shutting it slowly, laughing at something he'd said.

That night Maddy woke from a nightmare, crying out in her sleep. When Jada did not respond, she whimpered again, then realized Jada was not in the bed beside her.

A voice called to her from across the room. "What is it, sweetheart?" Brennan swung her thick legs over the side of her lofted bed. "Did you have a bad dream?"

Brennan climbed down from her bunk and pulled a book from among the clutter on her desk. She sat at the foot of Maddy's bed where Jada should have been, her legs folded like tan pretzels, and read to Maddy. Jung, *Modern Man in Search of a Soul*. Maddy could still see the book's white-lettered title seeming to glow in the hazy dark. She did not understand what Brennan was talking about, but she relaxed into the role of child in need, letting herself be lulled to sleep by Brennan's singsong voice, waking again at four a.m. when Jada let herself in and lowered herself onto the mattress next to Maddy, pretending she'd been there all along.

Even now, all these years later, Maddy remembered her jealousy of Jada—her room, her freedom, her boy. What had happened to Thomas, with his gentle eyes and his guitar? He'd never come home with Jada or met their parents. She'd just ditched him, probably, the way she'd ditched Maddy that night, the way she was now ditching Blake.

"I don't get it." Blake was standing with a slice of uncooked bacon in his hand, marbled with fat and dangling limply over the griddle. "Why does she get to be wishy-washy? Why does she get to change her mind? I love her."

Maddy shook her head sympathetically.

"If *I* said to *her*, 'I don't know if I want to be with you anymore,' I'd be an asshole," he said. "But if she's the one leaving, it's okay, she's finding herself, it's some act of female empowerment!" The bacon still swung from his fingers. "Why does she get to leave me, but I don't get to leave her?"

"You could leave her."

"Not if I want to be a good guy."

"Do you want to leave her?"

"No!"

At last, the hiss and pop of the meat hitting heat. She said, "You think if she left, everyone would blame you?"

"Of course. They'd think I cheated or hit her or had a drinking problem. Why else would she leave me?"

"I don't know."

"I'm a good person."

"I know," Maddy said. "I don't think anyone would assume you hit her."

"What would they assume, then?"

Maddy shrugged. "That she's crazy."

She had finished her toast and now moved through the house's main living area while Blake cracked eggs. Sleek shelves of blond wood lined the walls on either side of the gas fireplace, above which the huge TV was mounted, Blake's gaming console stuffed into a cubby below. Maddy searched the shelves for blemishes or dust and found none. She examined the pile of boxes Jada had packed and pulled back the flaps of the one on top, still unsealed. Psychology textbooks, a handful of hardcover novels, the Elvis snow globe their father had given each daughter after he drove to Memphis for a hardwood-grading workshop, the only time she could remember he'd left home. *What happens in Memphis stays in Memphis,* he used to say, as if the trip had been a bacchanal, a bender. She was surprised to find that Jada still had the globe, the tiny, tacky Elvis inside with his hips thrust and his rubber legs. It was the sort of thing she would have thought Jada would want to purge from her home, or at least hide.

Maddy opened a textbook to a page showing a diagram of the human brain, then shut it and put it back in its place. No thanks. She opened a novel, *The Bell Jar,* and read about Esther Greenwood perched in her fig tree, afraid to choose, going hungry as ripe figs blackened and dropped to the ground around her.

When the bacon and eggs were ready, Maddy and Blake ate at the island together. He had seesawed back to blustery optimism and was enlisting her help in keeping him there.

"I think it will be all right, though," he mused. "Things work out, you know?"

She nodded. The smell of the eggs was newly revolting to her (*Yolk sac*, she heard Pat say). She recalled the first time Blake had hosted her family for dinner at his condo, before his engagement to Jada. On the way, in the car, her mother: *You're going to eat whatever he serves, you got it?* Glancing at her father: *That goes for both of you.* Watermelon and feta salad, bacon-wrapped dates, baby greens, pink-middled meat. On the way home afterward, her dad to her mom: *Who puts cheese on watermelon?* And her mother had burst into giggles. It seemed so long ago.

He was watching her eat, now, and she felt the need to eat gratefully despite her queasiness. She speared a clump of eggs with her fork.

"I'm giving her what she needs," he said. "You think other men would do that? You think other guys would be this understanding?"

No, she did not think other guys would be this understanding. The guys she'd known had been happy to see her disappear. She thought of her package full of cash. She thought of the boys who'd come before *him*, boys who showed her their guns or spread her like a condiment across the seats of their trucks and sandwiched her there, pressing down, seat-belt buckles and metal tongues digging into her back; the boys she'd watched play video games; the boy who, dancing with her at a house party at somebody's parents' camp, his hand in her hand-me-down skirt, had reached under the waistband of her tights and gotten stuck inside the skintight nylon, herded her into a room full of bunk beds and deer heads with his hand still caught in the elastic, and with his free hand drawn his pocketknife and slashed the fabric from crotch to waist. The tights had had a pattern of tiny on-purpose holes in them in the shape of constellations, and Maddy had left their husk behind on the bedroom floor. She'd never seen that boy again.

"Anyway," Blake said. "Thanks for listening, Maddy. You're easy to talk to."

"So I've heard." She tried not to think about the last time a man had said that to her, and Blake didn't ask. But, just like the last time a man had said that to her, she felt her heart swell. "Can I ask you a question?"

"Shoot." He refilled her water, his bourbon.

"Did you ever go to church?"

"Sure did," he said. "Raised Catholic, went to Catholic school, a Catholic college." He crossed himself.

"But you don't go now."

"No."

"You didn't like it?"

He shrugged. "Just lost interest, I guess, as I got older. There were a lot of things you had to do, go to confession and whatnot."

"When was the last time you went?"

"A long time ago," he said, checking his phone.

"You aren't worried about stopping? You aren't afraid you'll, I don't know, go to hell?"

Blake leaned back on his stool. "I haven't done anything bad."

What she would give for just a crumb of that confidence! She wondered what he'd prayed for back in the day, what Pat prayed for now. What was there to say to God if you didn't have anything to be sorry for? Thanks, she supposed—you said thanks, and asked that the blessings you deserved keep rolling in. She thought of the pamphlets

Pat had given her, one with an image of Mary and a verse below: *From now on all generations will call me blessed, for the Mighty One has done great things for me.*

"Why do you ask?" he asked.

"No reason."

He studied her, then put a hand on her shoulder. A hotness spread through her, and she had the feeling that she should not look at him. But trying not to see him meant that she became hyperaware of his location, his every movement. You could not avoid something without knowing exactly where it was.

"You've been through a lot," he said. "If there's something you think might help you feel better, you should do it."

She studied a vein in the countertop and coughed to clear her throat. "Thanks for the eggs," she said. "Can I help you clean up? Load the dishwasher?"

"No, no." His eyes flicked to the door, then to his phone, and eventually Maddy caught on: he hadn't cooked for her, not really. He had cooked for her so that Jada would see that he'd cooked for her and be moved by his hospitality, see her error, and come back home.

This pissed her off. Absentmindedly she drew the rubber fetus from her pocket, arranged it in the fruit bowl behind a bunch of bananas, out of Blake's eyesight, and squeezed it flat. She had practically force-fed herself his scrambled eggs because she'd thought they were for her. She had wanted the bacon to be for her, the toast to be for her, the kind words to be for her, but they were all for Jada. Fucking Jada. Blake was right. Who had a man like this and left? Who had a house like this and moved? Who had a mom like their mom and let her die?

The sound of a car in the driveway. Jada, back to pick up some of her stuff. Only now did Blake rise and gather the dishes, letting them clang pointedly against the countertop. Maddy was nervous, sweaty. Part of her felt the too-familiar panic of a secret girlfriend on the verge of discovery; part of her felt like the child of parents on the cusp of divorce, dreading the impending split.

She said, "I could, you know. Be your eyes and ears."

He turned to her, downing the rest of his drink.

"I could send updates," she went on. "On how she's doing."

"You'd do that for me?"

"Of course."

He looked at her, then to the door. "I just want to know that she's okay."

"Right," she said. Jada's footsteps on the stairs. She would have seen Maddy's car out front. "Of course."

Then there was Jada, in yoga pants and a university tee, her hair washed and her skin unblemished and even her shoes clean, though Maddy could see dark circles under her eyes. Always, even now, that chilly regality—a repellent, perhaps, to men who were only looking for easy prey, men of the sort who liked Maddy.

"What are you doing here?" she asked, looking at both Maddy and Blake.

"I . . . I thought I could stay with you for a while," Maddy said.

Jada stood immobile for a long time, then ushered Maddy into the cool quiet of the bedroom she was vacating. "Why now?" she asked, pointing to some shoes in her walk-in closet, then to a cardboard box, signaling for Maddy to help her pack. She had closed the bedroom door behind them. "You've never just shown up like this before."

"I tried calling."

"I'm sorry," Jada said. "Things have been crazy."

"Why are you—"

"What did you want to talk to me about?" Jada asked. "What's going on?"

It was so much harder to say the words for real than it had been when she'd practiced this conversation in her head. Maddy watched as Jada studied her face; she watched Jada's own face change as she processed what she saw there. Maybe Maddy looked different or smelled different or glowed, or maybe Jada just had some spooky, moon-given gift of female intuition, but just as Maddy was about to open her mouth to finally speak the words, Jada said, "Don't tell me you're pregnant," and waited, and still the words didn't come, and Jada put one hand over her heart and the other on Maddy's arm and said, "Oh God, you're pregnant. You're pregnant, aren't you."

Maddy shrugged. "Surprise," she said weakly, and wondered where the sisterly superpower that had allowed Jada to see her situation had been all this time—why after lying dormant for nineteen years it should now spring into action.

"Did you tell him?" Jada tilted her head toward the door.

"Blake? No. Why?"

Jada shook her head. "Let's talk at my new place, okay?"

They loaded boxes and armfuls of Jada's things into both their cars and headed in a two-car caravan to the apartment, where it took Maddy three tries to parallel park behind a neighbor's parking chair. It was only when she'd gone inside and begun settling into the space—yarny brown carpet, chipped pressed-wood cabinetry, a water stain on the ceiling—that Maddy put a nervous hand to her pocket, felt for the fetus doll, and realized she'd left it in the fruit bowl.

# 8

## JADA

### April 2018

She'd passed an awkward Saturday, the day before Maddy showed up, packing items from around the house that she could identify as incontrovertibly hers—clothes, books, the stupid Elvis snow globe she couldn't let go of. She would pick up an object and set it down again, afraid to move it, like her house was a furniture showroom or a home goods store. She had thought about crashing with Catalina but was too embarrassed to ask. She had not told her father or Maddy what she was doing. She'd told only one person, this morning, the last person she should have told.

"I won't say I told you so," Drew said on the phone.

"You just did," she protested. "And you didn't, back then. You never predicted the future. You just tried to stop it from happening."

"Because I knew what it was going to be like for you."

"You knew what it was going to be like for *you*."

"Same difference," he said. "I hate seeing you unhappy. You deserve better."

She cleared her throat as if to warn him not to cross some line. But hadn't she known he would say this? And—whatever his motives, whatever hers—hadn't she needed to hear it?

"Jada," he said. "Tell me what I can do."

"Nothing. I just wanted to tell you."

"I can supply a truck," he offered, "and my enormous guns. Help you move furniture, haul stuff from IKEA, whatever you need."

"I don't know." Now that she'd heard his voice, she felt both revitalized and impatient to get off the phone. "I'll let you know. Thank you."

She'd come fresh from that conversation to finish packing, the key to her new place on the ring next to the key to her current one, her apartment ready for move-in. Blake was not supposed to be home, yet there he was, clearing Maddy's place at the table, rinsing her plate with a fatherly attentiveness that felt to Jada like a reproach: *I'd be a great dad.* As if, when she turned to Maddy and asked, "What are you doing here?" she was asking not only her sister but their child, the child she'd said no to, sitting in the kitchen she'd said no to, a living what-if.

She had not really believed the words as they'd spilled out of her—*You're pregnant, aren't you.* Yet here was Maddy, pregnant, hauling piles of Jada's clothes up the apartment building's stairwell, pants flung over her arm. Dresses slipped off their hangers; hangers clattered to the floor. In the center of Jada's new bedroom sat an uninflated air mattress, which, it turned out, she'd be sharing.

It was not a nice apartment, but it smelled like fresh paint, and it would do. A few pieces of furniture had been left behind by the last tenant: a dresser with a chunk missing from the corner of one drawer, a ring-stained coffee table, a cheap high-top kitchen table with two stools. When she'd first seen the place, she'd been instantly comfortable there. It reminded her of the bachelorette pad she'd shared with Brennan, the roommate she'd lived with on and off campus in State College, who'd loved Jung and eaten strawberry yogurt for dinner and walked on her heels, their heavy thump-thumping against the cold tile a homey comfort to Jada. Had she been more herself then, living with a woman and without money, or was her mind playing tricks on her, romanticizing the past, distorting the difficulties of her life before Blake? Had she been more herself when she'd last lived in a place like this one, or had she been someone else, someone who was gone now and would not return?

Maddy reached for Jada's box cutter and retreated to the living room to slash the tape on the boxes they'd brought in. Jada remained in the kitchen, wiping down cabinets. Best, she figured, for them to work in separate but adjacent rooms, able to hear each other but not to look each other in the eye.

"All right," Maddy said. "Why are you leaving Blake?"

"I'm not leaving him." But what did it mean to leave someone if not to seek out space away from them? Did she have to mean to leave him in order to be doing so? Maybe to leave someone was less about setting off with purpose, letting wind fill sails like so many pregnant bellies, rations stowed belowdecks and map in hand, and more about wearing down the frayed rope tethering you to shore, mindlessly pulling at a knot that might slip after a while without your realizing it. Maybe the leaving had begun long ago.

Maddy's head appeared in the threshold between rooms. "Then what the fuck are we doing here?"

"Maybe," Jada said, "we should start by discussing what *you're* doing here."

Maddy's head disappeared. Jada's heart thumped in her ears. "How did this happen?" she pressed.

"Well," came Maddy's voice from the living room. "When a man and a woman—"

"Maddy, please."

"I don't know what you want me to say."

"Weren't you on birth control?"

"I quit it. The hormones—"

"And you didn't use protection?" Jada's chest burned, like her heart was in acid. Maddy might have asked her the same questions; she just didn't know it. A small part of her enjoyed the sensation of her hypocrisy. Its false righteousness was almost convincing.

"We did," Maddy said, "most of the time." A pause. "Aren't you going to ask who the father is?"

"Who?"

"Just some guy. It's over, and he doesn't want to be involved."

"Okay." Jada's hands shook. She had an impulse to shatter something, so she picked a mug out of one of her kitchen boxes and dropped it on the vinyl. The mug bounced uncooperatively and did not break. Just sat there on the floor all proud of itself.

"Well," Maddy said after a while, "are you mad at me?"

"No. I'm mad at myself."

"Why?"

"I promised I'd look after you. I should have taken better care of you."

"I'm not a child."

It was true, technically, and yet in a sense Maddy would always be a child to Jada, in much the way that a child was always a child to its mother. When Maddy was born, Jada had been only marginally aware of sex, but she remembered the embarrassment she'd felt at the sight of Ellen's pregnant belly. To be seen in public with her was suddenly a humiliation, as if Ellen had been wearing a sign that read I HAD SEX! As Jada matured, she came to embrace the joy of her sister's existence; but Maddy had remained, in her mind, always the fruit, never the tree.

She said, "We can make this go away."

"I knew you'd say that," Maddy said. "But I don't think I can do . . . that."

"Abortion. You can say it."

"I don't think I want to."

"Then what?"

Maddy shrugged. "I could be a stay-at-home mom."

"Stay at whose home?"

"I was thinking I could stay with you."

"Oh, Maddy." Jada gestured generally to the empty apartment around her. "You can stay with me, but you can't . . . I can't have a baby. Not here, not now."

*Selfish,* hissed a voice in her head. You were supposed to drop everything to make room for a child, as her mother had done; twice, now, Jada was refusing. It was easy to feel good about choosing when a choice involved saying yes—yes, I will earn this degree, take this job, love this person, wear this dress—but harder when it involved saying no, and didn't all choices, however seemingly affirmative, involve saying no? *Yes, I will have a child* meant parting ways with your child-free self. *I will be with this person* meant, usually, not being with another. Still, rights of refusal felt like things that should remain perpetually in reserve, like insurance policies; you wanted to have them, but you didn't want to *use* them. If you did, you were supposed to do so wholeheartedly, triumphantly, owning your decision with pride, like a good feminist. Hold your sign, chant your slogan. No wishy-washy bullshit. No voices in your head yelling at you at a volume no single voice outside of it could reach.

She should try to recast her decision in positive terms—not *I failed as a wife*, not *I am selfish*, but something along the lines of *I am an intelligent woman who can trust her own judgment, and who used this difficult situation to learn more about who I am and what I want, and if and when I feel ready and able to be a good parent, I can make a new choice.* But that wasn't something you could write on poster board, that wasn't a sign you could hold or a slogan you could shout, and as such it didn't feel valid, didn't feel real.

Jada said, "You have plenty of time to become a mother. On your own terms, in your own time, when you have a supportive partner to help you. You have so much going for you. . . ."

"I'm not like you."

"What does that mean?"

"You know." Maddy had appeared in the threshold between living room and kitchen and was leaning against the frame. "I don't know what else I could be. I don't have some big dream like you did. Maybe I'd be a good mom. I like babysitting."

"It's not babysitting when it's your baby." It wasn't babysitting when it was your sister either, Jada had discovered, when at fourteen she had asked her father for an allowance in exchange for watching Maddy.

Maddy crossed her arms. "It would be Mom's grandchild."

And what could Jada say to this? She had worked through the logic herself; she had had the unreasonable yet unignorable thought that to end her pregnancy was, in a way, to refuse her mother a type of resurrection. Difficult to say how her dilemma might have felt different if her mother were still alive. Would she have felt more able to parent, more eager, or only more compelled by her awareness of the joy it would have brought her mother to have a grandchild?

She said, "Is that really what you want?"

Maddy shook her head. "I don't know. I could give it away."

"Why would you go to all the trouble of having it just to give it away?" Jada knew this was callous but tried not to care—*give it away*, as if a baby were a pair of outgrown pants. "Can you even imagine how hard that would be?"

"No."

Jada could feel Maddy watching her and suspected her suggestion was a test meant to gauge her reaction. She had a vision of herself and Maddy passing a crying infant back and forth, cooing and bouncing. Of having left her home, her husband for . . . her sister? "I just don't know why you'd do that to your body," she said, "or why you'd invite that kind of emotional turmoil into your life, when . . . if you don't want a baby, you don't have to have one." She closed her eyes, opened them. Everything still here. Her right hand found her left and squeezed. "Chiclet," she said, "you're only nineteen."

"Almost twenty."

"Almost," Jada said. "My point is, you have your whole life to live."

"I can live with a baby."

"You can live without, too."

"Yeah, and get cancer," Maddy said.

"What?"

Maddy went to her bag and fished out a stack of pamphlets. The one on top was designed like the front page of a newspaper, with a black-and-white image of the Virgin Mary, who the pamphlet depicted as lily-skinned and fair-haired, beneath the headline LOWLY MAIDSERVANT BEARS SON OF GOD. Mary, the pamphlet explained, had been an ordinary girl from Nazareth before she was elected to give birth to God's son and courageously accepted the role. It went on to summarize the Nativity story and spell out its relevance to women who found themselves unexpectedly pregnant: they should, according to Philippians 4:6, *be anxious for nothing.* Matthew 6:27: *And which of you by being anxious can add a single hour to his span of life?* "Mads," Jada said, "why would you go to this place? They're not a medical facility."

"They gave me an ultrasound."

"But they just want to get you to go along with their agenda. Their whole goal is to get you to have the baby."

Jada held up the LOWLY MAIDSERVANT pamphlet. Poor Mary, she thought, and wondered if Mary had a last name. Surely she did. And surely she *had* been anxious, and surely she'd hate to be used this way, manipulatively, to suggest that goodness lay only at the end of a narrow behavioral corridor along which all doors but one—to do as she did— were closed, all alternate routes immoral and thus unthinkable. By the logic of this pamphlet, the secret to happy motherhood was simple: resign yourself to the fact that because only one choice is moral, only one choice is available. Then you could make it and go on your way, feeling justified. Being able to choose was not just about objectively *having* options; it was also about psychologically perceiving them. Morality constrained those perceptions. It took options off the table.

Jada's mind raced. That limiting choices might lead to greater happiness was not a baseless insinuation: the fewer the options, the higher one's satisfaction with the choice made, as demonstrated in studies of consumer behavior using exotic jams and gourmet chocolates. But Maddy wasn't a Sunday shopper picking over jams, and perhaps, Jada thought, she was missing the real point of the pamphlet: to suggest that Maddy was like Mary not in that she lacked options, but in that she was special. Not a chooser, but the chosen one; not the consumer, but the chocolate. She and other visitors to New Dawn, the pamphlet

suggested, had only to locate in themselves the kind of humble gratitude for their special status that Mary displayed when she became the
mother of Christ, the ultimate miracle baby. It was the same tack Jada
had just taken when she'd said that her sister had her whole life ahead
of her. You're special, so have a baby. You're special, so don't.

The next New Dawn pamphlet presented pictures of fetuses at
each stage of development alongside self-indulgently graphic de-
scriptions of abortion procedures and lists of their supposed risks
and side effects:

CRAMPING

HOLES IN THE UTERUS (UTERINE PERFORATION)

TORN CERVIX (CERVICAL LACERATION)

PELVIC INFECTION

INJURY TO BOWELS

HEMORRHAGE

PUNCTURED BLADDER

INCOMPETENT CERVIX

FERTILITY PROBLEMS

RESPIRATORY PROBLEMS FROM ANESTHESIA

HYSTERECTOMY AS A RESULT OF COMPLICATION OR INJURY

INCOMPLETE ABORTION (FETAL PARTS LEFT IN THE BODY)

PREOCCUPATION WITH BABIES OR GETTING PREGNANT AGAIN

SEXUAL DYSFUNCTION

RISK OF CANCER

FEELINGS OF GRIEF AND REGRET

SUICIDAL THOUGHTS AND BEHAVIOR

POST-TRAUMATIC STRESS

DEATH

Jada tossed the pamphlets aside. "Maddy," she said, "do you have any idea how rare most of these 'side effects' are? Most abortions happen by pill now, so you probably wouldn't even need an operation, and women are more likely to die of childbirth complications than of complications from an abortion procedure. An overwhelming majority of women who get abortions stand by their decision years afterward. There are studies."

Maddy rolled her eyes.

"And sure," Jada continued, "like any big life decision, there's a chance you might have a lot of complicated feelings afterward, but a lot of women who *have* babies—even babies that were wanted—also go through a period of depression, and don't you think it's worth considering how many of the bad feelings women do experience after having abortions probably come from their not having a network of supportive and sympathetic people they can talk to about their choice, because they fear their partner's reaction, or their family's reaction, or society's reaction, and it's that stigma that makes them feel alone?"

It was like she'd started down a steep hill in skis without knowing how to turn. She went faster and faster. Her face was cold.

"As for this part about cancer," she went on, "your chances for certain kinds decrease if you have kids, but that doesn't mean they increase if you don't, and none of it has to do with whether you've had an abortion."

Maddy was looking at her. "How do you know?"

"It's common knowledge," Jada said. "It's science."

She had the feeling she was missing her chance. She should speak up, hold her sign. Wasn't that what you were supposed to do these days, share your story? The right she had exercised had been granted in the name of privacy, but it didn't feel private at all. On the one hand her story was populated by a crowd of unwanted secondary characters; she had been glared at and yelled at by picketers. On the other hand she felt like she'd been unwittingly drafted into a league of women whose obligation it was to publicly and vocally defend one another, defend their own humanity. No one had privacy anymore; hardly anyone even seemed to want it. Like, what good was a right these days, what good was an action, if it couldn't be tweeted about with bluster to the world?

She did not want to tweet. She did not want to tell. Hearing what she'd been through might make Maddy feel less alone, but Jada couldn't bring herself to narrate the experience, not in front of her sister. She picked up one of the pamphlets and began tearing absent-mindedly at its creases. Her legs felt like noodles.

Maddy was eyeing her. Eventually she said, "I'll think about it, okay?" and changed the subject: "Seriously, what's going on with Blake? Why are we here?"

"It just isn't working."

"Why?"

"We aren't on the same page about things."

"What things? What page?"

Jada shrugged.

Maddy shook her head, her eyes on a spot somewhere near the pantry door, which was missing a knob. The box cutter was still in her hand. Eventually she said, "If I had what you had . . . I don't know, I wouldn't just throw it away."

Jada had said the same thing before, to Blake. Though he tended toward stinginess and was a bad tipper, she'd seen him throw money away. It was dimes. Less than shiny, crusted in greenish brown, unsightly and one Canadian, but still. He had pulled them from his pocket and tossed them into the trash. After he left the room, Jada retrieved them. They'd fallen to the bottom of the basket, beneath orange peel and onion skin and bits of paper, and she put them in a change jar she kept in her closet.

What was wrong with her, that she could not want properly? That her wanting was confined to coins fallen to the bottom of garbage cans, career milestones, and—yes, she had to admit it, she had known Drew would want to help her, and calling him had been like testing a parachute before jumping out of a plane—ex-lovers? She wanted to have wanted the child she didn't want. She wanted to want Blake, with whom she had charted a future. But as she looked around the apartment at the weird picnic of belongings spread across the floor, the unboxed books in teetering piles, she thought that perhaps no option could be better than rejecting them all and staying here alone, answerable to no one, wanting nothing.

"I'd be a bad mother," she blurted.

Maddy looked caught off guard.

"I mean," Jada added, "I wouldn't be good at helping you. With a child."

"Maybe not," Maddy said, and Jada realized how badly she'd hoped Maddy would contradict her.

"Didn't I take care of you?"

"Yeah. But you would have rather not."

Was it true? Maybe. Caring for Maddy hadn't always been a chore, but Jada could not deny that much of the time, given the choice (and she had not been given the choice), she would have rather not. She had loved Maddy with a ferocity that caused her physical pain, true, but she had also resented Maddy, and she could see now that Maddy had absorbed the resentment she thought she'd concealed, osmotically, irrevocably. And developed her own, as well.

"You're never going to forgive me, are you?" Jada said.

Maddy crossed her arms and looked at the floor. Jada could guess what she was thinking: that what happened to Ellen could have been stopped, that Jada could have stopped it.

"Maddy, it wasn't up to me," she said. "Surely you understand that."

"No." Maddy had turned at an angle and was speaking to the wall. "I don't understand. She would have done anything for you. For *you*."

Jada sat on the floor by the mug she'd dropped. Her instinct was to flee, but this was her apartment. She'd been generous, taking Maddy in, for all the thanks she got. *That was really nice of you,* she told herself. *You're a good sister.*

"Look," Maddy said, "I'm sorry. But I don't need advice. I don't need you to save me. I don't want to talk about Mom. I just need a place to stay while I figure things out. I won't get in your way."

But you *are* in my way, Jada wanted to say. This is my way, and here you are, in it.

Sure, there had been times when she'd wished she could wish Maddy away; sure, she might wish her away now. But there were many others when they'd been as equals, when the decade of experience between them had contracted and seemed to disappear. Jada remembered the two of them lying on their backs in the snow, arms and legs spread. Angels. It was dark, and they'd been playing in the yard in the scant rays of the motion-sensing porch light, which had gone out. The only light came from the moon, illuminating the snow, the fat flakes floating down into their eyes. She had seemed to be moving though she was completely still, and the snowflakes rushed toward her like stars, like she was hurtling through space, faster than sound. Then she felt her sister's hand in her own, and Maddy started humming the *Star Wars* theme, and Jada knew Maddy had seen what she'd seen in the falling snow, in the stars, and they'd both burst out laughing.

Maddy retreated to the living room and commenced unboxing: more books, though there were no bookshelves; a desk lamp, though there was no desk. They needed to eat something, but there was no food. Jada had packed two of each type of cutlery from her wedding flatware, boxed them up in pairs like animals on an ark, and now that her legs had stopped trembling, she began placing them in drawers she'd disinfected. Most of what she'd owned in her life before Blake had been thrown away when they moved in together.

She was about to propose dinner when she heard a cry from the next room. When she entered, Maddy's back was to her, and she was hunched over, whimpering.

"What?" Jada said. "What happened?"

Maddy turned and slowly held up her left hand, her face draining of color, the box cutter at her feet. A deep, inch-long gash in the fleshy part of her thumb.

"Fuck," Jada said. Blood was running down Maddy's arm. Jada grabbed the arm and held it up, squeezing, trembling again, fighting back squeamishness.

"It's fine," Maddy was sputtering. "I'm fine."

"You need stitches." Jada pulled Maddy by the arm from the living room to the kitchen. Nothing there but tissue and newsprint and disinfecting wipes, an old rag soaking in soapy water. She towed Maddy into the bedroom. Blood was dripping over her own hand.

"I don't want to go to the hospital," Maddy wailed.

Jada scanned the open boxes in the bedroom and grabbed a sock on top of a batch of items waiting to be loaded into her dresser. Next to her, Maddy dipped and rose with her movements. Jada pulled the sock over her sister's hand like some evil puppet and watched a petal of blood bloom on the fabric.

"I'm okay," Maddy moaned. "I'm okay."

"Shh." Jada was on autopilot, her gestures swift, impersonal. She plucked the top item from a heap of clothing Maddy had dropped onto the air mattress, a blue marled linen tee. She wrapped her sister's socked hand in the shirt as tightly as she could and toted her, objecting—*it's okay, I'm okay*—out to the car, Maddy's hand raised over her head like she had an important question and was waiting to be called on.

"It's bad, isn't it," Maddy said after a while. "Is it bad?"

"It's not that bad."

"I'm a train wreck."

"No."

They drove in silence for a while, until Maddy said, "It was an accident. I wouldn't hurt myself on purpose."

Jada frowned, startled. In the corner of her eye, her sister's big hand floated like a stick of cotton candy. "I know that," she said, and hoped it was true.

In the urgent care waiting room, while a doctor put five stitches in Maddy's hand, Jada called Drew again.

"I do need you," she said, and told him about Maddy, the apartment, the box cutter. The day had been too big; she could not contain it. It spilled out. She spoke quietly, in a corner of the waiting room by the magazines (RADICAL SPRING BEAUTY: QUICK FIXES FOR HAIR & SKIN!), though the room was empty except for a woman in her sixties with rainbow-dyed pigtails who kept scratching at a rash on her arms and a young man with a face full of piercings whose ailment was invisible.

"I need help," she finished. "The truck, the guns, all of it."

"I'll come down tomorrow," he said. "Ma can cover for me in the store. Just send the address."

"You can't spend the night."

"Whatever you say, old pal."

She closed her eyes. "Why do you like me so much?"

Drew laughed, like it was a stupid question. "Because," he said. "You're the one."

A warm, liquid ache filled her nose and eyes. It was not true, as Maddy alleged, that she never cried, only that she did so at the wrong times and in the wrong places, without witnesses or before the wrong ones: on the phone with an ex-boyfriend; in urgent care with this pigtailed woman and this man with his lip rings; at the symphony; in the airport with her carry-on at her feet. Crying wasn't even the word for what she'd done there, on a bench by the Cinnabon, on her way to New Orleans for a conference last year—she had wept uncontrollably, broken all the way down. No one had stopped or spoken to her, and she still didn't know if she'd wanted them to, or what she would have done if they had: accepted their handkerchief, lashed out in anger, or followed them, like a found puppy, to some sort of authority: *Isn't there somewhere . . . else . . . you can put her?* But even now she felt jealous of those strangers passing by with their roller bags, courteous or indifferent enough to ignore her. She would like to be one of those people. She would like to be able to look at some other unraveling woman and be like, Wow, at least I'm not *that* lady, at least *that's* not me.

She would also like to think that if she did encounter a woman in the midst of such a public undoing, she'd stop and help, and would intuit what kind of care to offer. But then you never truly knew what you were going to do until you did it, did you?

She wiped her eyes and sniffled, trying not to let Drew hear. "You can't say that," she said. *You're the one.* "Please don't say things like that."

"Okay."

"It makes it worse." She was not sure whether this was true.

A nurse came out and signaled to Jada, and she hung up the phone.

"When was her last tetanus shot?" the nurse asked.

Jada looked around like somebody else might know. "I don't know."

"She said to ask you."

Jada was holding her hand over the speaker on her phone—the meaty part of her thumb, the same part Maddy had sliced open—even though she'd ended the call. "I'm just her sister," she said.

"If you had to guess. Last ten years?"

Jada swallowed. "You should probably give her the booster."

The nurse nodded. "Can't hurt," she said, and left the room.


It was late by the time they returned to the apartment and inflated the air mattress, and Maddy fell asleep minutes after lying down, her bandaged hand resting on a pillow above the level of her heart. Jada stared at her sister's body, splayed like a starfish, and felt a rush of tenderness, a fierce urge to protect. Also, a sinking dread. Barely settled in her novel half freedom, in the uncertain space of her separation, with Drew on the way, on the verge of who knew what trouble, look what she'd gone and done: brought home a baby.

# 9

## JADA

### May 2016

Jada and Drew, sitting in a tree. Not kissing, though he'd like to be.

The morning after the pizza at her mother's, her engagement announcement, the forced hug with her father and the talk of movie stars, Jada has fled her parents' house. The harsh light made plain the dusty sills and baseboards, the bathroom in need of cleaning, the crumbs ground into the carpet, and the dirt is a giveaway: her mother is letting go. Ellen looks terrible, her house looks terrible, and what's with Maddy that she can't be bothered to clean her own home, that she has to ruin a pleasant evening? Jada slid out the door this morning, Saturday, to escape these frustrations. And to tell this man, who she has known for as long as she can remember, that she's engaged to another man. It's a disclosure that she hoped would be cheery and casual—they're lifelong friends—but that has felt instead like a confession, somber and made in the shade of rotting beams in the tree house his dead father built.

"Anyway," she says. "I wanted to tell you in person."

They sit with their backs against opposite walls of the tree house, her left foot barely touching his. The walls are furred with lichen, the knotted rope swing frayed. The pulley's broken, the bottom's fallen out of the bucket, and she's not sure they should be here. She has kept her ring hidden throughout their conversation, both hands drawn inside her long sleeves. He has kept his eyes trained on a daddy long-legs making its way across the floor. Now he looks at her, and she's reminded both of why she loved him and why she left him: that look in his eyes, his arrogance, his conviction that he knows her better than she knows herself. The chance that he actually might.

As children they played together in his tree house and in the store-room of his father's hardware store. In third grade, he gave her a box of Hershey's Hugs & Kisses with a note inviting her to check a box: yes, no, maybe. She returned two boxes: the rejected candy, the "no." In ninth grade, he tried again; still no. *You're like my brother.* Then that changed. Junior year, new feelings, but it was too late; he was dating Chrissie Russo, blah, blah, blah. Finally, their senior year: to-gether at last, but only briefly; after a long-distance freshman year of college, they went their separate ways. He did two years in Behrend's engineering program before dropping out after his father died sud-denly of a heart attack. He took over his father's store and has been there ever since. Things briefly rekindled between them during those slumping postcollege years when Jada waited tables at Missy's Diner, paying down her debt, arguing with her father, and caring for her mother before moving away for grad school and abandoning her. Abandoning Drew, too.

Drew knows Jada in jeans with holes worn through them, and not on purpose; knows her with baby Maddy on her hip and spit-up down her shirt; knows her pressed against his back on the four-wheeler, arms around his belly, chin on his shoulder; knows her getting off to push when the wheels begin to spin, ankle-deep in mud, splattered brown and laughing. Knows her crying. The intimacy she's built with him is exhaustive, exhausting; when they're together, they are crowded by all the people they used to be. His interest in her is long-lived and intense enough that he can conjure her past selves up at will—which he does, periodically, in an effort to remind her who she really is. And if she really is who he says she really is, she is making a terrible mistake.

"Show me," he says, and points to her hand.

She peels back her sleeve to reveal the ring. He takes it in with a hint of a smile, the edges of his mouth tightening.

"You used to be so anti-diamond," he says, and just like that, college freshman Jada is in the room, drafting her petitions, climbing back on her old soapbox, hitting her head on the cobwebbed treehouse ceiling. "Child labor, human rights abuses, environmental degradation. Remember you wrote that—"

"It's not a diamond." College Jada poofs away. "It's a sapphire." The band, though, is rimmed in diamonds, as they can both plainly see. It's not Blake's fault he hasn't read Jada's college essay on conflict diamonds and the marriage-industrial complex. It's not his fault he didn't get a head start at knowing her.

This is what Drew does: pushes her buttons, then watches what happens. He loves her mind, he's always said; it is the only one he believes can rival his own. He loves her mind, but he loves it in the way one loves a dog: it makes an engaging companion, and he'll throw a ball for it once in a while, and he likes to see what it digs up from the yard he walks over without thinking of scavenging, but it's ultimately of a different species than his—high-strung, anxious. *Aww, come here, sit,* he'll say, and stroke her thoughts, and think how cute they are.

Then just when he gets cocky enough to piss her off, he'll turn around and surprise her. He'll read some study she's cited, or he'll acknowledge that of course he knows a president Trump would be a disaster, or he'll send a handwritten letter to her college mailbox, sharing his thoughts about the pros and cons of the Kimberley Process.

He can write a letter like you wouldn't believe. He can make her feel like . . . well. He can make her feel.

He's still watching her, his gaze darting between her face and her ring.

"What?" she demands.

He shakes his head.

"Say it."

He holds up his hands in surrender. "It looks like the old lady's necklace."

"In *Titanic*."

Drew nods.

"It does not," Jada protests, fingers splayed. "That one was heart-shaped. And a diamond."

He holds up his hands again, like, *Don't shoot the messenger.*

"Anyway, every girl alive in 1997 wanted that necklace."

"But you aren't like those girls. You never were. You're different."

She had thought they could do this, be friends, but now she isn't sure.

"Okay," she huffs. "I see what you're doing. Trying to make him Cal so you can be Jack Dawson. The resourceful and sensitive steerage guy, the artist."

Drew laughs. "Come on. I can't draw."

Which is a lie. She rolls her eyes. He can draw, he can write. He can carve shit out of wood with a chain saw. He could fix up this tree house if he took the time, and he'd make a great engineer if he finished school. And it's true that he has a certain DiCaprian glimmer in his eye, a "Meet me at the clock" swagger. It's there now, and she knows he knows.

*Damn you, Jack Dawson.* She was ruined from the start. How could any living man measure up? How could any girl of Jada's generation, whose sexual awakenings were set to "My Heart Will Go On," have been anything but doomed? And yet other women had turned out all right—look at them, with their kids and their stuff. They tempered their expectations, or at least appeared to. Yet here was Jada, ever on the verge of jumping off a lifeboat to be with some beautiful boy: Drew, looking at her now as if he knows all the contents of her head, knows that when the moment comes for her to spit in Cal's—Blake's—face and run off, she will.

Something stirs in Jada, something primal and unwelcome. She searches for alternative explanations for this stirring from the one that volunteers itself: that she wants Drew, plain and simple, in the same hopeless way that Rose wants Jack. No. Perhaps, Jada insists, this is nothing more than a classic case of misattribution of arousal: her heart racing from the sight of the ground below, threatening through the gaps in the planks of the tree-house floor that creak and groan with the slightest movement. The state of being vertiginous, of being nervous, is so physiologically similar to the experience of sexual attraction that it's easy to mistake one for the other. In ancient Rome, men were advised to take their love interests to arenas so that the would-be lovers would misattribute as sexual arousal the adrenaline rush of seeing a prisoner of war devoured by a lion or a gladiator run through with a sword. Dutton & Aron, 1974: When a beautiful lab assistant posted herself on a rickety suspension bridge rocking in the wind and offered her phone number to every lone man crossing it, a surprising number of them called her, compared to a very low number of men approached by the same hot researcher on a sturdier bridge.

Yes, perhaps it's that simple for Jada, too; she is feeling the effects of altitude. Maybe Rose felt them at the bow of the ship, as well, and that was all there was to it.

Maybe not.

She shifts her foot away from Drew's so that they longer touch.

"He's a good man," she pleads.

"There are lots of good men in the world. You don't have to marry them."

Now she's pissed. Who does he think he is? But she knows who he thinks he is: her soul mate.

He is one of the ones who cling. To guns, yes. To his father's legacy. And to her.

*We belong together,* he'd said more than once. He was a romantic, hard on the outside but gooey on the inside, like a fine chocolate moelleux. But Jada was versed in the science of love, knew it as a pulse in the reptilian core of the brain, a hot spot of light in the ventral tegmental area, a squirt of dopamine. Soul mates, she'd lectured, were a myth debunked by research, and there was a world out there, a big one, and even if there were such a thing as soul mates, what should make Drew and Jada think that theirs had been placed so conspicuously, offered so freely by God or some other grand design, with no search involved?

"I need you to be happy for me," she says. "Please."

It distresses her to realize how true this is, how badly she needs his blessing. It's as if she is asking him to walk her down the aisle, her hand in the crook of his elbow. She is asking him to give her away.

He says, "I think you're making a mistake."

"Based on what?" she says. "You don't know him. I can make my own decisions. You're only pushing back on this one because you don't like it."

"I'm looking out for you."

"You're looking out for yourself."

She watches his back straighten. "All right," he says, "maybe I am. Why shouldn't I? We're good together. I get you."

"He gets—"

"No, he doesn't. And when your mom—if your mom—is he going to get *that*? I *get* that, Jada. I want to be there for you, whether it's this year or next year or fifty years from now."

Her head fills with bees and stars, everything buzzing and blinking. "So we can talk about death together," she says. "That doesn't mean we should *be* together."

It is true that she has accompanied him through his grief. It's true that that grief is ongoing, that he moves through it as if through water, that he sometimes reaches for her as for a rescuing rope. It is true, too, that his grief remains a mystery to her, that she does not understand it, and that her own—when it comes—will be a mystery to him as well. She doesn't know yet what it will feel like for her mother to be gone, but she knows already that it will be a hell no man can understand, that her pain will be a room she'll occupy alone, like a bedroom with a sign on the door: KEEP OUT. And she knows that the years they spent together before she left for Pittsburgh, the days spent waiting tables and dropping off his ham and cheese at the hardware store, the nights spent watching *Jeopardy!* with his mother or tending to her own, were some of the most frustrating she's known. That taste of what their life together, their life here, might be like—it was bitter. Say what you will about Blake, she had run toward him in their early days together as if dashing for the cover of an awning in a rainstorm.

She had run away from Drew. What kind of fool would she have to be to run back now, like Rose hopping off her lifeboat and back onto the deck of the sinking *Titanic*? What kind of fool is he, to still be waiting for her?

"I never asked you to wait for me," she says.

"I'm not waiting. I date people. I just don't like anyone but you."

"Try."

"I do try."

"Try harder."

Where did he get the idea that she was so special? He kept a small pond. Plenty of fish in the sea, but their hometown was not the sea, and he was okay with that, and she was not, and as long as that remained true, they couldn't be together.

"Do one thing for me," he says.

"No."

"One thing."

"Fine."

"Kiss me."

She stares at him, summons indignation. She should have seen this coming. No, she *had* seen this coming. She had known this would happen and she came anyway, pretending she didn't. This is what always happens: they go months, sometimes a year without seeing each other, and then they come together in this tectonic collision, and everything is temporarily upset, the ground shifts, and after the dust settles she tells herself this meaningful look or that touch or that kiss didn't mean anything, it didn't matter, it was just a sentimental acknowledgment of their shared past, too pure to count as cheating.

She can't do this anymore. It has to stop.

It's not easy to storm out of a tree house made for children, but Jada does her best. She stands too quickly, bumps her head. "I'm sorry," she says, maybe to Drew, maybe to the beam she's run into. Drew remains seated, convinced she'll change her mind and stay.

She picks her way down the ladder, dodging loose steps and rusty nails. He doesn't come after her. Her heart aches, and there is no one she can offer that ache to, no one who can help her bear it—not her mother, too frail to withstand its weight; not Blake, who'd be wounded by its very existence; not Maddy, who is still so young and uncommitted and whose life stretches before her so full of options. She blows past Drew's mother on her way past the house, waves distractedly, doesn't stop to talk. At home she tells her own mother, *This summer. A backyard wedding at home.* She says, *I wouldn't have it any other way.*

That night a storm blows in, and Jada listens to the wind from the warm security of her childhood bedroom, tapping out emails by the light of a bedside lamp. It's an activity that lets her tell herself she's busy, she's working, she isn't thinking of Drew. She listens to the storm gaining force, cracks her window to let the sound and the breeze filter in.

She did it, of course. Kissed him. She couldn't have summoned that kind of anger at him if it hadn't been mixed with anger at herself, couldn't have stormed out of his tree house that indignantly if her indignance had been righteous. Why did she always feel like she owed them something, men—not just one of them but all of them, somehow, simultaneously? To Blake, her constant commitment; at the same time, to Drew, a competing fidelity, an equally constant reverence for the grand narratives they'd constructed with each other, about each other.

*Don't think about him,* she thinks. But she knows how attempts to suppress a thought often have the opposite effect, placing the thought at the forefront of the mind, rendering it hyperaccessible; thinking, "Don't think about Drew" was, ultimately, just another way of thinking about Drew. Wegner, Schneider, Carter & White, 1987: participants are asked to narrate everything that comes into their mind for five straight minutes into a tape recorder. Half of them are told to think of a white bear, while the other half are told not to, but when instructed to press a button each time they think of a white bear, the participants on both sides press it at equal rates. Later, once the participants in the suppression condition are given permission to think of the white bear, they discuss the bear at length, pressing the button at an overwhelmingly high rate compared to those who were never asked to suppress the thought in the first place.

Whatever you do, do not think of a white bear. Do not think of a white bear. White bear white bear white bear white bear white bear white bear.

A memory surfaces: her freshman year at Penn State, before the distance got to them. They'd come home for a weekend, and she was halfway through her first course in relationship psychology, and as they sat together on the floor of this very bedroom, right there—she glances at the spot—she told him she'd learned the secrets of human attraction. Familiarity: we love what we know. Reciprocity: we love the people who love us. Physical attractiveness: we love who looks good.

"Define 'good,'" he said. They sat with their legs crossed in front of them, knee to knee, his hands spread over her thighs.

"Height"—she made a show of sizing him up, head to toe—"and shoulder-to-hip ratio"—her eyes darted across his body—"and facial symmetry."

"But your face isn't symmetrical," he said. "Your left eyebrow is arched a little more than your right."

"Strike one."

"And you have this little mole"—he leaned forward to touch it—"by your lip."

"Strike two."

"And this spot in your eye, this fleck of brown."

"Strike three," she said. "I'm out."

"I prefer you this way." Drew turned his head to the left, then the right. "How's my symmetry?"

She scanned his face, looking for a flaw. "So perfect it's annoying."

He winked at her, victorious. She took a pen, uncapped it, drew a tiny blue star above his right eyebrow.

"There," she said, "I fixed it." By which she meant, *I ruined it.*

A clap of thunder she feels inside her body shakes her from her reverie, and lightning illuminates her bedroom. Then the wind carries a branch into a power line somewhere down the road—she hears the crack like the impact of ball against bat—and the house goes black. Blind while her pupils race to expand, Jada holds still, feels her other senses rise to the occasion. Smell of damp soil. Sound of slender trees creaking in the wind like old bones, stiff legs walking. She rises to shut the window, picks up her phone to light her way to the hall closet stocked with flashlights, batteries, candles and matchbooks, jugs of clean water. They were a family used to being periodically ripped from modernity; they lost power often, and with it went their well's pump, their water. As a child, during storms or heavy snowfall, Jada would sometimes wake alone in this room to complete darkness and absolute silence—no white noise, no light, nothing definite against which to define herself—and wonder if the world had ended. If she'd slept through fire and flood and four horsemen and survived unnoticed, the last one left. Or if while sleeping she had traveled through time—back before birth, before parents, before electricity—and when she went into her parents' bedroom for reassurance she might find in their places strangers in frilled nightcaps, slumberers from another century.

Smartphones make power outages less inconvenient but also less thrilling. Jada lights a candle and is about to open a crossword app when Maddy appears in her doorway.

"Are you awake?" Maddy asks.

"No."

For a moment Maddy just stares at Jada. Then she sits down on the bed. "I need to talk to you." She unlocks her phone, its light casting a white glow on her face, and hands it to Jada. On the screen, a website touts the benefits of apricot seed therapy to cancer patients.

"What is this?"

"Something she hasn't tried. I'm saving for it. If you want to pitch in."

Jada scrolls down a page of FAQs. *Why don't more treatment centers use this type of therapy? Why do some claim it's ineffective? Isn't cyanide poisonous?* She skims defensive answers: *You eat cyanide-rich food every day if you consume apples, pineapples, or any of the thousands of other foods found in nature.*

"It looks . . . medically dubious," she says.

"I knew you'd say that." Maddy snatches her phone away.

Outside, the wind howls and the trees groan. Jada studies her sister. She knows what Maddy is thinking: that Jada has no idea what it's like being here, caring for Ellen; that the constant fear and exhaustion are hers alone to bear while Jada traipses through life engaged and carefree. Jada knows this brand of resentment well; it's one that she shares, turned inward. And it's one she has felt toward Maddy.

When Ellen first got sick, around the time Maddy was born, her symptoms were easy to shrug off. Even the lump she noticed while breastfeeding had been easy enough to dismiss. Later, throughout her surgery and treatment—double mastectomy followed by chemotherapy, a brutal AC-T regimen—she was too ravaged, too weak to care for baby Maddy, and Jada had stepped up. She had changed the diapers, she had dangled the toys before the child, hating their bright colors and deranged smiles, their too-happy jingles. She had cleaned the bathroom, done the dishes, put Maddy and, after homework, her twelve-year-old self to bed. Later, in high school, the memory of her days of infant care and Cinderella-like domestic labor served as a kind of maximally effective birth control for teenage Jada, who stayed chaste until after graduation. Where Maddy now cares for injured owls, Jada had cared for a human girl—a human girl who, all signs indicate, is as unconscious or forgetful of that steadfast daily care as a bird would be.

*Don't be mad at her,* Ellen had told Jada at the time. *It's not her fault.*

When her mother's cancer returned after she went off her Tamoxifen, Jada was freshly graduated from Penn State and about to head to Michigan for her PhD. Instead she stayed, worked at Missy's, with its proud and widely mocked REAL MASHED POTATOES sign out front. She drove Maddy to friends' birthday parties and softball practice, accompanied her mother to doctor's appointments, administered anastrozole, watched her mother grow sleepless and moody. Eventually, once Ellen had convinced her it was okay to go, she enrolled in a doctoral program closer to home, came back on weekends when she could. Even now, she drives her mother to treatments at UPMC, shuttling her back and forth, helping her transition from one new drug to another, writing down her oncologist's every word, even the ones she does not want to hear, the ultimate white bears. That Maddy resents Jada, that she thinks she is the only one who suffers on behalf of their mother, is the result of a careful illusion that Jada and Ellen have agreed to curate for her. They have placed her behind a curtain. She will not know everything Dr. Will says. Ellen is determined that she should have as normal a senior year as possible.

Jada twists the ring on her finger. She should support Maddy's idea, medically dubious or not. At least, she should appear to.

She asks, "Have you talked it over with her?"

"I'm waiting until I have the money. I'm almost there."

Jada watches her sister cradle her phone in her hands, scrolling absentmindedly, pretending to read. They are on the same page about their mother's situation, she can see. Though they may not have access to all the same data or agree on how to respond, they're both getting desperate.

"Is Dad on board?"

"Of course not," Maddy says. "He doesn't know. I'd take her to Mexico myself."

The wind has died down, and the rain has stopped, though thunder continues to rumble and lightning continues to flash outside. Maddy puts down her phone. "Let's go out."

"Now?"

"I like this kind of storm."

Jada takes the candle and lets it light their way down the stairs, past their father asleep on the couch in front of the dark TV, and onto the back deck. Early fireflies blink in the wide-open yard and in the field beyond, which slopes down to a dense line of trees where they once watched a black bear stand on its hind legs and wiggle and scratch its back against bark. Maddy is right: it's the loveliest kind of storm, near enough to dazzle, distant enough not to threaten. Someone else's problem, now, though the power is still out and the only light comes from candle flame and fireflies. Jada imagines swallowing a mouthful of the insects, her belly like glass, all its parts on glowing display. Thunder rolls, low and hungry-sounding, and she and Maddy sit in weathered deck chairs and watch as lightning flashes in concert with the fireflies, illuminating everything in bursts of blinding white. It ought to be set to music, she thinks, and hears in her head, again, Chopin's raindrops. A cool breeze licks her skin.

She remembers teaching Maddy to catch fireflies: to transfer them through the mouth of a glass jar, letting them plink daintily against its base; to screw the lid their father had punctured with a screwdriver quickly back onto the jar. The first time Maddy caught one, she'd crushed it, too eager, a yellow-green smear on her skin. Does she remember? Jada glances at her sister. Does she remember the way Jada held out her cupped hands to deliver a trapped, blinking bug into her palm?

She is opening her mouth to ask when Maddy says, "I think I know what made Mom sick. I've been reading."

Jada takes a deep breath. "Not this again."

Maddy has worked her way through a number of theories about the cause of Ellen's cancer. Formaldehyde in shampoo absorbed through the scalp. Chimney soot, woodsmoke, the varnish on the living room furniture. It's not that Jada would contest the harmfulness of these things, only that she knows that once you opened that Pandora's box, you'd never reach the bottom of all that was inside. Maddy has let her hair go greasy, thrown out her mother's cheap perfume. Jada has tried to peer-review her sister's fears—no, underwire bras do not cause cancer; no, antiperspirants don't block the release of toxins from the body—but her fact-checking has done little to comfort Maddy.

"You know those rusty pipes in the yard?"

Yes, Jada knows them. Her family lives in a pincushion. The yard, woods, and entire region are full of holes, the remains of the oil and gas drilling that has gone on there for over a century. Maddy tells her that abandoned, unplugged oil and gas wells can leak carcinogenic benzene, methane, and other volatile organic compounds that seep into soil and contaminate ground and surface water. Old, leaking casings or crumbling cement can give oil, gas, and brine access to aquifers.

"And houses can explode," Maddy states. She smells like BO. "If an unplugged orphan well is close enough to a house, the migrating gas—"

"The house is not going to explode."

"Other people's have."

It could be any and all of the things Maddy fears that has caused their mother's cancer. It could also be none of them. What scares Maddy is that it might be the stuff around Ellen that's made her sick, but what scares Jada is that it might not be. That it could be just . . . being a woman. Having a woman's body.

"The wells should be plugged," Maddy says. "The ones on our property, and all the other ones. And we should . . . we should sue."

"Who?"

"Somebody."

"For what?"

"For putting them there."

"Those wells are over a hundred years old."

"And we should be drinking bottled water, just in case."

Jada nods—okay, fine. But if it's water that has made her mother sick, it's the same water they've all been drinking their entire lives. If it's abandoned wells that are killing her, they are the same abandoned wells Jada sometimes tripped over as a child playing in the woods. She thinks of the TRUMP yard signs she passed on her way to her parents' house—he's the presumptive Republican nominee—and that seemed to multiply in frequency the closer she got. They stood outside homes that had once seemed benignly sleepy, and it was tempting to be surprised by their sudden appearance, but Jada knows better. She is disconcerted, but she is not surprised, just as she is not surprised by Maddy's data on orphan wells. What's here has always been here, and has always been dangerous, even if you only tripped on it now.

Her phone lights up with a text message. Drew. *You're right, I don't want to lose you. Even after all this time I guess I haven't been able to let go. You are smart and you can make your own decisions. If you stand by this one and it works out, I'll do my best to respect it and be happy for you. If it doesn't, I'll be here to catch you.*

He has not said he's sorry. Jada had apologized instinctively, fleeing the tree house, but he had not. He will not.

When she looks up from her phone, she sees that Maddy is watching her.

"Who's that?"

"No one." Jada locks her phone and places it on the arm of her chair.

Maddy continues to study her. "What's wrong?"

"What? Nothing."

"Mom said you're having the wedding here."

"Yes."

"Why?"

Jada turns to look at her sister, her face dimly lit by candlelight, her eyes dark pits where little light reaches. "It will be easier for Mommy this way."

She checks herself. She had not meant to say "Mommy," a term that conjures the time when Jada was little and an only daughter, enjoying that singular bond.

"Is it what you want, though?"

"I don't know," Jada says. "Sure." She has never been a girl who dreamed of white dresses; she has nurtured no princess fantasies. "It's just a wedding."

"What does Blake think?"

He was hesitant when she told him. She promised him a second reception in Pittsburgh with his family and their friends, an event that she suspects will be more like a second wedding.

"He's fine with it," she says. "Why wouldn't he be?"

Maddy shrugs. "He just seems . . . you know."

"What?"

"*You* know. Fancy."

Jada does not respond.

"What kind of dress do you want?" Maddy asks.

"Haven't thought about it."

"How do you want your hair?"

"I don't know."

"Who's going to be your maid of honor?"

"Catalina." Jada had asked her right away—*you're like a sister to me.*

Maddy goes quiet, and Jada realizes her mistake. "You'll be in the wedding too, of course," she says. "Obviously. Will you be a bridesmaid?"

A silence stretches between them. Then Maddy says, "Yeah, thanks. I'm honored." Her voice is sharp. "I'm a maid, honored."

"I'm sorry," Jada says. "I didn't—"

"It's okay."

The storm is over. The fireflies' show has ended. It's almost completely dark, and so Jada is blindsided when, as she sits thinking of something to say, Maddy flies at her in an ambush, throwing her arms around her and squeezing violently. She taps Maddy's back with the tips of her fingers, waits for release. Maddy wields physical contact as a weapon against Jada, who prefers to live limned in a critical perimeter of personal space like a bumper, a padding aura. She flinches when anyone or anything penetrates it, and this flinching is endlessly amusing to Maddy.

"Mads," Jada says, and taps her back again. She can move her hands but not her arms, pinned tightly at her sides.

Maddy does not let go. Instead she laughs a deranged, witchy cackle and squeezes harder. The hug is aggressive, punitive—is this about the maid of honor thing? Is this laughter even laughter?

Has Maddy gone mad? Have they both gone mad? Where does her body end and her sister's begin?

"Stop," she gasps. "Maddy, *stop*."

At last Maddy pulls back. The boundaries are restored, the aura repairs itself. "Good night," she says, and leaves Jada alone on the deck.

Eventually Jada too goes back inside and crawls into bed. When she was little, her mother would tuck her into this bed, the ends of her long hair brushing Jada's forehead and cheeks. It was a game they played, her mother sweeping her face like this. Cleaning up, she'd joked. Ellen would toss her head, making a swishing sound— *shush, shush*—and Jada would catch the soft strands in her fists, gently pull her mother's face toward hers. The ritual is a reminder: she is not fundamentally opposed to touch. She's not a monster. Her mother can permeate her barriers, dissolve her boundaries. If other people can't—Maddy, her father, even Blake—well, that's on them. Jada's heartbeat slows. The memory is so sharp, the room so familiar even in darkness, that she is half tempted to reach her hands up now, half-convinced that she'll find Ellen's face there—circa mid-nineties, pre-Maddy, healthy. She is tempted, too, to go quietly to Ellen's bedside and let her own hair drape down, their roles reversed. It would be a way of saying, *I haven't forgotten. I will not forget.*

She lets her phone light her way to the room where her mother sleeps alone. Ellen is awake and turns to look at her. "I heard you girls go out."

Jada lowers herself softly onto the edge of her mother's bed and turns off her phone's flashlight. A curtain of darkness falls between them. "I think I upset her. I asked Catalina to be my maid of honor. Maddy—"

"She's your sister."

"I know."

"She needs to feel special. Can't you give her something to do?"

"Of course," Jada says. "I asked her to be a bridesmaid."

"Thank you."

"You don't have to thank me."

Ellen takes Jada's hand. "You're on your way up, baby," she says. They sit in silence for a long time, until Ellen asks, "Have you thought any more about what we talked about?"

"The wedding?" Jada says, though she knows this is not what her mother means.

"You know. The other thing."

No. She did not want to think about it when it last came up, and she does not want to talk about it now. "I can't," she says.

"You can." Ellen rubs the back of Jada's hand with her thumb. "My strong, smart girl. There's nothing you can't do."

This is, of course, untrue, but Jada does not want to argue with her mother, who seems to truly believe that she can do anything and everything. All her life Ellen has propped her up, the beloved bookish child, shuttling her back and forth from the library, so proud of her daughter, the teacher's pet. It was part of the contract they'd always had: Jada was Smart and would be Successful.

*Some people might say I live precariously through my kids,* Ellen wrote in the card she gave Jada when she graduated from Penn State, and Jada had felt a pang of love and shame at the malapropism. *Well I don't mind. I love your life as much as I love mine.*

"I need you on my team," Ellen says now. "I need you to do this for me."

"I don't want to."

"Well," Ellen says, and pats Jada's hand, and then lets go. "That doesn't really matter, now, does it."

They do not speak for a long time. Jada hears an owl outside. After a while, her mother breaks the silence. "I'm going to give Bachi's wedding ring to Maddy for her eighteenth."

Jada nods. Her grandmother, her Bachi, died when she was ten, before Maddy was born. "She'll like that."

"You don't mind?"

"Of course not."

"You have your own ring," Ellen says, and Jada hears the pride in her voice. "And we need to make sure her graduation is special. You should think about what you're going to do for her."

"Money?" Jada says. "And a nice card?"

"Take her somewhere. Do something with her. She's never seen the ocean. She's never been on a plane."

Jada nods.

"She needs you."

"I know, Mommy."

Ellen pats Jada's hand again. "You should go to bed," she says. "It's late."

When Jada returns to her own bed, she closes her eyes, forgetting that the lights were on in the room when the house lost power. When it returns hours later, startling her from sleep with a flash and a whir—the bedside digital clock blinking 00:00, the world outside still black, no trace of dawn—her eyes will snap open and burn, overcome by light. Disoriented, she'll have the sudden, irrational sense that she has died.

# 10

## MADDY

### April 2018

When she woke in the morning, it was from a dream of her mother, black-and-white and grainy like an old-time photograph, wearing a shimmering gown. She approached Maddy and stretched out her hands, held her for a long time. Then she said, *Undo me, baby*, and turned around, the train of her gown furled around her feet.

The bodice took the form of a corset and was done up with a thousand silver hooks and eyes. Maddy set to work unfastening them. She could feel the corset straining, bursting a little more open as each hook slipped out of its eye. But for each clasp she unfastened, another appeared, and another, until the trail of them seemed to stretch for miles. Endless fabric firmed with wire opened out from her mother's back like wings spreading. The fabric was soft as petals, its wires fine as fish bones, and when Maddy pulled what looked like loose dark threads at the hem, she found that they were not threads at all but her mother's lost eyelashes.

*I didn't lose any damn battle*, Ellen said in the dream, as she had in real life shortly before she died. *Got it?* Then she pulled on one of the wires that protruded from the corset the way the edge of a feather might poke through the case of a down pillow, dipped it into a well of ink, and began to write. Her hand moved with urgency, but Maddy couldn't read the words. When she opened her eyes it was to see them better, but they were gone, and she thought to her mother, *If you're trying to tell me what to do, you're going to have to find another way.* The dream receded, and she felt the throbbing in her hand.

She lay on the air mattress, watching the blades of the ceiling fan turn. She tried to slow it down with her eyes, to follow the path of a single rotating blade, but they moved too quickly. Her eyes darted helplessly; she grew dizzy, got the jerk-and-stall sensation of an old record skipping.

She'd slept until eleven. Jada was not home. Her things were still piled everywhere, though Maddy could see that she'd risen early and attempted to organize them, put clothes in the dresser and closet. In the kitchen, scrounging, she found a note: *Went shopping. Keep hand dry! Be back soon.*

Maddy sat on one of the stools at the kitchen table. Bits of her dream still clung to her, and she tried in vain to interpret them: words, wire, wings, dress. Wedding dress? Her mother had been asking her to take the dress off . . . so she could put it on herself? Maddy didn't know, and the dream probably meant nothing, but either way, she figured, she ought to find a boyfriend. If she kept the baby, she would need more than four thousand dollars and a housecleaning gig. She would need more than just herself.

She downloaded a dating app, poking at her phone with her good hand, one-fingered, like an old person. Unlikely that most normal guys her age were scouring the apps in search of pregnant girls, but you never knew. She uploaded a photo of herself taken at last year's

Owloween fundraiser at the wildlife center. She held a screech owl on her arm, jesses clipped to his legs, and was opening her mouth to speak to a crowd of guests and potential donors, the table behind her spread with plastic jack-o'-lanterns and bird-themed coloring sheets for kids. The sight of the photo filled her with longing and pride. Even that owl had had a girlfriend, a wild girlfriend who would swoop down to talk to him most evenings, the two of them calling back and forth from inside and outside the mews.

She uploaded three other photos—a car selfie, her head tilted and the light a syrupy orange; a bathroom-mirror selfie, one hand holding up her sparkle-cased phone and the other propped cutely on her hip; and a picture Jada had taken on one of Maddy's previous visits to Pittsburgh, where she held a huge sandwich with French fries on it in both hands, laughing, looking out of the frame to her right, at her mother.

She had other photos on her phone, too, a bank of nudes to draw on should she need them. The ones that had been shared without her consent, of course, and others she'd taken for herself. In the time since the incident with Bear she had honed her skills, and now, alone in Jada's kitchen, she opened her secret folder and scrolled, admiring both subject and skill. The fact was she liked her body, or at least she liked beholding it from the outside the way someone else would. She liked knowing how others saw her. There was power in this knowledge, or at least there could be if she could figure out how to use it, how to reconcile the body she admired with the body she inhabited. She liked the idea that, should she become separated from her body, she could pick it out of a lineup: that one, her, that's mine.

She closed the folder and turned around, as if someone might be looking over her shoulder. Then she published her profile and began swiping through others': *Tattoos, motorcycles, and livin free. The girls in the pic are my nieces FYI. I like boats, cars, vacations, and work.*

Overwhelmed, she closed the app and looked up one of the adoption sites listed on a pamphlet from New Dawn. Profiles of aspiring adoptive families greeted her. They were a lot like dating profiles: pictures of couples on their wedding day, couples in snorkeling gear. Couples or single people with pets, by campfires, in front of European palaces and fountains, on bikes, separate and tandem. Favorite snacks, favorite movies, favorite ice cream flavors, favorite holidays and holiday traditions. Favorite fruit, flower, family activity. *We enjoy going to the theater. We look forward to nightly family dinners and reading aloud by the fireplace. We're outdoorsy. We're foodies. We love long walks on the beach.* In the letters and videos they posted, many of them praised birth mothers for their bravery, their unselfishness. *If you choose our family, we would raise your child knowing how much they are loved by you. We'd be honored to be a part of your life and promise to love your child unconditionally.*

Some said "your" child, some said "our" child, some said "a" child. Maddy's head began to spin, and she turned her phone facedown, but the profiles and the voices stayed with her, all swirled together: *We love board games and cooking Filipino cuisine. I'm the funny guy at the office. We live down the street from a brand-new elementary school. Workin on my biceps u can touch if u play ur cards right. Garrett is a pediatrician and loves working with kids. Chelsea is a nutritionist who would make sure our child ate healthy, balanced meals. Let's have a tickle fight. Let's hit the gym. Let's curl up by the fire and binge trash TV. Looking to give a child the kind of happy childhood I was blessed to have. Looking for my partner in crime.*

She heard voices in the hallway, the sounds of a heavy object being moved through the narrow space, scraping the walls. The door opened, and Jada came in lugging a folded futon mattress wrapped in plastic, trailed by Drew.

"Drew came down," she said, dropping the mattress and holding the door for him.

Maddy felt her eyes narrow and thought of the promise she'd made Blake. "Why?"

"To help me."

Drew maneuvered three large boxes, one labeled ARMS and two BODY, through the doorway and plopped them on the living room floor. "Maddy-girl," he said, his nickname for her since she was little. "How's your owl?"

"Good," she said. "Dad and I saw you in the paper."

"You were in the paper?" Jada asked.

"He sure was."

Jada looked at Drew encouragingly, waiting. She waited a long time as he slashed open a box with his pocketknife and removed pieces of futon frame. "Something for the store?"

"Not exactly," Drew said, twirling an Allen wrench between his fingers, then caved: "Public urination."

"He peed in a potted plant," Maddy supplied. "On Main Street."

Jada looked confused. She stared at Drew as if waiting for a punch line and sat down beside him. "Nutrient rich," he offered.

"Dad showed me," Maddy said.

"Yeah? What did old Jeff have to say about that?"

"Oh, he thought it was hilarious."

"Did he," Jada said. Her knee was touching Drew's.

"Aw, come on." Drew gave her arm a nudge and began plugging holes in the futon slats with wooden dowels. "It's just one of those things."

"It's not, though." Jada rubbed a crumb of Styrofoam between her fingers. "It's not something people do when they're . . . in a good place."

"I'm in a great place." Drew spread his arms wide. "I'm here."

Jada's phone chimed. She tapped the screen to open a text, then jumped, startled, and held the phone back far from her face. "What *is* that?"

"What?" Maddy asked, but Jada was already charging toward her, pointing the phone's screen at her face.

"What is this thing, and why is it in my—Blake's—house?"

On the screen was a photo Blake had taken of her fetus doll, beneath which he had texted a quadruple question mark. Maddy didn't know whether to laugh or cry. She let out a weird squawk.

"You think this is funny?" Jada asked.

"I didn't mean to leave it there."

"Is this some kind of joke?"

"They gave it to me at New Dawn," Maddy said, "to remind me . . ." She touched her belly.

"Let me see," Drew said, and raised his eyebrows when Jada held out the phone.

"Sure," Maddy said. "Just show whoever."

"He's not 'whoever,'" Jada said. "And he already knows you're pregnant."

"Just tell whoever, then!"

"You're the one who put a baby doll on Blake's bananas."

"Hold this." Drew handed Jada a piece of the futon frame, helped her balance it where he needed it, and began screwing it to another piece of frame.

"You're giving these people too much power over you," Jada said, talking to Maddy but not looking at her. "Carrying around their souvenir just like they want you to, letting them get in your head, make you feel guilty—"

"I don't feel guilty."

"They want to make you feel like you don't have a choice." Jada dropped the futon slat, and Drew took her hand and gently repositioned it. "It's coercion. It's cruel. Things are hard enough for you already, and then they—"

"Okay," Maddy said. "Jeez. It's not that big of a deal."

Was it? She wasn't sure. A part of her liked the idea of being righteous in the way that Pat had seemed righteous, liked the thought of tending to a child as to a raptor or a songbird. But another part had doubts. That part looked at staircases and thought, if only for a flickering second, of throwing herself down. Women used to do that, Maddy had learned, to end their pregnancies; she'd watched a YouTube video whose host had explained it. Women had friends or partners punch them in the gut, drank special teas, pierced their cervixes with knitting needles. Women squirted bleach into themselves or lay in ice baths or pools of scalding water. Yesterday, in the stairwell with an armful of Jada's clothes slung over her arm, Maddy had paused and touched the wicked tip of a wire hanger with the pad of her pointer finger, remembering those women who'd had no other option. All she would have to do was take a pill, and she would be alone again, uninhabited. If that were really what she wanted, she wouldn't be so gullible as to let herself be swayed by a rubber doll—would she?

"They aren't God," Jada was ranting, "and they can't decide for you. They can give you a plastic baby and some secondhand onesies, but where will they be when you have an actual child to take care of?"

"It's just a doll. It doesn't bother me."

"Well, it should," Jada said. "It bothers me that it doesn't bother you."

"*Okay,*" Maddy groaned. "Why are you freaking out?"

*I'd be a bad mother,* Jada had said, and Maddy wondered if there was something her sister hadn't told her.

She spent the afternoon getting boba tea, wandering the neighborhood and the apartment texting with *Star Wars is my first priority* and *I can literally juggle* until the evening, when she knew Blake would be home from work. Drew was still at Jada's when Maddy excused herself and drove to the town house to retrieve her fetus doll.

The house was a mess when she arrived, transformed since the morning before: open containers of Chinese takeout on the counter and the coffee table, dumplings and orange chicken and scattered white rice, a large sticky mark where something probably alcoholic had spilled, socks strewn in unexpected places. A video game was paused on the TV screen.

"What's her apartment like?" he asked, leading Maddy into the kitchen.

She scrunched her nose, and he seemed pleased, and she wondered if she should tell him about Drew. She had pledged to be his eyes and ears. But the thought made her feel dirty. All Jada had done was ask for help; all Drew had done was help her. He had literally made the bed in which Maddy would sleep.

"What happened to your hand?" Blake pointed to her bandage.

"Box cutter," she said. "It's nothing."

He had placed her fetus doll inside a domed glass cake stand that could be overturned and converted into a punch bowl. He lifted the dome by the ball on its top with a flourish, like a chef presenting a meal kept warm under a silver cloche, and handed her the doll.

Whenever she forgot about it, a sign of failure flashed in her mind like a *GAME OVER* message at the end of a video game. *PLAY AGAIN?* asked the text on her mental screen, and she clicked yes, resumed, and failed again. Of course she knew a rubber baby was easier to misplace than a human one, which could cry and demand milk, but it was also more portable and less disruptive of her daily routine, and she worried that to think first of anyone but herself at this moment in her life might be a challenge she could not meet.

"So," Blake asked, "do you want to talk about what this was doing in my bowl?"

She shrugged, hating the thought of him feeling sorry for her. She wanted them both on the same page, a page on which she was a funny and generally functional adult coming to him for casual, chummy guidance rather than rescue or pity.

"Have you eaten?" He gestured toward the containers of Chinese food. "I'll make you a plate."

"Okay." She half sat on a stool while he filled a big bowl with rice and orange chicken and fished chopsticks from a drawer. Her stomach sank; she would have to pretend to know how to use them, and she would look like a hick.

"Who's the father?" He pushed the bowl toward her and motioned for her to carry it to the living room, where she joined him on the couch, cradling the bowl on her lap, balanced against her bandaged hand.

"Nobody."

"Virgin birth," he said. "No wonder you were asking about God."

"He doesn't want to be involved."

"God?" Blake chuckled. She didn't. "Do you want him to be involved?"

"No." She had never thought about it because she had always understood it as an impossibility. For a moment she tried to let herself imagine that she'd met him under different circumstances, but this too proved impossible. Different circumstances would have made him a different person. His impossibility had been the source of his appeal.

"How did your dad react?" Blake asked.

"He doesn't know."

"That's why you're here."

Maddy nodded.

"But you want to have it?" he asked. "The baby?"

"It's hard to answer that," Maddy replied, and he waited for her to explain. He was looking at her, watching as she struggled to balance a nugget of orange chicken between her chopsticks. "I don't *want* to *have* it—as in, the thought of giving birth is scary. But I don't want to *not* have it. I want it to go away, not by my doing anything, but by . . . an act of God, I guess."

"You want to pray the baby away."

"Maybe. But I don't think it works that way."

"No, I don't think it does."

If only she could magic her baby into an alternative paternity, someone available, who loved her. Sometimes she went through the day looking at boys and men—both IRL and online—just longing to absorb their genes, rewrite the letters of her child's DNA. In her most irrational moments she worried that her ugly feelings toward its father might print themselves on the child, rendering it a gremlin, all her pain expressed in its mean little face.

"Are you happy?" Blake asked, not joking anymore.

She shrugged. "In the movie version of my life, I'd have a convenient miscarriage."

"How does it feel to think about that?"

"Bad."

"Why do you think that is?"

"Everything feels bad," she said. "It feels bad to think about giving it up for adoption, too."

"Yeah," Blake said, "I don't think your dad would want that."

This surprised her—not the idea itself, but the fact that he'd expressed it, that that was where he went. "I don't want my dad to raise my child."

"He raised you."

"My mom raised me." Her voice sounded loud. "Jada raised me."

Blake held up his hands, like, *whoa.* "Sorry," he said.

"Lots of people want kids and can't have them," she said.

"Sure, but there are lots of kids out there already who need loving homes. And it's not your job to make a baby for somebody else. It's not just some supply-and-demand thing. It's a human life. It's *your* life."

Maddy dropped a clump of rice onto the rug. "I know that," she said.

"Do you need a fork?"

"No." She picked up the rice and folded it into her napkin.

"It looks like you do."

"I don't."

"Let me get you one just in case." He got up and returned with a fork, placed it delicately on the coffee table.

She would rather starve than touch that fork. She set her bowl down on the table.

"You want kids, don't you?" she said.

"Of course."

"With Jada."

"Of course. Who else?"

"It's just," Maddy said, "she's not here."

"She will be."

She had a vision of Blake lifting her baby like a dumbbell over his head, saw the child's toothless smile, heard its squeaky baby laughter. She shook the vision away.

"You should tell your dad, though," he said. "He needs to know."

She would not have guessed that such a female predicament would involve thinking and talking about so many men. The baby's biological father, the baby's future replacement father, her own father. "You're so worried about my dad all of a sudden."

"No," he said, and gave her shoulder a few friendly taps. "I'm worried about you."

Her fingertips tingled. She leaned back into the couch cushions as he played his game, then took out her phone and scrolled through dating profiles, needing not to look at Blake, staring down at the screen. *Regular guy just living life! People might mistake me for a rough guy, but in reality I'm just a big teddy bear. The question I hate most is did your tattoos hurt. You should expect me to play video games until 4 in the morning.*

"Anyway," Blake said. "You know what they say about it taking a village."

She had heard the expression, of course, but didn't care for it. It conjured a pastoral, thatch-roofed innocence that didn't seem to reflect reality. Where were these "villages"? Was this city a village? Had she grown up in one? It hadn't felt that way. Maddy picked up her bowl and tried again to eat. A piece of chicken tumbled out of her grasp and rolled to a gloating stop at the edge of the fork Blake had given her, practically begging to be impaled.

"Here," he said, pausing his game and turning toward her. "May I?"

She nodded. He took her good hand and positioned the chopsticks in her fingers. "Like that. See?" He puppeted her fingers, letting the sticks click together, then resumed his video game.

Maddy imagined herself in a village with Jada, knocking at the door of her timbered cottage or wandering barefoot into her mud-walled hut to hand off a newborn in exchange for a cup of sugar or a sack of yams. No. Then she imagined Blake a resident of the village—a peasant with a scythe, open-shirted, feeding her child a chunk of crusty baguette; a loin-clothed hunter come back to camp with a saber-toothed tiger hanging by its ankles from a stake propped on his shoulder. Into the fire it goes. Up fly the sparks. He grunts at her; he holds the baby; they tear the red meat with their teeth. Yes.

She was laughing through her nose to herself without meaning to. "What's funny?" he asked.

"Nothing," she said. "Should we eat these fortune cookies?"

They were sitting on the coffee table in their packages, unclaimed. Two of them. He picked one up, unwrapped it, and cracked it open. "'Feeding a cow with roses does not get extra appreciation,'" he read aloud.

She cracked hers and drew the slip of paper from inside. It resisted a little, and she felt an urge to apologize as she pulled. "'An agreeable romance might begin to take on the appearance.'"

"Ah," he said. "See? Things are looking up already."

She smiled.

He held out the controller and nodded toward the TV screen. "You want a turn?"

She shook her head, held up her injured hand. Her heart did a happy somersault in her chest, and she felt color in her cheeks. *Get ahold of yourself,* she thought.

To cool herself down, she reminded herself that he pooped. She reminded herself that he had once been a baby. She left her cookie uneaten and slipped her fortune into her pocket.

"You're not going to eat that?"

She said no, she didn't like them.

"If I eat it," he said, "do I get the fortune?"

"Nope."

He ate it anyway, crunching loudly. She brushed rice from her lap. *Someone is being born right now,* she thought. And now. And now. Another one: now. She was not special, she was not unique. Birth was boring when you really thought about it. Billions of people had babies; who would care if she did, too? She was small, smaller than an eyelash, smaller than a grain of sand. She had had these thoughts before, but then—as now—some scale would tilt in her mind, and her thoughts would shift, her sense of proportions changed, and she was clobbered by the great magnitude, the lofty miracle of life: she could have a *baby*. A BABY, a HUMAN, with the potential to change the world.

She was a tiny atom, she was a sprawling galaxy. She was made of stars. She was nothing, she was everything; her pregnancy trivial, planetary. She wanted everything to be just one thing. But which one was the right one? How did you know?

# 11

---

# JADA

**April 2018**

*Are you a single student who wants to connect with potential dat-
ing partners near you? You might be eligible to help the university
pilot a new, in-house online dating site,* Prowl*! Interested students
can earn extra credit in eligible courses and free* Prowl *membership
in exchange for two visits to a computer lab to complete a short
survey and browse an exciting selection of online daters from our
groundbreaking algorithm!*

At the beginning of each of her studies, once her research assistants
had learned their scripts and read the requisite background research,
Jada met them at the lab to walk them through the first few participants' visits. They role-played, Jada playing the participant, listening as the RAs rehearsed their lines, making corrections as needed.
She liked filling the role of mentor. She liked the backstage, pre-
game quality of these meetings, the sense of expectation, the insis-
tence on exactitude—everything to be timed and delivered just right,

monitored and controlled. All conditions kept consistent, identical except for whatever was being deliberately manipulated.

At first, when she had been an undergraduate RA looking up starry-eyed at her own grad student mentor, Jada had thought it was only her innate love of precision and control that drew her to research in the social sciences, but now she understood that it was more than that. She loved control, yes, but part of her was also drawn to the chaos in need of controlling. She loved the precision of numerical data, the cleanliness of the quantitative, but she also loved the human messiness that lurked underneath it. Always, there were the uncooperative participants, the hungover participants, the belligerent participants, the sleepy participants, the distracted participants, the eliminated participants who failed intention checks, produced incorrect responses, or did things like walk out mid-study or, in one case, lean forward and vomit onto a computer lab keyboard. Or, in another, when asked how many sexual partners they would ideally have, draw an ever-looping infinity symbol in the white space on their survey. You did your best to create conditions that would yield only the information you wanted, but you always got more than you asked for.

On Thursday, Jada met her RAs, Ola, Isla, and Minh, in a small, dim room just off a computer lab, hidden behind a one-way mirror and crowded with file cabinets, headphones, and rolls of old conference posters. In a corner of the room stood the spit refrigerator—a small fridge, papered with warnings not to open, in which her advisor stored samples of human saliva for measuring hormones in her studies on stress. Drew was coming back to the city and would meet her when she finished up in the lab. She had double-booked herself on purpose, fitting him in after this first round of data collection as a way of making seeing him just another thing she did on a busy day, something she did while "at work" and not at home, where Maddy loafed, eating prenatal gummy vitamins like candy. She had not quit her cleaning jobs, she'd told Jada, at least not all of them; she was "on vacation" indefinitely and could return once she'd decided what to do. Already Jada had begun to feel that by taking Maddy in she had burdened herself not only with a child to care for but also with a vigilant parent to whom she must report, who watched her carefully and might ground her if she misbehaved.

"Run me through the protocol one last time," she said, her RAs clustered before her like cubs in a clinical den.

"They fill out the survey, they browse the profiles, they pick one, they answer the questionnaire about how happy they are with their selection," Ola summarized, clutching a creased copy of the protocol, TOP SECRET typed in all caps at the top. Her nails were manicured to match her magenta lipstick, her eyes sharp and focused behind large wire-rimmed glasses.

"And we refer their questions to you," Minh said. He was over-dressed, in a smart blue suit over a white dress shirt and gleaming brown loafers, his hair gelled to a point that made Jada think of the top of a soft-serve ice cream cone.

"Questions about the website, yes," said Jada. "You can answer basic procedural questions yourselves. Take good notes. Anytime the participant doesn't do what they should be doing, write it down."

She thought of the man on the pool deck at that horrible party: *Why these questions?* Certainly the research path she'd gone down had not been arbitrary but had been bound up with her awareness of her own ambivalence, her own pain. The thing was, she had built up an extensive professional vocabulary, and yet naming her psychological and behavioral tendencies and observing them in others did little to make them easier to bear. (White bear.) She knew she was a maximizer, intent on pursuing not just a good option but the best one, meticulously examining all alternatives, disinclined to settle for the first option that crossed her threshold of acceptability—that was, in other words, good enough. She had thought she could overcome her maximizing tendencies, join herself to Blake, let her mother rest in the knowledge that her girl would be all right. She had gone on thinking she could do this until the world turned upside down and her mother was gone and she was pregnant and then she wasn't and suddenly her life did not make sense anymore. "Good enough" wasn't good enough. Something, possibly everything, had to change.

She knew that more choices did not mean more happiness but a greater likelihood of dissatisfaction with the choice made and self-blame for having chosen poorly. She knew this, but her knowledge did not inoculate her. She *was* dissatisfied, overwhelmed by the existence of paths not taken, one of which—one of *whom*—was traveling here right now, to meet her in secret. She was disappointed to find that she was not the type of person who could stop second-guessing when she found a good man to love, and who loved her; she had clung to the possibility, however stigmatized, of reversing her decision to marry Blake, and she had failed to deploy the ego-protective mechanism that would allow her to view that decision through a rosy filter, to convince herself of its rightness. Still, the idea that the study she was conducting might further confirm the pervasiveness of thinking like hers brought her some comfort. She did not believe in God, but sometimes she did indulge in a vision of a great, cloud-dwelling scientist arranging the accessories of her life before her and then observing as she scrabbled through them, a rat in an experiment. A rat, yes, but one that acted in basic accordance with most other rats.

Through the one-way glass, she watched with Isla and Ola as Minh welcomed the first participant to the lab. "Please leave your belongings in the control room so as to minimize distractions," they heard him say before entering the lab. Inside, he handed the participant, a young woman in dark sunglasses with a frizz of red hair, a confidentiality agreement and a note card containing the *Prowl* web address, a username, and a password.

"I just had LASIK," the girl said, taking the card, motioning to her sunglasses. "In case you're wondering."

"Okay," said Minh. "This is your private log-in to the website." He pointed to the card in the girl's hand.

"I just didn't want you thinking I'm some person who goes around wearing sunglasses indoors."

Minh smiled politely. "You're welcome to use this log-in to return to the site anytime throughout the next two weeks to revisit your options. This—"

"Great," said the girl. "That's great. Since I just had LASIK, I might want to look them over again, you know, once I can take these off." She pointed to her sunglasses again.

"Sure."

"I can see and everything, it's not like I can't see. I'm just taking precautions."

Minh gestured to the confidentiality agreement. "This is a confidentiality agreement."

"Yes, I can read," the girl said, laughing flirtatiously. She held the paper up before her face and read, "Confidentiality agreement."

Minh's eyes flicked to the mirror. Isla giggled, covering her mouth with her hand. *Just had LASIK*, Ola mouthed, and mimed writing the phrase in her open notebook.

"So," Minh persisted, "since our website is still in its beta stage of development, we must ask that you not reveal our work to anyone else at this point in time."

The girl tapped the confidentiality agreement, took the pen Minh offered her, and signed. "Got it." She sat down at a computer, fluffed her hair, crossed her legs. "Great suit, by the way."

"Oh. Thanks."

"You don't see a lot of guys our age wearing suits like that," she said. "It's too bad. It looks, like, really good. So are you one of the web developers?"

"I'm just here to administer this trial," Minh replied, puffing up at the chance to show off his fidelity to the protocol while Jada looked on. "You can direct any questions you might have about the site to the email at the top of your note card."

He waited until the participant had logged in, then said, "I'll check on you in five minutes. In the meantime, if you finish up or have a question, just raise your hand." Then he started a stopwatch, recorded the participant's start time so she could be scheduled to return to the lab for a follow-up exactly two weeks from her first visit, and returned to the control room.

The girl filled out her survey, clicked through faces for a minute or two. Before the sets of dater profiles could be distributed, Jada and her assistants had had to review them all, grouping them strategically to ensure that the good-looking ones were equitably dispersed. The study wouldn't work, Isla had rightly pointed out, if "all the hot ones" were concentrated within the same sets. This had meant rating all 166 of the unknown students' profile photos using a series of seven-point Likert scales: How attractive is this online dater? 1 = not at all attractive; 7 = extremely attractive. How willing would you be to date this online dater? 1 = not at all likely; 7 = extremely likely. Jada had pushed her way through the attractiveness scales, imagining herself

ten years back in time and still their age, and it occurred to her now
that she could have enlisted Maddy's help. She had averaged her answers with those of her RAs, whose circled numbers were accompanied by penciled-in exclamation points, smiley or frowny faces, and
other punctuating doodles.

Now they all watched as the participant took a spin in her revolv-
ing chair, then raised her hand.

"I think I'm pretty much done," she said. "I do have a question,
though."

"Yes?" Minh stood with his hands folded and his back straight,
like a security guard on duty.

"Excuse me if I'm being overly, you know . . ."

"Oh no," Ola whispered.

". . . but I can't help but feel like there's some chemistry here." The
girl drew a line with her finger from herself to Minh and back again.
"Is there any chance I can . . . I don't know. Pick you?"

Behind the glass, Isla cringed. Ola heaved with silent laughter.
Jada shook her head. Minh, flustered, stuck to the protocol. "I'm
sorry," he said. "I'm not . . . you have to choose from the options on
the site." He left the room, returning only when the girl had finished
to remind her not to misplace her note card and to confirm her return in two weeks' time.

"Lab coats," Jada said when the participant had left the room.
"All of you in lab coats for the rest of the study." Though even
this wasn't foolproof. You could cover the body, but the body was
still there, still a body, an object of allure and critique. Two years
ago, when Jada's former RA Avery had worn her lab coat over shorts
while collecting data unsupervised, appearing pantsless beneath the
white fabric, a participant had typed on his survey on sexuality, I SAW
YOUR BUTT CHEEKS.

She would tell Drew about this, Jada decided. She knew he'd laugh, and she knew just how, and she felt warm inside hearing the sound of that laugh already in her mind, white bear, white bear.

She did tell him, and he did laugh, when they met in Schenley Plaza after she left the lab. The sound and sight of his laughter so closely matched her mental preview that she was startled, grew nervous and fidgety, folding and unfolding her hands on the table where they sat together.

It was important, she said, that he know everything about how she'd come to be here. She told him about the abortion. It did not take long, and he did not interrupt her. He had hung a yellow plastic Dollar General bag over the corner of his chair, its contents sagging, and she wondered what was inside.

"I'm trying to tell you that this wasn't a random decision," she said, "my moving out. It followed from a specific thing that happened."

"A thing that happened because you aren't happy with him," Drew said. "He's not right for you. If he were, you wouldn't be here."

He said it with such sureness, despite his lack of data. She'd said similar things to herself, it was true, but they had been more like hypotheses than conclusions; saying them had been like testing ice that might turn out to be too thin to hold her. Suddenly the scientific method seemed to her remarkably feminine in its cautiousness— questioning endlessly, making no assumptions. Men were just like, *This is this because I say it is. You are this because I say you are.*

"I guess that's part of what I'm trying to figure out," she said. "How much of my choice was because of my feelings about him, and how much was because of my feelings about motherhood." She could see Drew's big-ass truck parked down the street, obscuring her view of Dippy the dinosaur in his spot outside the Carnegie Museum of Natural History. "I'm not sure I want children," she said. "With anyone."

"I get that," he said.

"You do?"

"Sure. A life can be about other things."

Jada nodded. "I said that to my mom once. She told me I'd change my mind."

"Maybe you will."

Her mother's eagerness that Jada should marry had been a late-in-life development. When she was in high school and college, and even for a while after, her mother had seemed discouraging of her love life, looking sidelong at Drew and the other men she'd dated as if each had some devious plan to derail her career. Near the end of her life, though, she'd been all marriage, marriage, marriage, a regular Mrs. Bennett, as if the shine had worn off whatever romantic vision she'd held of Jada as a go-getter going and getting it alone, an independent woman who could take care of herself. Sometimes it seemed to Jada that her own wants were indistinguishable from her mother's. It both heartened and alarmed her that this might be so, that her mother might have not only carried her body in her own but also determined all she'd do with it later. If this were so, what now—now that she was gone?

"There are times when having a child feels really, really important," she said. "But not in some instinctual, mammalian, feminine life-force way. It's not a biological urge I feel. It's a social urge. It's an eagerness to achieve the social capital that comes from having children."

Why couldn't she talk to Blake like this? He cared about social capital; he had a checklist. Jada had liked that at first, because checklists were for people with futures. Checklists were how people measured time, and their success moving through it: family, property, equity. You could use a checklist, like a rubric, to give yourself a grade at life. But challenging the premise or need for the checklist was, well . . . not on the checklist. It was not something she could do with Blake.

She leaned forward in her chair, talking with her hands. "In other words," she said, her voice rising, "I want to feel normal. I want to make myself normal by completing the normal, noble action that is having a baby. But that's not the same as wanting a baby. It's just wanting to get an A at being a woman. It's grade-grubbing."

"It's natural to want approval," Drew said. "Approval, social capital, whatever you want to call it. I say this as a grown man who lives with his mother."

"But you don't do that because you have to. You do that out of kindness. Anyone would respect that."

He shrugged. "Kindness, and the fact that she cooks for me. Speaking of which"—he handed her the plastic bag he'd brought—"she sent you these."

Jada opened the bag. Inside were two gallon-sized freezer bags, one filled with chocolate chip cookies and the other with snickerdoodles. A gift from a mother. A rush of grief and gratitude made it hard for Jada to breathe.

"Thank you," she said. "Please thank her for me."

"I will. And I'll take a snickerdoodle."

She unsealed the bag and handed him one, then broke one in half for herself.

"My point is," he continued, "maybe you can focus on how normal it is of you to crave normalcy. Every time you do, you succeed in completing a normal action."

"It's not an action, though," she objected. "It's just noise in my head. It's not something that can be recognized or rewarded by the outside world."

"Except me."

"Except you."

A thin vein bulged at his temple. She had the urge to press it.

"As soon as I think I've made up my mind that I don't want a child," she said, "I start to worry it's a fear-based decision, like I'm just afraid of having to make the sacrifices a child would require. But when I swing the other way and think sure, of course I want a kid someday, then that decision starts to seem fear-based, too, like I'm just afraid of the possibility of regret, or I'm afraid of becoming an object of disdain. Have you ever told a person with a baby that you're not sure you want one?"

He nodded, opened the bag of chocolate chip cookies, and broke one of those in half, as well. "Steph, of Steph and Kyle," he said. "A couple months ago."

"They had a baby?"

"Two," he said. "Twins. She came into the store with one of those big strollers."

"Remember when she—"

"Drove her car into the store window? Senior year? On her way to deliver a pizza? Of course. But you should have seen how she maneuvered that double stroller through the front doors. It was Olympic. I still might not trust her to deliver me a pizza, but if I needed a baby in thirty to forty-five minutes . . ."

Jada brushed crumbs onto the pavement. "But you told her you didn't want a child?"

"She asked, I answered honestly."

"Was she offended?"

"She pretended not to be."

"It's worse when you're a woman," Jada argued, "because you're supposed to want it that much more intensely. And if you don't, women who did feel hurt. They take it personally, like you looked at their child and vowed then and there to never have one of your own. When really your choice is just yours. It's not a referendum on anybody else's choice or anybody else's baby."

It would be nice if this were true, and she hoped it was, but when she said it out loud it sounded defensive, desperate. Perhaps there was an aggression inherent in opting out, whether you wanted there to be one or not.

Look, she said, she had nothing against babies. It was the discourse surrounding them that bothered her. People talked about babies like they'd always be babies, the unborn like they'd always be unborn, like they wouldn't grow into hairy, sweaty adults who hurt people and got accidentally pregnant themselves. Reach a certain age—a day, a decade? a minute?—and without doing anything to deserve it, you lost the right to automatic compassion, you lost the benefit of the doubt, you were no longer pure and were not supposed to need things like school lunches or medicine, you were not supposed to have—well, a body. *Precious baby*: in no time it, too, would be called upon to save the babies! As if babies were pandas or rhinos or any of the other creatures she'd been determined to save from extinction as a kid with a *Zoobooks* subscription—as if, if only they were allowed to live, and not poached or maimed, they could do so on their own, in the wild, munching peacefully on bamboo.

They sat in silence for a moment. A small brown bird approached a cookie crumb on the pavement, pecking tentatively, then backing away. "Why did you pee in the planter?" Jada asked.

Drew sighed deeply and loudly, leaned back, stretched his arms over his head. "One of those days," he said.

"Your depression."

"Eh."

"It's worse?"

"Nah," he said. "Just still there. And there's stuff with the store, things aren't great. Honestly, it's a miracle we've held on this long."

"I'm so sorry," she said. "You've done the best you could. Your dad—"

"Yeah," he said, "I know."

"Is there anything I can do?"

"Move home and buy a shit ton of tools."

The bird approached the crumb again, and Jada slid her foot away as if to signal her permission. *Come on, buddy,* she thought.

"It's fine," Drew said, "we're fine, and I'm not giving up yet. But maybe it's time for a new chapter in the old Life of Drew. Who knows."

"Back to school?" Jada tried to keep her voice neutral.

"Maybe, yeah."

She picked at her cuticles. "Are you taking your medication?"

"I am now. New stuff."

Jada nodded her approval and took his hand. She said, "I'm holding your hand in a comforting way, not a romantic way."

"That's a shame."

That squiggle of vein, an autograph at his temple. She felt guilty for being so at ease with him; she felt guilty for not feeling guilty enough about abandoning Blake, who could drive by at any moment. Around them, that current, that sizzling energy, both old and new, familiar and fresh. Somehow it felt more thrilling than sex—just the prospect of sex hovering, an energy zipping between bodies, raising the hairs on her arms: the bolt not yet struck, the static in the air. She didn't have to touch him to feel it. She dropped his hand.

"I just don't think you need to solve this big life mystery right now," Drew said, "or see it as a question you have to answer before you can acknowledge what you do or don't feel about him."

She'd never heard him say Blake's name—just *him* or *that guy*. She looked across the plaza again to where Dippy's long neck appeared to extend out of the bed of Drew's truck. That his truck should rival a life-sized diplodocus for the command of her eye unsettled her, and she felt a pang of—something (clarity or snobbery?)—that told her they still couldn't be together, they could never be together, she couldn't be with that truck. Could she? And what did it mean that she was even thinking about it? Had she done all this, on some level, for him?

She shook the thought away. He always drove with the windows down, her hair blowing everywhere, a mess of tangles and the wind pounding her eardrums. She'd hated it then. She would hate it now.

"I know you want me to say I never loved him," she said, "but I can't do that."

It would be easy to say this. It would make a tidy story. But she had loved Blake, *and* she had left him, and she could not ignore one of these facts in order to make the other simpler, for Drew's sake or her own. Drew wanted her to make her marriage exceptional, out of character, so that she could more easily distance herself from it, indulging in a fantasy of how her life would be different—better—if it hadn't happened. Kahneman & Tversky, 1982: Tell a story in which a man named Mr. Jones is hit by a drunk driver on his way home from work. Let some participants read a version of Mr. Jones's story in which he left for work unusually early that day but drove home via his usual route. Let others read a version in which he left at the usual time but took an unusual route. Ask the participants how Mr. Jones's demise could have been avoided, and you'll find that they construct counterfactuals around whichever antecedent to the tragic accident they consider anomalous: "Mr. Jones would still be alive if only he'd left at the usual time"; "Mr. Jones would still be alive if only he'd stuck to his usual route." We fixate on deviation; we hold it responsible for the messes in which we find ourselves. We shift exceptions to the norm via counterfactual thought.

What, then, was Jada's own deviation? On the one hand she might say, *It was so unlike me, marrying someone so . . . unlike me. If only I hadn't rushed into marriage, I'd be freer now, and happier.* On the other she might say, *It's so unlike me to be as spellbound as I am by Drew*, and discount her behavior where he was concerned as out of character and worthy of skepticism. If she let this thing with him—whatever this was—drive her once and for all off the cliffside of her marriage, perhaps she might look back and say, *If only I'd stayed the course. If only I'd been a better wife, a better woman.*

"All right," Drew said, "all right. I'm not trying to push you."

It was true that she'd left her own wedding feeling like she'd ticked a box, given a gift—to Blake, to her mother. But it would not be honest to pretend that she'd accepted Blake only to please someone else. Sure, she had felt obliged to say yes when the ring appeared— you didn't say *no*, for God's sake; a body in motion wants to stay in motion; it's physics, it's law. They'd been moving forward together at a certain speed, and to say no would have been like jumping out of a moving train. She'd felt a pinprick of doubt, and she'd felt a wash of numbing happiness: the needle inserted, the anesthetic spreading. Which was the authentic feeling—the pinprick or the wash? Did anyone ever really feel just one thing at a time, at this or any other pivotal moment of their life? How long did you have to feel something before it became The Way You Felt and not just a mood, a phase, and was there a difference between making a choice and making your best guess?

She watched the bird finally carry away the crumb. Maddy would know what kind the bird was, what song it sang. "It's not fair to him to act like I did this crazy, mindless thing," she said. "It's not fair to me, either. I did love Blake, even if not in the same way I loved you."

Drew stood, put his palms down on the table, and leaned forward. Her heart kicked in her chest. He was giving her that look, *his* look, that impossible combination of playfulness and deadly earnestness, swagger and sadness.

"So, not the good way," he said. "Not the real way."

She went around to his side of the table. He wrapped an arm around her waist. *This is something,* she thought. *This is not nothing.* He pulled her close and kissed her.

No. Come on, now; let's be honest. She kissed him.

# 12

## MADDY

**April 2018**

In the week after she set up her dating profile, Maddy had break-fast with *Extremely different/multidimensional*, dinner with *I floss and make the bed. Addicted to Jeeps!* seemed to be breadcrumbing her. She got a dick pic from *I'm pretty much a ball of fun*, another from *Not your typical meathead*, a glimpse of *I can literally juggle*'s balls. *I'm the tall one in the group shot* was the only one she told she was pregnant; in response, he wrote, *oo u little slut*, double winky face, double eggplant.

She swiped, swiped, messaged, deleted. *Laid-back generosity caring like to have fun at the lake. 6'2", ENTJ, one time at the beach I stepped on a stingray. Let's cross of each others bucket lists.* Even if she declined all possible options, they'd eventually recommend themselves again as her results refreshed, and so she swiped, swiped, trying, failing, dismissing, rejecting. She became more critical the more she used the app, swiping left, left, left, and she had the self-awareness to realize that this was the type of behavior she'd take offense to by a man—

this impersonal inspection of faces and bodies, not ill-intentioned so much as devoid of intention—but she chose not to care. *If your normal we won't get along. Only the crazy should swipe right.* She swiped left. *No crazy please.* Left again.

On Friday afternoon she left her disappointing date with *Extremely different/multidimensional* and went to meet Jada at the Carnegie Museum of Natural History. It was an outing Jada had proposed, and Maddy figured she knew why: to dip her into the swirling cosmopolis, to make her look at art and dinosaur bones so that she might realize Jada was right—there was a world out there, so many places to be explored, so many people to meet, so many things to see and make and learn. It was true that the commotion of campus was infectious, that as she moved among students in backpacks toward the museum with the help of her phone's GPS, which narrated in a British accent from her pocket, she felt the same pull she had on that long-ago visit to State College to be part of something—a student body, of which she might become an arm or a leg or just a humble pinkie toenail. In the near distance loomed the Cathedral of Learning, on the top of which, Jada had told her, a peregrine falcon kept its nest. Along the sidewalk, groups of students handed out flyers and sold plates of food at tables covered in the names of causes and organizations. Maddy moved past them, shielding her eyes from the sun with her bandaged hand, surveying club names and Greek letters. At the end of the line of tables, a handful of boys in fraternity swag stood around a hot dog stand bearing a poster-paper sign: SAVE THE TITTIES! $1 WIENERS, PROCEEDS FIGHT BREAST CANCER!

"Save the titties!" one of the boys hollered into cupped hands. He caught Maddy's eye. "Buy a wiener to save a titty?"

It occurred to Maddy that sometimes it is not the thought that counts. Sometimes it really is the gift, the gesture, and sometimes the gesture is all wrong. She stopped and stared at the boy, baseball cap on his head, the two-tailed loop of an awareness ribbon pinned to his chest. Behind him, his brothers in matching pins speared hot dogs from a charcoal grill and laid them with care, like precious penises, in store-bought buns.

At home Maddy had a pair of socks patterned with that ribbon. She had a pink umbrella with white polka dots and the ribbon in the form of a charm dangling from the handle. These things were supposed to give her hope, or to give other people hope, but when she wore the socks or carried the umbrella, when she watched these college boys stuff cash into envelopes, she did not feel hopeful, she did not feel charitable. She felt selfish and empty, her performed awareness of the sick only underscoring her own healthiness, and her mother gone no matter how many wieners were sold.

Her mother, walking down the road with Milk-Bones in her pockets, feeding the dogs the neighbors let run loose and that sometimes followed her home, hung around the yard, and stared through the screen door wanting in. Her mother, filling the yard and woods with plastic gemstones placed at the centers of flowers or among blades of grass, pretending fairies sent them.

It was too late for her mother. It was probably too late for this boy, too, with his lighthearted titty rescue mission and his lettered cap. But Maddy dug into her bag for the wallet into which she'd been feeding her payoff money, took out a fifty, and held it out to him. He probably had a mother, she thought with resentment, handing over the bill.

"You want . . . fifty hot dogs?" he asked.

"No, thank you," she said. "Keep your wieners. Just take the money."

*      *      *

At the museum, Maddy and Jada made their way through the Hall of Minerals and Gems—a gleaming reef, minerals like glittering brains, dick-shaped crystals, geodes full of hard candy—and into the Halls of African and North American Wildlife, full of taxidermized baby everythings feeding off their mothers. Most of the animals had been arranged into neat nuclear-family units behind glass: the watchful papa antelope, head high, horns horny; mama antelope by his side; baby antelopes suckling or at play. Jada walked slowly among the dioramas, doing weird things with her hands, and Maddy could tell she had something she wanted to say.

"How was your date?" Jada asked. She had come from a meeting with her advisor and wore a cream-colored blouse and denim skirt, hair in a neat ponytail, feet in pointy-toed flats.

Maddy did a thumbs-down and blew a raspberry. "He just kept summarizing movie plots," she said. "But I'll keep looking."

Jada frowned. "I wish you wouldn't look at your situation as one a man can save you from. And while we're on the subject of looking for things, it's probably time you started looking for a job. If you're going to stay here, that is."

Maddy ignored her, rubbed at a kink in her shoulder. Her back was sore from sleeping on the futon that Jada had bought and Drew assembled. The apartment's floors were uneven, and she had had to place some of Jada's books beneath the legs of one end of the futon so the blood would not rush to her head in her sleep. "I didn't realize you and Drew were still close," she said. A comment she'd been saving.

"I needed a truck for furniture."

"You could have rented one."

"He's a lifelong friend."

"But he's also more than that."

Behind the glass, a pair of amorous zebras posed coquettishly, eyes locked and nostrils flared. One zebra's neck rested on the other's back, where a saddle might go.

"Is there something going on there?" Maddy pressed. "With Drew?"

"I don't know," Jada said. "No. I don't know."

The fetus doll bulged in Maddy's back pocket. She focused on the glass in front of a termite mound, registered the fingerprints and nose prints there, thought of the person who would clean them up. She moved close to the glass, took a corner of her shirt, and rubbed at the cloudy smears, but the fabric only moved the oil around.

Again, she wondered if the things in this museum, combined with the swarm of students on the surrounding campus, were what Jada had in mind when she referred to the life of adventure Maddy might lead if she did not have this baby. There were certain things out there—like blue whales and snow leopards, Mount Everest, the rings of Saturn—that you just accepted, things you could see confirmed on Instagram or behind glass in museums like these animals, things you could point to on a map. Maddy had always acknowledged the existence of these out-there things with a blind assurance much like faith; she did not need to see them to know that they were real. And then there were other things, the abstract things Jada and her mother and Pat and other people spoke of— options, opportunity—of which she could find no solid evidence or credible cartography. She wished someone could show her these, capture photos of the versions of herself she might become if only she had the opportunity—photos taken by a paparazzi elsewhere in the multiverse, where her other lives might already be playing out. What *did* Jada mean when she said that Maddy had her "whole life to live"? What was she doing now, if not living it? Was it really so superior to see a zebra in the wild instead of on social or in the Hall of African Wildlife, where she could be safe and clean, and where she could push a stroller?

She paused in front of a water buffalo, globs of glue-drool on its lips, feet sunk in muddy puddles. Someone made this, she realized. Someone arranged the drops of snot rimming the buffalo's nostrils just so. Someone caringly placed this patty of dung at the animal's feet. This extreme attention to detail, this willingness to tend to dead animals with the same gentle affection with which she cared for real ones, moved Maddy almost to tears. Down the hall the glass on one of the dioramas had been removed, and a man in a surgical mask and cloth moccasins hunched on a wooden platform, spray-painting the pelt of a brown bear with a spray gun attached to a hose, and it dawned on Maddy that maybe this was what Jada meant for her to see—not just the diorama, but its restoration, the fact that the occupation of "brown bear diorama restorer" existed, one of the many life paths that she had not been exposed to back home and that might expand her sense of the possibilities for her own future.

"Is that that doll in your pocket?" Jada asked as they walked. A giraffe loomed over her shoulder. "You saw Blake?"

"Maybe." Maddy saw an opportunity. "Why did you get so upset about it the other day?"

"Why was I upset by the creepy piece of propaganda you were given at a nonmedical facility by people who don't know you, don't know what's best for you, and are okay with misinforming you in order to manipulate you into having a baby?"

Maddy rolled her eyes. "Yeah, that."

Jada took a deep breath. "There's something I want you to know," she said, "that I didn't tell you the other day. Remember when you asked how I knew all the abortion facts?"

Maddy listened, rested her good hand on the lump in her jeans.

"A little while back I got pregnant by accident. I missed a pill, and I didn't think it would be a big deal." Jada spoke slowly, looking directly at Maddy. "I knew—I *knew*—I wasn't ready for a child. And I couldn't tell Blake. I knew that if I told him, I'd be having that baby, one way or another. There would be no getting out of it. So I got out of it."

"So . . . ," Maddy said.

"So I had an abortion. And I couldn't tell him because he'd hate me, probably leave me, so I figured better if I left him first. That's where I was when you showed up."

Maddy's nose crinkled, and she stopped walking. "*You* had an abortion. Even though you're married. Even though your husband is rich."

"It was my decision," Jada said, "and I stand by it. I didn't die, and my intestines are intact, and I'm not infertile. Blake is a good person, and I don't want to lie to him, but I felt like I had to, and here I am." She turned toward the glass where they'd stopped and addressed her words to some grizzlies tearing apart a salmon, its needly bones exposed and its tweezer mouth open. "Sometimes I hate myself for the things I don't feel, the things I don't want. And I don't want to hate myself, or be ashamed."

Maddy tried to keep the look on her face neutral, but she must have failed, because after a few seconds Jada said, "What?"

"Nothing."

"If you have something to say, say it."

"Fine." Maddy gestured at Jada's belly. "It's just . . . You didn't even have an excuse."

"I don't need an excuse. It's my right."

Maddy shook her head. "It's not *for* you. It's for poor people, people who got raped, people who can't take care of kids. You can. You could. You had everything you needed."

"Well," Jada said, "it was my choice."

"I disagree."

"What do you mean, you *disagree*?" Jada crossed her arms and struggled to keep her voice low. "You don't get to disagree. I don't have to take this from you. I didn't even have to tell you."

Maddy's heart was in her throat. She had lost track of what she was upset about. "Why are you telling me now? Why didn't you say something before?"

"I wasn't ready."

"You didn't trust me."

"No, I didn't. And this is why."

"You want me to see what you did so I'll feel like I can do it too."

"Yes," Jada said. "Because you can. Because you aren't . . ." She gestured to the hall around them, to a screaming sea lion in a glass case. "A wild animal. You have the power to choose the life you want."

Maddy turned her back to her sister and stared at some walruses posed in a painted seascape. She did not know how she felt, or should feel, about what Jada had said. Her feelings had become mush, and her thoughts were not thoughts but a whirling, wordless blur. She steadied herself, focused on the here and now: the objective yet uncanny fact of a walrus's bald head. It was the dioramas' very hyperrealism that rendered them unrealistic—no intrepid traveler to the Arctic would see for herself the droplets of salt mist on the tusks of a live walrus or the precise texture of its mustache, with its hairs like porcupine quills, or be able to pause to count the wrinkles in its skin while it stood frozen, modeling patiently, looking her in the eye.

What might she be like as a mother? Maddy set aside the logistics—where she'd live, what to do about work—and tried to dream herself into the role. Perhaps there was an instinct deep within her, as there was in a walrus or a wildebeest, that would rise to the occasion when the time came.

She thought of her mother, the guided meditations she'd done for a while—two of them, which Maddy had thought of as the nice one and the mean one—that she listened to in headphones or pumped through the house. *"You are the commander of a robust army of fighter cells,"* said the narrator of the mean one, which was mean only to cancer but which Maddy nevertheless found unsettling in its militancy. *"Mobilize your private, faithful troops. Watch as they gather around clusters of cancer cells, penetrating them, poisoning them."* The narrator's soft voice, like the tinkling, sparkly music in its background, seemed ill-matched to the meditation's content. *"Watch the enemy cells as they shrivel and die."*

Here Ellen would lift her hand, L'ed in the shape of a gun, and mime shooting the deviant cells. *"Your army ingests the remains, purifying tissue, purging the body of disease, purging it of fear and pain,"* the narrator said, and Maddy would retreat like an enemy cell, disturbed by the juxtaposition of the cannibalistic imagery and the narrator's soothing tone.

All around her, claws and teeth. The Halls of Wildlife had begun to feel oppressive, confusing. Time, the dioramas suggested, was somehow both circular—death enabling life, and so forth—and stationary: the sparring elk's antlers would never lock, the fight would never be won. The circle of life was brutal, the violence at its center undeniable: a dead bull elk run through with an arrow, eyes glazed and tongue hanging out, perched upon by vultures; a litter of jaguar cubs ripping apart an iguana, tearing its skin with their razor claws. *Watch the enemy cells as they shrivel and die.*

She couldn't with the circle of life right now. She was done with the circle. She wanted life linear, a clean line stretching into infinity.

"I'm sick of blood and milk," she said, and to her relief Jada said, "Me too. Let's get out of here."

Just outside the museum, Maddy saw the poster, taped to a lamppost. BRIDGING THE PARTISAN DIVIDE: A ROUNDTABLE DIALOGUE WITH YOUNG PA POLITICIANS. Below the words, a date: two weeks from now. Below the date, a vertical row of photos. At the bottom of the row, *his* photo. Jason's.

Maddy got sweaty, her veins got icy. She was standing on the pavement by the lamppost, the street and the sidewalk swirling, her hands beginning to vibrate, her chest tight. As quickly as possible, so as not to be noticed, she peeled the flyer from the lamppost.

"I need a minute," she told Jada, stuffing the paper inside the waistline of her jeans and dashing back toward the museum. "I have to go to the bathroom," she called over her shoulder, hurrying into the building, when Jada called after her.

Inside, she shut herself in a stall and breathed, unfolded the flyer again. His face in that little square. Once, in her spare time, she had googled him so that she could look at his photo from the privacy of her bedroom; now the sight of him made her sick. Once, she had offered him photos from her bank of nudes, but he didn't want them; her thing with him had been old-school in its pure physicality. When she offered—*u want a pic?*—he'd texted back, *I've already toured the venue, it will work great, thanks!* She was in his phone as Butterfield Events and Catering. When it came to cleaning, she corresponded exclusively with Meghan, who had her saved in her phone as Maddy Cleaner and who, when Maddy told her she was leaving, said she was sorry to see her go. She had done such a terrific job.

She thought of him moving on with his life, just going about business as usual, taking speaking engagements, bridging the partisan divide, sleeping well at night next to his wife. It occurred to her that what he had, what he took for granted, was a freedom she'd never know: a snug sureness that he was safe—not just safe as in not needing to carry pepper spray, but safe as in certain that his secrets were keepable. Her own secret—she put a hand to her belly—was not one, or at least it wouldn't be for long, because her body would out her, the choices she made were corporeal, and she would have to live with them for the rest of her life.

She had told herself she didn't care. She had known what she was getting into, accepted the risks. She had reminded herself, again and again, of her accountability for her own actions, and yet here she was, struggling for air in a bathroom stall. She didn't really know what his responsibilities as a state senator were other than to hold strangers' babies and shake strangers' hands and probably sign his name on a lot of documents. Fucking a cleaning lady who had asked for it wouldn't be a stellar line on his résumé, but it didn't necessarily disqualify him from doing these things; couldn't he still sign his name, regardless of where his dick had been? Couldn't he still shake hands? Couldn't he do the things he had promised her he'd use his power to do? Who would believe the cleaning lady, anyway?

But then, she had not destroyed the proof.

What would he do if he saw her in the crowd, so near to him and so still-pregnant? He might notice the slight pudge at her midsection, even if other people wouldn't; he knew her body well; she had shown it to him again and again of her own volition, no force involved but the force of her own desire, her own sadness. What right did she have to be mad? she asked herself. What right did she have? And yet she thought of bloody claws. An iguana's shredded skin, an arrow in the side of an elk. The blade of a box cutter.

She could tell on him, scream at the top of her lungs, but all the things she'd have to say were so embarrassing. For so long, even when she told the story to herself, she saw herself as the villain, doing what she'd done in someone's nice house, where she was hired to make things clean. Why had it taken her so long to get this scared, this angry at him? Why had the worst had to happen in order for her to finally understand that their relationship was not one? And now that she did, she could not think of what to do. Tweet, scream, humiliate herself. Cut him open like a diorama salmon. Jada had said she was not a wild animal, but even Jada could be wrong sometimes.

So far Jada had not followed her into the restroom. Maddy's heart had moved from her throat to her hand; the thought of the cut sent it pulsing. She took out her phone and called Pat. It rang once, twice.

"Maddy!" Pat answered. "It's—"

"I want to pray." Maddy's voice was low and firm and seemed to come from someone else. She breathed in, breathed out. "Please, pray with me."

She ignored the cooing satisfaction in Pat's voice, ignored the noise of a mother-daughter pair entering the neighboring stalls and, later, washing their hands, the daughter singing the happy birthday song as she scrubbed, the mother praising her, handing her a paper towel. She mashed her phone against her ear and closed her eyes and breathed, and she listened. "The Lord is my shepherd," Pat said, "I shall not want," and the words grew wings and flew around Maddy's head, beautiful and impossible: *I shall not want, I shall not want.*

# 13

## MADDY

*June 2016*

Few things that seem sudden actually are. Maddy will learn this when her mother dies—when after years of slow struggle, she blinks out like a light. "Cancer cells double, you see," a nurse will explain. "Two, four, eight, sixteen. But think about what happens when those numbers get bigger. Double one million to two million, and boom. At the end, the chronic illness becomes acute."

It's the same way with Jason: both gradual and sudden. It starts as many small things, things that aren't things, looks, vibes, doubling and doubling, slow until they're fast. The day he presses a big tip into her hand and tells her to treat herself—that look in his eye. The way she starts coming early, finding him always there and Meghan always out. When she turns eighteen a month after Jada's engagement and the week before her high school graduation, he gives her a muffin with a candle stuck in it, and she knows something will happen.

"Sorry for the candle," he says, handing her the muffin. "It's all I could find." It's a deformed white number one left over from his son's birthday, rimmed in green and melted at the top. He leans over to light it. She makes a wish and blows. On the wall hangs one of the many hand-lettered signs Meghan has made and displayed throughout the house: THE DISHES ARE LOOKING AT ME DIRTY AGAIN in loopy letters. Beneath it Jason removes a packet of cigarettes from a drawer, opens the kitchen door, and sits down on the cement stoop outside. "Do you mind?" he asks, and lights one.

"I didn't know you smoked."

"I don't." He pats the spot next to him.

Maddy sits down, unwraps the blueberry muffin, and breaks it down the middle. It was the last from a package of four from the grocery store and is slightly stale; he had not known it was her birthday until she told him when she arrived and had had to improvise. She keeps the half with the hole where the candle was and hands him the better half. They split it, purple stains on their fingers.

"Want to know what else I don't do?" he says, muffin in one hand, cigarette in the other.

She waits.

"This is a secret."

She makes a zipping movement over her lips with her free hand.

"I don't hunt," he tells her. "I never have."

Maddy has seen his campaign ad—Jason and his gray-haired father carrying rifles. "But that commercial," she says, "with your dad—"

"That's all made up."

She smiles tentatively. "Is that your real dad?"

"Oh, yeah, that's my dad." He laughs. "The dog is my dad's dog. So I guess it's not *all* made up. I guess the made-up part is just . . . me."

There's a gun safe in his den; Maddy has dusted it, buffed away the odd fingerprint. She says, "The guns."

"Oh, I have them. I just don't use them."

She studies him. He isn't that good-looking, but he is assured of his own good looks in a way that seems to make a strong case for them. His sleeves are rolled in that politician way, showing the sleek muscles of his forearm. Behind him, on the panes of the open French door, she sees baby handprints where his son has pressed his palms against the glass. In front of them is Meghan's vegetable garden, backed by a wall of pines. The neighbors' house isn't visible through the trees.

"You can't tell," he says, "about the hunting."

"Or what? You'll shoot me?"

It isn't funny, and she feels bad as soon as it comes out of her mouth. But when she looks at him, preparing to apologize, she sees that he is laughing.

"People don't vote for you because of what you *do*, anyway," he says, finishing his muffin, talking with his mouth full. "They vote for you because of who they think you are."

"And they think you're a non-smoking hunter," she teases. "When, really, you're a non-hunting smoker. The scandal."

He drops his cigarette on the stoop, stomps it out. "I told you," he says, "I don't smoke."

They sit in silence for a moment, listening to birds. Maddy can identify their songs and thinks of telling him what she hears— black-capped chickadee, catbird, mourning dove—but fears seeming nerdy. She says, "I hunt. I mean, I have."

She learned to shoot at her school's Wonderful Wilderness camp, where for three days her class had taken a hunter education course and learned gun safety and archery, how to use a compass, how to build a fire. She'd gone hunting only once, to please her father, his orange cap too big for her, his old camo jacket too baggy. But she just ended up disappointing him, refusing to shoot a doe in plain sight.

She prefers the Maxwell House can he uses as a target in the back yard, the clay pigeons he throws for her in a field down the road. There is a BB gun by the door at home that she uses to deter the squirrels that raid her mother's bird feeder. She fills the feeder with seeds she digs out of a bulk bag in the garage, scooping them with an old cream cheese container, and when the squirrels come, she stuns them away, the report ripping through the yard. Where they live, you can fire as many times as you want and no one will hear or, if they do, care. Everyone is always shooting.

"I'm a pretty good shot," she adds, and he says, "I bet you are."

More birdsong. She moves to get up, but he says, "Oh, don't worry about cleaning."

"It's my job."

"You can't clean on your birthday."

"Technically, it's the day after my birthday."

He waves the fact away. "Same difference."

Maddy freezes, uncertain. "What about—"

"She's not coming back today," he says. "She took Theo to her sister's. I'll tell her I canceled, or I'll clean up myself. You take the day off."

"Thanks," she says, "but I could use the money."

"I'll pay you. Call it a birthday gift."

She looks down at her right hand, at her grandmother's ring, a ruby set in a thick gold band. Yesterday, on her actual birthday, her mother presented it to her wrapped in leftover Christmas paper, snowflakes in June. It slid right off her ring finger, so she wears it on her middle one instead.

"That's a beautiful ring," he says.

"Thank you."

"Who gave it to you?"

She tells him, and he smiles. "I thought maybe you had a boy-friend. Or a girlfriend."

"Nah." She's been talking to the boy who'd been in line after Bear, but her heart still isn't in it, and with graduation around the corner, she feels both blissfully untethered and a little regretful, like she's missed out on something. For a long time, especially since quitting softball, she prided herself on being a girl who made friends with the boys, forgoing the knotty challenges that came with female friendships in favor of lighter, looser, uncompetitive bonds with guys. But this strategy, too, had been ill-fated; she'd come to feel that most of her straight guy friends viewed her not as a true friend but as a sort of girl piñata to be poked and prodded in what seemed like play but was really a greedy hope of breaking through to a prize inside.

She should go, she thinks, but she doesn't get up. He talks about his campaign; she talks about school. A few weeks ago, she finally met with the school counselor, filling out intake paperwork that required her to rate how frequently—always, often, sometimes, seldom, never—she'd experienced things in the past month: Social isolation or loneliness? Fluctuating moods? Frequent worry or tension? Feeling that you have let yourself or your family down? *Yikes,* she'd thought, checking "often" more often than she would've liked, feeling proud whenever she found an opportunity (Heart palpitations? Hearing voices when alone?) to check "seldom" or "never." *Good job,* she told herself. *There are some things that aren't wrong with you. You are doing okay.* Then she returned to "Low self-esteem?" to revise her answer, moving the *X* from "often" to "sometimes." But she doesn't tell Jason this. She tells him, instead, about the wildlife center and its upcoming summer fundraiser, which she invites him to attend; the eagle-owl; Jada's wedding plans.

"I'm not even the maid of honor," she complains. "I'm just a bridesmaid."

"Count yourself lucky," he says. "You don't have to plan the bachelorette or give a toast."

"I could give a toast." She isn't old enough to drink, legally, but she is old enough and smart enough to string a sentence. "And there isn't going to be a bachelorette party."

"Why not?"

"Because Jada," she scoffs.

"So, she's not fun."

Maddy shrugs. "I don't know."

"You are, though," he says.

"She didn't even consider me. It was so obvious. As soon as she told me, you could see this light go on in her head—like, 'Oh, shit, I forgot I have a *sister*.'"

She's being loud, weird, without meaning to. She feels him looking at her. She gathers herself, tucks her hair behind her ears.

"Weddings," he says dismissively.

"You had one."

"I almost had another one, too."

Maddy waits for more.

"I was engaged before Meghan." He laughs. "I don't know why I'm telling you this."

But he is. She is thrilled by the intimacy of the telling. "What was her name?"

"Angela."

"What happened?"

He lights another cigarette. "So," he says, as if he is not beginning the story but continuing it, "a month before the wedding, she goes to this psychic. The psychic tells her she sees a yellow dress, is anyone in the wedding planning on wearing a yellow dress? And Angie says yeah, her mother-in-law. My mom. She'd bought a yellow dress and shown it to Angie, all excited." He takes a long drag. "So the psychic says, 'You have to tell your mother-in-law not to wear that yellow dress. If she wears the dress, the marriage will fail.'"

Maddy blinks. "What did she do?"

"She said I had to tell my mom to buy a different dress. My mom was sick, diabetic, she'd just had a kidney transplant. I wasn't going to tell her she couldn't wear the dress she wanted to wear." He exhales deeply, slowly. "Fuck that."

He sits close to her, not touching her but close enough that she can feel his heat. It seems they've been inching—not even inching, centimetering, millimetering—closer together, without her quite realizing it. Has she moved, or has he?

"Anyway," he continues, "one thing led to another. Angie came around, apologized, but in the meantime all sorts of other problems had surfaced, and we realized neither of us really wanted to get married."

"Wow," Maddy says, and is disappointed in the blandness of her reaction. She should give him more; he has confided in her. "So your mom never wore the yellow dress?"

"No, she didn't."

"What did she wear when you married Meghan?"

"Nothing," he says. "She was dead."

It is the first time he's talked about his mother. Maddy had not known she was dead, had imagined her cooking up whatever game or fowl his father, the hunter in the campaign ad, killed. She wants to touch him but doesn't know if she can.

"I don't talk about this with anyone, not even Meghan," he goes on. "My ex, my mom. Let's keep it between us, huh?"

Later, she will hear him refer to his mother's death in a speech, but she does not know this now. She nods: yes. *Between us.*

"You're easy to talk to," he says.

"You are too," she breathes, and sees that a door is open, and chooses to go through it. "Actually," she says, "can I ask you something?"

"Okay."

"Before, you said people don't vote for you to do things, they just vote for you to be something. But there's something I wanted to ask you to do. If you can, I mean. If you win."

He shifts a little farther away from her. "What's that?"

She tells him about the abandoned wells, the same facts she reported to Jada. "There are literally hundreds of thousands of abandoned oil or gas wells out there," she says, "a lot of which aren't even accounted for. Most of them were drilled before there were any environmental regulations in place in the state and plugged improperly or not plugged at all. It's a problem in other states, too, but it's worst in PA since we've been drilling here the longest. All these holes in the ground are leaking methane, and contributing to climate warming, and potentially contaminating water and soil."

His eyes narrow, and an eleven forms between his brows. She's losing him.

"They lower property values, too," she adds. "And there are studies showing that frack water can come up through old wells. It can't contaminate groundwater on its own because it would have to travel upward through rock, right? But when you have unplugged wells that are old and rusted and give upward access . . ."

"Yeah," he says, "that's not really part of my platform."

". . . and surcharges on new well permits are not enough," she persists. "The state plugging program for old wells needs better funding."

"I didn't know you were such an environmentalist," he says.

"I'm not."

"You're so passionate." He smiles.

"It would create jobs," she says weakly. "Plugging wells."

He moves closer to her again. "Look, I'll see what I can do."

"You will?"

"Sure. I admire your conviction. And, yeah, you're probably right about all this." His leg touches hers. "Just don't expect to hear me making a big thing of it on the campaign trail."

"Right."

"Because the fact is, honestly, most people—"

He is going to say they don't care, and she can't let him. She can't hear it. She cuts him off: "Thank you for listening to me."

"I like listening to you." She feels like she has unloaded something—and, at the same time, taken something on, something new and heavy: her debt to him. There is more she would like to ask for—funds for the wildlife center, for example, which struggles to make ends meet and which must rely on donors to sponsor its residents—but she doesn't dare to ask for more than what she already has. Her eyes fill with tears. The reaction is reflexive, so much so that she doesn't even realize she's crying until he says, "Oh, Maddy. Don't cry."

"I'm sorry," she says. "I'm sorry about your mom."

"Thanks," he says, "it's all right. I'm okay." He puts a hand on her back and rubs, gingerly at first. "Is this okay?" he asks, and she nods. He squeezes her shoulder.

She sniffles, shudders, breathes in, out. "I'm sorry," she says again. "It's just this stuff with my mom, my sister's wedding . . . I guess it's getting to me."

"All right, Maddy," he hushes her. "You're sweet."

The tears keep coming. She wipes her nose, laughing a little to lighten the moment.

"You feel things deeply," he says. "I knew you did. I saw that in you."

Yes, she thinks, this is the kind of person she is: one who feels deeply. This is why she is like this, falling apart in front of Jason. Her pain makes her special. She might clean his house, but she is a part of the club he's in, the club of people who feel things deeply, good things and bad things, and it is such a relief to be a member that she is overcome with gratitude and pride. She wants to give him something—he has given her his secrets. She pulls herself together, wiping her eyes, laughing at herself. She feels sick in a good way, and also in a bad way, because she knows what is going to happen, she knows what she is going to do.

"I have a secret, too," she says.

He waits. His hand on her back. Near where his jaw meets his right ear is a small, shallow crater she never noticed before, as if someone has bitten off a chunk of his flesh.

"Sometimes I try on her clothes," she confesses. "Meghan's. When you aren't home."

A slow smile spreads across his face. Her insides feel fiery but her skin feels cold. Her body feels heavy but her head feels light, like a balloon tied to her body with a flimsy string, a string that's about to be cut.

He traces a finger down her arm. Her skin prickles.

"Show me," he says.


In the bedroom, she undoes the button on Meghan's purple suit, removes it from its hanger, unclips the skirt from where it hangs beneath. She goes into Jason and Meghan's bathroom, and behind the closed door, in front of a mirror that's huge and round and glowing like a portal to another world, she puts the suit on—a little big, the skirt sagging low at her hips. In the mirror behind her reflection is one of Meghan's signs: HOME IS WHERE YOU POOP MOST COMFORT-ABLY, in cutesy calligraphy. She breathes in, breathes out. He's not *that* much older than her; twelve years, thirty to her eighteen, the same age as Jada, who doesn't know him; he didn't grow up here, he's from Johnstown. And yeah, he's married, but . . . that's his problem.

The black-and-white penny tile feels cool and pebbly against her feet. Her polo shirt and jeans—she came straight from the wildlife center—lie in a heap at the base of the vanity. There is a fine white splatter of toothpaste on the mirror that she is not going to clean, a dusting of powder blush on the marble, hairs in the sink. Do they even try not to make a mess? Or do they try *to* make a mess, actively, so that she'll have something to do when she comes, so they'll get their money's worth?

Breathe in, breathe out. The suit's single button falls just above her belly button, the little bow at the center of her bra showing in the V of the fabric. She debates: bow or no bow, bra or no bra. This is crazy, but who cares. Everything is crazy, and no one cares. Why should she have to care all the time when nobody else does? Why must she care about every baby robin, every rusty pipe coming out of the ground, some man's marriage, some woman's spilled makeup powder, her own so-called virtue? Yes, she feels deeply, but she should get to pick what she feels, not just take it all on unquestioningly. She should get to choose, the way Meghan chooses not to care about her hair in the sink she pays Maddy to clean.

She takes the bra off. She takes her panties off. She takes off the ring her mother gave her and places it carefully in the pocket of her jeans but leaves her wraparound snake ring on. She beholds herself in the gold halo of the mirror, and a warmth rushes up from the base of her, a reverse lightning bolt: she's aroused by the sight of herself, and she knows he will be, too. She feels a surge of power. She chooses this man, this feeling; she chooses this mess. She opens the door and he's sitting on the king-sized bed, as she guessed he would be, leaning back against an assortment of vaguely tribal-looking throw pillows that are arranged around him like he's part of a gift basket, and she wonders if he fretted over where to sit, how to position his body and what to do with his legs, the way she fretted over whether or not to take off her bra. Is this how Jason Mayhew spontaneously sits on a bed, or is this how Jason Mayhew sits on a bed when he is trying to look a certain way, playing a certain role. Is this Jason the person in his home, or is this Jason the character in a campaign ad, a commercial for a person. Is his marriage a marriage or a commercial for a marriage, is this house a house or a commercial for a house. She wonders if he has done this before.

He takes her in. His eyes go down her body, up her body. He makes an impatient swirling motion above his head and says, "Your hair."

She takes the hair band from where it lives on reserve around her wrist, gathers her hair into a ponytail.

"No." He points to a duckbill clip on Meghan's dresser, and she pinches the end so that it opens like a crocodile's mouth. Click, click; chomp, chomp. She turns away, annoyed, to twist her hair atop her head the way she's seen Meghan's. The tiny teeth bite down. She had not expected feedback, especially feedback that would make her look more Meghany, and the balloon that is her head loses a little air, descends a little closer to her shoulders, but she stops the leak just in time. She's an adult. She can put her head where she wants.

When she turns around, his dick is out, and she has that unintended moment of mild disappointment she always has, seeing a new one: like, Oh, that's it. Like the ones she'd seen before were not professional penises but mere penis understudies, and eventually she'll encounter one spectacular enough to clarify what all the fuss is about. But not today. He works his hand up and down the shaft, watching her, and she breathes in, breathes out; she turns from side to side, lets the jacket hang open and slide down one shoulder and then the other, one boob out and then the other. She starts to run out of ideas. She slips the jacket from her shoulders. The silk lining licks her arms. She smells like dead rats and bleach.

When she goes to remove Meghan's skirt, he says, "Leave it on," and irritation flares in her again—she's not interested in pretending to be some other woman. She's not interested in being a commercial for Meghan. She leaves the skirt but pulls the duckbill clip from her hair, shakes the strands loose, and climbs onto his lap, the tweed bunched around her hips, the waistline of the skirt riding up and covering her belly, grazing the bottoms of her small breasts, and she hates herself a little bit, but not enough to stop. There's a picture of his son by the bed, in a soft white sun hat cinched below his chin, sitting in the sand on some beach with blue water, and she tries not to look at it. She unbuttons Jason's shirt and kisses him, his mouth stale and smoky, and he says, "Put the jacket back on," and she says no, and then he is inside her, and then he stops and says, "Is this okay," and she says, "Yes," then, "Do you have a condom," and he says, "No, we don't use them." His nipples are small, like the copper rivets on jean pockets, and his chest is broad and hairy, and she fits her tongue into the crater on his jaw. He's quiet, too quiet, his eyes glazed over and his hands on her hips, moving her, and she wishes he'd make a noise, any noise, verbal or nonverbal, a piggish grunt, anything. He moves her faster, and she whispers, "Say my name," and he mumbles something between breaths, and she says, "Please," and he doesn't, and she waits, and he doesn't, and she shouts, surprising herself, "Say my name!" and he pulls out and shudders, not saying it, and he comes into his hand, not saying it, and some shoots onto her thigh and the lining of Meghan's skirt, and she dismounts and unzips it, the tweed stretched and creased, and goes to the bathroom to wipe herself off. *Spilled seed,* she thinks, the biblical phrase insinuating itself into her consciousness from some place where it has apparently lain buried.

While he lies back on the bed, recovering, she stands naked at the bathroom sink and scrubs at the purple silk. Her floating head returns to her body. She scrubs and scrubs the lining, dark with wet and frothed with suds, until he comes up behind her and touches her hair, rests his hand at the base of her spine, and says, at last, "Maddy."

# 14

## MADDY

### April 2018

Maddy found the church online the day after she prayed with Pat. There were so many, and she was not well-versed in their differences, and so she chose one at random, still hearing Pat's words in her head, *I shall not want.* On the church's Facebook page they emphasized themselves as a tight-knit family, and Maddy imagined them gathered smiling around a table with Jesus at the head, carving a turkey.

All right, she thought, why not. If there was no earthly person she could go to for answers, she'd go over their heads, like asking to talk to the manager. Absent a mother, a man in a robe might do. He would tell her what to do and then make her feel right and just for doing it. *Pray,* Pat had said, and so she would. *I shall not want.* In the lobby of the cancer pavilion where she'd sometimes gone with her mother, gift-wrapped boxes had been set out to collect prayers. People wrote them on index cards and slid them through a slit in the top of the box. Maddy had never filled out these cards, and now she wondered if things might have turned out differently if she had.

Her mother had gone through a religious streak; it had been short-lived and eventually tilted toward a New Age spiritualism that hadn't seemed to serve her any better before fizzling out altogether. But maybe there was something to be found here after all. Who was to say? What did she have to lose?

The church occupied a large share of a strip mall, flanked by a Vietnamese restaurant and a dialysis center, in a building that seemed itself to be a recent convert to the faith—in its previous life, it might have been a furniture showroom or an office supply store. Tall, rain-streaked windows lined the building's face, and above its front doors a wide portico stuck out, beneath which it was easy to imagine shoppers pushing buggies to their cars or men loading couches into moving trucks. At the entrance she nearly turned and ran, but a man opened the door for her and welcomed her in with such cheerfulness that she entered just so she didn't have to let him down. Inside the entrance stood an easel bearing a whiteboard that read *Quote of the Week: Don't just Go through it, GROW Through It!*

There was no stained glass—no windows at all, in fact, once Maddy stepped inside the inner room, just rows of red curtains pulled shut to hide bare, thin walls. No pews, but metal chairs with faded green padded seats arranged in neat rows. No organ, but a group of middle-aged men and a teenage boy with guitars and a drum set getting ready to jam on a low stage at the front of the room. Maddy took a seat near the end of a row at the back, locating the room's red EXIT signs in case she had to make a run for it.

She looked around at the curtained walls, the scuffed blue carpet on the stage up front, the men warming up on their instruments, the podium, the dirty vinyl beneath her feet that resembled the kitchen floors in Jada's apartment. The room began to fill with a great variety of faces and bodies, and Maddy was torn between an

intense fear of being spoken to and an equally intense longing for
recognition—by the woman in front of her, for instance, in bright
pink pants and a floral top, a quilted paisley purse in clashing colors pinched beneath her arm, her gray hair held back by butterfly
clips. Maddy herself had worn a skintight, lime-green cotton tee, a
tattoo choker necklace, her peanut butter and jelly earrings, and a
pair of thrifted black slacks that had begun to feel too small. She'd
put on some orangish lipstick and tucked the pink streak of hair,
oily and mud-brown at the root, behind her ears. She'd been unsure
of her wardrobe choices and was relieved to see that there was no
clear dress code here. People wore, she supposed, what the Lord had
moved them to wear.

She wanted that—to be *moved*, to something, by something or
someone. Not Jason, not her father, not Pat or Jada or even Blake but
some deep and mysterious force. She had no idea what she was doing,
where she was going; she wanted someone else to drive. To curl up in
the back seat of her life, fall asleep with her head against the window,
wake up wherever.

To make herself look busy, she checked her phone, opened the
dating app. *Bigfoot? Let's discuss. I've been told I resemble Ben Affleck.
6'3" and great at tossing pizza dough. I am a master on the ukulele.*
She swiped until the lights dimmed and music started up and the
woman in front of her was joined by what must have been her husband and daughters, girls who looked to be just a few years younger
than Maddy, rolling their eyes when their mother reached out to
embrace them. Maddy felt a hot shock of anger. How intolerable that
these ungrateful girls should get a mother when she didn't, that this
woman should be alive to carry her ugly purse and hug her stupid
kids when Maddy's own mother was not. But she checked herself.
It was this anger, more than anything—more, even, than the fetus

inside her—that she hoped God would zap away. She could not go through the world mad at girls just for having mothers, mad at mothers just for being alive, mad at hers for being dead.

So far the service was nothing like what Maddy had expected. Stage lights flashed, a spectrum of colors fading one into the next. The woman with the butterfly clips threw her hands up and swayed. On the platform at the front of the room the band jammed away, led by what seemed to be a father-son ensemble, sons on drums and electric guitar and dad on lead vocals, belting out "Come into me, O Lord" to the tune of "Louie, Louie." No, this was not what she had bargained for, the swaying worshippers with their closed eyes and outstretched hands, the way even songs of praise evoked sex. Maddy grew self-conscious, fearful of standing out by standing still. She had expected to sit quietly, contemplating her misery to organ accompaniment. She eyed a glowing exit sign and gripped the back of the seat in front of her with her good hand. What the fuck had she thought was going to happen here?

She remembered the words from a song they'd sung back at the Methodist church, before Jada had refused to continue attending and Maddy, five or six and wanting at the time to be just like her sister, refused, too. *Create in me a clean heart, O God*—that archaic *o* without an *h*, that solitary circle like an open mouth. Different from the peppier songs they sometimes sang about morning and blackbirds, backed by organ or piano, this one had been in a minor key, and Maddy had cried to it, held on to the back of the pew in front of her and let her head dip beneath her arms and kicked her feet, which had not touched the floor then, and watched the tears drop onto the clay-colored tile and leave rusty puddles there like drops of blood.

The music stopped, and the man in front of her sank down onto his chair, dropped like a man-bomb, crushing the fingers on Maddy's good hand between the chair's metal back and his sweaty one. She pulled back her hand, rubbed her pinched fingers. The preacher took the stage and asked all visitors to please stand.

*God,* Maddy thought, exasperated, and then wondered: Was this prayer? Was it enough simply to use his name?

The preacher was looking at her. She stood, arms crossed at her middle, hugging herself.

"Welcome, visitors!" he said to Maddy and another newcomer across the room. "We love you, folks. We may never have met you before, but we love you. I love you." The congregation applauded.

His name was Dan, and when he said so, Maddy realized she'd been hoping for something more grandiose and apostolic, like Thaddeus or Bartholomew. He liked to repeat things in pairs, echoing himself, with those echoes echoed in turn by members of the congregation, who riffed off his declarations as if in a game of telephone. *Children of the most high God. Children of the most high God. Children of God. God's children. Amen, amen.* Beneath the mumbling and incanting, Maddy could make out a sound like the fizz of radio static. It had begun to rain.

"An abundance of rain," Dan said, wrapping the weather into the service in a kind of spiritual jazz, improvising. "He will rain down his favor upon you. My friends, God's gonna fill you with his love. Fill you to overflowing. Rain down healing and forgiveness and favor. He's gonna rain it down, my friends."

After more music and dancing came an energetic sermon in which Maddy and the other congregants were encouraged to think of Abraham and Sarah, the biblical couple gifted with a child despite Sarah's infertility. *Abraham considered not the weakness of his own body,* quoted Pastor Dan, *nor the deadness of Sarah's womb.* "Friends," he urged, "let us all be more like Abraham—not fussing over the little things, the hurdles or the tough times, only trusting God. Putting our trust in God. Because what did God do for Abraham? God gifted him with a child in due time. God performed a miracle for Abraham and Sarah, who never lost faith in him."

Typical, Maddy thought of Abraham, *considering not*. Hard for her to identify with Sarah, aging and longing for a baby—if Sarah had longed. Who wrote these stories, anyway? What did some man know about how some other man's wife felt about her pregnancy? Then Maddy thought of her mother, surprised by her own late-in-life fertility, gifted—or cursed—with Maddy.

"You see, my friends," Dan went on, "it's easy to blame ourselves for failing to make things happen. Why didn't I get that promotion, Lord? Why didn't I score the winning basket? Why can't I get my drinking under control? Why don't I have the house I want, God, or the marriage I want, or the job I've dreamed of? But, friends, I ask you: Who makes things happen?" He paused. "Not us," he said. "No. Who's in charge? Who brings the rain?"

"*He* makes things happen!" someone called. "*He* does!"

"He does. He's in charge. He brings the rain that heals the earth, that nourishes the roots of the trees. And he's going to rain down on you, just like he rains down on the oak tree, the fern, the flowers, all the good things that grow on this good earth."

Maddy let herself be carried on the rhythms of Pastor Dan's voice, let her body unclench. *The oak tree, the fern, the flowers, this good earth*. Her heart sped up, her palms grew damp. She looked at the girl next to her, whose eyes were closed. Maddy closed hers, too.

"You can't make it rain yourself, friends!" Dan cried. "You can't break your chains! He has to break them. He has to break them. He'll break your chains, friends. He'll heal your broken heart as he healed Sarah's womb. He'll guide you down the path toward healing, toward success. Plant your seed in him, friends. Sow your seed and let him bring the rain that makes it grow!"

A hitch in Pastor Dan's voice. Maddy's eyes snapped open. Yes: he'd begun to cry, then wiped away the tear and held it shining on the tip of his finger, a tiny crystal offering to God. The congregation began to cheer, and, scandalized, Maddy wondered how Dan did it. How he could get away with weeping nakedly like this, a grown man. Her father would not be caught dead crying red-eyed on a stage. He would not be caught dead crying at all.

A woman behind Maddy began to chant, "God, I'm coming! I'm coming into your presence!" and Maddy held down a laugh that made its way out of her all the same, unbidden, like a burp. The woman in front of her turned and flashed her a look you could file your nails on, and Maddy fought to keep a straight face. Did these people not understand innuendos? Why did things persist in being funny even when your mother was dead, even when you had gone to church with an open mind and a broken heart, ready to be good?

She should not be here, she thought again. She was bad, she was nasty, just as Bear had told her, just as *I'm the tall one in the group shot* had told her. She was beyond salvation.

That first day with Jason, changing out of Meghan's suit—she had gone home feeling like she'd conquered him. Like she was the one in charge. Wham, bam, thank you sir. When eventually she realized that she had not really chosen him but been chosen, the realization didn't bother her as much as it probably should have; in fact, she'd been flattered. Like she'd won some kind of sex election. He'd had so much to lose—marriage, family, election—and yet he had trusted her. Only when he handed her that envelope full of cash did she understand, at last, that he'd chosen her not because she was strong or dependable, but because she was weak.

It had been so embarrassing to go to him the second time and see him produce a box of condoms from the nightstand, because he had known she would come back for more. She had wanted to leave him wondering, the ball in her court; she had wanted him to feel lucky when she deigned to give him another go. But he had known what cloth she was cut from.

She had made things so easy for him. Taking his money, going away. What did this say about her, Maddy wondered, as Pastor Dan pastored on and the rain pounded overhead—that she was good, loving her enemy, sparing him ruin? Or that she was evil?

"God works in the dark, my friends," Dan incanted. "You might not see him working. You might not feel the rain falling down, feeding those thirsty roots of yours. But he's working for you. And believe me, friends, what he begins he will complete. It might be tomorrow, it might be next week, next month, next year. It might be in the next life, your eternal life! But what he starts, he will finish. He is with you, friends. He's been with you, he's been working for you, since before you were born. Psalm 139: 'For you created my inmost being; you knit me together in my mother's womb. I praise you because I am fearfully and wonderfully made; your works are wonderful, I know that full well. My frame was not hidden from you when I was made in the secret place, when I was woven together in the depths of the earth. Your eyes saw my unformed body.'

"My friends, God says to each of us, you are one of a kind. God says to each of us, as he said to Abraham and Sarah, I could have chosen anyone, but I chose you. I made you in my image, and what I start, I will complete."

Maddy put a hand to her belly, her secret place, and let the cadence of the psalm wash over her. *I know that full well.* Oh, O, to know anything full well; to know anything even half well! And what did Dan mean when he said she had been chosen? For what higher purpose had she been knit together? To be her mother's baby? To have a baby of her own, *fearfully and wonderfully made*? She had seen no angelic apparition. There was no donkey for her to ride to Bethlehem, no shining star for her to follow, and yet Maddy had a vision of herself as a modern Mary if not a modern Sarah, legs slung over a big-eared ass, riding sidesaddle to an inn where she would give birth on a bed of straw because she had been chosen to do so.

She imagined holding her child's clammy hand in hers, lifting it in her arms, balancing its warm heft on her hip. If she died, when she died, the child would remember her.

"'All the days ordained for me were written in your book before one of them came to be,'" Dan quoted, eyes closed, palms up. "You are precious, God says to us. From the moment you took shape in your mother's womb, you were mine. You have been chosen."

She imagined her child learning to speak, looking at her and saying, *Mama*. She had always wanted so badly to be loved; in a child, she reasoned, she'd have a love hostage. Knowing no better, at least for a while, it would worship her.

But this was unfair of her—to want to be worshipped. God was a man. Her job as a woman, as a mother, she supposed, would be to give love selflessly.

The music started up again, a softer song now, "Amazing Grace," and people started singing, and something stirred inside Maddy. She glanced at the girl next to her as if to ask permission for something, and the girl returned a smile as if to grant it, nodding a little: *yes*. A tiny flame in her chest flared. Something moved her, something shook her, and she was cracked open, gut-punched by what she could only assume was grace—a dizzy, drunken weightlessness, the sense of being lifted from her seat. Amazing. That she might have been chosen not because of her body but before it; that she could belong to someone who would never leave her, who—if Dan spoke the truth, and wasn't that his job?—had been with her always, even when she hadn't recognized him. Jesus looked down at her from a framed print on the wall. Her wounded hand took on a new, towering significance. She raised it into the air. Yes, this song was better; this song she liked. *How sweet the sound.* A few people began pushing their way to the ends of their rows to queue up in the aisle, and Maddy watched as someone at the head of the line collapsed into two fellow worshippers' arms with a fishy limpness.

She had an urge to run not from the commotion but into it, and she rose to her feet and drifted toward the prospect of forgiveness, purity, goodness, making her way down her row of chairs and into the church's central aisle. She floated to the front of the church, hardly knowing what she was doing, *moved,* and when she came to the front of the line she fell to her knees, the music swimming inside her, her body slack and trembling, bathed in colored light, now yellow, now pink, now blue. *Your body is a temple,* Pat had said, but it hadn't been, not then. She had been only a blueprint. She would take the pieces of herself, these shitty bones, this viable fetus, her pink hair, her many mistakes, and make something of them. Rebuild herself from the ground up.

Someone touched the top of her head—Dan? God? Odd, she thought even then, that a man's hands on her should be both the way in and the way out of sanctity. But if this was the path, she'd take it. A hot stream of tears oozed up and out of her, trailed by a puppyish whimper, a sound like air leaking from a valve, a sound like something dying.

Back at her seat, the girl next to her hugged her. The bald dad and the paisley-pursed mom hugged her. Other people Maddy didn't know hugged her, singing: *a wretch like me*. What a hideous lyric; what a hideous word, *wretch*. What a way these people had of making hideous things oddly beautiful, couching the word in this song that ran over her like clean water in this moment, this hour, the hour she first believed.

She hadn't been back at her seat five minutes when she came down from her high and was slammed back into her body. She had to pee again. She squeezed her legs together until the service ended, then pushed through the crowd and hurried to the bathroom. She made it just in time, made it rain, rain down. *Amen,* she thought. It occurred to her that she should not draw mental parallels between Pastor Dan's sermon and her urination, that this was not what a good girl would do. And she saw how hard it would be to maintain the image of herself as a temple that she'd had in the sanctuary, imagining herself unsullied, while meanwhile her body went on doing body things. How did you reconcile high and low, purity and pee? How did you hold on to the feeling she'd had moments ago?

But maybe these questions were too much too soon. *God works in the dark, my friends,* Dan had said, and Maddy pictured God gray-bearded on a dimly lit sweatshop floor, sewing feverishly, coaxing a piece of pearly fabric through a machine. Silver needle stabbing, stabbing forever. The point was, he had a plan, there was a pattern.

Maddy felt exhausted, washed ashore on the coast of her new faith. She zipped her fly and stood in the stall, waiting for the sounds of bathroom socializing to die down, not ready to be seen or spoken to. She had the feeling she got after seeing a good movie, when the lights came on in the theater and you became aware of the fact that all the strong emotions you'd imagined you were feeling privately had in fact been shared with strangers, and you rushed to hide the signs of those emotions, because they belonged in the dark.

When she emerged from the restroom, it had stopped raining. A few churchgoers hung around the lobby, talking to Pastor Dan. Maddy slouched and scuttled around the perimeter. She had a sort of one-night-stand feeling toward Dan: they had shared something intimate; he had laid his hands on her, but she didn't know what she'd possibly say to him now. She slunk past him, pushed through the front doors, and stepped outside. The sun beat down on shrinking dark spots on the sidewalk. The world looked brighter, colors were sharper, the smells in the air were stronger. Tires hissed over wet streets. A bass beat thumped from the stereo of a passing car and pulsed through Maddy's body, and she felt it beating inside her, received it in the way her child must receive the world—through sound as vibration like a next-door bass beat, a thrumming transmission from a place not seen. The light poured down, white and watery, touching everything. She stretched out her arms and touched back.

# 15

## JADA

In their 1994 study on the allure of secret relationships, Daniel M. Wegner, Julie D. Lane, and Sara Dimitri instructed mixed-gender pairs of research participants, two pairs at a time, to play cards while seated at the same table. In each group, one pair received written instructions to communicate with each other via under-the-table foot contact; the other did not. Of those pairs instructed to play footsie, some were told to keep their contact a secret from the other pair of participants seated at the table, while others were permitted to conduct their footsie game with the full knowledge of their fellow card-players. At the end of the experiment, the participants were asked to rate the degree of attraction and closeness they'd felt to their partner during the card game. As hypothesized, those who had been encouraged to play secret footsie reported significantly greater attraction to their partners than those who hadn't and were the most likely to consider themselves and their partners a plausible romantic match. Secrecy was in essence an aphrodisiac. And outside of the laboratory, as survey data had shown, the deceptive practices required to maintain secrecy demanded an intense, near-constant focus on the secret, an obsessive preoccupation, that was fuel to the flame of desire.

Because of this fact, and because of Maddy's newfound religious zeal, Jada had not told Maddy that she was continuing to see Drew—that last week, after their heart-to-heart over cookies, they'd gone to Phipps and made out frantically among cacti in the Desert Room like teenagers with the sun beating down through the greenhouse ceiling; that she would see him again tonight. *Thou shalt not covet*, etc. She hid her rendezvous from Maddy the way she would have hidden them from Blake if they still lived together, the secrecy both thrilling and disgraceful.

The peace in the apartment felt precarious. Jada washed and folded the laundry, she prepared and served the meals, she scheduled Maddy a doctor's visit. As the spring semester drew to a close, she spent the days analyzing her data, working on her article. She had tried to get Maddy to do the dishes, but after a few days went by during which they crusted in the sink, she'd given in and done them herself. At first she had been pleased with herself, had read her maintenance of a clean and stable dwelling place for Maddy as a sign of her own ability to nurture. But more recently she had come to understand it as the result of a compulsive desire to keep things, to the extent possible, the way they'd be if Maddy had not come; to erase her.

"'Early in the morning,'" Maddy read now from the Bible she'd bought, "'as Jesus was on his way back to the city, he was hungry. Seeing a fig tree by the road, he went up to it but found nothing on it except leaves. Then he said to it, "May you never bear fruit again!" Immediately the tree withered.'"

She was pacing around in a pair of cherry-print pajama pants and an old softball shirt with WETZEL WRECKER SERVICES printed in cracked white letters on the front. She looked up from the Bible at Jada, drinking a glass of grapefruit juice and typing half-heartedly at the kitchen table.

"So?" Jada asked.

"It was a miracle."

"But why wither a tree? Weren't there disciples to feed? Hungry villagers?"

Maddy looked down at the page. "'When the disciples saw this, they were amazed. "How did the fig tree wither so quickly?" they asked. Jesus replied, "Truly I tell you, if you have faith and do not doubt, not only can you do what was done to the fig tree, but also you can say to this mountain, 'Go, throw yourself into the sea,' and it will be done. If you believe, you will receive whatever you ask for in prayer."'"

She closed the book. Jada could feel Maddy's eyes on her but didn't look up from her screen. Ever since she'd told Maddy about the abortion, she'd had the feeling Maddy saw her as some kind of fallen demon-woman. She had not expected that Maddy would come to the city only to find the same Jesus that lived in the country and that she could have found a thousand times over back home if she'd cared to go looking.

"You hate this, don't you," Maddy said proudly. "You hate that I've entered a personal relationship with Christ."

"No." Jada's mouth twitched. "I'm happy for you. But, like I've said, I think you need a job."

She bought figs at Trader Joe's and served a fig and arugula salad for lunch, whole-grain fig toast on deck for tomorrow's breakfast. Before digging into the salad, Maddy closed her eyes tight—praying, Jada guessed. Watching from across the table, fork in hand, Jada got the feeling she'd had once, years ago, when she visited a friend's house for a birthday party, helped herself to a plateful of confetti cake, and saw above the family's dinner table a placard portraying folded hands and emphatic capital letters: AS FOR ME AND MY HOUSE, WE WILL SERVE THE LORD. Jada had sat below the sign and felt below the family, savage and unwelcome, an outsider whose lifestyle—her own family's church attendance spotty, their food unblessed—was the shadow to contrast the pure light of *me and my house*. In the house, but not of it, she'd been afraid to touch her cake.

She was clearing the lunch dishes when Maddy's phone rang from among the salad bowls. Maddy snatched it away, refused the call, but not before Jada caught a glimpse of the screen: Pat from New Dawn. She looked at Maddy; Maddy looked away.

Jada turned to the sink, chewed her lip, felt an energy building inside her that she needed to release. Why should her stance on her sister's pregnancy matter less to her than that of a stranger with a handful of pamphlets and too much time on her hands? Who would end up taking care of the baby, taking care of Maddy? Not the crusading stranger. Not Jesus. It was time their father knew. Things were getting too hard for Jada to handle on her own.

"I'm going for a run," she said. She left the dishes in the sink and Maddy at the table and fled the home she'd fled to, exorcised.


She took the hills with determination, savoring the feeling of her body shifting gears—certain muscles engaged on the way up, certain others on the way down, her center of balance shifting, the air in and out of her lungs. She ran as far as her old neighborhood, to the street where she used to live and where some of her things still did, timing her visit so that Blake would not be there to see her huffing by. She paused, squinted up at the empty building. And let herself in.

He hadn't asked for her key, and she wondered whether he assumed she came here. Inside, her body prickled with the shock of the conditioned air. The cat slid in and out of her legs. To her surprise Jada found that she enjoyed the role of impostor, the vitalizing tension, the thrumming alertness, all her senses engaged.

In the kitchen, she filled a wineglass with cold water and drank, moving through the space they'd shared, observing the nicer household items, the cut glass and candlesticks. These things had been gifts from members of Blake's family, and many of them—the set of champagne flutes, the fluffy bathrobes—were monogrammed with an *M* for Macauley, his name, the one she had not taken. There was an *M* crystal bowl from Tiffany's, a sterling-silver *M* cake knife and server that Jada had looked up online after unwrapping them, finding that the set had cost $350. She'd resolved to return them, but Blake had stopped her, reminded her how she'd dropped the ball on the registry, compiled too late and with not enough items; people had had to improvise. That she might end up with monogrammed cake servers had not occurred to her.

She could come back here. There was still time. Back to the cheese knives with *M*s on their handles, back to the *M* cake stand. She touched it now, lightly. *M* for marriage, *M* for mistake. She lifted the glass hemisphere, flipped it, and settled it carefully into the stand, plate turned to punch bowl, *M* turned to *W*. *W* for wife, for woman; *W* for who, when, where; *W* for why was she in this kitchen now, wiping down the quartzite countertop until it shone, pouring herself a second glass of water in a thin-stemmed wineglass? She dipped a finger into the water, ran it around the glass's rim, and listened to the crystal whine. She washed and dried the glass, replaced it in the cabinet, and walked through the house touching *M* objects, *M* for mine, *M* for memory. She took off her clothes, left them lying on the hardwood in the hallway—oak beams she still couldn't look at without thinking of her father assessing, grading, foam plugs in his ears—and went into the bathroom with the big tub and the heated towel rack and the his-and-her sinks, and ran herself a bath.

Inside, she let her toes bob to the surface. She was failing as a wife, a sister, a daughter; she was failing as a Good Woman, sneaking away from Maddy, sneaking around the Japanese Garden under Drew's arm. Perhaps if she thought about it enough she might refashion her failure, paradoxically, into a kind of success, a thing she was doing thoroughly and well. If she could shed her shame, frame failing as a thing she could get an A in, she could take a defiant pride in it—be a Master of failure, a Doctor of it. But the shame hung on. She had made a promise to Blake, with the full intention of keeping it. If she could get that wrong, what else might she have gotten wrong? What might she get wrong still?

The way she'd felt these last few weeks, with Drew—like she just woke up. Guilt, yes, but also relief: the freeze could thaw. She should try to harness this new desire, treat her arousal as a general thing—a lamp that would glow as brightly plugged into any outlet, a match that could light any candle—and not as specific to Drew. If she held this spark to the wick of her marriage, she might yet be able to save it.

She sat up so that her chest rose out of the water and nudged her nearby phone into selfie mode. Extended an arm and snapped: lips, jaw, neck, clavicle; top of a breast, droplets of water; star of a mole, vines of wet hair. A lacy froth of bubbles where the bathwater line had been. She studied the photo and was pleased to find herself turned on by the sight of her own skin.

Here was the spark, the wick. All it would take was this photo. She tapped the image, hit share, but she could not send it to Blake. The thought of his seeing it made her sick, and the fact that this thought made her sick made her sad, and her sadness propelled her to Drew, who had offered himself as its antidote, but the thought of sending him the picture instead of Blake unleashed her mental mob: *Terrible person, terrible woman, this is your husband's bathtub.* She kept the picture to herself. She liked the idea of carrying it with her in the way Maddy had carried the rubber fetus through the Halls of Wildlife, a reminder of her responsibility: she had a body to take care of.

Jada drained the tub, changed back into her running clothes, wrapped her towel around her head. Then she sat down in the linen reading chair in the corner of the bedroom and called her father.

Right away, he asked about Maddy. "She okay?" he said. "I mean, it was weird. How she just woke up one day and took off."

Jada paused. *Just do it.* They were on opposite sides of everything; here was a chance to change that, to bond through the glue of shared knowledge.

Maybe there was still time for them. Time for him to become a more motherly father, someone who could love her uncompetitively and without conditions. Time for her to do the same for him. Besides, if Maddy was going to have a baby, he was going to find out sooner or later. She was helping Maddy, really, by giving him a heads-up.

So she told him. A long silence unfolded. She said, "Dad? Are you there?"

"Yeah."

"Don't tell her you know." She began to panic. "I wasn't supposed to say anything."

"Why didn't she tell me?"

"She will. She'll tell you in her own time."

He was quiet again, then said, "You'll take care of it, won't you?"

She should have known he would ask this of her. Anger set in, then regret: she had taken something from Maddy—control of her story, as precious as control of the body—for the sake of ingratiating herself with her father, who had no qualms about asking her to clean up the whole mess herself.

She said, "It's not my baby, Dad. Surely you can't expect me to take care of it. I have school, I have work. . . ."

"But that's not what I mean," he said. "I don't mean take care of it. I mean, take *care* of it."

Now it was her turn to go silent.

"You know," he repeated, but she wanted to make him say it. Why wouldn't anyone just say it?

He said, "It's still early, right? She's not ready. And I—I can't . . . right now."

"Care for a child?"

"A baby. I can't. I don't expect you to, either."

So there they were, on the same page, with nothing to say to each other, only euphemisms and pregnant pauses. She imagined a bridge stretching between them, so long she could not see the other side. If she started across it, would it carry her back to him? Or did it end halfway across the ravine between them, crumbled, impassable?

She remembered something he'd said shortly before the election. *I'd move to Canada,* he'd ranted, *rather than have that woman for a president.* She had not been sure, once he'd said it, where the emphasis lay—*that* woman, or that *woman,* not that it really mattered—and she had noted with scornful bemusement his apparent misunderstanding of Canadian politics, and she had fought back: *How do you think it makes me feel that you'd support someone who brags about grabbing women by the pussy?* She was not sure, now, whether to be relieved that his convictions could bend, or whether to be appalled that they were so flimsy.

"I'm not sure what you want me to do," she said. "It's her body."

"Just . . . I don't know. I don't know what to say."

His voice was too loud. Her reflex was to grow defensive, but she checked herself; it was probably his hearing. During Trigger the dog's twilight years of deafness, master and pet's shared disability had bound them in a silent, brotherly bubble; call them both and neither would come. Jada had been so jealous of that dog, her father's chosen companion.

She envisioned him alone in the house, the freezer packed with TV dinners, cans of pop stocked as if for the apocalypse in the basement fridge, mice setting off traps, sawdust in his hair. She missed him. She missed being too young to see herself as different from him, or for her difference to matter. He had loved her most in her days of least consequence, when she had been opinionless, reliant. She could resent him for this only so much: she had loved him best then, too.

"It's okay, though?" he said. "Having her there?"

"Yes, it's okay."

"Make sure she helps. Don't let her loaf around."

"She's fine. I told her if she wants to stay, she needs to look for work."

"She could work at the zoo," he said. "All that time with those birds."

It wasn't a bad idea. "I'll help her look into it."

"Tell her she can come home whenever she wants."

"You can tell her that yourself."

"What?" he said.

"I said you can tell her that yourself."

A memory popped into her mind: she is nine, and her father is folding a napkin into a tight triangle, a football; the two of them zing it back and forth across the table of a Pizza Hut, a rare dinner out. They've gone to get her free BOOK IT! pizza—she reads voraciously;

they've just dropped off her latest stack of books at the library—and even at this age she is fastidious, brushing clumps of Parmesan from the tabletop. Her father joins his hands at the thumbs, palms facing her, inviting her to flick a field goal through the space between his index fingers. He's in a good mood, singing along with Sheryl Crow's "All I Wanna Do," though this is very much not L.A. Jada flings the paper football through her father's goalpost fingers, and her parents throw their arms in the air, cheering open-mouthed, her biggest fans.

"Well, what about you?" he said. "Everything going good?"

"Yeah, good."

"You got that paper done?"

"I'm working on it."

Muffled noise on his end of the call—a hammering, or a knocking. "You're the one who should be having a baby. When are you and Blake gonna start a family?"

Heat in her face. "I don't know, Dad."

"A baby's good for a marriage."

She was quiet for a while. "That claim isn't supported by research."

"It can still be true," he said.

"It's not. There are studies."

"Well. I think it is."

She closed her eyes and saw that imaginary bridge again. He would believe what he wanted to believe no matter how many studies she cited. To learn, to build knowledge, it must be possible to prove one's theories wrong, as she wished she could tell him: falsifiability is fundamental. But her father was not a man of theory. He was a man of ideology, which was impossible to prove *or* disprove, like the existence of God.

"Who is it, anyway?" he asked. "The father."

"She won't say."

"I didn't know she had a boyfriend."

"I don't think she does," Jada said. "She says the guy doesn't want to be involved."

Then he was fuming, as she'd known he would—he ought to this, he ought to that, he was going to track him down, etc., and she said, "No, you aren't," and he asked again why Maddy hadn't told him, and she said, "This is why. You're raving, you're threatening," and they were both angry when they hung up the phone.

She rose from the chair, patting the memory of her form out of the cushions. She did not want Blake to find her used towel, so she took it with her, draping it like a heavy scarf around her neck. She ran with the weight of it on her shoulders, its ends flying out cape-like behind her, all the way home.

She met Drew on the Strip for a walk, dinner, and drinks. They strolled up and down Penn Avenue and browsed the pasta aisles at Penn Mac, ate oysters at Wholey's and biscotti from Enrico, shared gnocchi from a bread bowl for dinner. She bought him a shirt with Super Bowl rings on it that said CITY OF CHAMPYINZ; he bought her one with a Heinz pickle on it that said I'M KIND OF A BIG DILL. Eventually they ended up in a bar off the Strip. He ordered a Yuengling with a shot of Jameson, she ordered a vodka tonic.

"Remember how I used to . . . ," he started, and she interrupted him: "Yes."

"What was I gonna say?"

"How you used to make up those fake cocktails for me to order."

Drew laughed. "The Tuesday Night," he said. "The Murder She Wrote. You'd be all nervous and cute, all 'What should I order?' and you'd saunter on up to the bar, so serious, 'Hello, I'd like a—'"

"Whatever," she said. "You're a bad influence."

She could not stop thinking about her conversation with her father, which she summarized for Drew. "I shouldn't have told him," she said, stirring her drink with her two cocktail straws.

"It's not like he won't find out," he said, "if she's really going to have a baby."

Jada shook her head. "She's still in touch with some woman from the crisis pregnancy center. Sometimes it seems like she cares what everyone thinks but me."

"She's smart, though. She knows she doesn't have to do anything she doesn't want to do. Maybe what she decides is just . . . what she decides. It's like you were saying the other day, about mothers feeling hurt when other women don't want to be mothers. Maybe you don't need to take it personally."

"It will be personal if I have to help her raise a kid."

"You don't *have* to help her," he said. "But you would. Because you love her."

He was scrutinizing her in the way Blake sometimes did, as if there were complicated math problems on her face that he was trying to solve, carrying ones and moving decimals. Sometimes Blake would study her like this for a long time before asking her what she was thinking: something about the way she'd looked must have suggested she was deep in some profound and consequential reverie. In fact, much of the time she'd been thinking about little life things, like what to add to the grocery list; but when a man looked at you like that, like you were such an interesting riddle, you couldn't very well tell him the answer to the riddle was Raisin Bran and a stick of butter, and so she'd just look away. Then she would feel pressure to hurry up and start thinking something big enough to match his expectations.

"Do you think you're a good person?" she asked. "I mean, *I* think you are. But do you?"

He smiled, took a drink. "You're baiting me."

"No, I'm not."

"You're trying to get me to say you're a good woman because you're afraid to say it yourself. You want me to tell you you're brilliant and beautiful so you have permission to believe it too." He picked up the pen the guy next to him had used to close out and began sketching on a napkin.

She felt annoyed. "You seem to think you have a lot of power over me."

Drew shrugged, smug, still drawing on the napkin. "For what it's worth, I do think you're a good person. And I do think you're brilliant and beautiful. I think I'm all right, too. Not that any of this should come as a surprise."

Dion, Berscheid & Walster, 1972: what is beautiful is good, or so we assume. We ascribe favorable qualities to those we find beautiful. His whole life he had looked at her and liked what he saw and assumed those likeable features were signs of virtue; she'd looked at him and assumed the same. In theory their mutual admiration for each other's beauty should have helped manifest the very goodness they'd believed in, a self-fulfilling prophecy: years of being assumed good and treated accordingly should make it easy to be so. It took little effort to confirm a bias in your favor.

"Remember how I used to draw those squirrel cartoons on your science notes?" he said. She tried to see what he was drawing now, but he blocked her view with his hand.

"And how we used to hang out at Walmart," she said. When it opened when they were in tenth grade, it had become their indoor playground, though they never bought anything. They'd walk down aisles and turn all the boxes upside down. They'd take stuffed animals out of bins and hide them around the store: in freezers, riding kids' tricycles, zipped into orange vests on racks with their furry heads poking out. They had not been cool, didn't drink or get high, just rode around in the woods on his used Polaris and got kicked out of Walmart and talked about books—he liked *Dune* and *American Gods*; she liked Sylvia Plath.

"God," she said, "we were so bored."

He took a long drink. "I wasn't," he said. "I was happy."

And that had been their problem. He wanted to rest, while she'd been restless; he wanted to stay, and she had felt with every part of herself the need to go.

He slid the napkin toward her on the bar. It was her face, rough but recognizable. A-plus work for five minutes on a cocktail napkin. It felt good to recognize herself in his hand, and it felt bad, too; she should not need a man to tell her she was good, to draw her so that she could know what she looked like. As he replaced his now-gone Yuengling with an Iron City, she tried to imagine him moving here to be with her, or moving to another city, far away, so she could pursue a postdoc or a teaching position. It was hard. He was part of a landscape.

"I know your mom thought I wasn't good enough for you," he said.

"That's not true."

He held up a hand. "Just let me finish."

She felt suddenly afraid. It was the terror of recognizing a moment as important while still inside it.

"I know I haven't been . . . ambitious. But it's not my plan to live with my mom forever. I do want something else, and I'm open to all sorts of ideas about what that might be. And it would be really nice if it could be with you."

Jada couldn't speak. Too much all at once to think of commitment, when it was commitment she was fleeing. Sometimes she worried that what she really wanted was not a second chance, a second wedding, but something impossible and unfair: to dwell in a permanent prelude like the one she now occupied with Drew, a beginning without an ending or even a middle, a lingerie life perpetually on the verge of disrobement: not contact, but the idea of contact; not the body, but a dream of the body. Not sex but sexual desire made more intense by the knowledge that she could act upon it at any time if she chose to. Not the challenge of a choice committed to but the mere electrifying presence of possibility, of ripe unseized options hanging like figs from a tree.

"You don't have to say anything," he said. "I just want you to know."

He'd let her stay here, then, a little longer. This smoky box, this unnamed state. This plush red vestibule wherein she had no label for him and he had none for her, where everything was anticipation, where their past was a romantic film they'd watched and memorized, and nothing was a disappointment. Unsustainable, unreasonable, but this was where she wished Drew would remain, at least for now, and where she wanted to remain for him: perfect, suspended, nowhere. A kind of sexy airport, duty-free.

They ordered nachos and another round of drinks, and she switched to a margarita and relaxed into drunkenness. People were dancing somewhere behind them, and the place had grown hot and close, and the bar was littered with chip crumbs and puddled with water rings, and even drunk she couldn't keep herself from wiping them up with cocktail napkins from their stack on the bar until Drew took her hand and held it and she breathed deeply: it's not your mess, let it go.

Maddy texted: *When will u be home?* and Jada texted back, *Don't know.* She tried not to think about Maddy, about Blake. She tried to mute her brain.

Drew was describing being a boy and watching his father club a caught trout in the head with a metal baseball bat for the first time. ". . . and I cried," he said.

"You cried." She gave him a melty look, half sympathy, half mockery. They were both laughing loudly, though the story was not that funny.

"What can I say. You know what my dad used to call fishing?" he asked. "*Ripping lips.* As in, 'Let's go rip some lips out on the river.'"

"No!" she cried. "Ew!"

He nodded. "It's been ages since I went," he said. "I never go. I should go. He used to take me all the time."

"So fish."

"Maybe I will."

"It's been ages since I swam," she said. Her bra strap slipped from her shoulder.

He put his hands out, palms upturned. "So swim."

"Swim!" said a drunk woman behind him. "Swim!"

She looked at the bartender, who shrugged. Next thing she knew she was on the small dance floor performing a front crawl, beating the laminate with her hands and kicking her feet like a child throwing a tantrum. Then a breaststroke, humping the floor with froggy kicks, her breasts mashed against the tile, strange men egging her on. The floor was a collage of broken tortilla chips and spilled booze and shed hairs and earring backs and a lost press-on fingernail. She was a fish, a writhing body, a spectacle.

Was this who she was—the fun girl at the bar? Perhaps she had been too rigid in her sense of self. Perhaps she had suppressed something and now was finding her way back to a truer self. In the morning she would relive her indignity in fragments with a mix of shame and pride—how unlike her to put on a show, get herself indoor-dirty. *How out of character,* she would think with shame. *How out of character!* she would think with pride. It was squalid and embarrassing and just what she'd wanted, without knowing it—to become, for once, all body and no mind.

In time she rose to her knees, flustered, and the cheering died down, and Drew helped her up. Her vision was tequila-woozy, the limes swimming in their crate behind the bar.

"Look at you," he said, and looked at her. His arm around her waist. She leaned into him and they swayed together, dancing where she'd swum, her arms draped over his shoulders and then snaked around his neck, his face so close to hers. She could hardly hear the music, a ringing in her ears. She was laughing but didn't know what at—the memory of their slow dancing to K-Ci & JoJo in middle school, maybe, her hair twisted back in a rainbow of mini butterfly clips; or the thrill and panic of their closeness now; or to chase the thought of Blake (What was he doing right now? Was he alone?) from her mind. Thank God she wasn't pregnant! But there was no God. There was *no God*, Maddy. There was no celestial domain from which their mother watched them. Why did people want that— to be looked down upon? Surely Ellen had better things to do in death, if death was a state in which one did things, than surveil her daughters.

"I'm not driving home tonight," Drew said into her ear.

She pulled back from him. "You can't stay over," she said. "Maddy."

"Come on."

"I'm serious, Drew. She's like . . . watching me. She'll beat you with her Bible."

He shrugged. "I'll sleep in my truck."

"You can't sleep in your truck."

He moved back to the bar, closed their tab, then headed to the restroom, sliding his wallet into his back pocket in that easy way men did. His signed bill was on the table, wet and warped. Blake was a bad tipper, and Jada always added a few dollars, keeping bills on hand out of habit to offset his cheapness. This was a test, she thought through the murk of her inebriation: rate each man's generosity on a seven-point scale, with 1 being stingy, 7 saintly. As covertly as possible she grabbed the slip and took in his blue-penned numbers, her heart surging at the sight of the roofed peaks of his close-topped fours. Six, she rated, and placed it back on the table.

She wanted her mouth on something of his, anything. In a mad rush she picked up his glass and licked the rim. This was her life. Her life! It was changeable, as all things are changeable. She could vote the old life out if that was what she chose to do. She could pick Drew. She could pick this version of herself.

She went to the bathroom, washed her hands, her arms, her face. She scrubbed gunk from her knees and thighs with watered-down orange soap and wiped down the most visibly dirty parts of her top. As she dried her shirt under the hand dryer, a nervousness set in that rivaled her drunkenness. On the one hand, blissful oblivion, an agave-induced optimism: she was having fun! She was a badass who went after the things she wanted and away from the things she didn't! On the other hand, a fearful agitation—was this what she wanted? To go back to Drew? To go back—it sounded like the opposite of what she ought to be doing. But then, he was not the same as he'd been before. She had bailed before he was fully formed.

*You overthink everything,* Blake used to complain. And probably he was right.

Drew drove her home with the windows open like always, the sound of the wind in her ears. He parked on the hill and followed her up the stairs, and she fumbled with the key until Maddy opened the door. She was back—or still—in her cherry pants and softball shirt.

"Where were you?" she said. "I was worried." She looked at Drew.

"He's going to sleep on the floor," Jada said.

"That's where *you* sleep," Maddy pointed out.

Jada looked at her sister and felt a creeping nostalgia for all the versions of her that had preceded this one, when she was younger, sweeter, easier. She reminded herself that one day she might feel a similar nostalgia for the current Maddy, and she tried to bypass the vast psychic and temporal territory between then and now in order to harness the feeling.

She brushed her teeth, changed into her BIG DILL T-shirt, then stumbled into the bedroom and tossed Drew a pillow and blanket. He was singing, "He was a floor sleeper" to the tune of "Day Tripper." He fluffed his pillow and collapsed.

Jada lay down on her air mattress. There was a glass of water next to it.

"Thanks for the water," she said to Drew.

"It's from Maddy."

He reached to his left and held up another glass, his own. Then he set it down and reached to his right to pull Jada to the floor. He held her close, and she turned on her side to face him. He ran a hand over the curve of her hip, let his fingers dip beneath her shirt and skim her side until she trapped his hand with her arm and pinched it against her rib cage. She shook her head ever so slightly.

"You want to," he said, his words a warm cloud in the space between his mouth and hers, his hand hot against her skin.

"Yes."

His eyes caught the light coming in from the street. "You do," he whispered. "You want it."

"Yes."

It needed to be enough, the wanting, not because of Maddy, not because of God or even Blake, but because she was not ready to leave the incubating space of her desire. It had taken so long to get back here. The familiar ache, the delicious pain of coming home—the place she'd craved, the place she'd run from—she needed to linger in it. Fucking him would put her on a trajectory, and she didn't want a trajectory. Like most women, she'd been conditioned to think in terms of destinations: get *there* as soon as you can, as directly as possible—to love, marriage, shelter—and lock yourself in. Now she'd seen how the walls could come down, how the structures could shatter, and she needed not to move, to lie still in her longing, warm by a fire built from rubble. Yes, she wanted it, but *it* wasn't the point. The point was the longing, the capacity to burn.

She curled into him, her face in the damp heat of his neck, her leg slung over his legs, her arm slung over his chest, until she woke, dry-mouthed and still burning, and climbed onto the cool raft of her mattress.

# 16

## MADDY

**April 2018**

Maddy woke at dawn from a sex dream of a faceless man-smudge, coveting, sweating. Purity was a bitch. She had hoped that after God blew her apart he might Picasso her pieces back together in some different, better order; but her salvation, she was sorry to find, had so far not translated into any significant modification of her behavior, only a heightened sense of her usual behavior's wrongness. Masturbating, for instance, mashing herself against a pillow, now seemed weighted with consequence; what had once felt like a mildly undignified but ultimately natural act now felt like cheating on Christ. *To the pure, all things are pure,* Pastor Dan had paraphrased in church, *but to those who are defiled, nothing is pure.*

She turned on her side on the futon, faced Jada's closed door. Normally they slept with the door open, Maddy's head lined up with the hallway that connected living room and bedroom, and she took comfort in the sight of her sister's legs and feet on the other end of that short corridor. Now, it was like she'd been thrown back to that night in State College: waking up to find Jada off with some guy. This time there was no woman there to read her back to sleep; she would have to read to herself. Two books under her futon: the Bible and *The Bell Jar*, Esther Greenwood on the beach in her filthy skirt. There was enough light coming in from the streetlights that she could read by it if she wanted to, and she thought with longing of the darkness and silence of home, the people who waved when you passed them on the road. The raspberries that would soon ripen in the bushes in the backyard, their fine hairs and sticky juice, the seeds stuck in her teeth. Her father coming and going from the house, the squeaky handle on the screen door, its slap against the frame. Removed from these things, from the place where she was once so lonely, she felt lonelier than ever.

She had to pee, and to get to the bathroom, she had to pass through Jada's bedroom. Maddy opened the door timidly and slunk inside. Jada slept nestled against Drew. She was still in her clothes from the night before, he was still in his. Neither of them stirred.

*They lay together*—it was Bible for sex, a euphemism that made Maddy smirk. She remembered her promise to be Blake's eyes and ears, but as she watched Drew and Jada literally lay together, she couldn't summon outrage. One of Jada's shoes was still on her foot, her compulsions overcome by drunkenness, or maybe by happiness. Maddy pulled the shoe off and set it next to its partner, which had been kicked against the wall and lay on its side by the dustless baseboard. She bent and pulled the blanket up over Drew's and Jada's sleeping bodies and hurried into the bathroom, the old glass doorknob detaching in her hand like a chunk of warm ice when she pulled the door closed behind her. A layer of silver leaf or tinfoil pasted inside the doorknob's hub seemed meant to make the glass shine like crystal. She knelt on the floor and pushed and worked the knob, the illusion, back in place.

Its metallic bed called an image to mind: the foil balloons, filled stiff, that Ellen's coworkers at the bank gave her when her cancer came back when Maddy was twelve. Her mother had asked her to pop the whole bundle—because, as she'd said, "They're glad I'm sick."

"No," Maddy had protested. "They care about you."

She'd looked around as if to prove her point. Roses at Ellen's bedside. The cheerful script on the front of the balloons: *Get Well Soon.* But her mother persisted: "They're glad it's me. As long as it's me, it's not them."

At the time, Maddy had dismissed her mother's words as empty expressions of fear. Wanting to be dutiful, she'd removed the balloons from her mother's sight, not popping them but shepherding them, knocking against each other, to her own bedroom. She'd tied them to a bedpost, where they stayed until, like the thirsty roses in Ellen's room, they wilted. She had not known what her mother meant—that people might need her sick so that they could be well—until last week in church when, hearing about how Jesus had died so that she, they, everyone might live, she had thought she understood.

Back on her futon, she could not fall back to sleep. The light coming in between the blinds was brighter now, and she heard Jada stirring, climbing onto her mattress. She went into the kitchen and drank juice straight from the carton, chewed her gummy vitamins, sliced a green apple into wedges and placed them in a plastic baggie. She did not feel like being home when Jada and Drew got up, so after getting dressed she took her phone and her fetus and her apples and walked down the hill to the nearest park.

There was a deer in the park when she got there, and it gave her a long stare, ears twitching, then went back to eating, picking over the ground on spindly legs. A movement in some brush behind the doe revealed a fawn, big-eared and spotted. Except for the deer, the park was empty, and Maddy could see why Jada liked it here: city, but not *too* city, deer crossing neighborhood streets and munching on people's petunias. She liked the idea of the wild infiltrating the man-made; she preferred it to the idea of the man-made infiltrating the wild, and so she chose to view the deer's presence in the city park as a triumph rather than a defeat, to see the two as things harmoniously intertwined rather than in fierce competition. She sat on a bench, took out her phone, and swiped and scrolled, first men and then, for the second time, couples looking to adopt.

"Have you thought any more about adoption?" Pat had asked the last time they spoke, after they'd prayed together. So now, to do her due diligence, she was thinking about it, recalling Pastor Dan's story about Abraham and Sarah. Not every couple benefited from miracles, and she liked the idea of creating or at least contributing to a family, even if it wasn't her own. Until she began browsing adoption sites, she had not realized that a birth mother could choose her baby's family or continue to be involved in their life; she had not bothered to think of such a choice as an act of love. She'd been ignorant, and she wanted to be better.

Couples carving pumpkins, couples playing Monopoly, couples hiking, swing dancing, flipping burgers on a grill, pulling fresh-baked cookies out of ovens. *Our rescue dogs love children. We own a home in a safe and tight-knit community with caring neighbors. We live on a cul-de-sac in a diverse neighborhood in an excellent school district. We've tried for ten years to conceive a child naturally. We believe that adoption is our calling. We can't imagine how you must be feeling right now and admire your heroism and selflessness in the midst of a challenging situation.* Potential parents wearing cheesy holiday sweaters, cheering on football teams, throwing a ball for a border collie, eating tacos, training for triathlons.

The profiles moved and troubled Maddy. Some couples posted videos that made her cry. What was the right thing, the good thing? Would she be good if she gave one of these couples the baby they longed for—would she be, as some of them had written in their letters, a hero? And if she was so good and so heroic, if she had the capacity for selfless love many of them cited, why should she—or anyone—think she could not be a good mother?

She looked up from her screen. The day was heating up, the park was getting busier. The doe and her fawn were gone, and Maddy was flooded by a sudden fear on their behalf, surprising in its intensity: of cars and buses, all the material perils of the world, the things that could smash and kill. That Bambi's-dead-mother horror: she couldn't stand it. She imagined taking both deer home to Jada's apartment, feeding them from bottles, building for them a nest of blankets, branches, leaves, converting futon to feeding trough. Corn to eat, salt to lick. She remembered the apples she'd brought and pulled out the bag only to find that the wedges had already begun to brown. Their softened edges sickened her, and she tossed them in the direction of a squirrel.

She closed her browser and called Pat. It rang once, twice. The sun beat down, and sweat chilled the space between her breasts. A bead of it rolled, slimy and sexy, down Maddy's back, dipping beneath the silk line of her panties, and she was stricken by an urge to undress. To stand naked in a garden full of snakes! *That* was an apple she would have eaten, she knew for certain; she would have plucked the Edenic fruit from the branch in a heartbeat, even as she threw her own to rodents.

A third ring, a fourth. So far there had never been a time when Pat had not answered her call, and Maddy wondered whether Pat slept or had sex. Pictured her enormous dough-ball breasts bouncing. Then Pat answered—"Maddy!"—and the bouncing ceased.

"I've been thinking about what you said," Maddy said. "About adoption. I just don't see how I could give my child away."

"Maybe don't think of it as 'giving away' the baby," Pat said, "but as choosing adoption *for* your baby. It would be a tough choice, but giving it a lot of thought and choosing a great adoptive family would do a lot to help alleviate those feelings of regret."

FEELINGS OF GRIEF AND REGRET: Maddy recalled the words from one of the pamphlets Pat had given her to warn her against abortion. Why should the prospect of those feelings give her pause in one context but not another? Why should she be made to feel that she could overcome them in one context but not the other?

"Can I ask you something?" she asked Pat.

"Of course."

"Why is adoption regret 'good' regret but regret over an abortion 'bad' regret?"

"Well," Pat said, "because you and Blake would be doing what you deemed best for your baby."

Maddy covered her face with her hand. The lie she'd told, the name she'd given—she'd had no idea how it would come back to tease her.

"Anyway, most adoptions are open these days," Pat went on, "which means birth parents can have some form of ongoing contact with their children."

Maddy knew this, thanks to her research. "It still makes me sad."

"Well," Pat said, "you could always wait until after you've had the baby to decide."

She felt a sudden need to distance herself from Pat's voice, and she held the phone out from her face. That Pat would encourage her to kick the can of her decision that far down the road, to wait until after she had pushed her body to the limit, after she'd seen the child's face—it made Maddy's chest feel tight and stony. That Pat would work so hard to save her from having to choose whether or not to keep her fetus, only to see her have to choose whether or not to keep her baby—it made her sick.

Her own separation from her mother broke her heart. It re-broke it every day. She could not imagine inflicting another separation like it on herself, or on a child.

"You know," Pat continued, "that feeling of holding your baby for the first time—there's nothing like it, Maddy."

She could not ask her mother what this feeling was like, she could not ask her grandmother or Jada, so she asked, "What was it like for you?"

"For me?"

"Yeah."

"Oh, I don't have children."

Maddy was confused. "You . . . you're not a mom?"

"No," Pat said. "I'm a volunteer."

Maddy was quiet.

"I have lots of nieces and nephews. I love babies. I just don't have any of my own."

It didn't matter, Maddy told herself; why should it matter? A woman could have any number of reasons for being childless. But *this* woman?

She could not help herself. "Why?"

Now it was Pat who went quiet. "Well, Maddy," she said, "that's personal."

Maddy held the phone out from her face again, saw her reflection in the screen, her hair frizzed with humidity. She examined it as if it were the phone that had spoken, and not someone's voice through it, and she saw how she had made herself a window for Pat, showed her everything inside. *Personal* was an ultrasound wand inserted into her vagina. Personal was a photograph of the inside of her womb, the sound of her baby's heartbeat. Her embrace was personal; her tears were personal; her prayers were personal. Personal was a phone call on a Saturday morning, made from a park bench where she had gone to give good-faith thought to a thing she'd been encouraged, in seeming good faith, to think about, a thing that could forever change her life. *That's* personal.

She could hear Pat's muffled voice issuing from the speaker: "Maddy? Are you there?" She slid her finger over the screen's hot, glassy surface, and tapped to end the call. She realized she was crying—because of hormones; because of God, who brings the rain; because of baby fawns braving urban parks; because she had lost someone, not a mother but a woman who had sometimes served as one, who had held her, answered her calls, given her counsel; because of all the people out there who had felt unable to parent their children and so, in love and pain, relinquished their care; because of all the others who wanted a child and didn't have one; because she was alone.

She did not want to be Pat's baby bird. She blocked the number and deleted the conversation from her recent calls and felt, as she did, both a profound loneliness and a starburst of power in her chest. Maybe she had EMPOWERED HERSELF after all, just as the sign at New Dawn had promised, if not in the way they'd hoped. She could choose not only what to do about her baby—to have, to keep, to let go—but what to do with the living people in her orbit. Have, keep, let go.

\*       \*       \*

Jada and Drew weren't there when she got back to the apartment, and Maddy was glad. She had one more call to make, and she wanted to make it without an audience.

She would do it, she told herself, once she'd had a cup of tea. She heated water in the microwave, plopped in a bag of Earl Grey. Once the tea had steeped, she told herself she'd call once it was cool enough to sip as she talked. Once the tea was cool, she told herself she needed a snack—toast baked with butter and cinnamon sugar, a longtime favorite. Her stomach turned at the smell of chilled leftovers and the sight of a squeezed mayonnaise bottle when she opened the refrigerator door, and she hurried to the toilet, thinking she'd puke. Once she'd not puked, once she'd buttered and baked the bread, she told herself she'd call after she'd eaten it.

She squeezed her eyes shut. *Pray,* she thought, but no prayer came. *Pray!* What better time than now? *Oh God,* she thought, *Our father—* she thought of her father—*give me strength.* She clasped her fingers and felt her palms slurp together. She concentrated, but she did not know what to say, could not summon the same ecstasy she'd felt in church, that sense of being swathed in a love that would shelter her from harm. He loved her, she reminded herself. God. He worked in the dark, and apparently, also, in silence. He would not give her words. She would have to come up with her own.

When her father picked up, she started speaking before he could say hello. "Dad," she said, "there's something I have to tell you. Please don't freak out."

He waited.

"Will you promise not to freak out?"

"I promise."

She gathered her courage, but the words wouldn't come. She anticipated his *I told you so.* After all, he had. How many times had he told her, *You're not going out of the house like that*, when in fact she very much was, one foot already out the door? She'd be at the threshold in a skirt like a lampshade or a tank top that exposed her belly, clothes she'd bought with her own money, and he would issue this nonfactual statement as if casting an ineffectual spell. One night as she prepared to bolt from the heat of the house to the heat of her already-running car in the driveway, he threw his Carhartt at her and said, *For Christ's sake, you're half-naked, you want to end up pregnant?* and she said, *Clothes don't get you pregnant*, and sprang out the door.

"Chiclet," he said.

"Dad."

"Is this about the baby?"

Maddy felt sick. "You know?"

"Jada told me."

"Why didn't you say anything?"

"Say what? It was up to you to tell me."

"Apparently not." Her voice rose. "Apparently it was up to Jada." Maddy wiped her face, snot streaking her arm. She had lost control of her body, which peed and peed and cried without her consent, and now she had lost control even of her secret, which had been sneaking around behind her back, circulating like a naked selfie.

"Don't be mad at her," her father said. "She just wants to help. She's willing to help you, you know . . . take care of it."

"She doesn't want to. It's not her kid." Her father was quiet, so she said again, loudly, "Jada doesn't want to take care of it."

"Chiclet," he said after another pause.

"Don't call me that."

"You're so young."

"I know how old I am. I don't need a lecture."

"Maddy—"

"There isn't anything you can say that I haven't already said to myself," she said. "I'm not asking you for anything. I don't need you."

"Maddy," he said again, sternly.

"You don't have to help me," she went on, "but you also don't have to yell at me."

"I'm not yelling," he yelled. "Please just listen. When I graduated—"

"Not this again." She had heard this story a hundred times. Now she listened as he told it again: when he graduated from high school, his father had given him an itemized bill for all the things he and his mother had bought for him as a child, from diapers to tennis shoes. And he had paid it back.

"Every cent," he said.

"I know, Daddy. You want a medal or something?" She remembered hearing the story for the first time. At the end, he'd said, *And you girls live like princesses.*

"What I'm trying to say," he said, "is that you can ask."

"For my bill? My big fat debt?"

"*No,*" he said. "Goddamn it, Maddy. You can ask for help. From me. If that's really what you want."

Why wasn't he mad at her? "Thanks," she said with caution.

"And if that's not what you want . . . that's okay too."

She sniffled, wiped her nose again. "What?"

"You don't have to have the baby if you don't want to."

She was too surprised to know what to think or feel. It was like there'd been a small explosion in her head, everything smoky, debris scattered. "So you're pro-life except when it's your grandchild?"

"It's complicated. It's a gray area."

"But what's the point?" she gasped. "What's the point of having principles if at any time you can just ignore them?"

He sighed. "I guess it seems different when it happens to you," he said, "than when it happens to other people."

"Why, though? What other people?" She did not know why she was raising her voice, or even if she was angry. "I am the other person, Dad. We are the other people."

The smoke had begun to clear, and she saw how badly she had needed him to give permission: to be a mother, but also, to not be one. Whether or not she used it was almost beside the point; it was the having it that mattered, that meant that her choice could truly be one. She should not need this permission from him. Jada had gotten and ungotten pregnant without thinking about men or their feelings about it; she did not need to go to their father as before a judge, hadn't told him and never would. A stronger woman than Maddy might need approval only from herself, dads be damned, but the truth was she *had* needed his, or at least wanted it, and it would not help to beat herself up for it.

*There's nothing like it, Maddy*—Pat didn't know what she was talking about, but Maddy's father knew. He had held her when she was brand-new, red-faced and sinless. He'd held her later, bigger, a difficult daughter, climbing the furniture, running where she should walk. *Be brave,* he said in her memory, *hold still*—she was seven, running on the deck, where she'd tripped on a warped board and fallen—and she did, trusting him, and he held her firmly against him, pulled the angry shiv of a splinter from her palm.

"Dad," she said. "What did it feel like when you held me when I was born?"

A pause on the other end of the call. "What's that?"

He hadn't heard her. Maybe she hadn't meant him to. "Never mind," she said, and then yelled, "I love you" in the tone and at the volume that a different person in a different family might use to say the opposite, and hung up.

\*          \*          \*

She was so mad at Jada she could hardly see straight. Though the call had gone better than she'd expected, her news had not been shared on her own terms. Jada had taken something from her, and she wanted it back. She could speak for herself, and Jada wasn't the only one who could share news that wasn't hers.

She went straight to Blake's, rang the bell.

"There's something I think you should know," she said. "Can I come in?"

They sat at opposite ends of the couch. Jake clawed at the living room rug. Blake's facial hair was growing out, looking patchy and cute. "I used to hate facial hair," he said when he caught her looking at it, "but then it grew on me."

She smiled, hesitated. Already her anger was cooling.

He looked at her expectantly. "There's someone else," he said, "isn't there."

"It might be nothing."

"Or not." His eyes narrowed. "What did you see? I want to know."

She was quiet. She felt both righteous and dirty—a defender of truth, a deserter of sisters. What if he went apeshit, hurt Jada? He wasn't like that, yet Maddy thought of something Jada had said to her, years ago: in some ways, the good guys could be their own kind of bad. Their mommies had told them they were nice boys, and it went to their heads, and they grew up to assume that their niceness would be redeemable. They wanted a prize.

"I deserve to know," he said.

Her father's voice: *Jada told me.* Her mother's voice, when Maddy presented her with the printout about the Tijuanan apricot extract treatment, the money she had saved, that Jada had let her save, believing Ellen still had a chance: *Oh, honey, no. It's just more poison.*

"It's Drew," she said.

"That guy."

"They're friends."

He snorted. "Are they . . ."

"Just hanging out. A little. Here and there."

He searched her face. She tried to guess how to mold her expression into one that was knowing and sympathetic, to say with her face, *See how faithful I am?* She felt her loyalties shifting—to him, to Jada—and told herself this was okay, she had made him a promise and needed to keep it, he had always been so nice to her, to Wilson. . . .

"Women are like monkeys," she paraphrased. "Won't let go of one branch until they've got ahold of the next one."

*"Mission Impossible II."*

"The branches are men," she said, and immediately felt stupid, shitty—stating the obvious, and stating it against her sister, her flesh and blood.

"She's leaving me for that guy," he said, "is what you're telling me."

"It's just a movie line."

"The thing is, I don't know if she ever let go of that branch. Of him, I mean."

"She married you," Maddy said, not knowing what she was trying to say, or on whose behalf.

"Thank you, Maddy." He went upstairs, and she heard their bedroom door open and slam closed, and then she heard nothing for a very long time.

She sat on the couch, hand on her belly. Was she supposed to leave? It wasn't like him not to see a guest off. Was she supposed to go in there? She took a few tentative steps toward the stairs, a few tentative steps up them. They did not creak like the stairs in her parents' house or Jada's building; she could move stealthily, like a robber. She stopped outside his door. She didn't know how long she stood there, motionless.

"Blake?" she peeped.

No answer. She opened the door.

He was sitting on the bed, staring at the white wall. The bedroom smelled like feet and cologne. Clothes were strewn on the floor. The face of his bedside digital clock was blank until she moved in front of it, her movement lighting up white numbers. Next to the clock, a full glass of water, his phone on a charger. The bed was unmade, the pillows sunk down in the gap between the headboard and the mattress. She sat next to him, tried a dad joke. "I don't trust stairs."

He looked at her like he'd just remembered she was there.

"They're always up to something," she finished.

He didn't say anything. She studied the curve of his jawline, stubbled yet sharp. She traced it with her eyes, following it from ear to ear, a kind of throat slitting. A huge bronze-rimmed floor mirror leaned against the wall, reflecting Jada's half-emptied dresser across the room. A few forgotten photos in frames still sat on its surface. Maddy squinted into the glass, studied the pictures, and recognized, rimmed in wood, her own face: her senior portrait.

"Can I get you a drink?" she asked, and immediately hoped he'd say no; she did not know how to mix what he liked, or much of anything.

"No, thank you." The screen of his phone lit up with a Tinder notification, and Maddy felt nearly choked with relief: he had his own thing going on. By telling on Jada (and what had she really told?), she had not, it seemed, become the thing that would end their marriage. She hadn't done anything wrong.

He followed her eyes, flipped the phone upside down. "I'm not using it," he said. "I don't do anything."

"I'm not judging."

"Why would she be unhappy with me?"

"I don't know."

"I deserve better."

"I know."

It felt intimate, sitting on the bed with him, the sheets vaguely musky. "At least she didn't get you pregnant," she tried, and put a hand on her stomach.

He smiled ever so slightly. Hands clasped, elbows on his knees, shoulders slumped, he turned to look at her. "You're a good kid, Maddy," he said, and her irritation at being called a kid barely had time to kindle before he followed up the compliment with a better one. "You're going to make a great mom."

She felt gooey, joyful, sneaky, sad. There was more she could tell him, but she couldn't bring herself to do it. She'd done enough already.

"You'd make a great dad, too," she said, and then she reached out, touched his arm just a hair too tenderly, a hair too long. She knew it as soon as it had happened, as soon as she saw the shine of her grandmother's ring against his skin; she felt him tighten, scoot away, and her stomach sank.

"You should probably go," he said.

She stood and looked around the room for what she was certain would be the last time—the artless walls and casement windows, the midcentury dressers with their tiny knobs and thin gold handles, the floor mirror propped against the wall, his hunched back turned to her—and hurried out. She rushed down the stairs, past the cat perched on the windowsill with its tail tick-tocking side to side. She was still the girl who'd gone to Jason despite knowing she shouldn't, staring in the face of her own self-destructiveness and self-destructing anyway. She dashed out the door with a hand over her heart—her heart still, after everything, a stupid slut, bare naked, wide-open, too eager by half.

Outside, trembling, she placed her final call of the day. It went straight to voicemail.

"This is Butterfield Events and Catering," she said at the tone. "We found . . . a typo in your contract. Please call us back at your earliest convenience."

# 17

## JADA

**April 2018**

Drew was gone and Maddy was nowhere to be found when Jada got the text from Blake: *We need to talk.* Not at the apartment, he said, and not in public. In their home. She took three ibuprofen to try to banish the headache she'd woken up with. The sensation she had of moving in slow motion as she prepared to drive to the town house sent her back, in her mind, to the end of her pregnancy.

She'd had to make three trips to the clinic to get her abortion. One to confirm her pregnancy and receive counseling mandated by the state. One to take her first pill, a progesterone blocker, and to receive the second, which was to be taken at home. One for a follow-up. Each time, she made a playlist. She rallied herself with the sound of women's voices while she got dressed, ate oatmeal. With her earbuds in and a cheerleading chorus in her ears, everything down to dried cranberries seemed imbued with a special power, and she became like an audience to herself, a woman watching a stirring movie montage about a woman who happened to be her. She was fired up on her behalf, ready to go. Then the music stopped and the world got quiet, and she became self-conscious, tiptoeing around the house like she was trying not to wake someone sleeping, tiptoeing to the clinic, tiptoeing past the protesters.

They were required to respect the city's buffer zone ordinance, positioning themselves at its edges, leaning toward her with their upper bodies and their shouting signs: EMPOWER YOURSELF: CHOOSE LIFE or ABORTION LEAVES MEMORIES OF A DEAD BABY or LOVE THY UNBORN NEIGHBOR AS YOU LOVE YOURSELF. One man held a sign that said I WILL ADOPT AND LOVE YOUR CHILD. A surprising number of the protesters were men in their fifties or sixties, though there were also kids in the crowd, crammed in next to their parents like examples of something—like she did not know what children were and needed to see a specimen in order to understand their appeal. Mostly, the picketers stood quietly, holding their signs, though a few attempted sidewalk counseling, calling to her in cruel or kind tones. Someone held out a white rose with a note tied around the stem. Someone prayed a rosary. Someone pushed a stroller in which plastic baby dolls of different sizes were displayed. Someone shouted something about clinic staff eating babies. A woman about Jada's age had leaned out and spat on the pavement in her direction. A small buzz then, people chastising her; spit was not part of their strategy. They were there, as they saw it, to educate her.

By the time she got inside, she was shaken. She had thought that if you didn't consider something a sin yourself, it shouldn't matter if other people did, that if she rejected the premise of others' disapproval, it could not touch her. But people spent energy hating her, they took time out of their day to make her feel bad, and she was not a block of concrete, okay? She could not have anticipated, at the time, how in the weeks to come it would be as if the protesters had exclusive access to her every thought and action. When she was in the closet, they were in the closet. When she was in the bath, they were in the water with her. She could not have known when she went to the clinic that she would have yet another choice to make even after the pregnancy had ended, as grave as the one she'd already made: she could trust herself, or she could believe the story they wanted to tell about her. It should have been an easier choice than it would turn out to be.

The waiting room looked like a classroom. Recessed lighting, carpet trying to be fun, chairs arranged in rows, a whiteboard that visitors were invited to draw or write on but that was empty except for a handprint someone had traced there. In the exam room, a nurse named Tina cited measurements and probable gestational age, noted cardiac motion, informed her of the medical risks of carrying a child to term, read from the state informed-consent script. A framed beachscape hung on the wall. Jada was offered an illustrated packet published by the PA Department of Health, *Abortion: Making a Decision*, that included a calendar of fetus photos and that she refused.

"I read up on this online," she said. "The state publication."

"Did your homework," Tina said. Though her voice remained cheerful, she seemed unimpressed.

Jada answered a string of questions, which Tina was artful enough to fold into something resembling a naturally flowing conversation: she was safe at home; no one had hit, slapped, or kicked her; she lived with her husband; he had never forced her to have sex or made it difficult for her to use her contraception. She could feel Tina probing as neutrally as possible for the information she needed, careful not to lead her in any particular direction, and she appreciated her precision. It was good data collection.

"I just can't have a child right now," Jada said.

Tina nodded.

"I know it might seem like I can, but I can't."

"You don't have to explain, baby."

Jada had been agitated throughout the rest of their conversation, hung up on the need she'd felt to explain herself. As if her reason were any different from anyone else's; as if she were different from the clinic's other visitors—like they didn't have their lives together in the way she did, made bad choices where she typically made good ones, were poor where she was poor no longer, slept with bad men while she slept with her good husband. The clinic was a place where she did not have to explain herself, where to do so was not only redundant but narcissistic, and yet she had sacrificed this safety, she had spoiled this respite from judgment. She had been a snob.

She had an urge to apologize to Tina but feared the apology would make things worse, and so she sat there feeling guilty for not wanting a child, feeling guilty for feeling guilty for not wanting a child, scolding herself for her snobbery and scolding herself for endlessly scolding herself, because why couldn't she just acknowledge her error and move on, why should she self-flagellate in an unending loop when her very self-flagellation was itself narcissistic, a sign that she held herself to a higher standard than she held others not just when it came to preventing unwanted pregnancy but when it came to being a good person, a good liberal; a sign that she couldn't look beyond herself and her problems, that she insisted on magnifying them when other people had bigger problems, and she should focus on those people and those problems, and meanwhile she couldn't get the image of those awful baby dolls in the protest stroller out of her head, the spit on the sidewalk, and she was angry at herself for still thinking about them, giving them power over her, when she was supposed to know better than that, be stronger than that. Her anxiety mounted, her head hurt, and she felt terrible, but not for any of the reasons she might have expected going into the clinic, and this was her state when she went out of it; put *that* on a pamphlet.

At home, while Blake was in Tampa, she sat in her living room with Catalina and held the pill inside her cheek until it dissolved. It tasted bitter. When she felt the clot pass, the relief and the pain took her breath away.

When Jada got to the house, Blake was waiting for her. "Your sister was here," he said.

"Why?"

"You tell me."

"I don't know." She sat down in the chenille tweed swivel chair, turning it a bit with one foot, the other propped beneath her. He sat on the couch, his hair unkempt, his facial hair spotty.

"She's fucked up," he said.

"All right," she said. Her headache was fighting back, and she rubbed her temple. "That's not helpful. She's doing the best she can."

"She came on to me."

Jada winced. "No, she didn't."

"Her hand on my arm, like . . ." He mimicked what Maddy had done.

"She's confused. She didn't mean anything by it."

"She needs help."

"I know. But I don't understand . . . when did this happen?"

"Just now. Today." He got up and stood before the unlit fireplace, one hand on the mantel. "And she told me something interesting."

Oh no. Jada felt herself go pale. Maddy couldn't have—could she?

"You've been seeing that guy." Just as Drew had never said Blake's name, Blake had never said Drew's. That guy, that other guy.

"I've been hanging out with Drew," she said, rocking in the swivel chair. A tentative relief pulsed through her.

"A lot, according to Maddy."

"A bit."

"Are you sleeping with him?"

"No." Not in the way he meant. Not that it mattered. Anything where Drew was concerned was so fraught with significance that even if they'd only met for coffee, Blake's feelings of betrayal would be almost as justified as if she'd *slept*-slept with him. It was true that lying next to him last night had felt like a kind of coming home; but so, somehow, did sleeping alone, head and toes at a diagonal across the mattress, taking all the space for herself.

But it seemed Blake didn't know the other thing. If she was going to tell him, this was the time, but what could she say to him that would make him understand? What could he say to her that she hadn't said to herself a hundred times? *If you spent five minutes inside my brain,* she wanted to say—to him, to the picketers, to the whole world, with their opinions—*if you could crack the door to my head and hear all this noise, you'd shut up.* Her decision had been not impulsive, as he would assume, but reasoned through and informed—by her knowledge of herself, and by her knowledge of him. *Please. It's so loud in here.* But he would ask why, why, as if there could be no reason for what she'd done; blinded by his own pain, he would not see the ways she had suffered.

Why, why? There was so much she could say. Why: because she might have half-assed marriage and half-assed sisterhood, but she wanted to whole-ass motherhood, and she did not have a whole ass to give right now. Why: not because she had no reverence for life, but because she had plenty—including reverence for her own.

Why: when she remembered her march up the path to the clinic like a canceled celebrity on a hellish red carpet, Jada thought of the backwards birthday party her mother had thrown her when she turned eight, hurling herself into the planning and execution of the party with as much zeal as she had hurled herself into pretty much everything before she got sick. She'd made invitations by hand that read

*You're invited to Jada's Backwards Birthday Party!*

There was a note at the bottom: *If you can't read me, hold me up to a mirror.* At the party, Jada and her mother wore their shirts backward and inside out and greeted guests at the door with goodbyes, and when it came time to eat, Ellen spread a tablecloth on the floor, and the kids sat underneath the table eating burgers on upside-down buns and singing, *You to birthday happy, you to birthday happy.* When Jada thought of children, of the type of parent she'd want to be, she thought of this scene and of the photo memento she still had of that day, a picture of her and her mother with their backs to the camera and their arms around one another. She thought of the scavenger hunt her mother had set up. The kids had set off to gather clues, words written backward on notes hidden around the house and yard that they had to unscramble to determine the cake's location. Most of Jada's friends had found notes, but Jada had not, and with only one remaining, she wandered the yard, frustrated.

Then she saw the garden, the gazing ball: her favorite place, a place her mother would not have left empty. She ran to it and, sure enough, saw the corner of a note sticking out from under the reflective blue globe, where so many times she'd stood with her mother and seen their faces distorted and reflected side by side. With both hands she unseated the ball from its pedestal, removed the clue. She ran back to her friends, victorious and full of love for her mother, who had arranged a charmed world around her, who had made her feel, however temporarily, like she was at the center of something, safe, and that someone would do their best to stash the clues to life in a place where she could find them. If she were a mother, she would want to give her child that same assurance of being central, of being propped up by a firm foundation of love. She would want to do for the child the things her mother had done for her. But when she imagined doing those things, organizing enchanted birthday parties, she knew she wasn't ready. She was not yet ready to be anything other than her mother's daughter.

She missed her mother. She missed the mirror ball in the garden and her mother's face and her own inside it. She missed the yellow columbine at its base, the dirt under Ellen's fingernails. She missed the trick candles she could not put out no matter how hard she blew and the scoops of strawberry ice cream her mother served that day in bowls with upside-down Joy cones stuck on top. She missed the happiness she had seemed to generate for her mother simply by being happy herself. She missed being happy. She did not miss the cell cluster that had clumped in her uterus or the prospect of the modified life it had asked her to envision.

She could tell Blake this. But then she thought of him stripping on the pool deck, sitting at the bottom of the pool with bubbles coming up from his nose, and she felt that to tell him would be unbearably cruel, when she had caused him enough pain already. Making him her judge would not serve either of them; neither would making him her confessor. Unloading this weight on him for the sake of clearing her own conscience would not change what had happened, and her reasons could not buy her his empathy, just like they could not buy her the goodwill of the person who spat at her.

Why had she gotten rid of it? Why had she said no? Of all the possible answers, there was only one that mattered, and at the end of the day, she was the only one who needed to accept it. She had done it because she wanted to.

He was giving her the math-problem look, eyes roaming her face for answers, signs of her feelings for Drew. "Do you love him?" he asked.

"Yes," she said, and watched him shatter, hurting, not knowing the final hurt she'd spared him.


Back and forth they went until late into the night, again—his point of view, hers. Why don't you want what I want, what does he have that I don't. Eventually he landed on, "We could go to therapy. We could work harder."

She had not expected him to say this and found that her heart fell at the proposal. "I don't want to go to therapy," she said.

"You're always advocating counseling to everyone else."

"I just don't see the point. This isn't working."

"We could fix it."

"I don't know if that's true."

"Of course it's true."

"Well," she said, "I don't think I want to fix it. I'm sorry."

He looked at her vacantly, his hands at his sides. "Why?"

Because there were times when the sick body must, at last, refuse the medicine, and she had learned to recognize those times. There was a time when, like her father who rose each morning to trudge to work at the sawmill, she would have done what he'd always told her and Ellen and Maddy to do—*suck it up*—and done her duty without heart and without objection, but this was not that time. What she had acquired over the years through experience and education, what she had exercised in her abortion and now would exercise again in her marriage, was a kind of privilege that should not be one. It was the privilege of being able to say no.

"But, Jada," he said weakly, "we belong together."

When she didn't respond, he stiffened. "You're going to be with him."

"This isn't about him. It's about me and you."

"You're leaving me for him," he charged again. "Aren't you?"

"I don't know," she said, and meant it.

He went tearing through the house, picking objects up and setting them down, breathing so hard. How hard was too hard? Ever since the incident at the party, he had seemed newly erratic to her. Would he jump off the balcony? she wondered, and her panic increased when she concluded that she didn't know. Anything seemed possible. Her head pounded, a throbbing behind her eyes.

"You aren't even grateful," he said, picking up the TV remote, a half-burnt candle, "for what I did for you." She looked around, trying to think what to say, but he cut her off: "Not the house, Jada. I'm talking about loving you."

After a while he started throwing away the things he picked up: the candle, some too-brown bananas, a wedding photo in a frame. "I don't want these," he said, and looked around for something larger. "I don't need a crystal bowl." He dropped it into the trash. She heard a heavy thunk as it met the bottom of the can.

"Stop," she pleaded.

"What was the point?" he asked. "Why did you marry me? Why did you waste my time?"

She wanted to say that she'd had every intention of making it work, but he was busy throwing out a cheese board.

"Please stop," she said. "Couldn't one of us still use a cheese board?"

"Not this one. This is a wedding cheese board."

"You're being irrational."

"And this is a wedding cheese knife."

She grabbed the garbage can and pulled it away, stepping in front of it. It cowered behind her like a child as the knife hit the floor.

"A waste," Blake said. "Waste of time, waste of money."

Back and forth, back and forth. She followed him as he paced around, inventorying. "I don't even like this bedspread," he said in the bedroom. "I like prints. Geometrics."

"I didn't know that."

"I like color. Big, bright flowers."

"I'm sorry," she said, sitting down on the bed. "I thought you liked white."

"And why are these things still here?" He held up a picture of Maddy she'd forgotten on top of her dresser, some tubes of Chap-Stick, a pair of snow boots, the toes melted where she'd propped them too close to a campfire. "Move out or don't move out. Don't leave your things in my house."

"Okay."

He sat down next to her. "You're going to regret this."

"Maybe." He looked at her like he'd won something, but she went on, "But it's what I have to do."

"That doesn't make sense," Blake said.

She felt herself growing impatient, kept her mouth shut. What she'd tell him, if she thought he'd listen, was born not only of her experience but of her research: dispense with the notion that humans are rational choosers. Dispense with the idea that we will inevitably, out of practicality and self-awareness, reject what will hurt us and embrace what won't, reject what doesn't make sense and embrace what does. Dispense with these things and the sad, strange world will, paradoxically, make a little more sense.

For years, until recently, Jada had seen a therapist, Deena. They spoke mostly of her mother, but Blake had come up, too. Jada had liked Deena because she didn't just hide behind a clipboard but shared her own experience where she thought it might be helpful. She told Jada that on the day she decided to leave her marriage, she had had an epiphany: she had looked across the dining table at her husband picking the baby corn out of his Thai noodles, and she had known that the marriage had to end. *And I didn't look back.* She had challenged Jada to keep her heart open for such a moment of clarity in her own life. *I want that for you,* she'd said. *Certainty.*

After that session Jada had not gone back. She did not know at first what it was about Deena's story that had disconcerted her, but eventually it sank in that there had not been a single moment when she'd been as firmly, lastingly, liberatingly certain about anything as Deena had described. The lightning bolt she spoke of seemed enviable but unachievable in Jada's own life. When clarity had come to her—as when she had known she would have the abortion, as with the thing with her mother—it had been painful and guilt-ridden, not a triumph but a reconciliation, ongoing and arduous. She was going to leave, but not without looking back, and not without fear.

He was looking at her with begging eyes. He put his hand on her knee, slid it slowly up her thigh.

At first she shook her head, but then she softened. One more time, then; one more yes. Off with her shirt, her jeans. It was cold in the room. He had turned the thermostat down with her gone, its usual setting the result of a compromise they'd made that he no longer needed to honor. He tipped her back on the bed. Her head struck the headboard.

"Ow," she breathed, and he said, "Sorry," and she centered herself on the mattress, and her bent knee stabbed his thigh, and he said, "Ow," and she said, "Sorry," and it was almost too sad to bear. They had been good once. His bedside water sat untouched on the nightstand, the sheets were creased and oily. His hands were like ice, and the AC blew chilly air on her bare skin, and she said, "It's too cold" and tugged at the duvet beneath her, and he climbed off, let her climb under, then got in beside her, hands still so cold. She focused on her body. Goose bumps on her skin. He was crying.

In their famous longitudinal study, psychologists John Gottman and Robert Levenson determined a ratio of positive to negative affective experiences that predicted relationship stability and success. Stable couples, they determined, were those who demonstrated a 5:1 ratio of positive to negative experiences. What those experiences consisted of hardly mattered; the formula had less to do with what was said or done by a couple than with how much and how it felt. As long as positive affective experiences outweighed negative ones by a factor of five, the relationship typically remained intact. As Jada pushed against Blake, she ran the math in her head, ran back through time.

That time at Acadia; he'd just lain in the tent and whined. That time at trivia; she had been embarrassed of him. That time at his parents'; he'd been embarrassed of her. *Couchette, croquette,* but also: the time she brought home the cat; the time he tied her shoes; the times they'd stayed up all night talking. The two of them on the beach in Positano, when they'd stood with their feet sunk into pebbles up to the ankles, holding hands and swaying like trees, the waves lapping at their calves, balconied homes in shades of orange and yellow climbing the cliff behind them. She'd just eaten a lemon cake garnished with a spiraled peel and a heart-shaped slice of strawberry on a terrace overlooking the sea, her tongue sweet and sour. "Where should we go next?" he'd asked. She couldn't remember her answer, just that the question had exhilarated her, and that after she'd answered, he'd asked, "Where next?" again, and they went on like that, planning to see the world together. Jada remembered the moment as a pure one, one she had occupied willingly and completely, no distractions. In all likelihood, though, this moment she traveled to now had itself been stuffed with other moments, anxieties, preoccupations she couldn't quantify or arrange in the necessary ratio to mathematically determine her marriage's odds of survival. In all likelihood, as her body swayed on the Amalfi Coast that afternoon, her mind had been, as always, as now, half somewhere else.

Their honeymoon, Florence. She went back to a lazy morning, a rumpled bed, an open window. The terra-cotta shingles on Brunelleschi's dome, the marble of the Duomo, green and white and coral pink. Pigeons on the balcony, the iridescence of their puffed chests, the vibrations of their voice boxes. The streets coming alive, the hum of early-risen tourists, a man shouting, *Sandro? Sandro!* as the light stretched into the room. Even from inside it the scene had felt stolen or constructed, a set of something—so cinematic, so perfect it hurt. What had she done to deserve this moment, this light, this life? Why had he chosen her?

She'd asked, "What would you do if I died?"

Blake had rolled onto his side, propped himself on an elbow. "Well," he said, "I'd be devastated."

"Would you remarry?"

He'd studied her, looking for the right answer in her eyes. "Would you want me to?"

"Of course. I wouldn't want you to be lonely."

"Then I guess I would. For you." He'd paused, then asked, "Would you?"

Jada put her hands together and framed the view from the window with her thumbs and forefingers. "Would you want me to?"

"No."

"No?"

"No way," he said.

"What if I did?"

He'd grabbed her, pulled her close. "I'd haunt you."

Now he labored over her, his cheek pressed against hers, his stubble chafing. *Labor,* she thought—for men, this was it, the work, the birth pain that was not one. She could not remember what came next that Florentine morning. Sex, maybe; an argument. The passage of an hour, a day, a year. But in her memory of the moment, his words coincided with the clamor of the seven bells of the campanile striking the hour—which hour?—in a chorus of chimes and peals.

That life was ending, the bells' toll a memorial. She grieved for it as he would have grieved for their child, because she felt then that, whatever your politics, to end a marriage was to end a life.

"Pull out," she reminded him, pressing at his chest. Her fingers dug into his skin. When she drew her arm back, it bumped the glass of water on the nightstand, and it toppled and fell to the floor. He came in a hot rush on her stomach, filling the crater of her belly button, then collapsed onto his back beside her, her skin cold again where the warmth of his body had been.

*I'd haunt you*—yeah, maybe he would. The great counterfactual, the what-if-I'd-stayed, a ghost to rival her mother in his omnipresence. Maybe he would.

"Thank you," he said, and she knew it was over.

# 18

## JADA

*July 2016*

It could never have been a backyard wedding. The day Jada brings
Blake home to explore the idea, there's black smoke and a toxic smell:
the neighbors have brought a recliner outside and set it on fire. Her
mother has stopped gardening, and the beds are overgrown. It's been
a wet summer, and the mosquitoes are ravenous, and the ground
in the yard is soft and muddy, not suitable for guests' heeled shoes
or clean slacks or parked cars, and there's no shoulder on the road.
There's nowhere nearby for guests to stay. The colorful paint on the
house's deck railings is peeling, put there during her mother's summer of painting, when she was well and sat outside with a caked
brush and tubes of acrylic paint and an old yogurt cup full of cloudy
water, marking everything in bold primary colors: Maddy's bedroom
furniture, the railings, random stones in the driveway, striped and
polka-dotted and zigzagged. Ellen doesn't have the energy to fix it,
and no one else has the heart or the time to paint over it. Then there's
the junk in the yard: the Ugly Car no one's driven for years, the burn

barrel in back, the neighbor dog popping over to say hi and poop. Someone has painted *TRUMP* on the side of the big barn down the road in gigantic letters. And shortly before the wedding, the township pours tar over the unpaved road to tamp down dust, leaving a sticky black film dotted with flecks of gravel that cars must crawl over slowly, the gravel making rain-stick sounds in wheel wells, the tar sucking at tires, a spray of black gunk on fenders and rocker panels no matter how slow you go.

There could never have been a backyard wedding, so Jada reserves a pavilion in a county park by a creek that babbles over moss-fuzzed rocks. She orders white folding chairs, muslin tablecloths to cover the picnic tables, lacy table runners, paper lanterns, citronella candles, mismatched glass bottles and jars to stuff with wildflowers.

The weekend before the wedding, on the third of July, she comes home with Blake to confirm details and support Maddy at the wildlife center's summer open house, which will coincide with the release of a bald eagle that has recovered from lead poisoning. In honor of her graduation, Maddy has been trained to handle the release.

Attendees are encouraged to bring gifts from a wish list of items posted on the center's website. Jada would not have to buy her donation items from Drew's store, but she does, heading into town with Blake in the passenger seat, the road tar fresh and stinky on her Outback's tires. Many of Main Street's storefronts are vacant, but some are still occupied. The ice cream place with the teaberry ice cream; the bank that leaves a jar of toy soldiers next to the lollipops at each teller's station (TAKE ONE AND PRAY FOR THEIR SAFETY); Gino's sub shop with its green, white, and red awning; the thrift store (in the window: red, white, and blue rubber flip flops, silk flowers in a vase, a hand-painted sign that says MY WIFE SAYS I NEVER LISTEN— AT LEAST I THINK THAT'S WHAT SHE SAID, and an Uncle Sam yard statue made of scrap wood, holding a wooden flag). The military recruiting office (START YOUR ADVENTURE); the hair salon with the old-fashioned barber's pole (HAIRS TO YOU); the food bank; a row of sunbaked, paint-flaked bars; a carpet and mattress store that Jada can't recall ever having seen anyone enter or leave, still with a sign from the eighties above the door that says WATERBEDS!; a brewery that opened, then burned down, and now is open again. At the end of the block, the diner where Jada used to work. Farther on, the rusty bridge over the creek, a billboard (ADDICTION IMPACTS 1 IN 4 PENN-SYLVANIA FAMILIES) across from a billboard ("MY KID WOULDN'T DO DRUGS"—YOU SURE? ASK). The Presbyterian church across from the Catholic church, both decorated with Fourth of July wreaths stuck with miniature flags. The McDonald's across from the Burger King, the CVS across from the Rite Aid, the Dollar General across from the Dollar Tree.

Jada pulls to the curb outside Drew's hardware store. On the sidewalk are the remains of burst bang snaps that kids have thrown, teardrops of cigarette paper split open on the pavement, little bombs of sand and silver fulminate. A shaggy man walks by in a T-shirt depicting Trump holding up the head of Hillary Clinton as Medusa, snake-haired. But, also, here comes Jada's fifth-grade teacher carrying dry goods to the food bank in a bag she sewed herself, asking after Ellen's health and Jada's studies, shaking Blake's hand, admiring Jada's ring.

She used to hate it here. Over time she made a tentative peace with it. Now that she no longer lives here, she sort of loves it, but not out loud. She came to care about it just in time—thank you, man in Medusa shirt—to realize how little it cared about her, and this position is both part of her struggle and an expression of her privilege: that there had ever been a time when she'd thought that a whole world or even a whole town could consist entirely of people like her fifth-grade teacher, asking how she's doing and caring about the answer, reminds her that though she's had less than many—less, for instance, than Blake—she has had more than many others. She had not thought of herself or her family as poor until in college and afterward. Before that, most of the houses she'd seen or been in had looked at least approximately like hers; most of the people she'd met had looked like her. Class differences were signaled largely through the quality and quantity of pickup trucks parked in driveways. She'd waited tables and lifeguarded (the pool now filled in) for the mup'eres who came "up here" from Pittsburgh and elsewhere to the camps they owned in the area, running out the maggots and mealworms from the live-bait vending machine outside the video-rental-place-turned-Little-Caesars, floating down the river with coolers full of beer, shooting off fireworks on the Fourth of July, but she had met them on her own turf. She had gone to school and played with kids who were the same as her, or pretended to be; she had come of age in the era of dial-up, her mother and father yelling at her to get off, they needed the phone. Cloistered, she had lived under the illusion of relative if low-ceilinged equality, defining poverty as something elsewhere, something other. It had taken her too long to understand how her illusions had insulated her, to perceive their violence. Now here it is, the violence, in the open: a woman's severed head screened on a man's chest.

"Cute," Blake says, peering in the window of the thrift store at an embroidered hand towel that reads I'M A TENT PITCHIN', BEER DRINKIN', S'MORE MAKIN', CAMPIN' KINDA GIRL. Jada isn't sure what else she'd want him to say.

There's no one behind the counter when she turns between piles of mulch and potting mix to enter Drew's store. There's a random, sun-bleached picture of a turkey in the front window, a Sharpied sign that says FIREWOOD FOR SALE—CALL LARRY with an 814 number scribbled below. The bell dings as the door opens, then swings closed. Often when she comes in, he'll ambush her over the PA: *"Cleanup on aisle two"* as she walks down aisle two; then, when she turns down aisle three, *"Cleanup on aisle three,"* and so on down the line. He'll count her change entirely in pennies. Once he hid behind the counter while she stood waiting, too polite to ring the bell by the register, and when she finally did, popped up and scared the shit out of her. She's not sure whether she wants Blake to witness these antics—would they make him jealous, or could they be a way of saying, *See, we're friends, look how goofy and unthreatening our friendship is?* Why has she brought Blake here, the weekend before her wedding, and why does she still feel like she needs Drew's permission to walk down the aisle?

Although Jada has told Blake about Drew and Drew about Blake, they have not met, and Drew has not been invited to the wedding. His uninvited status was discussed and agreed upon by her and Blake, and yet here she is, grabbing a garden hose and some duct tape from the shelves of his store while Blake follows her, dressed in a mustard-yellow shirt of rough-hewn linen with elbow patches that she knows Drew will notice and make fun of. As if to shield Blake from mockery, she slips her arm through his, gives a suede elbow patch an appreciative pat. It is a relief, this urge to protect him, and she snuggles into the feeling. She loves this shirt, this mustard linen, this man. She is on his side.

When she rounds the corner, Drew is up front at the register. He looks at Blake, who doesn't look at him, doesn't know he has a reason to. She passes him the hose and the tape.

"Taking on a home hose-taping project, Ms. Battle?" he asks, scanning. He wears a plain, heathered navy tee, stretched tight around his biceps.

"It's for the wildlife center."

Now he has Blake's attention—*Ms. Battle*—and she introduces them. Her head feels wobbly as they shake hands.

"Ah," Blake says, "so you're—"

"Old friends," Jada says, handing Drew her credit card. On the checkout counter, on-sale bug spray and tick repellent, a dish full of pennies, a tray of Lion Mints. No one says anything else for a long time that is probably actually only a short time but doesn't feel that way. "Bad Moon Rising" plays on the store speakers.

"I used to think they were saying, 'There's a bathroom on the right.'" Jada points upward, as if the band or the bad moon might materialize in the air. Drew hands over her card, the bag.

"Congratulations, man," he says, and nods at Blake, who nods back: "Thanks, man."

Jada takes the bag. They're waiting for her to say something, do something, so she forces a smile and walks out the door with Blake and feels, as she does, the sensation that she is stepping out of one life and into another—as if this is the wedding, and what is happening next weekend is simply a reception. The sun disappears behind clouds that lumber bearlike across the sky, then emerges in slow splendor, and she watches the light spread over her world again one object at a time, a curtain opening to illumine each set piece: knick-knacks, sub shop, bank, ice cream, bars, Blake, and her. She says a line in her head—*I am walking into my life*—and feels hopeful and afraid, moving across the stage of her life. Feels the sun on her face, too hot. The sidewalk is more crowded than usual, with the mup'eres up for the Fourth, and she studies them as they walk by, lifts a hand to shade her eyes.

They're halfway down the block when Drew steps onto the sidewalk behind them. "Jada," he calls, and she drops her hand. "You forgot your wallet."

She didn't. "One minute," she says to Blake, and walks back to the store. Drew has come around the counter and is standing in a rhombus of sunlight just inside the door, in front of the key-making station.

"So you're really doing it," he says.

"Of course."

"Why?"

She backs closer to the door, touches the handle. "We've been through this."

"I still don't understand."

She pivots to check the sidewalk. Blake is nowhere in sight. "We broke up, Drew. Twice."

"And I regret that."

She tries not to look at the fabric of his shirt straining over his broad chest. She tries not to think about how she has bitten into his shoulder. "You and me—it didn't work out."

He shakes his head. "Those are just the early chapters in the book, Jada. Ships in the night and whatnot. They get together in the end." The light in the store dims as another cloud covers the sun. A row of hummingbird feeders on a shelf between Jada and Drew goes from bright to dull red. "We get together in the end."

"I don't believe that."

"You're what makes me happy."

Jada touches her ring. She touches her chest, to make sure her heart is there. She has made the registry, bought the dress, cut the muslin to the length of the tables. "You can't do that to me," she says. "It's not fair."

"Do what?"

"Hold me responsible for your happiness."

He crosses his arms. "Why did you come here, Jada?"

"I don't know."

"Sure, you do," he says. "You want me to release you."

"I want to know there's peace between us. I want closure."

"I'm not going to give you that," he says. "I'm sorry."

They stand facing each other in sunlight that blinks on and off. Blake is waiting for her. She doesn't know how she wanted this interaction to go, but it wasn't like this.

"Maybe you're right," he says. "You're not responsible for my happiness. But I'm not responsible for yours, either."

She is feeling around for something to say when she senses a pressure on the other side of the door and looks through the glass to see Blake's face. She steps aside to let the door open.

"Lunchtime?" he asks. He looks at her, he looks at Drew.

She nods, peeling herself away. "Wings?" she says. "We can drive out to the Forest Inn." Her throat feels scratchy as she turns back to Drew. "Good to see you."

The bell chimes as the door closes behind her.

The wildlife center is a large, squat wooden building that was once a restaurant and some sort of clubhouse. The kitchen's been turned into a medical clinic, and opaque, diamond-shaped clings have been stuck on all the windows to cut down reflective glare and prevent bird collisions. A sign outside the door reads QUIET: HOSPITAL ZONE! On the grounds surrounding the building are feeders for wild birds, fountains and water features that double as decorative and rehabilitative for soft-released songbirds, and white dishes hidden among tree branches for almost-recovered patients who stick close to the center before flying away when they're ready. Inside, in a large central gathering space with a stone fireplace and rustic wooden ceiling beams, Jada sets the garden hose and tape on the donations table alongside the other items people have brought: jugs of bleach, dish and laundry detergent, blankets and towels, sunflower and thistle seed, gauze pads, cat food for food mixes, surgical masks and gloves, trash bags, office supplies and light bulbs.

"See, this is why registries exist," Blake says, and Jada shoots him a withering look.

"I'm just saying," he says. "People need to know what we want. Like how the folks here told us they needed tape and . . . toilet paper." He motions to a stack of double rolls on the floor by the table.

"I'd be thrilled if our guests gifted us toilet paper," Jada states.

"Ha ha."

She's been off all afternoon since Drew, and if Blake has noticed, he hasn't said anything. She needs to get her shit together, she knows, but she doubles down: "I'm serious. If the point is to get us things we need, well, that's a thing we'll always need. Slap a bow on top and bam: an instant, objectively useful gift."

Blake looks at her with worry in his eyes. Then he smiles, kisses her forehead. "You're so funny."

They mill around the center with cups of lemonade, looking for Maddy. On the wall above a table covered in informational flyers and volunteer sign-up sheets, screens stream video footage from monitors inside the enclosures where rehabilitating raptors are kept. An array of labeled feathers is laid out on display on a sideboard. A whiteboard on the wall presents a drawing of an open-mouthed fledgling, gangly-legged, stump-tailed, and fuzzy, underneath the words "I DO NOT NEED HELP!" *I am a fledgling,* reads the speech bubble by the fledgling's head, the handwriting charmingly lopsided. *I can't fly, but my parents are caring for me, even if you can't see them. You don't need to rescue me!*

The guests are not allowed to view the center's patients, but they can meet their trained ambassador raptors, and they can watch birds preparing for release fly around a screened, high-ceilinged aviary on the other side of some one-way glass. Through a pair of double doors, on a patio in back, a volunteer addresses a group of observers while holding a kestrel with a partially amputated wing on her outstretched arm. At a table in the middle of the room, kids trace their hands with crayons, turning them into turkeys. Others glue felt and googly eyes onto pine cones to make owls. Still others run around in bird masks they've colored and covered with craft feathers, with cutout eyes and card-stock beaks.

"They're scary," Jada says at the same time Blake says, "They're cute."

"You don't have to be so cynical," he tells her.

"What?"

"They're kids." He gives her a look.

"It's the creepy masks," she says. Her face and neck feel hot. "It's not a big deal."

"I thought you wanted kids."

"Sure, someday. That doesn't mean my ovaries have to catch fire every time I behold other people's."

There's that look again, part concern, part disgust. "Why are you being like this?"

"I'm sorry," she says, and takes his hand. "I'm just nervous."

"About marrying me?"

She shrugs. "It's normal. It's human."

"*I'm* not nervous."

This makes her more nervous, his rock-solid certitude, the pride he takes in it. "Not even a little?"

"No," he says. "Forgive me if I don't want my fiancée to be, either."

Jada spots Maddy across the room, serving squares of cake from behind a table strung with crepe-paper streamers, two-toned twists like bright DNA spirals: pale pink and red, light blue and navy. Jada catches her eye, and Maddy runs out from behind the table, still holding a paper plate.

"You guys came!" Maddy greets them with quick hugs, deposits the plate upside down on Jada's head. She wears a smocked sundress of dusty beige cotton with purple flowers tumbling down the bodice and accumulating at the hem, and their grandmother's ring. Her hair is twisted up with a duckbill clip in a way Jada has never seen her wear it before, and Jada is struck by her sister's beauty, how she seems to glow here in this space where she is an insider, an expert. Even the crust of dried sweat where her hairline meets the curve of her forehead seems oddly lovely.

"We brought a hose," Jada says, abandoning the paper plate on a nearby ledge.

"Thanks." Maddy links her arm through Jada's. "Come on, I'll give you a tour."

She leads them down a hallway, past a row of dinged-up volunteer lockers with flowers stenciled on their doors, the fridge and freezer where the clinic rodent supply is kept, the industrial sinks where tubs and bowls drip dry, bookshelves jammed with labeled binders. She points out the exam room, where through another pane of one-way glass Jada sees crates lined up beneath a counter, metal instruments laid out on a long table, a collection of machinery she doesn't recognize, a registration log and detailed admission protocol with instructions for intake on clipboards. In the back, the mountains of dirty laundry Maddy has complained about having to do. Jada thinks of her lab and feels a kinship to this space. It warms her to enter the sanctuary where Maddy spends so much time, to observe the place of refuge she maintains for creatures who cannot thank her.

"And this is a ghillie suit." Maddy lifts a fringed green suit made of scraps of camouflage fabric and burlap from a nail on the wall. "We wear it when we feed baby birds to prevent imprinting." She holds the suit up in front of her and shimmies, the fabric bits fluttering like leaves in a breeze.

"Look at you," Blake says. "You're quite the expert."

"You really are," says Jada. "I'm proud of you."

Maddy turns to her, radiant, a smile breaking across her face, and Jada is either paranoid enough or wise enough to sense the precious-ness of this moment, to understand it as the calm before a storm some part of her already knows is on its way.

Maddy holds a finger to her lips. "No talking in here, okay? Don't scare the babies." She takes them through a room full of screened cages containing baby birds and ducklings, then offers to show them her eagle-owl. She leads them back into the main room, inside which a tall, slim man in shirtsleeves is shaking people's hands. Maddy stops short, her cheeks redden, and she grabs Jada by the arm again. "That's Jason Mayhew. I clean for him and his wife."

Jason spots them, comes over, shakes hands with Jada and Blake.

"Congratulations on your upcoming wedding," he says jovially.

"Oh," Jada says, "thank you."

"Meghan and I love Maddy. She does great work."

Maddy beams; Jada smiles politely. There's something unpleasant about this man, something she can't put her finger on. Then again, she's not sure she can trust herself right now, so twisted up inside. Blake won't stop looking at her; she can feel him trying to see into her mind, where what he'd find is a picture of the hurt in Drew's eyes, the sound of his words, *I'm not going to give you that.*

She's thinking of something to say to Jason when the center's director, who resembles a skinny Santa Claus in a purple plaid button-down, snowy hair and bushy white beard and kind eyes behind rectangular frames, invites everyone to join him in a meeting room, where folding chairs have been set up before a projector screen for a presentation on bald eagle rehabilitation. Jason nods at Jada, nods at Blake, nods at Maddy, and excuses himself.

"What do you think of him?" Maddy asks as they follow Jason and the rest of the visitors into the room with the screen. She unpins her hair, puts the duckbill clip in her mouth while she retwists it.

"What do you mean?"

"He's running for state senate."

This, Jada figures, must account for her unease; it's the practiced charisma of an aspiring politician she's reacting against. "I don't know," she says. "He seems all right, I guess."

Maddy clips her hair in place, and the three of them sit near the back and listen as the director explains that, like the eagle the center will be releasing, nearly half the eagles examined across the United States suffer from lead toxicity. It can take six months to remove lead from an eagle's system, he says. On the screen is a video of a shuddering eagle wrapped in a blanket, unable to stand or breathe properly, its head tucked into its body. Jada looks away.

"He's a secret smoker," Maddy whispers from Jada's right.

"Him?" Jada tilts her head toward the director, trying not to look at the screen.

"No. Jason."

Jada glances at Jason again as the director implores the crowd to use non-lead ammunition and tackle to protect avian scavengers. "So?"

From her left, Blake mumbles, "What were you talking about with that guy today?"

"Nothing," she mumbles back. "Just wedding stuff."

"Cigarette stash in a kitchen drawer," Maddy says on her right, "behind the pot holders. Housecleaners know all."

"How do you know they aren't his wife's?"

"I just do."

"Did he do anything to you?" Blake asks, and both Jada and Maddy look at him.

"What?" Maddy loud-whispers.

"No," Jada says. "No, he didn't *do* anything to me."

"I don't trust him."

"Who?" Maddy asks, as at the front of the room the director encourages visitors to take up mealworm farming and donate their homegrown mealworms to the center.

"Nobody," Jada mutters. She turns to Blake. "You don't have anything to worry about."

"The way he looked at you."

She shakes her head. "I shouldn't have taken you there today. It was inappropriate. I'm sorry."

He nods, but she can tell he's not appeased. On the projector screen is a photo of someone's cupped hands holding a bunch of light brown mealworms.

"Wait," Blake says, squinting at the photo. "Why is he showing us a picture of crispy chow mein?"

Maddy laughs so hard that people turn to stare. The director looks at her, his eyes amused behind his Santa Claus glasses.

"Even though we humans do a lot of damage," he says, still smiling genially, wrapping up his speech, "we can also give a lot of help." Then, of course, he asks for money. In addition to the wish-list items the guests have been generous enough to supply today, he says, the center is saving for a new blood-testing unit that will aid in the treatment of lead-poisoned wildlife. In the front row Jada sees Jason Mayhew make a show of whipping out his checkbook.

"Look." Maddy scoots to the edge of her seat. Her face is flushed— again, that glow, one that raises Jada's suspicions but that she's so glad to see on her sister, so rare and so bright, that she brushes her misgivings aside. "I knew he'd help us."

Blake looks at Maddy and perks up. He seems about to say something when the center's education programmer brings Maddy's beloved eagle-owl out on her glove, explaining that he is the center's only non-native resident, purchased as an owlet and imprinted on human owners who couldn't care for him. The eagle-owl flaps its wings and jumps from her arm, dangling by the tether, flapping furiously while upside down, then rights himself with his handler's help. Her forearm is in the range of the projector light, and half the bird's head and one of its ear tufts are silhouetted on the screen.

"And of course," the director says, "we're always looking for sponsors for permanent residents like this one, our treasured Eurasian eagle-owl. Sponsors can give as little as five dollars a month to earn a photograph of their chosen bird and help keep them fed and cared for, or, for those feeling extra magnanimous, rise to our Soaring Hawk giving status to earn naming rights for residents in need. See me for details!"

He introduces Maddy as one of the center's valued young volunteers and wishes her a happy graduation. She waves, beaming, does a silly curtsy, and everyone moves outside. The grass is damp from recent rain, and the onlookers are swarmed by gnats. Jada watches Blake swatting at them with both hands and, though she wants to do the same, feels compelled to play the country girl and act unbothered.

She thinks of her mother, at home resting. She has rallied for Maddy's birthday and graduation; she will rally for Jada's wedding, but she spends more than half of each day in bed.

"I wonder how many birds they don't release," she says as Maddy carries the bald eagle outside in a crate with a blanket thrown over it, flanked by the director and another volunteer. "How many they can't save."

Blake puts his arm around her, continues swatting gnats with the other. The crate in Maddy's hands bobs and swings until she sets it on the ground a small distance from the center, facing a large field to the west of the building.

"Don't worry about that," he says. "Focus on this one."

"I can't help it." She can't get the image of that sick eagle out of her head, its ragged breaths and drooping head, the vacant eyes.

As the small crowd arranges itself in an arc behind Maddy and the eagle and counts down from three, Jada thinks of the suffering bird rather than the strong one, of Drew, of her mother. Of all the things that can't be saved, all her white bears. Of the words of Ellen's oncologist, Dr. Rochelle Will, at that fateful appointment two months ago, a few weeks before Jada's engagement. *The capecitabine isn't working the way we'd like.* Jada had clutched her mother's hand on the other side of Dr. Will's desk. *That's three drugs in a row with no real benefit. We have more choices, but with the way things have gone, I'm afraid it's time to start considering the possibility that nothing is going to work.*

Jada with her notepad, her hundred questions, the hundred studies she's read, the hundred more that Blake has read. Dr. Will's white coat, her magnificent black curls tumbling down her back and over her shoulders, fabulous with health. *We can try IV chemo,* she'd said, *since the less aggressive options have not been effective. But I should warn you that infusions are hard on older patients facing recurrences. This would be a last resort.*

The eagle thrashes in its crate; Jada can see its movements through holes in the side. Blake takes her chin in his hand and lifts it. He looks at her, and in his eyes Jada sees love, fear, frustration, exhaustion. "Just be here, now," he says. "Please."

Then Maddy opens the door to the crate, and the eagle bounces forward tentatively and takes flight. It's not a mature eagle, only three years old, and it lacks the classic white head and clean brown body. White and brown feathers are scattered patchily over its head and body, and as it flies away it looks scrappy and speckled and defiantly beautiful.

It's over in seconds, the bird here and gone. People clap and cheer, scan the empty sky, then wander back into the building.

"You okay?" Blake asks. His arm is still around her.

Jada nods, waiting for the crowd around Maddy to clear. Blake releases her to slap at a mosquito on his arm, hard and fast, a splatter of blood and torn wing left behind on his skin.

"I'll see you inside," he says, and hurries indoors.

Jada waits at a distance for Maddy, who is talking to Jason Mayhew. When he leaves, she congratulates her sister and walks with her back into the building, where things are winding down, a volunteer gathering art supplies, a worn-out child crying. The cake has been ravaged. Jada scans the room but can't find Blake, and a cold fear strikes her—she's chased him away; she's blown it. She is turning to Maddy to ask if she sees him when the director reappears at the front of the room and asks everyone left in the building for their attention.

"Now for a bit of fantastic news!" he exclaims. "Before all you folks head home, I'd love to share a happy development in the life of our beloved eagle-owl. As of a few minutes ago, he has secured a sponsor who has generously offered to finance his stay here at the center and give him a much-needed name." He waves someone into the room, and everyone turns to stare—at Blake.

He's looking right at her. Jada feels light-headed. Everyone is clapping. A few people follow his gaze and look at her, too. She looks at Maddy, who is luminous.

"So, wait," Maddy says, wide-eyed. "He's going to be named . . . Blake?"

"No." Blake chuckles, then grows sober. "I was thinking we'd name him after your mom."

"Ellen?" Maddy crinkles her nose.

"I thought we could call him Wilson." Ellen's maiden name.

"Because he's a fighter." Maddy nods, her eyes brimming with tears. "Like her."

Maddy runs to Blake and hugs him, hugs the director. Blake's eyes stay locked on Jada's. *Here,* they say. *Now. Choose this. Choose me.*

The ceremony is brief, held beneath overcast skies. It's a self-uniting marriage, a relic of the state's Quaker past turned secular: they are declaring themselves married, with no need for a middleman between themselves and, as the Quakers would have it, God. Blake's older brother, Peter, officiates anyway, reading his script from beside the stone-studded stream where they've staked a rustic arbor draped with chiffon, though Blake's parents disapprove of the self-uniting license and want a wedding Mass. His mother, Bernie, sits sternly regal in a dusty-rose shift and beaded bolero, fanning herself with one of the cheap folding hand fans Jada selected as favors, their names and wedding date laser-engraved on the side. Jada's mother holds her fan in her lap, the eggplant-toned fabric of her dress showing dark through the filigreed sandalwood. She is smiling but exhausted, even with the steroid shot a doctor gave her, and though she says she feels fine, when a fly lands on her hand she does not move to swat it away. It's hot, even with the sun behind the clouds, and sweat glazes her face.

Their vows are traditional; Jada did not suggest that they write their own. She wanted to hear him say *in sickness*. She tells herself that if she says the words sincerely enough, if she applies her intellect to the fullest extent and harnesses her good intentions, she can vanquish the parts of herself, surely irrational and thus defeatable, that still aren't sure.

Concentrate. An image of Drew flits through her mind, and she zaps it. *From now on,* she tells herself, *I will be the person I want to be.* He flits through again and she says, *From* now *on. Now.* She stands flanked by Catalina and Maddy, who hands her Blake's wedding band. Maddy wears a hot-pink A-line cocktail dress of shiny satin that hits well above the knee, her legs brown with summer; Catalina, a plunge-necked electric-blue sheath. Next to Jada, who wears a bridesmaid's maxi of lightweight navy nylon tulle, wrapped bodice and cap sleeves, they are vibrant as parakeets. She does the thing with the ring. He does the thing with the ring. No one pronounces them anything; they pronounce themselves, and Peter and Catalina sign as witnesses. She is married.

After the ceremony everyone gathers in the pavilion, eyeing the cookie table spread with anise and vanilla pizzelles, Russian tea balls, frosted sugar cookies, jam thumbprints, peanut butter blossoms, almond crescents, and apricot kolaczki like Jada's Bachi used to make, dusted with powdered sugar and resting on paper doilies. The guests drink from plastic wineglasses Maddy put together the night before, jamming stems into bases, breaking a few and swearing each time. They eat wood-fired pizzas cooked in seconds in a mobile brick oven and sit at the picnic tables set with wildflowers in Ball jars and dishes of mixed nuts and chalky after-dinner mints. It's a sit-where-you-want situation, which annoys Bernie and a few others, who mill around waiting futilely for instructions. There's no cake, just the cookies, so Blake and Jada feed each other slices of Neapolitan-style pizza, holding them by their charred crusts, buffalo mozzarella sliding off the drooping triangles of dough.

"Ugh," Bernie huffs as Blake wipes a fleck of crushed tomato from the corner of Jada's lip, and her contempt is so brazen that Jada sort of loves her, or at least respects her.

It is a lovely wedding, a pure patch of happiness in the tapestry of her life. Nothing, not even the eventual end of their marriage, will undo its loveliness.

She sits next to Blake, and they eat together. Waxy threads of cheese, leaves of fresh basil. Romaine and shaved parmigiano, plastic forks against plastic plates. She is laughing, feeling light and accomplished. A few drops of rain begin to fall, barely enough to feel or to see on her skin.

"What's on your mind, wife?" Blake asks, chewing.

"I was thinking about the day we got engaged, at the symphony."

"Chopin." He smiles. "It was a good day."

She nods. "I'm grateful to you," she says, "for not saying anything when I cried. For giving me the space to feel. It meant a lot to me, that moment."

He looks at her. "You cried?"

"During the prelude? I had to let go of your hand to wipe tears away."

Blake frowns.

"Repeatedly," she goes on. "I was sure you'd noticed."

"Sorry." He shakes his head. "I had no idea. But that's an odd thing to fixate on, isn't it? Considering it was the same day I, you know. Took you to the house I'd bought us?"

"Yeah." She laughs lightly. He is probably right. She had wanted the moment to mean something, and maybe it did—but what? And why? It was just a moment. He'd had his aesthetic experience, and she'd had hers. He was not responsible for what she'd felt, and hadn't she just thanked him for respecting the privacy of her reaction? Why should it matter that that respect had been unconscious?

"You should have told me," he says. One of the tines snaps off his fork as he jabs a crouton. "I would have comforted you. We should share those things."

He looks uneasy in a way he shouldn't look on his wedding day. She stabs her salad, kisses his cheek, changes the subject. "Thank you, also," she says, "for the thing with the eagle-owl. Maddy's telling everyone. She's thrilled."

"It was nothing." He beams.

"You didn't have to." In fact, she is still not sure she would have wanted him to cover the sponsorship, let alone give the owl her mother's name, had he asked her. She knows he bestowed the name as a memorial and not, as Maddy had declared, to indicate some essential similarity between the bird's resilience and Ellen's.

He looks at her, holds her gaze. "I'd do anything for you."

After dinner and toasts, she makes the rounds through her guests, ending at her mother, who is seated next to Bernie. "Our friends the Doyles have a camp near here," Bernie is saying, fanning herself again, this time with a pizzelle. "Do you know the Doyles? Joe and Kathleen?"

Ellen shakes her head no.

Jada sits down next to her. "Mind if I steal her away?" she asks Bernie, who smiles tightly and shuffles toward the cookie table. By now Maddy's started up the playlist she made and begun dancing with Catalina. Gradually, others join them on the other half of the pavilion, beneath the white Christmas lights and paper lanterns, and in the grass. They give Jada and Ellen a wide berth, and Jada takes her mother's hand. It's thin and frail, and she sees the veins there. She thinks of fallen leaves, an oak leaf encased in a sheet of ice, and she knows what she has to do.

"Okay," she says, still looking down at Ellen's hand.

Ellen waits for her to elaborate, and it's like they're back in Dr. Will's office again. The clean glass topper laid over the big mahogany desk, the diploma on the wall, the framed photos of her golden-doodle. The proposed return to traditional chemo, the review of risks, and Ellen's reply: *Absolutely not.*

Dr. Will had wheeled her leather chair around the side of her desk to face them without a barrier. "We call it shared decision-making for a reason," she said. "It's my job to inform you of the full range of available options, their risks and potential benefits. But at the end of the day, it's your body. We'll take your values and preferences into account now just as we've done all along."

"Let's not rush into anything," Jada had said.

"She just said." Ellen nodded toward Dr. Will. "The treatment's not working."

"It's keeping you alive."

"But I'm not getting better."

"But you're not getting worse."

"Worse." Ellen pivoted to address Dr. Will. "I can't work. My daughter is cleaning houses for me. My other daughter"—she spoke about Jada as if she were not in the room—"drives hours to bring me back and forth for these appointments. We're broke. I have nothing to leave my kids. I give them nothing but responsibilities."

"That's not true," Jada protested.

"Oh, Jada," said Ellen. "It's time to be a grown-up."

She was right. It is.

"You have my support," Jada says now, watching Maddy take off her strappy sandals and throw them, Catalina do the same, dancers migrating barefoot into the grass; Blake dancing with his four-year-old niece, Aubrey; Peter swaying with his youngest, still an infant, in his arms. "If it's really what you want, if you're really ready—"

"I am."

Jada turns toward the dance party, Maddy's updo now a scraggly down-do, fireflies blinking in the dusk. "What about this?" she says, and lifts Ellen's hand as if to fill it with the scene.

"It's yours."

"But—"

"See, there's a predictability here," Ellen says. "It's new, and it's comforting. Like I'm writing a story, and I know how it ends." She speaks quietly but with a confidence that calms Jada. "For the first time in my life, I'm in control of the story."

"It could be longer. There could be more."

Ellen shakes her head. "I saw my daughter start her career and get married. I saw my other daughter graduate and turn eighteen." She pauses for breath. "This is the happy ending, Jada."

Jada rests her head on her mother's shoulder, her mother who has always counted her accomplishments like coins and considered herself wealthy. When really, in those moments when marriage seems little more than a symbolic milestone, when her research and career pursuits begin to feel trivial, Jada wonders if her ultimate, defining characteristic and primary contribution to the world might just be that she has really, really loved her mom. It is one of the only things she's done wholeheartedly, without vacillation, and that has had a visible positive effect on the well-being of another human. *I love your life as much as I love mine.*

"When the dog is sick, you put the dog to sleep," Ellen had said that day in Dr. Will's office.

"You're not a dog."

"So I don't deserve the same compassion?" she'd asked. "'It's the humane thing to do'—that's what you tell yourself when you let an animal go. It's humane."

Darkness falls. Moths to light. Jada feels awake, at that picnic bench under the pavilion, in a way she has never felt awake before. She studies the moment in a way she's never studied anything. Mentally, she scrambles to sweep up every detail and sensation—the raised veins in the backs of her mother's hands, the smell of sweat and citronella, the June bugs clicking in the rafters. She will memorize everything, she resolves, from now until the end. She must keep every speck, every word. This pattern of veins: memorize it. This blue light: memorize it. Her senses feel overloaded. Sound and odor bombard her. Seconds that would previously have ticked by unregistered now feel heavy with importance, with value, and she banks them like coins. *Save everything,* she thinks, even as she knows she can't—it's like trying to make out every individual tree as you speed through a forest, down a highway, the landscape slipping past. Every object you note is ten you miss, and once they're behind you, they're behind you.

"What about Maddy?" she asks.

"She can't know yet." Ellen shakes her head. "She'll want to fight. I don't want the conflict."

Catalina approaches, her feet grass-stained, her skin glowing. "Care to dance, Mama?" she asks Ellen. "We can set you up a chair on the dance floor if you don't feel up to getting on your feet."

The conversation is over.

At the send-off, the guests wave smokeless sparklers in the buggy darkness, and Jada braces herself, waves goodbye. In their room at the inn they've booked, decorated in dense Victorian florals and smelling of cat pee and potpourri, she thinks of telling Blake about the conversation with her mother, but the words don't come. In bed she begins to cry, and this time, he sees her. He wipes the tears with a tenderness that breaks her heart. He strokes her hair and touches her cheeks, so moved, so pleased to have brought his wife such joy.

# 19

## MADDY

### April–May 2018

As Maddy waited for Jada to come home, she thought of the day her mother had driven her to her old house. She'd been twelve at the time, and they'd been on their way home from somewhere, she couldn't remember where, when her mother had taken the unexpected detour. Dirty gray siding, shutterless windows, a sinking front porch, the yard mostly mud. A dog barked at them from a box at the side of the house, pulling at its chain. Some crooked plastic candy canes lined the path from the driveway to the house, faded remnants of Christmas arranged at wacky angles, though it must have been February or March.

"I used to live here." Ellen leaned over to take in the house through the passenger-side window, so close Maddy felt her breath against her cheek. "Before your dad."

The dog snarled. Maddy regarded the house with mild aversion. "You lived here?"

"With a different man."

"Your boyfriend?"

"My husband. My ex-husband."

There was a cat in the window, watching them from beneath a sagging set of Venetian blinds. Into Maddy's head, unbidden, came the word *pussy*. It had always made her think of a battered pink silk sachet, smelling of rotten potpourri.

"What happened to him?" she asked.

"I left," Ellen said. "And then he died."

Maddy scrunched her nose. "When?"

"Just last month. In fact"—Ellen shifted the car out of park—"would you mind one more stop before we go home?"

Her curiosity piqued, Maddy consented. She pitched questions at Ellen, and Ellen bunted, giving back minimal information: the man's name was Travis Johnson, though everyone called him TJ, and they'd dated in school and married as soon as they graduated.

"Till I was twenty-four," Ellen said. "Six years. It took me that long to get up the courage."

"Why? What happened?"

"Oh, honey," was all Ellen said, and Maddy had seen that she should go no further in her interrogation.

They drove another ten minutes down back roads to a cemetery. There he was, the grave fresh. A simple stone, no flowers. Naked trees, buds closed tight. The soft earth sucked at Maddy's shoes, and she thought of quicksand—that thing that as a child, not knowing better, she'd feared most in the world.

"He had a coyote," said Ellen.

"TJ?"

"Yes."

"A pet?"

"A decoration. The mouth open, the teeth. On this log with one leg bent, like"—Ellen held out an arm, bent an elbow, let her hand droop like she was a queen holding it out to be kissed—"mid-step. I'd get up at night to pee and there it would be, staring at me." She drew a shiny penny from her coat pocket, her hands cold and chapped. "You know how those eyes are. Always watching you."

Maddy had scooted closer to her mother—that old blue jacket, she could picture it still, with the dirty collar and big, loose buttons, one missing at the bottom. The cold made her nostrils burn and her head smart in the space behind her eyes.

"That was a different life," Ellen said.

"I want to go home," Maddy said.

Ellen bent and squatted before the headstone. Without her mother's body next to hers, Maddy shivered and wedged her ungloved hands into her armpits. The tips of her ears were fiery cold. Ellen placed the penny Abe-side up on the stone.

"Good luck," she said to the grave with an edge in her voice, and walked away, Maddy trotting behind her like a puppy. At the car Maddy climbed with relief into the passenger seat only to watch her mother pause, turn around, walk back to the grave, and retrieve the penny. A light, cold rain beaded on the windshield.

"Changed my mind," Ellen said when she returned, and tossed the coin into Maddy's lap. "Put that in your piggy bank."

"I don't have a piggy bank."

Ellen started the car and let it run for a while, farting filth into the cold air. She wiggled her fingers in front of the vents and looked at Maddy for a long time, waiting for Maddy to look back.

"Don't ever let anyone hurt you," she said when Maddy finally did. "Do you understand?"

Maddy nodded. She had thought she understood. But she had thought she understood a lot of things, then, that had turned out to be wrong.

"Did you tell Jada this?" Maddy had asked on the way home. "About your other husband?"

"She knows I broke up with my high school boyfriend, that he treated me badly."

"Not that you were married?"

"No."

"You didn't show her the house?"

"Nope. Just you."

This was the answer Maddy had been hoping for. "Did you tell her the thing about not letting anybody hurt her?"

"She knows."

"Because you told her?"

Ellen had looked thoughtful. "Jada wouldn't let anyone hurt her," she said. "Jada's struggle is different."

"What's her struggle?"

"To let people be kind to her," Ellen said. "And to be kind to herself."

But not letting people be kind to oneself had seemed to Maddy like an okay problem to have—Jada not only stronger than her, not needing to be warned about abuse, but also more virtuous, righteously self-denying—and she had stopped asking questions.

"Don't tell Dad I took you here," Ellen had said as she turned down their road.

"I won't," Maddy promised. And she hadn't.

She should not have told Blake about Drew. She should not have touched his arm. She should not, really, have done any of the things she'd done since that summer two years ago when her mother was dying. She should not have let anyone hurt her. When she thought of herself two years ago—hell, when she thought of herself two hours ago—it was like thinking about a different person. Two years before that, a different person again, and two years before that, again . . . she imagined a string of selves, linked at the hands and the hems of their skirts like a chain of paper dolls, connecting her past selves to present.

Not one of them seemed able to help her when Jada came through the door. Maddy was sitting at the kitchen table, uninstalling her dating app—she didn't need more men right now, didn't have the stamina, didn't trust herself—when Jada came in and opened a bottle of red wine, the corkscrew like a little guy whose arms rose in protest as she turned his silver head. She laid him on the table, his arms still up like those of a diver about to spring off a board, his legs tapering in a silver spiral. She poured herself a glass and didn't speak until after she'd taken a long drink.

"Why did you tell Blake about Drew?"

"Why did you tell Daddy I was pregnant?"

"You *are* pregnant."

"But I should have been the one to tell him," Maddy cried.

"I know. I'm sorry, Maddy," said Jada. "I truly am." She took a drink, picked up the corkscrew, and rotated its bottle-opener head absently, watching the coil spin.

"Now you and Blake can have an honest conversation. You can make up. Jesus," Maddy pronounced, "teaches forgiveness."

"Good for him." Jada took another gulp of wine. "We're not making up."

"Because you love Drew," Maddy said quietly.

Jada didn't answer, just stared into her glass. "Blake said you came on to him."

"I was trying to be nice. I was comforting him."

"Inappropriately."

Maddy rolled her eyes. "Oh, these poor men," she said. "Poor Blake, so innocent!"

"Of course he's innocent. What has he ever done to encourage you? Why would you think . . ."

"That he'd want me?" Maddy's voice shot up, shrill and razored. "I'm not good enough?"

"He's fourteen years older than you."

"So?" Maddy shouted. "News flash, Jada: men like me. Older men like me."

Jada studied her, brows furrowed. Maddy could see a little alarm going off behind her eyes, a light blinking on. "What's that supposed to mean?"

"It means what it means."

"It's a weird thing to say," Jada said. When Maddy didn't elaborate, she asked, "What older men?"

Maddy said nothing.

"What older men, Maddy?"

It was time to open the box. She couldn't keep this to herself any longer. Maddy went to her futon, took out her Bible, pulled the creased BRIDGING THE PARTISAN DIVIDE flyer out from inside, and handed it to Jada. The event was in five days. Maddy jabbed Jason's name with her finger.

"Remember him?" she said. "From the eagle release?"

She told Jada the whole story while the sun set outside. When she finished speaking, the sudden absence of noise left her feeling frightened. It was too quiet in the room; she had the sense of being overheard. The hairs stood up on her arms.

Jada began gathering dirty dishes from around the apartment, stacking them by the sink. "Why didn't you tell me this before?"

"It's embarrassing," Maddy said. "And I guess I wanted to protect him."

Jada filled the sink with soapy water. "I'm listening," she said, plunging her hands into suds. "I need something to do with my hands. Did you consent?"

"Yes."

"You said yes?"

"Yes."

"With words?"

Jada scrubbed a dish while Maddy leaned against the stove next to her. "He didn't rape me. And it went on for a long time, since before Mom died."

Dishware had begun to accumulate in the drying rack. Jada scoured, rinsed, and added to the accumulation. "Help me," she said, and tilted her head toward the pile.

"Just leave them."

"Why, Maddy?"

"I hate drying dishes. Why do a pointless chore when they could just drip—"

"No," Jada said. "I mean, why Mayhew? I just want to understand."

"Sure," Maddy said, "blame the victim."

"You said you weren't a victim."

"But you are blaming me." She yanked a towel from a hook and set to drying dishes.

"I just want to know what you got out of it."

Maddy stared at Jada, dripping dinner plate in hand. "Sex," she said, like, *duh*.

Jada washed lipstick from a mug. She picked up Maddy's fetus doll from the counter and washed it, turning it in her palm, wiping its closed eyes. "I just want you to respect yourself."

Maddy laughed a dry, wry laugh. "Yeah," she said, "the body is a temple. You sound like the women at New Dawn. Want to tell me who I can sleep with, when, how . . ."

"He was your married employer, in a position of power over you."

"Who are you to get all high-and-mighty about cheating?"

Jada's face reddened. "He took advantage of you."

"I took advantage of *him*," Maddy argued. "I saw an opportunity, and I took it."

"But you were . . . vulnerable."

"I was an adult."

"Barely. And it's about more than your age. You were . . . it was a very difficult time for you. With Mom. He took advantage of that."

When she'd finished speaking, Jada looked sheepish. Clearly she knew she'd opened the floodgates, and Maddy did not have the self-control not to be the flood.

"You just let her go," Maddy said. "How could you just let her go?"

"You know it wasn't that simple."

"No, I don't."

Each time she thought of it, the wound felt fresh: her mother's decline, the turn for the worse after Jada's wedding. The proposed trip to Mexico, the experimental treatment shot down with almost no discussion. The humiliation of returning the money she'd raised to the donors on her crowdfunding site. Maddy's panicked commands (*You have to keep fighting*), her mother's objections: *Enough with the war metaphors, it's not a war, I didn't lose any damn battle.* Jada's refusal to intervene, her postponed honeymoon. The shift to hospice care. It had been impossible to comprehend. Ellen had always been able to manage her sickness; why not now? Even before Maddy had understood, she'd lashed out at Jada: *Why are you not losing your shit right now? How can you just sit here and watch her leave us?*

"I've told you, and she's told you," Jada said now. "Stopping treatment wasn't some impulsive move. It was a careful decision made in consultation with Dr. Will. I know you know that."

Maddy shook her head.

"You do. You just don't want to admit it. Because if you can't be mad at me, you're going to have to find another place to put your feelings about her being gone. You're mad at me because it's easy to be mad at me."

"You cut me out of everything."

Jada had left her out, it was true, but in the end it had also been Jada who told her the truth: that she had to stop begging her mother to fight, that to stop fighting was not the same as losing, that it was she, Maddy, who would need to put on her armor.

Jada let the stopper out of the sink, let the water rush down the drain, rinsed the basin clean. The dishes shone where Maddy had stacked them on the table. "That was her choice, not mine."

"So I should be mad at her, then? Mom?"

"No. She wanted to protect you."

"I was an adult," Maddy repeated.

"You were vulnerable. And volatile. She wanted you to have a normal senior year, a normal summer."

"There was *nothing* normal about my senior year. I was obsessed with an owl, I was up to my elbows in Pine-Sol, and I was fucking a married man. I spent the first months of my adulthood watching her die."

Jada dried her hands on a kitchen towel and then, for good measure, on her jeans. "Maybe you're right. Maybe leaving you out of the conversation was the wrong thing to do. But how do you think I feel? How would you feel, really, if your mother asked your permission to die? What would you have said?"

"I would have said no!"

Jada looked at her with so much sadness in her eyes. "Exactly." She poured herself another glass of wine. "I don't expect you not to be angry," she said. "But please don't accuse me of not caring about

Mom. There's a lot of things you can criticize me for, but that's not one of them."

"I'm not accusing you of not caring about Mom," Maddy said. "I'm accusing you of not caring about me."

She could see that they were at a crossroads, that if they did not do something or change something now, they could lose each other more completely than they'd already lost each other after Ellen's death, speaking only stiffly on holidays and birthdays—or Maddy's birthday, anyway; Maddy had not called Jada on hers. It was true that she had become attached to her anger; it had become like its own gnarly entity, a teammate she'd drafted. With it on her side, she outnumbered Jada. She was winning.

Jada's eyes welled, and she covered them with her hand. "Of course I care about you," she said. "Of course I do."

As she watched Jada cry, Maddy's antagonism began to feel petty, and she saw what it took from Jada, and what it took from her. Maybe some part of her had known all along that what she'd suffered from these past few years was not only the loss of her mother, but the loss of her sister.

*You're going to have to find another place to put your feelings about her being gone*—maybe this was what had happened to Maddy that day in Pastor Dan's church, when she fell to her knees: the carving out of a space where she'd thought she was solid, and where she could hold what she had not been able to hold before. All these caverns inside her, suddenly! She had not known there could be such space there, opened up in invisible places like the hollows in a bird's bones.

Maddy handed Jada a napkin, slowly, staring. Like her crying sister was a bubble, translucent and fragile, that might pop if she moved too suddenly or too sharply. She watched Jada fold the napkin and dab her cheeks. Then she took out her phone and held it up, recording.

"What are you doing?" Jada asked.

"I want this on the record." The timer in its red box at the top of Maddy's screen counted the seconds. "You're *crying. You're* crying."

"Stop it." Jada sniffled.

"Stop what?"

"Studying me."

Maddy tapped her screen and put down her phone. She had begun to cry, too.

Jada rubbed her face again. "Don't you start."

"I can't help it. It's like a yawn, it's contagious."

They stood there sniffling, noses dripping. Maddy had lost track of what time it was. She felt disembodied in that way fighting can make you, feeling at once aged, haggard, and stuck in time. They might have been standing in the kitchen for five minutes or five years.

"When she was sick the first time," Jada said, "her tears turned pink. It was a drug she was on. It was so scary. She was like one of those religious statues."

"Sometimes when she would cry," said Maddy, wiping her eyes, "Dad would get all, 'Don't you think a better attitude would help?'" She imitated his voice. "And she'd go—"

"'I do *not* have to stay positive. I do *not* have to be happy.'"

"She put her foot down," Maddy said. "I admire that. But I wish she had, you know. Been happier."

Jada had explained to her many times that correlation is not causation. That her mother's cancer was pregnancy-associated did not mean that pregnancy was its cause. But Maddy still felt culpable, and she had a persistent sense that she had never really known her mother, that what she'd experienced of Ellen was less an expression of her true self or personality than of drug side effects, and of the fact that every day since Maddy was born Ellen had had a sense of her life as on loan and of herself as both lucky and eternally under threat, living it.

What Maddy would need to reckon with now that her mother was gone was not only the stark fact of her absence but the only slightly less stark fact that often, when she was alive, she was sad. Dead mothers in books and movies were always living loving laughing, cooing lullabies (Maddy cannot remember Ellen ever singing to her), baking well (Ellen didn't), jumping on beds while singing into hairbrushes. Maddy was sometimes tempted to make Ellen into such a mother in memory. Certainly she had modeled an enhanced gratitude for life, breathing deeply on spring mornings as if to drink the air, planting flowers. But this gratitude had often expressed itself through a weepy sensitivity to the mundane that annoyed Maddy. Ellen would cut into a ripe tomato and cry. She would see a sad story—or, for that matter, a happy story—on the local news and cry. It was as if she'd broken through some membrane between life and death and stayed suspended there. Everything hurt her. She was not, like dead women on *Dateline*, "always smiling." Did she love to laugh? Sure, but who doesn't? Who do you know who hates laughing?

Movie Maddy would go through her mother's impressively curated vintage record collection and pick out something folksy-cool to enjoy in her memory, but real Maddy remembered her mother scrubbing toilets to the music of Amy Grant, an embarrassing CD in a cracked case that skipped on the player. Movie Maddy would bake some elaborate cake or warm, yeasty bread to commemorate her mother, but real Maddy craves Ellen's crappy casseroles made with Campbell's cream of mushroom soup, even though she used to pick the mushroom chunks out and push them to the side of her plate while Ellen rolled her eyes: *Just eat them, they don't even taste like anything.* Nine times out of ten Ellen didn't finish her own dinner, just watched Maddy and her father bicker over wasted mushrooms or uneaten peas and shoveled the contents of her plate into a container stained orange from old spaghetti sauce, then into the fridge, then into Maddy's father's lunch box the following morning. Nine times out of ten Ellen didn't eat lunch.

Her mother was now the stuff of story, and everyone wants their story to have a strong protagonist, a peppy female lead who takes no bullshit. But some people are tired and some people are sick and some people do take bullshit, and those people need stories, too; those people deserve to be remembered, too.

"I don't think it was the case that she wasn't happy," Jada said. "She wasn't happy about being sick. No one would be, and no one should have to act that way for the sake of making other people feel better."

"Not even daughters," Maddy said.

"Not even daughters."

She sat down across from Jada. The PARTISAN DIVIDE flyer was on the table between them, flipped over. She picked it up. "This thing," she said. "It's Thursday night."

Jada examined the poster again. "'Bridging the Partisan Divide.'" She snorted. "Please."

Maddy shrugged. "Maybe there's some good he can do. He said he'd look into the thing with the wells."

"You still think some old oil wells are the reason Mom got sick?"

"They could be."

"Or it could be any of a hundred other things," Jada said. "Or all of them."

"I just want—"

"I know. You want to get to the bottom of things. But, Maddy, there is no bottom."

"You're the researcher. You of all people should understand. I just want an answer."

"And if you find it?" Jada said. "Then what?"

"What do you mean?"

"Say you find your smoking gun. What difference does it make? It's smoking because it already went off. Because she's already dead."

Jada was right, Maddy knew, whether she wanted her to be or not. What would she do if she could isolate a culprit? Bring her mom back? Never go home again, back to the site of the crime? Maybe this was what it meant to be from somewhere—to be of a place, or of a person. At least, maybe this was what it would mean for her, and for Jada. A fear of what it might have done to you, the damage it might have inscribed on the cells that make you. An aching love in spite of that fear.

"We should go to this," Jada said, holding up the flyer.

"Yeah, right," Maddy scoffed. "And be like, 'Mr. Mayhew, what's your position on a woman's right to choose?'" She did a silly voice. "'Mr. Mayhew, how do you plan to help PA's single mothers?'"

"'Mr. Mayhew,'" Jada said, "'how much do you pay your housekeeper?'"

"I was thinking of asking him for more money," Maddy said, serious now.

"You mean, like . . . in a blackmail sort of way? Or in a child support sort of way?"

Maddy shrugged again. "I don't want to be one of those women."

"What women?"

"Alleging things."

"You mean telling the truth? About what he did?"

"I did it too. I betrayed Meghan. She put her trust in me." Maddy put her hands to her belly and stared down at the kitchen tile. "I called him earlier. He didn't answer. I was thinking I could just, like . . . re-mind him what happened. But I don't want to break up a family. What if Meghan left him?"

"Don't you think she deserves to know?"

"I guess."

"Whether or not it breaks up his family is the least of your con-cerns. You don't owe him anything," Jada said. "You don't owe his family anything. You owe *your* family." She motioned to Maddy's belly. "And you owe yourself."

"My family," Maddy repeated, and felt, for the second time that day, a sense of permission. She had wanted it from her father; she had also wanted it from Jada. Now here it was. Her choice could be a true one, and she could make it without losing her father or sister.

"Mom got divorced, you know," she said.

"What?"

"She was married before Dad."

She could feel Jada looking at her. "She never told me," Jada said.

"I think the guy abused her. Her high school boyfriend."

"Why wouldn't she tell me?"

"I think she was embarrassed."

"But she told you."

"Because she thought there was a lesson in it for me. Not to let a guy hurt me. She knew you never would."

Jada hesitated, then said, "Blake wouldn't have hurt me."

"I know. But still. You shouldn't be there if you don't want to be there."

Jada wiped at her eyes again. "It's so embarrassing, Mads," she said. Maddy could not recall the last time Jada had spoken to her like this, so open. "On top of being so fucking sad, it's embarrassing. I don't want to be pitied. I don't want people to look at me all, 'How could this happen?' and then go home and hug their partners a little tighter because they're so glad they're not me, they're so determined not to end up like us. I don't want to be someone's cautionary tale."

Maddy shrugged. "You're probably overestimating how much people care about what happens to you," she said. "You have Good Student Syndrome."

"What?"

"You think you have to meet all these people's expectations, you have to please everyone. But you don't." She touched the PARTISAN DIVIDE flyer again. "Especially when everyone has gone completely fucking batshit."

Jada was quiet.

"Plus," Maddy added, "Mom always thought you and Blake were an odd match."

"She did?"

Maddy nodded.

"But she was all . . . gunning for me to get married."

"Doesn't mean she wasn't surprised who you picked."

How much more did one of them know that the other didn't? Remembering that day at the cemetery with her mother, telling the story to Jada, Maddy felt that an essential balance had begun to be restored. They should do more of this: add new pieces to the mosaic Ellen had become. The picture it made was their inheritance. How much fuller it could be, and more vivid, if they put together the pieces they'd kept for themselves.

"Hey," Maddy said. "This might seem like a weird question, but did we ever ride on a train across Kinzua Bridge?"

"Sure," said Jada. "You remember that?"

"Not exactly." She thought of telling Jada about her night on the bridge, but held back. She had not jumped, and she would not jump; that was what mattered. "It's more an impression than a memory. I didn't know if it was from my life or yours, some family story I hijacked."

"Oh, you were there," Jada said, and painted the memory for Maddy: They are on the railroad bridge, still intact—the four of them, a family, having boarded an orange-painted car of a quaint, old-fashioned tourist train that is, though they don't realize it, not long for the world and that carries them, though they don't realize it, across a gorge on tracks that will one day crumble, through space that will be nothing but air. Ellen, white-knuckled in an aisle seat, eyes closed, fearful of heights. Jada sulking, denied a snack from the café car; her mother has packed bologna sandwiches, which sit baggied and stacked in a cooler at her feet. Maddy a toddler in their father's lap, screaming at the top of her lungs, an earsplitting shriek that vibrates against Jada's eardrums and turns all the heads in the car. Papery green shades on the windows. Jada pulls hers down, snaps it up again, pulls it down, and her father says, *I paid for that view, and you are going to look at it,* so she snaps the shade up again on its roller and leaves it, the sun beating in hot through the glass, and her mother says, *This is why we shouldn't leave the house.* Her father hands Jada screaming Maddy, and she takes her on her lap, and Maddy goes quiet.

"You cried when anyone but me tried to touch you," Jada said. "I held you the whole way. It was summer, it was so hot, but I held you."

"Thank you."

"It's not like I had a choice."

"No," Maddy said. "For telling me."

If it was possible, as Jada had once told her it was, to implant false memories—of being lost in a shopping mall you were never lost in, or riding in a hot-air balloon you never rode—via subtle suggestion, it must be possible to pool real ones. In time Jada might absorb the memory of her mother's cocked eyebrow at the idea of her marrying Blake as if she'd witnessed it herself, and Maddy might absorb the memory of being held by Jada on the train as if it had blossomed naturally from her own mind instead of having been planted there by the sister who shared it—not a false memory so much as a true one disinterred.

She thought again of that chain of paper dolls she'd pictured earlier, all her hand-to-hand selves sometimes folded and collapsed in a pile, sometimes stretched in an endless line. Maybe, she thought, you are more than parts of a single whole—tits, womb, wounded hand, pink hair. Maybe you are a multitude: a pregnant woman on a bridge screaming into the darkness, a child on a bridge screaming in her sister's lap. You are all these things at once, not shedding your skins but wearing them in layers. You are all the people you've ever been, always.

Her fetus was in the dish rack. She picked it up. "I don't think we should go to the roundtable," she said. "I have another idea."

On the evening of Jason's appearance in Pittsburgh, they headed out of town on the same roads he took in. Jada drove; Maddy sat in the passenger seat, clutching a letter she'd written Meghan the day before, denting the folds with her thumbnail. The letter was part apology, part logbook. She spared few details, chronicling the major plot points of the affair, including dates and numbers when possible—what he'd paid her, when. Jada had helped her write it. She did not ask for anything other than the assurance that she and the baby, should she have it, would be safe. She was telling Meghan, she wrote, out of respect.

She watched through the windshield as if they might pass Jason's car in the opposite lane. He wouldn't recognize Jada's Subaru, but

Maddy hunkered low in her seat anyway. It was after ten when they arrived, after his event must have concluded, Jason still three hours away and likely to stay over in the city. If Meghan and Theo had gone with him, Maddy reasoned, the house would be empty, and she could run her errand without fear.

"There." She pointed. "That's the house." The windows all dark.

Jada slowed down.

"Don't pull in," Maddy said. "Pull up there." She indicated a graveled turnoff a few yards past the Mayhews' mailbox.

"You're sure about this?" Jada said.

Maddy opened the door, pushing it against some raspberry bushes, and stepped out. Thorns scratched her arms. "Wait here."

"Why don't you just leave it in the mailbox?"

"He could get to it before she does. I want it someplace only she will find it."

"Can't you just text her? Call her?"

"I don't want to hear her voice. I don't want to read her initial reaction. If she wants to reach out, she can do it once she's processed everything."

"But what if they're home? Meghan and the baby?"

"*He's* not home," said Maddy. "That's all that matters."

"She could call the police."

"She won't. She turns me in, she turns him in." Maddy moved to close the door.

"Wait," Jada hissed, waving Maddy back. "Do they have security cameras?"

"What? No."

"He's in politics."

Maddy rolled her eyes. "He's a state senator."

"She could have a gun."

"I've been through her bedside drawers," Maddy said. "The guns are all locked in his safe. At most I'm at risk of being stabbed by a calligraphy pen."

Jada climbed out of the car, crossed to Maddy's side, and hovered, looking unsure what to do with herself. She wore a black halter and jeans, her arms pale in the moonlight. "I'm going with you."

"You have to drive the getaway car."

"You'll have to run back to the car first, anyway, before I can drive."

"Fine," Maddy said. "But stay in the bushes. Don't come in."

"We should have a code. If you get caught, if you need backup."

Maddy rolled her eyes again. "I'll call you."

She nudged Jada into the undergrowth where the woods met the Mayhews' yard, watched her duck into the shadows, and made her way down the long driveway. Checked the side window of the garage. Meghan's car was inside, but they might have driven together to Pittsburgh; the house might still be empty. Maddy was surprisingly calm—and really, she asked herself, why shouldn't she be? She still had her house key, and she knew the property well, knew to use the kitchen door rather than the front door with the motion-sensor light, to lift up on the doorknob as she let herself in to keep the rubber weather strip from brushing too loudly against the tile. Once she was in she felt a rush, almost an ecstasy. She was emboldened, playful, slipping her shoes off by the door to creep barefoot through the kitchen, opening his cigarette drawer and stealing the two packs she found there, flipping the kitchen knives on their magnetic strip point-up to point-down, shaking salt on the table. A cookbook was open on the counter, *The Amish Cook's Essential Book*, and she turned the page from shoofly cake to knee patches. She stashed the cigarettes in the front pocket of her hoodie, which grew fuller, like a mama kangaroo's pouch. Also in the pocket: her tell-all letter to Meghan, her ultrasound photo from New Dawn, her fetus doll, and the box cutter, blade retracted but ready.

She rounded the corner into the foyer, just inside the main door, stepping lightly. Meghan's gym bag was packed for the next day's Pilates class. From the hooks above it hung three purses, a suit jacket, a child-sized bucket hat. A sign hung on the wall above them, that fucking calligraphy again: THANKFUL. Like the fact that the family, or at least Meghan, appreciated the things they had meant that they deserved them, and this sign was evidence of both—you couldn't begrudge her; she was THANKFUL.

But she shouldn't be too hard on Meghan, who had only ever been civil to her and whose life she was about to upend, whose gratitude she was about to shatter. Maddy slid through the living room, past the big TV and the lamp she'd almost broken (her mother's first rule of cleaning: always bring tape and glue), dodging Theo's toys, their colors muted, his kid books overflowing from their woven storage basket. She passed the French doors on the far side of the living room and froze when the outdoor motion sensor clicked on. She narrowed her eyes and peered into the night. A raccoon stared back, trash-bound, wiggling its creepy fingers.

When the light went off, Maddy started up the short flight of stairs. The euphoria she'd experienced upon first breaking in (was it breaking in if you had a key?) had passed, and her body felt tight and trembly. She reached into her pocket, rested a hand on the box cutter. Be brave. Don't touch the handrail, skip the squeaky step. She knew the house the way she knew his body, with an intimacy that was slightly embarrassing, slightly sad—she moved things, she touched them, but at the end of the day, they weren't hers. Few things were. Even her baby did not belong to her.

Four doors in sight from the landing. His office; their bedroom;

Theo's bathroom, with the rubber duckies and the wind-up swimming shark, the magnetic fishing rod and bobbing fish; Theo's bedroom. Somehow the house seemed more than ever Theo's: his toys and clothes she noticed now, his room she felt drawn to. She slipped inside, praying he was either not there or fast asleep, feeling a twinge of guilt at this abuse of the power of prayer, asking God to help her trespass.

His room was peaceful, lit by the glow of a star-shaped nightlight. Maddy switched off the baby monitor. Her shadow loomed against the gray-blue walls. The soft rug, the stuffed animals lined up in rows, their round, staring eyes. The woodland-animals mobile above the toddler bed: felt foxes and bunnies, acorns and red-capped mushrooms. The tree stenciled on the wall, painted branches curling whimsically. The gliding chair in the corner, the knit blanket flung over one arm. The stuffed black bear bigger than Theo.

He slept with his arms up by his face as if ready to defend himself, his head thrown to the side, his cheeks rosy. Maddy had the urge to lift him but only peered at him from the side of the bed. She felt like a fairy or a guardian angel, presiding benevolently over his sleep. She had rarely seen him up close, though she'd been in his room many times, and now that she did, she felt her fear that she could not love a baby that was Jason's begin to lose its grip on her. She watched Theo sleep and wanted to rub the tip of her nose against the smooth of his cheek, his sleep-damp forehead. He was a regular boy, a good boy, who might yet grow up to be a good man.

Who would he become? What would he do, how would he live? Before, these questions might not have mattered to her, but suddenly they mattered immensely. This boy who didn't know her name, who knew her at best as a shadow, a straightening, sanitizing presence, might now know her for the rest of his life.

One hand in her pocket, she stroked the box cutter, the glossy photograph. She thought of her mother's words: *Don't let anyone hurt you.* In the end, they had been the wrong words. She studied Theo, focused on his closed eyes and long, little-boy lashes, and concentrated, as if she could beam a message into him the way one sent a silent prayer to God. *Don't hurt anyone.*

A painful certainty singed Maddy's chest. Her skin prickled with knowing, a chill up her spine, and she searched for someone or something to credit for the transmission. Then she realized: it was not Jada or her father or Pat or Pastor Dan, it was not her mother, it was not even God. It was her own heart. She was going to keep her baby, this sleeping boy's half sibling, because she knew in her heart of hearts, in her secretest secret place, that though there might be someone out there who could give her child more than she could—more money, more material comfort, more opportunity of a certain kind—there was no one who could give it more love.

She shivered, suddenly cold, her knees newly shaky. He could wake up any minute. Meghan could come in. She backed out of the room and hurried across the hall, through Jason's cluttered office to the Jack and Jill bathroom that connected the office and master bedroom. The door to the bedroom was closed, and she tiptoed over the penny tile, trying not to breathe, and took his toothbrush. She could use it in a DNA test to prove his paternity. She and Jada had looked it up online—99.99 percent accuracy, results in six days.

Down the stairs, then, on wobbly legs. She tucked the letter and the ultrasound photo into Meghan's gym bag, where she knew she would find them in the morning. She was halfway to the kitchen door when she turned around, worked their house key from her key chain, reopened the bag, and dropped the key between the folds of the letter. She would not come here again.

She imagined Meghan finding the letter and the photo. Turning them over in her hands, unfolding the paper. The key clattering out. She imagined the sign above the coatrack changing letters, the calligraphy morphing: PISSED.

On her way through the kitchen, Maddy opened the contraband drawer one last time. She reached into her marsupial pouch and removed the fetus doll, tucked it in the space where the cigarettes had been. She closed the drawer, then the door behind her, and ran.

She sprinted up the side of the driveway, clutching Jason's toothbrush. Jada popped out from the weeds, a shadow, and they ran together, panting, whispering, and, the farther from the house they got, laughing.

"Ohmygod," Jada kept saying, "ohmygod, ohmygod."

They jumped into the unlocked car, and Jada fumbled with her keys in the driver's seat, still going, "Ohmygod, ohmygod."

"You're a terrible getaway driver!"

"Ohmygod, I'm sorry!" The car started, and Jada peeled out. "What happened?"

"I left the stuff in her gym bag. And I took his toothbrush."

"What took you so long?"

"I put the fetus where he keeps his secret stash." Maddy's whole body was buzzing. She pulled the cigarettes from her pocket. "Want one?"

"No."

"Me neither."

The seat-belt alarm in Jada's car was chiming. "Buckle up," she said. Maddy obeyed, rolled down her window, whooped and hollered into the night.

"Shh." Jada laughed.

"Why?" She felt wild, reckless. No clue what would come next, but she had leverage. He did not know where to find her. She had made her choice, told her story. Now she made one bird sound after another, watching Jada's face, watching her laugh as they sped down the dark road, knowing every dip and curve. Bird noise after bird noise, *brrrrt, breeet, preeet!* Jada laughing, her laughter powering some crazy engine inside Maddy. *You, then,* Pastor Dan had preached last Sunday, Romans 14:10, *why do you judge your brother or sister?*

"Let's go somewhere," Maddy said.

"Where?"

She thought of her unused passport, the money she'd saved. "Mexico."

They passed the New Dawn billboard, still standing: PREGNANT? SCARED? YOU'RE NOT ALONE. "Honk the horn," Maddy said, and reached across Jada to the steering wheel to hit it. Again and again, blaring into the night. Pitch-black, the headlights illuminating sprays of Queen Anne's lace, nothing but trees and trees beyond, and no one to hear them but deer and owls, but fuck it—they laid on the horn, both of them, jabbing at the wheel, rocketing past the yelling billboard, the yelling yard signs in front of sleeping houses. They could yell, too.

Maddy put her feet on the dash, felt the wind in her hair, breathed in the scent of honeysuckle, closed her eyes—pregnant, yes; scared, very. But not alone.

# 20

May 2018

The Mexican beach they travel to is the first one Maddy has seen out-side of the one her parents took her to on Lake Erie when she was ten and that they left after a matter of minutes, once the poison ivy she ran through to get there manifested in a seething rash on her legs. All she remembers is her mother slathering her shins in calamine lotion and that brief and unsatisfying glimpse of waveless gray where she'd imagined thundering blue. *It's just a lake,* she'd said that day, and her father said, *Ships have sunk in there,* as if it were only a capacity for destruction that made a thing great.

Here, at last, is the endless blue she dreamed of. She and Jada claim beach chairs behind their bougainvillea-draped bed-and-breakfast, where they share a room with purple walls and a painting of the Virgin Mary backed by sunbeams in an elaborate pressed-tin frame hanging above their twin beds. In the mornings they sit at an antique dining table clothed with a joyful-bright Otomí runner and eat breakfast with the innkeeper and a few other guests: vanilla conchas, perfect cylindrical pan omelets, hot drinking chocolate. Black-and-white photographs of the hosts' ancestors watch from the walls.

On the beach they place sunglasses and bottles of sunscreen and books on the corners of their towels to keep them down in the breeze, buy micheladas and aguas frescas from a palapa, and sip beneath the thatched roof. *Playa,* Maddy mouths, *playa, mariscos*—she's like a baby here, pointing at objects, saying their names, learning to speak. And to taste: the sweetness of agua de sandía, flor de calabaza quesadillas, turkey in chocolatey-rich mole, fresh lime squeezed over grilled octopus tacos (hold the queso fresco), the rubber-stamp circles of tentacles nested in warm tortillas. "Embarazada," she says when she orders, touching her belly.

In the two weeks since she broke into Jason's, he's called more times than she can count. He's very displeased with Butterfield's services. Maddy does not answer his calls. Her only contact has been with Meghan, who left her a voicemail shortly after she and Jada landed in Mexico and with whom she's been texting ever since. She didn't believe Maddy at first, until she confirmed the four grand missing from their savings, the date of the transfer to his checking account matching the date Maddy cited in her letter. *I trusted you inside my home,* she said in her message, and Maddy realized she'd never had a real conversation with Meghan, had assumed she spoke only and always in the platitudes she painted on signs. *You took something from me, but I can't take my anger out on you. The only person that serves is him.* She and Theo have moved in with her mother.

Jason has money, Meghan has made it clear. She will see to it that Maddy receives support, one way or another. *Not for you,* she said, *but for the baby.* It is not the job of a child to suffer for the sins of a father, or a mother.

Maddy's own father hugged her when she came by the house

to get clothes and a swimsuit for Mexico, their first embrace since her mother's funeral. It felt strange, and his role in her life and her child's life remains uncertain, but she knows there will be one. He'll be there. She'll stay with Jada as long as she needs to, a folding screen blocking off her corner of the living room, and their life together will be a mess, but when has it not been? She's got a part-time job lined up as a Kids Kingdom attendant at the zoo, with the help of a recommendation from the wildlife center's director; she'll conduct public programs with live animals, supervise the playground. Eventually, she'd like to study wildlife biology.

The coastline stretches forever. Birds run on long legs through wet sand, tracks like arrows behind them, needle beaks stitching the murk. A shrimp boat bobs far offshore, swarmed by screeching gulls, pelicans queued on rigging. Maddy pulls her sundress over her head, exposing her bare belly to the sun, crosses the hot sand in her blue gingham bikini, and walks until bubbles fizzle at her feet.

*Go, throw yourself into the sea*, she thinks, as Jesus said to the mountain.

She walks in. The waves are low. Clouds like opals in the sky, the sun firing through. El sol; la nube. She is using those flash cards she made in Señora Swartzentruber's Spanish class after all, if not in Tijuana and if not with her mother. The world is both bigger and smaller than she once thought. She walks until she's on tiptoe, her chin lifted above the chop. Breathes the salt air. Then she holds her breath and goes under.

Behind her, Jada lets the surf wash her feet, wiggles her toes in the sand, and watches Maddy walk into the ocean she is seeing for the first time. What Jada has seen for so long, when she's looked at her sister, is the absence of choice: because she did not choose sisterhood and cannot reverse it, she has viewed it as an obligation, grimly binding.

Now she sees that it can also be a choice, this bond more indissoluble than a marriage—she may not have chosen Maddy, but she can choose to love her. Each day, with agency, she can make this choice. In some things, research has shown, as un-American as it may seem, it is better to be constrained than to be unconstrained: she chooses this constraint. There can be more men, but there will be no more sisters.

A hawker in a straw hat approaches her with a basket full of jaguar noisemakers, sounding one so that she startles at its harsh growl and waves the man away. No, gracias. Her heels sink into the sand. She splashes out beyond where the waves break, beyond where Maddy floats, her belly a small island rising out of the water, her breasts two gingham peaks. She walks until she can't anymore, and then she takes off. She kicks, strokes, reaches ahead as if pulling herself along an invisible rope. Gulps air. Her blood thumps, her lungs fill and deflate, fill and deflate. She opens her mouth and tastes salt and fishy grime. In the back of her throat, a tang of tamarind lingers.

She has failed at marriage. Soon, back home, everyone will know. Watching other people be and stay married, counting their years together, will be newly painful. It will give her the feeling of losing a race, and she will have to work to remind herself that she chose not to run. It will be yet another grief she learns to live with. She will make a list of things she loves—things to eat, things to do—and that list will help her live, disentangling herself and her wants from him and his. And Drew's. She will keep some of what Blake has shown her, some of the ways he's changed her. Others, she'll let go.

*A waste*, he said, but it has not been a waste. It has been an education.

She swims until, all at once, her body stops swimming. It's as if she has been wound by some great hand, a toy woman, and now her gears have stopped turning. Her eyes scan the shoreline for Maddy's blue gingham. She thinks of riptides, of sharks, and turns back the way she came.

Though her academic study is ongoing, the data yet to be analyzed and conclusions yet to be drawn, the article yet to be published, her personal study is over. She files away her results. They are many; she's learned a lot, but there's one finding in particular that gives her hope: there can be more love. Whether it's with Drew or with someone she has yet to meet, there will be more love in her life. You can find more if you're brave enough, or stupid enough, if you're cold enough to freeze your life and walk over it like water to something new and blurry on the other side, small with distance, indistinct but glowing. Perhaps to go forth into the beautiful mess of your life—not knowing if you're right, only sensing, hoping, that you're not wrong, and letting yourself love yourself either way—is not a matter of certainty or knowledge. It is a matter of faith.

Back onshore, Maddy sheds her weightlessness, feels her body grow heavy again. She turns her head in the direction Jada swam and sees the distant dot of her form cutting through the water, watches as it grows larger. Psalm 139:8: *If I go up to the heavens, you are there; if I make my bed in the depths, you are there.* She looks up at the sky again, bright to the point of blinding despite the gathering clouds. She breathes in, breathes out. One hand to her belly, one hand to her heart. *Beat on, heart,* she thinks.

Break open, sky. Rain down.

# AUTHOR'S NOTE

The studies and laboratory experiments referenced in *How to Care for a Human Girl* are representative of real academic studies published in peer-reviewed journals and cited on the References page. While I have attempted to represent the researchers' findings and methods as accurately as possible, scenes of individual characters conducting or discussing research are my own creation and fictionalized.

Jada's study is inspired by a real study conducted by Jonathan D'Angelo and Catalina Toma at the University of Wisconsin-Madison and published in *Media Psychology* under the title "There Are Plenty of Fish in the Sea: The Effects of Choice Overload and Reversibility on Online Daters' Satisfaction with Selected Partners." I am grateful to Dr. Toma for providing essential insights into the research process for this study, which has also been fictionalized for narrative purposes.

The study conducted in the novel by the fictional Catalina is also inspired by an existing study, "Perception of Our Own Body

Influences Self-Concept and Self-Incoherence Impairs Episodic Memory," conducted by Pawel Tacikowski, Marieke L. Weijs, and H. Henrik Ehrsson and published in *iScience*. I wish to acknowledge and thank these scholars and all the others listed on the References page, whose work informed Jada's (and my own) thinking about choice, interpersonal attraction, and intimate relationships.

The information Jada cites on abortion procedures, their risk levels, their general relationship to women's mental health, and the burdens of abortion stigma also comes from peer-reviewed sources cited on the References page. Resources from the Guttmacher Institute and the Informed Consent Project also shaped this work. The largely inaccurate information Maddy receives at the fictional New Dawn Women's Care Center represents paraphrased information from the websites of actual crisis pregnancy centers.

# REFERENCES

Aronson, E., Willerman, B., & Floyd, J. (1966). The effect of a pratfall on increasing interpersonal attractiveness. *Psychonomic Science, 4*(6), 227–228.

Biggs, M. A., Brown, K., & Foster, D. G. (2020). Perceived abortion stigma and psychological well-being over five years after receiving or being denied an abortion. *PLoS ONE, 15*(1), e0226417.

Biggs, M. A., Upadhyay, U. D., McCulloch, C. E., & Foster, D. G. (2017). Women's mental health and well-being 5 years after receiving or being denied an abortion: A prospective, longitudinal cohort study. *JAMA Psychiatry, 74*(2), 169–178.

Clark, R. D., & Hatfield, E. (1989). Gender differences in receptivity to sexual offers. *Journal of Psychology & Human Sexuality, 2*(1), 39–55.

D'Angelo, J. D., & Toma, C. (2017). There are plenty of fish in the sea: The effects of choice overload and reversibility on online daters' satisfaction with selected partners. *Media Psychology, 20*, 1–27.

Dion, K., Berscheid, E., & Walster, E. (1972). What is beautiful is good. *Journal of Personality and Social Psychology, 24*(3), 285–290.

Dutton, D. G., & Aron, A. P. (1974). Some evidence for heightened sexual attraction under conditions of high anxiety. *Journal of Personality and Social Psychology, 30*(4), 510–517.

Else-Quest, N. M., Higgins, A., Allison, C., & Morton, L. C. (2012). Gender differences in self-conscious emotional experience: A meta-analysis. *Psychological Bulletin, 138*(5), 947–981.

Erber, R., & Erber, M. W. (2018). *Intimate Relationships: Issues, Theories, and Research.* New York, NY: Routledge.

Garry, M., & Wade, K. A. (2005). Actually, a picture is worth less than 45 words: Narratives produce more false memories than photographs do. *Psychonomic Bulletin & Review, 12*(2), 359–366.

Gottman, J. M., & Levenson, R. W. (1992). Marital processes predictive of later dissolution: Behavior, physiology, and health. *Journal of Personality and Social Psychology, 63*(2), 221–233.

Kahneman, D., & Tversky, A. (1982). The simulation heuristic. In D. Kahneman, P. Slovic, & A. Tversky (Eds.), *Judgment Under Uncertainty: Heuristics and Biases.* New York: Cambridge University Press, 201–208.

Kouchaki, M., Smith, I. H., & Savani, K. (2018). Does deciding among morally relevant options feel like making a choice? How morality constrains people's sense of choice. *Journal of Personality and Social Psychology, 115*(5), 788–804.

Lane, J. D., & Wegner, D. M. (1995). The cognitive consequences of secrecy. *Journal of Personality and Social Psychology, 69*(2), 237–253.

Loftus, E. F., & Pickrell, J. E. (1995). The formation of false memories. *Psychiatric Annals, 25*(12), 720–725.

Markus, H. R., & Schwartz, B. (2010). Does choice mean freedom and well-being? *Journal of Consumer Research, 37*(2), 344–355.

National Academies of Sciences, Engineering, and Medicine, Health and Medicine Division, Board on Health Care Services, Board on Population Health and Public Health Practice, & Committee on Reproductive Health Services: Assessing the Safety and Quality of Abortion Care in the U.S. (2018). *The Safety and Quality of Abortion Care in the United States*. Washington, DC: National Academies Press.

Niranjan, S. J., Turkman, Y., Williams, B. R., Williams, C. P., Halilova, K. I., Smith, T., Knight, S. J., Bhatia, S., & Rocque, G. B. (2020). "I'd want to know, because a year's not a long time to prepare for death": Role of prognostic information in shared decision making among women with metastatic breast cancer. *Journal of Palliative Medicine, 23*(7), 937–943.

Rocca, C. H., Samari, G., Foster, D. G., Gould, H., & Kimport, K. (2020). Emotions and decision rightness over five years following an abortion: An examination of decision difficulty and abortion stigma. *Social Science & Medicine, 248*, 112704.

Rocque, G. B., Rasool, A., Williams, B. R., Wallace, A. S., Niranjan, S. J., Halilova, K. I., Turkman, Y. E., Ingram, S. A., Williams, C. P., Forero-Torres, A., Smith, T., Bhatia, S., & Knight, S. J. (2019). What is important when making treatment decisions in metastatic breast cancer? A qualitative analysis of decision-making in patients and oncologists. *The Oncologist, 24*(10), 1313–1321.

Schwartz, B., Ward, A., Monterosso, J., Lyubomirsky, S., White, K., & Lehman, D. R. (2002). Maximizing versus satisficing: Happiness is a matter of choice. *Journal of Personality and Social Psychology, 83*(5), 1178–1197.

Tacikowski, P., Weijs, M. L., & Ehrsson, H. H. (2020). Perception of our own body influences self-concept and self-incoherence impairs episodic memory. *iScience, 23*(9), 1–38.

Wegner, D. M., Schneider, D. J., Carter, S. R., & White, T. L. (1987). Paradoxical effects of thought suppression. *Journal of Personality and Social Psychology, 53*(1): 5–13.

Wegner, D. M., Lane, J. D., & Dimitri, S. (1994). The allure of secret relationships. *Journal of Personality and Social Psychology, 66*(2), 287–300.

Williams, C. P., Miller-Sonet, E., Nipp, R. D., Kamal, A. H., Love, S., & Rocque, G. B. (2020). Importance of quality-of-life priorities and preferences surrounding treatment decision making in patients with cancer and oncology clinicians. *Cancer, 126*(15), 3534–3541.

# ACKNOWLEDGMENTS

This novel has benefited from the care of so many people. Above all, I'm grateful to Caroline Eisenmann, who guided me through the writing and publication processes with grace and patience, and whose wise insights were instrumental in shaping the book; to Daniella Wexler, for believing in this novel even before it was fully formed; to Lindsay Sagnette, Libby McGuire, and the whole team at Atria, for taking a chance on me and believing in my work; and to Natalie Hallak, for the empathy and respect you showed Jada, Maddy, and me—I'm so lucky this book and I found our way to you.

For gifts of time, space, and money in support of this work, I thank the University of Montevallo, the University of Houston, Inprint, and the Corporation of Yaddo. For their formative feedback, I thank Antonya Nelson, Robert Boswell, Chitra Divakaruni, Ann Christensen, Gregory Spatz, Ramona Ausubel, Victoria Patterson, Casey Guerin, and my workshop group at the Community of Writers.

I am fortunate to be surrounded by supportive colleagues whose knowledge helped me write about psychology. I'm especially thankful to Melissa Shepherd for lending me resources, patiently answering my many follow-up questions, and sharing your perspective on my work not only as a psychologist, but as a trusted reader and friend; and to Betsy Richardson and Rachel Jubran, who also contributed essential insights into the field. I'm infinitely grateful to Dr. Catalina Toma for her generosity in discussing her research, and to the many researchers whose work is referenced in these pages and whose contributions to psychology and public health can help us better know ourselves and care for one another.

Judy Paulich provided vital insights on oncology and palliative care; thank you, Judy. Dr. Gabrielle Rocque shared her expertise on metastatic breast cancer, supportive care, and shared decision-making to help me write realistically and compassionately about Ellen's experience and the experiences of those caring for her. My sincerest thanks to Dr. Rocque, for your time and passion in discussing your work, and to Emily Wykle.

Doug Adair gave generously of his time to talk to me about the work of the Alabama Wildlife Center. I'll always be grateful not only for the information he provided but for the interest he took in Maddy as a human girl with a backstory that would color her experience as a volunteer. The Tamarack Wildlife Center and the Pennsylvania Game Commission provided virtual resources that helped me imagine Maddy's experience at the fictional Pennsylvania Wilds Animal Rehabilitation Center.

One of my purest childhood joys was to spend the weekend at my aunt Cindy's apartment in Shadyside, going to Station Square to pick out bath beads and eat alphabet fries at Houlihan's, or peeking in Kaufmann's windows at Christmas. My love of Pittsburgh will forever be rooted in these treasured experiences. Thanks, AC and

Donna Kielar, for sitting down with me at the Chinatown Inn to talk about all things Pittsburgh, yesterday and today.

Thank you to all the others who lent expertise and encouragement as I wrote this book: Harold, for providing tips on Pennsylvania flora and fauna and life inside a sawmill; Vinnie, for offering perspectives on my writing and characters that were never "people's," but only yours; Steve Forrester, for introducing me to the "Raindrop" Prelude; Sara Beringer, for contributing valuable insights on women's health; Leigh Miller, for teaching me as much about my own mind as any study or textbook could do; and Alex, for keeping me in pizza, giving me bubbles to pop, and supporting my "Shirley Jackson lifestyle." And, as always, I'm thankful to my family, human and canine, for their unwavering love and support.

# ABOUT THE AUTHOR

Ashley Wurzbacher is the author of *How to Care for a Human Girl* and the short story collection *Happy Like This*, which won the 2019 Iowa Short Fiction Award and was named a National Book Foundation "5 Under 35" honoree and a *New York Times* Editors' Choice. Born and raised in Western Pennsylvania, she currently lives in Birmingham, Alabama, and teaches at the University of Montevallo.